PROVINCES OF NIGHT

William Gay is the author of the novel *The Long Home*. His short
stories have appeared in *Harper's*, *Atlantic Monthly*, *GQ* and *New
Stories from the South 1999* and *2000*. The winner of the 1999
William Peden Award, he lives in Hohenwald, Tennessee.

Also by William Gay

THE LONG HOME

Provinces of Night

WILLIAM GAY

faber and faber

First published in the United Kingdom in 2001
by Faber and Faber Limited
3 Queen Square London WC1N 3AU
This paperback edition first published in 2002

First published in the USA in 2001 by Doubleday, a division of
Random House Inc.

Printed in England by Mackays of Chatham plc, Chatham, Kent

A CIP for this book
is available from the British Library

ISBN 0—571—21214—X

1   3   5   7   9   10   8   6   4   2

This book is for Lee, Chris, and Laura
and William Blake
and for
Renee Leonard

Were there darker provinces of night he would have found them.

> —Cormac McCarthy,
> *Child of God*, 1973

Sometimes I think you're just too sweet to die
Sometimes I think you're just too sweet to die
Another time I think you oughta be buried alive.

> —Richard "Rabbit" Brown,
> *James Alley Blues*, 1927

PROVINCES OF NIGHT

PROLOGUE

THE DOZER TOOK the first cut out of the claybank below Hixson's old place promptly at seven o'clock and by nine the sun was well up in an absolutely cloudless sky and it hung over the ravaged earth like a malediction.

The superintendent walked over to a white flatbed truck and leaned his numbered gradepole against it. He filled a Pepsi-Cola bottle with ice water from a cooler on the truckbed and drank. He took out a red bandanna and mopped his face and throat. Behind him the scraped bottomland stretched as far as the eye could see like a dead wasteland, a land no one would have. A blue pall of smoke shifted over it and no tree grew, no flower. A bird would not even fly over it.

A swamper named Risner came up carrying a widemouth Mason jar. Its surface was impacted with earth and Risner was mopping at it with the tail of his shirt.

What'd you find, Risner?

Dozer cut it out on that slope yonder, Risner said. *Likely it's money. These old folks always used to bury their money in fruit jars.*

These old people never had any excess money to put up in fruit jars, the superintendent said. *Likely you've found you a antique jar of green beans.*

Risner was holding the jar beneath the cooler's spout and running water over it.

You'll want that water long about three o'clock, the superintendent said.

Risner was mopping the jar with his shirt again. The shirt came away muddy. He was squinting into the jar then the wet jar seemed to slip in his hands and shattered between his workboots.

What the hell is that, the superintendent said.

In the splintered glass of this transparent crypt lay diminutive human bones of a marvelous delicacy. Bones fragile and fluted as a bird's, tiny skull with eyeholes black and blind, thin as paper, brittle as parchment. Scattered as if cast in a necromancer's divination, as if there might be pattern to them, order.

It looks like there was somebody in there, Risner said lamely.

BOOK ONE

BOOK ONE

*J*UST AT TWILIGHT Boyd came up the graveled walk, the chain with its plowpoint weight drawing the gate closed behind him, before him the shanty black and depthless as a stageprop against the failing light. On the porch the old man in the rocking chair sat staring burnt-eyed at him like some revenant out of his past.

Which he was, but Boyd went on anyway. Behind the shack the horizon went left and right as straight as a chalked line and as far as the eye could see, the furrowed earth tending away toward a hammered sky that looked like turbulent waters at land's end. The old man just watched him come, sepia felthatted old man like a curling Walker Evans photograph, brittle and fragile as memory.

Come up, Boyd, the old man said.

Boyd strode up to the edge of the porch. He stood for a moment as if awaiting invitation to sit and when none came sitting anyway, taking a bag of Country Gentleman smoking tobacco from his shirt pocket and uncreasing papers and beginning to construct a cigarette.

Looks like they about plowed you under, he said. He'd not had occasion to speak aloud for two days and the sound of his own voice seemed almost to startle him. He struck a match and lit the cigarette. He could not see the river but he could sense it, dank and yellow-smelling, rolling somewhere out of sight in the gathering dark.

They claim they need all the land for cotton, the old man said. His voice was thin and whispery, like cornhusks rustling together. I reckon when I'm gone they'll doze this mess down and plant it all.

Boyd smoked in silence. The momentum that had carried him for days, for miles, settled upon him like an enormous weight, and he was seized with weariness. Now that he was here he saw that he had reached not some final destination but simply a waystation that had drawn him miles in the wrong direction. If she was here he would have read it in the old man's face, but nothing at all was written there, not even what Boyd had expected; bitter recriminations, who knew what. All there was was a stoic calm he didn't know what to make of. As if the old man had come to some kind of terms. Then he studied the face closer. The yellowed skin was drawn tight across the cheekbones, the face sunken and caved, the blade of nose like something an undertaker had sculpted of wax then studied with a critical eye. All in all the old man looked like something recovered from the earth in gross resurrection and set arock on this porch in the middle of a cottonfield.

Boyd drew on the cigarette. You been sick, Ira? His voice was blued and furred by the smoke.

I'm fixin to die. I got a cancer.

Well I reckon you finally got something everybody else didn't get one of first, Boyd thought. I hope you're satisfied.

What's it of?

I got it in my lungs. I wish you'd put out that cigarette. I ain't let to smoke, and it makes me want one.

Boyd toed the cigarette out in the packed earth yard, a small vicious black smear. A lamp was lit inside, he could smell the smoky burning kerosene. He had forgotten about the old woman, but now he could sense her presence, see her bulk vaguely outlined against the screen of the door.

You afoot, the old man said. I knowed your walk the minute I seen you. You always walked like you had the world in your hip pocket. You ain't though, have you? Last time I seen you you was in a fine car. You had big plans.

Times is hard, Boyd said.

Times is always hard for some, the old man observed.

They sat in silence. Boyd was watching a blur of cypress past the cottonfield and beyond the cypress soundless lightning flickered the sky to a pale metallic rose. After a while a whippoorwill called out of the trees like something Boyd had been listening for without knowing it, or even some sound he'd summoned by sheer will, and he felt he'd crossed the entire state just to hear this lone whippoorwill mocking him out of the falling dark, and now he must turn around and go back the way he'd come.

How's that chap? the old woman said through the screen door. He must be about grown by now.

He's right at seventeen.

Who's he favor? We never had no picture nor nothin.

He looks a right smart like his mama.

She ain't here, the old man said suddenly. I reckon you've made a long trip for nothin.

If she ain't here I have. And you ain't seen her?

The last time I seen her her belly was swole up with that boy you spoke of and you was helpin her into that fine car. Looks like several things has changed since then.

Boyd stood up. He brushed dry flakes of tobacco off the front of his dungarees. He looked back the way he'd come. A dim wagon road fading out in the cottonfield. I got to get on, he said. We'll see you.

You take care of that chap, the old woman said. You need to be worrying about him stead of traipsin around the country.

Boyd raised a hand in farewell, dismissal, and took the first step away from the porch. No one bade him stay.

You do find her tell her I got a cancer, the old man said.

Boyd didn't say if he would or he wouldn't. He trudged on woodenly. He looked back once and no one had moved, the whole scene fading into a mauve dusk that seemed to be rising out of the earth itself like vapors, bluely transparent, slipping into invisibility now that it could no longer serve him any purpose.

DAPPLED BY the first warm light of the season Fleming Bloodworth lay on his stomach on a shelf of limestone that formed the summit of a bluff overlooking Grinders Creek. He was propped on his elbows watching the road through his father Boyd's binoculars. This road was red chert and it snaked in and out of sight through the cedars shrouding the bluff. A wooden bridge on concrete pylons crossed the creek downstream from where he was lying and through the powerful binoculars he could discern the heads of the forty-penny spikes the timbers were secured with, trace the grain that ran through the weathered wood.

He was waiting for the mailman. In actuality he was waiting for a lot of things: he was waiting for his father to return from wherever he had gone and for his mother to turn up from wherever she had gone and for himself to decide whether or not he was going back to school. His immediate concern, though, was for the mailman, for the U.S. Mail adhered to a schedule the rest of his life did not. The rest of his life seemed to be in limbo, waiting for one event to take place so that other events would sequence themselves behind it, a recognizable pattern coalesce from swirling chaos.

He had been up and about this day before good light. The day gave promise of being warm, and the remnants of a dream still swirling in his head touched it with portent.

He had dreamed that the mailman brought a check with his name on it, a check from a magazine called *Country Gentleman,* and he had little doubt that somewhere in the mailman's sorted box of fertilizer ads and burial plan duns such a check existed, needed only the delivering to bring into his possession a typewriter he had seen in the window of a five-and-dime store in the town of Ackerman's Field.

Some months back he had come into ownership of a stack of back numbers of this magazine *Country Gentleman.* He had read them cover to cover and written a story so cynically devised that he did not see how it could fail. This story had everything. It had a love story involving a boy and girl from two feuding families, a collie dog falsely accused of killing sheep, a sentimental resolution wherein the accused dog saves a child from drowning. It was Romeo and Juliet moved to the backwoods with a sheepkilling dog and a flood thrown in for good measure, and it would not have surprised him to learn that his name was being bandied about editorial offices in Atlanta, Georgia, where the magazine was published.

The mailman's car hove into view in a stretch of road between the cedars and almost immediately it began to honk its horn. The boy scrambled up. He was an habitual joiner of book clubs and requester of catalogs and sample copies of magazines but he couldn't think of anything he'd sent for that would not fit in a mailbox. Perhaps a check from a magazine required a signature.

He was scrambling down the shale bluffs going tree to tree. All right, all right, he yelled. The mailbox was set up by an enormous poplar tree at the foot of the hill and the mailman's car had parked before it and continued to honk dementedly until Fleming arrived out of breath at the driver's side window.

Young Bloodworth, the mailman said. Got a package here for you. He was holding a flat manila envelope and now he scanned the return address. The boy was regarding it with a dull loathing. *Country Gentleman,* the mailman said. Didn't know they took to boxin em up like this.

Fleming received the package with some reluctance, stood regarding it balefully as if he did not quite know what to do with it.

That all you got?

That's it, the mailman said. Your mama ever come back, Fleming?

Thanks for the package, Bloodworth said, turning away toward the hill. The car remained still for a few seconds then the mailman raised a hand and drove away.

Crossing the ditch before the hill began its steep ascent he opened the flap of the envelope. The first thing he saw was his own handwriting, the second a note that had been paperclipped to his manuscript. *We regret that we are unable to read handwritten manuscripts,* someone in Atlanta had written. *All submissions must be typewritten.* He threw the manuscript into the ditch and went on up the hill but after a few steps returned and recovered the manila envelope and went on.

To reach this house you came from either of two ways. If you came by the cherted road you left it at the foot of the hill and climbed up through patches of limestone and a grove of cedars where the footpath led. It was an almost vertical ascent and the house came into view by increments, first a green tarpaper roof, hipped from the four corners of the house to a peak in the center, then weathered board walls, a house cobbled up from odds and ends, homemade, as happenstantial as something left by the recession of floodwaters. I reckon it'll do till we find somethin better, Boyd had said, but the boy had been six years old then.

If you approached from the rear, came down from the heavily timbered woods, you followed a footpath that in turn followed the spectral shadings of an old wagon road, a ghost of a road, a rumor of a road. This house had been constructed by and for folk for whom a footpath would serve as well, folk who did not acknowledge the invention of the internal combustion engine, to whom the value of the wheel itself was still in question.

The day that had begun with such promise now yawned like an enormous vacuum that he was called upon somehow to fill. He took down a slingblade from the porch and began to cut weeds, clearing the yard then progressing on toward the garden spot, the air full of bits of weeds like anomolaec snow. The day warmed as it progressed and he took off his shirt and resumed work as if he'd rid the world of weeds once and for all.

In the late afternoon he finally put up the slingblade and went into the house. The house was dark and cool, cavelike, scarcely lit by the windows. He took up a book and with it a cold cup of the morning's coffee and went to a chair where light fell through a windowglass and began to read.

The day drew on, was swallowed in dusk, in silence. No bird called, no insect. Life in abeyance, the world itself grinding to a halt, who knew what would follow. Light through the glass grew dim but he read on as if the passage of day into night was of no moment. The world was winding down, and young Bloodworth wound down with it.

NIGHT. Boyd hunkered in a viaduct watching beaded rain swing slant off the concrete lip above him. Through the silver curtain this made he watched the lights of a town wax and wane like something dimly perceived through deep waters. Thunder rolled hollowly across the flat countryside. An inch of dirty water coursed beneath him and his feet were wet. He tried to roll a cigarette but his fingers were wet as well and the paper shredded in his hands. I wouldn't have this Goddamn country if they boxed it up and sent it somewhere I could use it, he said. If they shoved a deed to it in my shirt pocket. Cars went by with tires sluicing the water, gleaming and newlooking in the rain, stark in the surreal clarity of the lightning, like images that were imprinting themselves behind his eyelids.

The concrete was too low to stand erect in and when his legs grew cramped he stood stooped with his hands clasped on his knees, staring into the black water that coursed between his feet. Lightning showed him cigarette butts, scraps of paper, an unrolled condom trailing like some weird sealife.

I reckon by God it's set in for the night, he told himself.

It hadn't though. The intervals between the blind white stabs stretched farther and farther, he thought the low rumbling was growing more distant, rolling on eastward the way he planned to go himself. When the rain tempered itself to a slow drizzle he came out of the viaduct and rubbed the stiffness out of his legs and clambered up the sloping shoulder of riprap onto the blacktop and walked off toward the lights of town.

Such town as there was and what there was of it asleep. He trudged through a high-class section of town, into a neighborhood where watchdogs from the dark porches they watched refused even to acknowledge his passage, as if he'd achieved some measure of invisibility. Or was utterly alien to their frame of reference, emissary from some race set apart. He put his hands in his pockets and hunched his shoulders in the wet coat and coming into what appeared to be the business section of town looked for something that might be open. A cab stand, a bus station, an allnight diner. The wet black sidewalks gleamed where the streetlamps pooled and particolored neon pulsed in the streets like a gaudy heartbeat.

Tires sloughed softly on wet macadam. An engine slowed, almost pacing him, the engine idled down so that he could hear the lick the full-race cam was hitting, and he thought *cop* without even turning to look. A soft breeze had risen in these western flatlands and in the street-lamp's globe of yellow, rain swung slantwise in a silver spray.

Hey.

Boyd turned. A blue and white cruiser was creeping along, driver's side window down, slab of beefy red face peering out. Jowly as a bull-dog. Hard cop's eyes, like shards of agate splintered off by the blow of a hammer.

Can I help you?

Not in any way I can think of, Boyd said.

Where are you going? Boyd had increased his pace but the cruiser compensated to match him, the cop's face intent as if he'd commit him to memory should he be called upon to identify this visage from a wit-ness stand or as if he'd compare it to some handbill seen long ago on a post office wall.

Somewheres it's dry, Boyd said. Am I breaking one of your laws or something?

None that I know of. It's just that it's three o'clock in the morning and most folks is in bed asleep. I seen you walking and thought you might have troubles of some kind. Be looking for a doctor or some-thing.

I don't reckon I need one, Boyd said. He took a deep breath, held it, forced himself to contain his anger. I was visitin some folks out by the levee, he said. Got caught out in the storm and sheltered under a bridge back yonder. I live east of here, in Lewis County, and I figured there might be a Greyhound station here.

There ain't no bus station as such. They sell tickets out of the Bob-White Cafe and the bus stops there for pickups. But not till seven thirty in the morning.

And there ain't nothing else open?

There may be somebody hangin around the cab stand. Get in, I'll drop you off.

Boyd knew the difference between an order and an invitation. He got in. He sat clasping the door handle. Thinks I'll steal his fuckin town,

Boyd thought with sour amusement. As if they had anything he wanted. The cruiser eased through the sleeping streets, Boyd's eyes cataloging a five-and-dime, a jewelry store, the aforementioned Bob-White Cafe. Closed, closed, closed, please call again. The entire town of Tiptonville, Tennessee, posted off-limits this April morning in 1952. If he pulls up in front of city hall he's goin to be one surprised son of a bitch, Boyd thought. He won't know what hit him.

The cop didn't speak again. He stopped in front of a small rundown storefront where a sign said TAXI and Boyd knew he was meant to get out. He did. He closed the door and the cruiser eased away. The plate-glass front of the cab stand was cracked in myriad fissures mended with duct tape and the entire window bulged slightly outward as if barely containing some internal force. There was a padlock through the hasp on the peeling green door but a cab parked at the curb before it and Boyd could see a pair of shoe soles propped against the driver's side window.

When Boyd rapped with a knuckle on the glass the shoes moved and a man raised up in the front seat and rolled a bleary eye up at him. The man wiped a hand across his face as if he'd erase sleep and cranked down the glass.

You needin a ride?

You know where a man might buy a drink of whiskey this time of night?

I might. Get on in here, no, get up here in the front with me. It's fell a flood ain't it? Looks like it fell a good bit of it on you.

I got caught out in it, Boyd said, getting in and pulling the door closed. How far is it to this bootlegger's?

It ain't never far to a bootlegger, the driver said, cranking the engine and pulling out into the street. Won't be no more than a fifty-cent run.

They drove out past the railroad tracks. A string of boxcars and flatcars stacked with crossties was pulled onto a siding and Boyd turned and watched them out of sight. They rode on past poultry houses with rows of lighted windows that looked long as freight trains and past cotton-fields wet and blacklooking in the headlights and across a rickety bridge that popped and snapped ominously under the cab's passage and to a bricksiding house in a treeless earth yard.

He don't sell nothin but halfpint bottles, the cabby said. I think it's a dollar and a half for a halfpint.

Boyd walked toward the porch beneath a bare lightbulb suspended from a wire that seemed to descend out of the dark heavens themselves. When he knocked a tiny door within the door opened immediately as if they'd had word here of his coming and a moleshaped man stood regarding him benignly from among his stacked cases of bottles.

Let me have two halfpints of whiskey.

I ain't got nothing but peach brandy left, the man said. I sold a sight in the world of whiskey tonight. Everybody in this part of the country must of decided to get drunk.

Just let me have whatever you got then.

When he'd paid for the brandy and paid the cabdriver Boyd had one lone dollar left and this he folded and slid carefully into the watch pocket of his jeans. In the cab he cracked one of the bottles and drank and offered it to the cabdriver but the cabby waved it away.

Lord no. I ever started drinking when I was behind the wheel I'd likely drive clean off to Asia or somewhere. I can't be trusted drinkin and drivin an automobile.

Shit ain't worth drinkin anyhow. Kind of sickly sweet. I bet enough of this stuff'd give a man a hell of a hangover.

I'll tell you what it'll give you in Lake County, the cabdriver said. A few days in the crossbar hotel. Where do you want to go? They'll vag you in this town, you ain't got a pocketful of money.

About two hundred and fifty miles from here, Boyd said. I guess that's more than a fifty-cent run, ain't it. How often they run that train out?

Ever day. Them flatcars of ties leaves some time in the mornin headed towards Jackson. You goin to have to get somewheres until then.

Let me out at the railroad tracks then.

HIS MOTHER had gone in the night with no word of her intent though the signs were there if you cared to read them. In his mind Fleming could see her covert departure. Perhaps carrying her shoes, tiptoeing toward the door past the moonlit windows, light to dark, light to dark until she vanished. Until the night negated her, made her transparent as the shade in some old grandmother's ghost story, sucked her down where the light goes when you lean and blow out a candle.

She had long been a silent woman, in her early thirties but old before her time, life passing her by, the world going its way without her. She had grown stingy with words, whole days spent in sullen silence, as if her supply of words was being exhausted and she must parcel them out one by one.

He had watched the sallow mask she wore for a face and wondered what went on behind it. A year ago he came upon her burning a box of his books, feeding them one by one to the wood heater. They struggled for a moment over the book she was proffering to the fire. He wrested the box away from her and she threw the book she was holding and slammed him hard in the side of the head. You dreamyeyed little fool, she spat at him, expressing once and for all her contempt for the written word, those who would read it and those who would attempt to transcribe it in spiralbound notebooks.

The night she vanished Boyd had shaken him awake, holding aloft the kerosene lamp, something strange in his face that was echoed in his voice when he spoke.

Where's your mama?

Fleming didn't know anything to say to this. He got up and followed Boyd into the front room. Boyd was searching all about the room though there was no place for her to be. He seemed in the throes of a grief so grotesque it was almost comic, and Fleming watched him with a dispassionate emotion approaching contempt.

If this don't beat any damn thing I ever seen, Boyd said.

The boy went back to bed. After a while he heard the door close when Boyd went out and then close again when he came back in. He waited for the sound of the bedsprings creaking when Boyd went back to bed but he never heard it. At length he turned his face to the wall and went to sleep.

BOYD WAS half asleep when the cars were coupled to the engine, a loud metallic shunting and a series of jolts he could feel in his teeth. He raised up from the straw he'd been lying in when the cars began to move, the dark landscape of light and shadow sliding past the open door. He drank from the opened bottle and put it back inside his shirt with its brother where he could feel it cold and smooth against his belly. He took out his tobacco and began to build a cigarette, watching past the flare of the match sleeping houses streaking past like islands afloat in the moving sea of night, the train's speed increasing, so that he was caught in a rising tide of exhilaration at its sheer movement.

I wouldn't mind one of them smokes, a voice said.

Boyd leapt involuntarily at the sound; he hadn't known there was anybody else in the world. At length he could make out a shape, a darker shadow among other shadows.

I ain't goin to bring it to you.

The shadow stirred, and Boyd could smell the man, a rank sour compound of perspiration, whiskey. He reached the tobacco across when the man hunkered before him, the man separating out a paper and sifting tobacco into it, light slant across his bearded jaw, long lank strawcolored hair that fell like a shadow across his eyes.

I had some money I'd buy a sack of my own. You ain't got a quarter you'd let a man have have you?

All I got is a dollar bill and there ain't no way of breakin it. If I had some change I'd give it to you.

That dollar'd work, the man said. His face was wolfish in the orange flare of the match, somehow unreal through the exhaled smoke, not like a man but the malevolent embodiment of one, just another obstacle the angry fates had stood in Boyd's path.

Boyd was gauging the man's size and he didn't reply. He was confident of his own size and strength, once when he'd worked at the tie yards he'd on a bet shouldered and walked off with a seven-by-nine crosstie on each shoulder. He could feel the tensing muscles of his thighs, the rockhard biceps, and he drew comfort from them. Boyd was as fastidious in his personal habits as circumstances permitted and he thought, if I can get past the smell of him I'll be all right.

How about a little drink of that whiskey?

I ain't got no whiskey.

The hell you don't. If there's one thing I ain't never mistook about it's the sound of a whiskey bottle lid bein screwed off. There ain't nothin else in the world sounds like it.

Why don't you just get away and leave me the hell alone? I ain't botherin you.

Let's have that dollar you been braggin about.

Boyd shoved him hard backward but the man seemed to have been expecting it and when he came up he was opening a hawkbill knife that just appeared from nowhere. Boyd crouched and waited for the thrust of the knife and when it came he grasped the arm as hard as he could and broke it across his knee. The knife spun away. As he stooped to pick it up the man gave a cry of animal rage and butted him so hard he went backpedaling away until his feet ran out of surface and he was falling, a nightmarish vision of the door receding not only upward but jerked hard to the right, the wheels clocking and gears gnashing like hell's jaws and abruptly he was rolling knees over head down a stony slope, pain that was liquid fire flaring in his sides and strange lights flickering behind his eyelids. He fetched up at the bottom of the slope sitting on his haunches and watching the vanishing train with a stunned disbelief.

At length he rose and pulled his shirt off and shook the glass out of it. Blood black as tar in the starlight was tracking down his ribcage from myriad cuts. He studied his wounds as best he could to gauge the seriousness of them and when he was satisfied stood picking the shards of glass out of his skin. The shirt was soaked with blood and peach brandy but there was nothing for it. He pulled the shirt on and buttoned it.

He turned left, right, trying to pinpoint the four points of the compass in all this dark. This world was flat as a pool table and as featureless. He wasted a few minutes searching for the tobacco and on the faint hope that only one of the bottles had shattered but gave it up when he found both bottlecaps.

It seemed a long time before the faintest wash of light appeared in the eastern sky and when it did he rose and walked off toward it.

WHEN E. F. BLOODWORTH came up the concrete stairway from the basement carrying the cased banjo she was sitting in the swing on the end of the porch waiting for him the way he had known she would be. He could hear the peas she was shelling begin striking the tin bucket set beside the swing but she had commenced only upon hearing him close the door to his rented room. The thought of her sitting there with unshelled peas held at the ready and waiting for the sound of his footfalls was a little disquieting, and he began to feel boxed in, a way he did not like to feel. And never had for long.

The day he had carried the guitar to the freight office to be shipped to Ackerman's Field she had been at work but she had missed the old Martin double-F immediately and inquired about it. He had shipped the guitar first because he could not carry both instruments at once, and he hated worse being separated from the banjo.

You'll fall out in that sun, she said. You know what the doctor told you.

Bloodworth was coming around the end of the porch, fending his way through the box elders with a walking stick. He only told me that because I was about broke, he said. If I had had twenty more dollars I could of got a more favorable report.

He crossed between the box elders and the porch. You planted all this mess so I couldn't fight my way through it and escape, he told her. He set the banjo case down on a cracked and wonky sidewalk and seated himself with some difficulty on the edge of the porch.

She went on shelling peas. It don't seem to be working too well, does it? she asked.

He took off his hat, a pearlgray Stetson fedora, and ran a hand across the long black strands of his hair. The sun was in his face and he shaded it with a hand. He had a craggy, hawklike face. His black eyes were heavylidded and sleepylooking, but watchful as a predator's. He sat for a long moment watching her out of these hooded eyes.

She was as square and solid and unlovely as a wooden packing crate. Her high-complexioned moonshaped face bloomed with the high blood pressure she suffered from and her hair was dyed a hard bright orange that nature would have been hard put to replicate. But she sat in the shade of a rose trellis and the shadows of roses and the shadows of their leaves climbed her clean white nurse's uniform onto her face and her eyes were a clear bright blue that reminded the old man of Indian summer skies he had seen long ago as a boy. On top of that she was as kind a human being as he had ever encountered and he had thought long and hard before deciding to make this move.

You are a fool, she told him. But then you don't need me to tell you that.

Where were you fifty years ago? he asked. If you'd told me that then it might have done some good. I might have straightened right out.

You couldn't be straightened out with a block and tackle hooked on each end of you. The only way you'll ever be straightened out is when they arrange you in the box and clasp your hands together.

Damned if you wouldn't cheer a feller up, he said. I bet in your spare time you set around making up sayings that would look good carved on tombstones.

I spend too much of my time taking care of people who die in spite of all they can do, she said. It aggravates me to see a man with a choice just set out to kill himself. You'll die on that bus. They'll take you off on a stretcher in some place where nobody gives a damn about you. It looks to me like if a man's set on dying he'd want to do it where there's somebody cares something about him.

I don't want to do it nowhere, Bloodworth said. And ain't about to.

You know I care something about you. I'd take care of you. And I can do it right, that's what I do for a living.

The amount of care I need has been way overstated, the old man said. I believe I'm capable of taking care of myself.

He fell silent, watching her. He didn't want to tell her that what she did for a living was part of the problem. Cora worked in a hospital in Little Rock, in the wing where patients were sent to die. It was Cora's job to help them, and he guessed she was good at it, they all died, but he didn't want any help from a professional. An aura of death hung about her like a plague. The smell of dying folks had soaked into her clothes, her lungs were saturated from breathing the last breaths of too many men, when she got up to cross the floor the unquiet dead she'd helped ferry across the Styx struggled up and followed obediently after her. She moved always encumbered by a legion of the invisible dead.

The tunes and words to songs ran perpetually through the old man's head and he thought of one he used to sing: *who'll rock the cradle, who'll sing the song*? and he wondered when the time came who would bind Cora's slack jaws, who would lean to close her eyelids forever.

It's just somethin I've got to do, he said. I want to see the country where I was a boy. And I guess maybe I want to see how long hard feelins can last.

They last a long time, she told him. I've no doubt that you'll learn that, at least.

He stood up, took up the banjo. I've got to get this thing shipped, I can't set around here jawing with you all day. I'm not even leaving till I get a little more of my strength back. Likely the way it'll go is I'll stay a month or two and come back before winter. Or maybe send for you, Cora, how about that? Would you come if I sent for you?

I'd go to wherever you sent for me from, Cora said, half amused and half angry. But God, what kind of fool do you think I am? You never needed anybody bad enough in your life to send for them.

I'm goin to town before this heat gets worse, he said, taking up the stick from where he'd leaned it against a porch stanchion.

You wait up, she said. If you're so set on going I'll call you a cab.

He went on. He did not want to die here in this boarding house. Cora was a good woman but he did not want his last vision of the world to be her moonshaped face floated down to his, leaning to whisper the password that would permit him access to a world that was in all probability even stranger and darker than this one.

TWO DAYS LATER just as he was falling asleep Fleming heard Boyd whistling his way down the footpath from the barn. The whistling was fiercely evocative, an artifact out of his childhood, and he thought at first he had dreamed it. He was out of bed and lighting the lamp when he heard Boyd's heavy step on the porch. The room leapt into yellow relief as the door opened and Boyd came in. The room was suddenly smaller, the house less empty and dead. Boyd filled it with raw and jagged-edged life.

Who cut all them weeds? Looks like the place was attacked by a bunch of mowin machines.

I did. I ran out of anything to do.

You'd do better to be in school unless your plan is to set your ass in the same seat next year. It does look some better, though. You've probably run up property values all up and down Grinders Creek.

Fleming didn't reply. Boyd had a bundle wrapped in white butcher's paper and a loaf of bread. He set all this on the cooktable. Build up a fire and let's cook some of this beefsteak, he said. I'm about starved away to nothing.

He removed a paperback book from the back pocket of his dungarees. I brought you this. I don't know whether it's any good or not.

Thanks, the boy said. He turned away from the cookstove where he was lighting kindling and took the book and tilted its cover toward the light. *Yellowhair* by Clay Fisher. The cover showed a yellowhaired man the boy judged to be George Armstrong Custer beset by a horde of marauding savages. It looks pretty good, he said. I may start on it tonight.

Let's get this steak floured up and fried. I've toted it halfway across the country and we might as well get some good out of it.

While the stove heated up Boyd sliced the steak and tenderized it with the edge of a saucer and breaded it with flour and pepper and salt. He sliced potatoes into a skillet of melting grease. The boy watched him. He was waiting for Boyd to ask the question he knew he was going to ask and finally Boyd asked it.

You not seen nothin of your mama?

No.

I ever catch the son of a bitch she run off with I'll cut his throat. I aim to catch him, too.

Fleming didn't say anything but he heard this with a sinking sensation in the pit of his stomach. Another man might say these words and have them mean any number of things but if Boyd said it it just meant he was going to cut somebody's throat.

Where were you at?

I been through hell and just barely got scorched. I learned that hell is real flat and somebody has planted cotton all over it. How come you ain't over at Ma's like I told you to be?

I don't know. Brady's a little hard to take at times.

He is that. At most times. Any clean shirts around here?

In that box by your bed. Old man Overbey was by here looking for you. He wants us to set out some pines.

Pines, Boyd said. He was turning the sizzling steak, stirring the potatoes. It'll be hard times indeed when I work for that stingy son of a bitch. Is there any coffee left?

We're about out of everything.

Something'll turn up.

They ate the steak and potatoes by lamplight, fending away one-handed moths and candleflies the light drew through the window. Boyd wiped his plate with a slice of lightbread and rose still chewing and filled the wash basin from the water bucket. He pulled off his shirt and balled it up and raised the stovelid and dropped the shirt onto the coals.

Great God, the boy said.

I fell off a train, Boyd told him.

Fleming judged there was a story here could he but hear it but Boyd was a man whose fences you broached at your peril and he guessed if Boyd wanted him to know he'd tell him.

NOTHING TURNED UP and Monday morning they came out of Hubert Overbey's barnlot and climbed a hillside to the edge of the woods where night still hovered, their shoulders laden with great burlap bags of pine seedlings, mattocks swinging along loosely in their hands. They fell to work on a slope of ravaged red clay, a blasted heath where nothing seemed to thrive save sawbriars and ditches.

An ascending sun burned off the early chill and as he warmed Fleming fell into an easy rhythm of working, a blow with the mattock, a dropped seedling, earth raked and tamped with a booted foot. Boyd worked savagely as if he bore each separate seedling some bitter grudge, as if he'd inflict pain to the earth each time he sank the mattock to the eye in the hard red clay.

At noon they ate a silent lunch of leftover breakfast bacon and biscuits and watched clouds form in the west, a thunderhead that rose and lay above the lowering hills like a tumor. Boyd threw away the rest of his lunch and poured out his coffee and got up. We'd better get it before that rain blows in here, he said.

By midafternoon they had covered scarcely a quarter of the slope and Overbey's supply of seedlings seemed to have diminished not at all. They laid aside their tools when all the sun there was was a fierce chromatic rose flaring behind the thunderhead and by the time they reached the roadbed night was seeping down out of the trees and nighthawks came slant out of the mauve dusk like flung stones. When they reached the house full dark had fallen and the house was cold and dark and enigmatic, like some house abandoned, like some house where no one lived at all.

The boy was cooking when they heard a car door slam at the foot of the hill. Boyd started at the sound and Fleming said, it's not her. Likely it's Dee Hixson.

I don' believe I feel like fightin them pines all day and contendin with that nosy old loafer all night. I believe I'll just run him off.

Fleming was standing in the doorway peering into the darkness where a figure was climbing the hill, shoeleather clicking on stones, a shape gaining corporeality as if it were forming itself out of shadows.

It's Brady, Fleming said.

On the other hand Dee might not have been so bad, Boyd said.

Brady Bloodworth was Boyd's younger brother though you would not have known it to look at him. He was small and freckled and intense. Slightly hunched as if something inside him was winding itself up and as it tightened drawing him toward his own center. His curly red hair sprang out wildly from beneath the felt hat he wore and his eyes burned incandescent as a cat's eyes in the lamplight. Childhood polio had marked him with a warped leg that limped still when he walked and left him perhaps as well with other warpings not as visible to the naked eye.

He sat on an old replevied car seat that served as a sofa and took off his hat and hung it on his knee. He ran a hand through his tangled hair. Still bachin, I see, he said.

Still bachin, Boyd told him.

What's that boy cookin up?

I don't know. We won't know till it's done. We'd ask you to supper but our grub's probably a little rough for you. You used to Ma's cookin and all.

It's just as well. I believe he's fryin up candleflies and everthing else. I seen a big one fly into that pan and I ain't seen it fly out yet.

We're a little loose in our ways around here. We wasn't expectin company.

What I come about was Pa. He's finally comin back.

That's a little hard for me to believe.

Believe it. He's had a stroke of paralysis and he ain't got nowhere else to go.

Well, hell, Boyd said, with a curious note in his voice that made Fleming turn and look at him. It must have been a bad stroke to make him do that. Pa always had more pride than was good for him and he never was one for backtrackin. How bad is he?

He ain't goin to die, if that's what you mean. I talked to him on a telephone, long-distance from Little Rock, Arkansas. He just called right up on the telephone. Lucky I was in the house and answered it. It could just as easy have been Ma.

That wouldn't have been the end of the world, Boyd said dryly. I expect she's noticed by now he's gone. It has been twenty years.

He's stove up but he's got all his senses and everything. His faculties. Got a limp on one side and goes with a stick but he says he's gettin better. He thinks he's goin to die, but he's not.

He's not? It must be nice to know stuff like that that other people wonders about. To have God lean down and whisper secrets in your ear.

Well. I run it out in the cards and he ain't fixin to die.

Jesus Christ. You run it out in the cards. Everbody dies sooner or later.

Brady had taken the packet of cards from his shirt pocket without noticing, slid them from their satin slipcase, rippled them smoothly from one hand to the other. He seemed to draw strength and confidence from them.

The cards don't lie, he said, apologetic but at the same time a little condescending. He may die later but he won't from this stroke.

I believe you're glad he's had a stroke. You seem to relish the idea of him bein a cripple, a broken old man.

The Bible says as ye sow so shall ye reap. He sowed it, not me.

It also says fortune tellers and soothsayers are an abomination before God.

Then it turns right around and says don't hide your light under a bushel. He gave me this secondsight, which is light in a way, and I ain't about to hide it.

I give up. How come him to call you, knowin the way you've felt about him for twenty years?

You ain't got a telephone. I guess he didn't know Warren's runnin that show in Alabama. He must have made a little money all them years he was pickin the banjo and singin all that crazy stuff nobody wanted to hear. He's wirin me the money to buy him a little housetrailer and set it up somewhere on the place.

Oh Lord. He's sendin you money and trustin you to do that?

Well, Pa always favored me over the rest of you. Always petted me, right up to the day he walked off and not a word out of him for twenty years. He done me and Ma sorry and you know it. Walkin off like that without a word. Not goodbye, not kiss my ass. Nothin.

Nothin to us, you mean.

Nothin to anybody. I can't believe he's got the nerve to come back. The gall. He probably expected to move right into the house with me and Ma.

Well. It's a pretty big place, two hundred and seventy acres. And I believe he bought and paid for it.

He'd have lost it over that penitentiary business if it hadn't been for Warren. I paid the last of it off myself.

He stood to go. I just thought you'd want to know he's comin back, he said. That boy there ain't never even seen his grandpa.

Don't rush off, Boyd said. I was just teasin you about the food, it's fit to eat. Just stay and eat with us.

I eat hours ago. I have to see about Ma. I have leavin her by herself at night. She's gettin old and childish. Absent-minded.

She's got more sense than me or you either one.

She's also over seventy years old and ain't realized it yet. I'm always afraid she'll fall or somethin. I'll let you know when I hear from Pa again.

Well. Come back, Brady.

When Brady was down the hill and they heard the car start Boyd said, That stroke must have kicked the hell right out of Pa. For him to swallow his pride and call Brady on the telephone.

He took a pan of water off the stove and set it on the table and positioned a mirror by the lamp. He lathered his face and began to shave. Fleming could hear the faint scrape of the straightrazor against Boyd's beard.

Poor old Brady, Boyd said. One minute you're feeling sorry for him and then he'll start that crazy mess about cards and hexes he's put on folks and about how the Jews are takin over the world and the Pope's takin over the world and you just want to wring his neck.

After supper the house was hot from the cookstove and to cool Fleming went outside and sat on the doorstep. The wind was at the trees like something alive and faint light quaked and died, flared and diminished far to the west and he held his breath waiting for the thunder. It finally came, so faint it was like a dream of thunder, a hoarse incoherent whisper, just a madman mumbling to himself in the eaves of the world.

The rain commenced sometime in the night and it was raining when they ate breakfast in a cold damp halfdark and raining still when they fell out with the mattocks. Fleming thought Boyd might wait for a break in the weather but there was no mention of this and they garbed themselves in old coats and hats until they looked like animated scarecrows starting up the roadbed. There was already a yellowish tinge and a quickened urgency to the water in the creek and a steady rushing sound of rain in the trees.

They labored like men demented over the muddy slope. There was no letup in the rain or even a rumor of it and the day seemed to chill as it progressed and the boy felt cold and wooden in his outsize clothing. He was loathe to move against the waterlogged clothes but he felt he'd freeze if he stopped working.

They had brought no lunch but at what they judged to be noon they sheltered beneath a huge cedar and watched the slope go to water, a thousand red rivulets coursing down the muddy hillside. In the ruined hat collapsed about his face Boyd seemed the very embodiment of human misery. A pale wash of hat dye was seeping down his face and he wiped it away and grinned ruefully. I don't know why it's so damned cold, he said. Blackberry winter ain't till May.

Maybe it's some other kind of winter. Toad frog winter.

Whatever winter it is it's a cold son of a bitch. And I believe that somehow it's managin to rain harder under this tree than it is out in that field.

The boy scanned the sky in the faint hope of a lightening but the sky was just cold weeping slate and if there was any sun behind it there was no indication of it. Why don't we call it a day and go to the house, he said.

We will here in a while, Boyd said. His face was cold and determined, as if he'd set himself some goal beyond the capabilities of ordinary men and would settle for nothing less than its completion.

When only twenty or thirty bundles of seedlings remained Boyd paused for a moment and considered them in speculation. What I ought to do is throw the damned things in a sinkhole and be done with them. But I contracted to set them out and by God I'll set them out.

They finished the last of them in red sucking mud and shouldered the mattocks and walked toward Overbey's farmhouse. Climbing the high steps onto the porch Fleming's legs felt as if they were asleep and his feet felt numb and wooden. They stood on the porch. Boyd knocked and waited. Pools of muddy water formed around their feet. The boy could hear the rushing of the creek somewhere off in the trees.

Overbey opened the door and stood regarding them with a bemused wonder. They looked like refugees, worse, like something exiled from the very fringes of human society. Something chimerical and insubstantial engendered out of the windy rain.

Overbey was cleaning the lenses of his glasses on the tail of his shirt. He looked warm and dry, cozy as a badger in its den. Beyond him a warm hearth, the flickering flames of a fireplace. There was a strong odor of steaming coffee.

I've heard of people willing to work but you two are about the beat of any I've seen. There wasn't that much of a rush to it. You get them all?

We got them all.

Well. Wait here and I'll get your money.

He went back in and eased the door to. Right, Boyd said. We wouldn't want to drip on your Goddamned carpet.

When Overbey returned Boyd was wringing water out of his hat. Overbey proffered a thin blue slip of paper and Boyd looked at his hands and tried to dry them but there was no place that did not have water running out of it. Finally he shoved them beneath his coat and dried them as best he could in the armpits of his shirt. He took the check gingerly and folded it and stowed it in a glassine envelope in his wallet.

You men want a cup of coffee?

We got to get on, Boyd said.

I do, Fleming told him.

Boyd glanced sharply at him but waited stoically while Overbey brought the coffee and impatiently while it was drunk. Fleming's hands were shaking and he held the cup with both hands and drank the coffee. It was hot and strong and he imagined he could feel it coursing through his veins and thawing out the parts of him that were frozen.

Overbey just looked at them and shook his head. I'd give you a ride but I expect it's over the bridge by now. It's fell a world of water last night and today.

Tell me about it, Boyd said.

Fleming reached Overbey the cup and they went down the steps into the rain. The day was already beginning to wane and they could see past the greening trees white fog rising off the creek like smoke and the very air felt dense as water in their lungs.

When they got to the crossing the creek was far out of its banks and they didn't even suspect where the bridge might be. The creek was a roiling mass of leaves and tree branches and once an entire tree, its dislodged roots twisting into the bank and the tree clocking around wheellike in the swirling yellow foam. All the sound there was was the angry roar of the water. Boyd stared disgustedly at it as if this was just one more cross to bear, one more obstacle laid in his path.

A drowned cow went by, its legs jutting stiffly upward. One of Overbey's, Boyd said with satisfaction. You want to try that swinging bridge?

Fleming decided that his father had gone mad. Something had simply broken in his head. Finally he said, I don't think so.

Then it's either sleep here tonight or go back to Overbey's and come around the bluff. Which'll it be?

The swinging bridge was a quartermile downstream. In the flooded bottomland sycamores rose white as bone out of the turbulent water. By the time they reached the platform the bridge was swung from they were slogging through thighdeep water. The ladder rose dizzily to the top of the platform where cables were suspended tree to tree. A relic of some older time, the bridge was seldom used anymore and sections of its flooring had fallen away and what remained were rottenlooking and questionable.

It seemed a long climb to the bridge. Farther still across the swaying cable to the other shore. Boyd crossed first, as if he'd defy these waters to take him. Fleming went cautiously, trying each board before he entrusted it with his weight, hanging onto the cables that served as handholds while the bridge creaked and yawed drunkenly over the mutated stream that went in a dizzy rush beneath him. He looked down once and the moving water appeared in some perversion of gravity to be tugging the bridge downstream and when his head reeled with the unspooling water he forced himself to look at the farther side until the shifting trees halted their spinning.

Going down there was water again but nothing to do but wade it and when they again reached the roadbed Fleming felt like some shipwrecked mariner struggling onto the reefs of a lost and barren island.

In the house he lit the lamp but was too tired to eat and too tired to build a fire and he stripped off his sodden clothes and put on dry ones and fell into bed. He'd thought he'd known before what exhaustion was but he'd been mistaken. He was immediately in a dreamless slumber but woke sometime far into the night at what he thought was some sudden sound but what woke him was silence. The rain had stopped.

The next morning the first thing he noticed was that he was warm. He got up and went into the front room and saw that Boyd had already been up and about. There was a fire in the heater and the room was filled with the strong evocative odor of coffee and chicory. He did not see Boyd anywhere.

He took a cup from the cooktable and filled it from the coffee pot on the stove and went outside. It had cleared in the night and the sun was bright though it was still very cold. A steely rime of frost lay upon everything. He didn't see Boyd and he went back into the house.

The first thing he saw was a note taped to the mirror by the window. Now what the hell is this, he thought. He took down and unfolded the sheet of foolscap.

> I have gone to get your mama. From what I can learn she is in Detroit Michigan with that peddler. I hate about taking the money but it is all I can do and I've got to have it. I will send it back when I get work. I will be back soon but till I do you go over to Ma's and stay there. I mean stay there.

He stood holding the note for a time with no look at all on his face. Then he crossed to the heater and opened the door. He balled the note up and threw it into the flames.

WHERE THE WOODS ended abruptly the field began, so that Fleming Bloodworth stepped from a thick viney undergrowth awash with birdsong into an open meadow lazy in the sun, cows grazing placidly below him, the new grass shading the rolling slopes with the palest of green. Tilting blackbirds burnished by the noon sun gleamed like contrivances of tinfoil, somewhere behind him a dove began to call, soft and mournful as something lost.

He sat for a time on the splitrail fence that bound the pasture, idly watching the house and its attendant buildings sleeping this warm day away. A great gothic farmhouse, of whitewashed lumber, its steep green roofline and gables like something moved intact from New England, its windows curtained and shuttered like drowsing eyes. He waited patiently to see what life would show itself. Some of Brady's dogs milling below the kennel, a wild motley of strange dogs of no exact color and no determinate breed, perhaps some breed Brady had invented. Or invoked from the mismatched parts of other dogs, he thought, raised like Lazarus from roadkill dogs by the dark alchemy he boasted of. Fleming smiled to himself, in no hurry, feeling the sun on his shoulders, postponing the moment when he must rise and make his way down to his grandmother's house.

Suddenly the screen door of the house opened and his grandmother came onto the porch with a broom, tiny, silent, furiously animate. She lit into one of the dogs with the broom and he could hear its startled yelp, see it scrambling madly for the gate down the doorstep. The gate must have been latched, for it finally scrambled over the porch railing and went streaking for the kennel. He didn't see Brady about but he judged him somewhere around the place, for he could see the sun hammering off Brady's black Buick, turtlebacked and gleaming, parked beneath the huge pine tree that shadowed the house.

He rose, in no haste, and ambled down the slope, letting the day sink into his pores as he went, cataloging the smells and sensations. The warm weight of the sun on his back on what might have been the first day of summer. The citrusy smell of the pine woods, the raw loamy earth smell of a field turned darkly to the sun by Brady's tractor, the faint call of distant crows that was all there was to break the silence.

He came up past the kennel in a wild cacophony of noise, the dogs yelping and throwing themselves in a frenzy against the heavy wire netting stapled to the two-by-four studding. Unconfined dogs milled about him and he kept turning to kick them away savagely and to watch his back. Some of them would bite and some of them wouldn't but he had never gotten it straight which were which. The dogs shifted about his feet like dirty water, a tide of dogs that bore him past the pear orchard and the grape arbor with its knotted armsize vines and crested at the kitchen doorstep.

The old woman had come onto the back porch to ascertain who'd authored this bedlam and stood watching him with her hand raised to shade her eyes from the sun. She fixed Fleming with a look of mock ferocity.

You get yourself in this house, she said.

He went through the back door into the long narrow kitchen, feeling as he always did the sudden onslaught of time, enthralled by the myriad smells of the kitchen: coffee and cloves and cinnamon, the heavy fruity odor of basketed apples and the faintly sour smell of dried peaches, and some other odor, rich and dark and mysterious, that was the odor of time itself, of days the old woman had stacked into years as carefully as a mason lays one stone atop another to construct a wall.

The old woman had come through the house from the front porch and she grasped him into a rough embrace and he could feel the wiry strength of her though she appeared frail and the top of her head only reached to the level of his breast.

What's the matter with you? I ought to take a withe to you. I've sent Brady after you twice and he come back both times emptyhanded claimin you wasn't there. I'd thought maybe you had more sense than Boyd but I'm beginnin to wonder about you.

She had released him and flustered about the table, setting out a plate and silverware, peering into covered dishes as if to see was there anything worth serving him. Get around here and eat, she said. I can feel ever bone in your body. You was always a skinny child but turned sideways you just ain't there atall.

I'll eat in a while, Grandma. Where's Brady at?

I reckon he's out there in the barnlot makin that dog a rock. There's peach pies in that safe in the pantry.

Makin that dog a what?

A rock, a rock. A tombstone, you know what a tombstone is, don' you? The mail carrier run over that Brownie dog and killed it and he's been havin a fit ever since. He's had me so nervous I'd strike out for Detroit myself, if I knowed which way it was.

The old woman claimed Cherokee blood and Fleming studying her now had no reason to doubt it. The thin gray hair pulled tightly into a bun behind her head had once been as black as shoepolish, her eyes fiercely alive, her tiny body barely containing the energy that animated her every waking moment. With her leathery face and beaked nose she looked less like an Indian woman than some old chief, the repository of the summed knowledge all his forebears had passed on by the flickering light of council fires.

I might get a piece of that pie and go out and talk to Brady a while.

Don't aggravate him. He's bad enough as it is.

Looks like he still has plenty of dogs underfoot.

We're about to founder on dogs around here. They're takin the place. I believe they're mixed with rabbit the way they litter ever few days. But that Brownie dog was about his favorite. He raised her from a pup with a baby bottle.

He got a wedge of pie from the safe and crossed through the living room and out into the bare earth yard beneath the pine tree, smiling to see the broommarks in the smooth earth where the old woman had swept it as you'd sweep a room.

On the shady side of the barn he found Brady kneeling before the tombstone, troweling grout onto its already smooth surface. His thin intent face gave no sign that he acknowledged the boy or was even aware of his existence. His congested blue eyes were focused on his work, a red curl had come uncombed and lay across his freckled forehead. He sprinkled water from a bowl delicately as an artist might, troweled smoothly around the letters BROWNIE. The rectangular form lay to the side, the reversed letters laboriously carved into the wood.

I get it slick and then when the water dries off it don't look like I want it to, Brady said.

You'll have to let it dry and then polish it with a grinder.

Brady laid aside the trowel and studied him. I reckon you've made a world of these things.

That just seems the way you'd do it. I don't know anything about it, and I never meant anything by it. I know how much you thought of Brownie.

I doubt you do. She was just a dog to you. To me she was family. She was like my child. When I seen the carwheels run over her stomach it was like they was runnin over mine. I felt somethin twist in me, and it ain't untwisted yet.

How come him to hit her?

Harwood never hit the brakes or nothin. Just drove across her. He's been onto me about my dogs before. He even had a feller from the post office come out here and talk to me about it. I reckon Harwood thought he'd teach me a lesson. But we'll see. We'll see.

What do you mean, we'll see?

You'll see too. It's a omen anyway, bad luck. All because of that old man makin plans to come back here.

It was on the boy's tongue to say that a person who claimed clairvoyance as strongly as Brady did should simply have gotten up yesterday morning and penned the dog up but he remembered what his grandmother had said and so kept his silence. Then he said: When's the funeral?

Brady searched his face for guile or irony but Fleming's face held only a studied bland innocence.

I buried her and said a few words over her this mornin. A few words of scripture then I told her how she'd be avenged. She can rest easy on that score.

Avenged how? You taking Harwood to court?

I'm takin him to a higher court than old Judge Humphreys. I'm puttin a hex on him, already got it in the works. He's got some hard times ahead of him.

What kind of hex?

He run over Brownie's stomach and busted her all up inside. She died and died, takin on. I'm goin for Harwood's stomach, too. His stool will set up in him like concrete, his insides will petrify like wood turnin into rock. If you don't think that'll give him reason to think about what he done, then you don't know nothin about the workins of the human body.

Hellfire, the boy said.

Hellfire is right, Brady said. I don't know if he'll die or if he'll finally get well. I can start em but I can't stop em. It'll be out of my hands.

He's crazy as a shithouse rat, the boy was thinking. And if I don't get out of here I may catch it myself.

Brady rose and unpocketed a small glass vial. He held it before the boy's face but did not relinquish ownership of it. Do you know what this is?

It looks to me like a pill bottle.

What's in it?

The boy looked closer. A Lucky Strike cigarette butt, he said.

Yes and no. It's Harwood's cigarette butt. I seen him when he flipped it out and I was on it like a duck on a June bug. It was still afire. Harwood touched it, it's got his essence all over it, and it's all I need to put a hurt on him.

The boy rose, simultaneously angry at Brady and yet touched by the grief that ravaged his face. Remind me not to leave anything of mine around where you can find it, he said.

You don't own anything to leave, Brady pointed out.

For supper the old woman had fried country ham and made red-eye gravy. There were baked yams and huge cathead biscuits that threatened to float out of your hand and tall cold glasses of buttermilk. The boy took a deep breath and buttered up one of the biscuits and fell to and fairly outdid himself eating. Even the old woman seemed mollified by his performance. If I can keep you around for two weeks I'll have you lookin very nearly like a human bein, she said.

And the rest of us knockin at the poorhouse door, Brady said sourly.

After supper they sat on the front porch and watched a long purple twilight descend on the world, swallowing the distant treeline first and sweeping across the fields toward them like mauve clouds. The boy watched the known world of shape and form vanish like something slowly dissolving in acid.

You mind if I listen to the radio?

Why Lord no, boy. You just help yourself.

He found the Grand Ole Opry out of Nashville, fiddles and guitars and advertisings for miraculous patent medicines. Country comedians that made him smile faintly, his eyes closed, sitting in an old willow rocking chair, here in this house of the dead and dying. Here within these walls time was of no moment. The walls were adorned with calendars but they had measured years already immured in memory, five years old, ten years old. The house was full of clocks but some of them were stopped and of the ones that worked no two kept a similar hour. A simple request for the time of the day was a cause for consternation, for much comparing of the accuracy of one clock with another to arrive at some approximation of the hour. Here time did not matter. Here another set of rules was in order, out of another century.

Right out that window's where I seen that warnin that night, the old woman said. He opened his eyes. She had come in silently and she was reaching a cup of coffee toward him and in her other hand she held one of her own. The coffee was black and so strong it seemed to have its own thick viscosity. He imagined the spoon he stirred it with vanishing away to nothing.

You always made the strongest coffee.

If I wanted to drink muddy water I'd just drink muddy water.

He sipped from his coffee. What was it a warning of? he asked, though he knew, knew all this by rote.

It was when old Mr. Bloodworth, Elbert's daddy, that would have been your great-granddaddy, was laying abed. He'd had pneumonia but the night I'm speakin of he seemed to be some stronger. He'd knowed Elbert that day and spoke a few words. He was layin right there by that window, in that very bed.

When the boy looked at the daybed a cold bone hand lay on his shoulder, ice crept the back of his neck. The window had gone opaque with night, reflected light threw the room back at him, a dark gangling boy and an old woman holding coffee cups.

It was nearly one o'clock in the mornin. Everbody was asleep but me, I was settin up with Mr. Bloodworth. It was hot, in August, and so stiflin you couldn't hardly breathe. Heat lightnin in the west. That was before Warren got the electricity and we didn't have no fan or nothin. I looked about Mr. Bloodworth and thought I'd go stand in the door a minute to see if I could get any air and that was when I seen it.

Brady was reading a farm magazine or pretending to but as well seemed transfixed by the old woman's voice. His glasses had slipped far down his nose and he had stopped turning pages.

It was a white shape. Like a woman in a white dress or gown. It was comin across that field on the other side of the garden there, kind of glidin, comin faster than a person could walk. But when it come to the garden fence it stopped like it was goin between the woven wire and the strand of bobwire at the top, the woven wire was loose there then and it was just like a person pushin the wire down and climbin through it. Mr. Bloodworth made some kind of a racket and that brought me to myself. I turned around and when I looked back Mr. Bloodworth was settin up in bed lookin at the window there. Then he just fell back with his eyes open. He had died.

I always wondered why a haint or a warnin had to crawl through a barbed wire fence, Brady said. It looks to me like it would just hit that fence like it never amounted to nothin and keep on goin.

I never made the world, the old woman said irritably. I don't know why everthing does what it does. All I know is what I seen.

Before he went up to the attic to bed he went outside for a time in the deepening silence. Far to the south lightning flared and died in photoelectric brilliance, relit the clouds briefly before the night sucked them back down to darkness. So far away no thunder came, so far away it was unreal. He thought of dark hollows, lightning on rainwet leaves, rain, and Boyd crouched for shelter under a dripping cedar, his fierce vexed face already impatiently scanning the night for a road the lightning might show him.

An owl called from somewhere out of the telluric dark. He imagined shapes in the shadows, a white form telescoping toward him out of the night, and he turned and went back in.

He was to sleep in his Uncle Warren's old room, and the stairway to it led out of the room his grandmother called the pantry. He stood for a moment looking about the room in a kind of wonder. Here was largess beyond measure. Shelves and shelves of canned foods. String beans and peaches, strawberries in their rich amber juice. Sugar-cured hams hanging on the walls, a side of bacon cured with smoke and brown sugar, bins of potatoes and apples, a barrel of flour and one of meal. He thought wryly that Boyd certainly hadn't inherited this trait: he seemed to want nothing the world had to offer. He wanted nothing but the clothes on his back and he wasn't terribly concerned about those. He seemed to feel that his movement through life should be unfettered by the ownership and accumulation of objects that slowed him down.

The room he slept in was shaped like a triangle, its sides formed by the rafters that framed the roof. He found a box of magazines and read the second installment of a serial by George Sessions Perry: he could find neither the first nor third segment but he read it anyway. It began to rain gently, he could hear it on the roof, a comforting murmur of faroff thunder. He read on, while his Uncle Warren watched him from a gilt frame on the bureau, until he lowered the magazine and studied the photograph.

Warren handsome in his Army uniform, his Congressional Medal of Honor pinned to his tunic. The smooth wing of his hair, clipped mustache like a nineteen-forties matinee idol. The boy thought of the invasion of Normandy that Warren had told him about, scrambling up the beaches over the bodies that had gone before, mortar fire that lit the night and exploding artillery shells that trailed out of the velvet sky like strings of phosphorus.

He slept but awoke sometime before day in this strange room and for a time he didn't know where he was. How he'd come to be here. He had no idea what time it was. The room began to feel like an enormous womb that was keeping him alive with its warmth, its comfort. It seemed alive, he imagined its stertorous breathing, he could feel its dark heart's blood coursing through the wiring, the plumbing. He got up and moved through the sleeping house. In the kitchen he made sandwiches of biscuits and slabs of ham and he cut two wedges of dried peach pie and put all this into a flour sack.

He went outside and struck out past the dog kennel toward home. The rain had stopped. A few of the dogs awoke as he passed and they roused themselves and followed him sleepily for a time. He paid them no mind. His feet were sure and confident on the path his eyes could barely see. They knew every turning, every windfall tree that lay across it. One by one the dogs fell away as if he was bound for some world they wanted no dealing with, and they turned and went back toward comfort and civilization.

SPRING THAT YEAR was a strange and solitary time. There were days when the only car that passed below his house was the mailman, weeks when he spoke or heard no word of human speech. Boyd did not come and he did not come and there was no letter, as if the border of trees he'd walked into had fallen closed behind him like a curtain that shrouded the mysteries of one world from the mysteries of another. Brady was sent to check on the boy but Fleming did not return to his grandmother's. He was sent again but this time the boy watched from the shade of the woods and did not acknowledge his presence. Brady stood on the porch and knocked and waited a while, the sun like a fire in his bright red hair, and then he went away. If he returned Fleming was not there to see it.

The house was full of odd silences, dark corners. The house seemed to be listening to him. To be waiting. As if he'd begun to tell some tale and the house was waiting for him to continue, listening patiently to hear the end of the story. But he'd lost the thread of the narrative and he could not go on.

The books he'd read no longer comforted him. The progression of the words had been subtly altered so that they deceived him, sentences had been shifted like pieces in a jigsaw puzzle and arranged into lies. He forgot to eat until finally things began to look subtly different to him, their edges shimmering with a bluegold aura. There seemed imponderable mysteries veined in a leaf, he watched light that fell through a gauzy curtain onto a tabletop with a bemused wonder. He watched its sweep across the rough pine grain of the wood as if he couldn't fathom where it came from, what purpose it might possibly serve. He began to suspect another, deeper layer of time, a time of stone and cloud and tree to which the time of clocks and calendars was a gross mockery cobbled up by savages. He felt the ways of men fall from him like sundered shackles.

He stayed out of the house, he was much of the time in the woods, he felt like some animal half domesticated but ultimately unable to resist the feral ways of the forest. The spring nights were fecund and warm and alive, and there were nights he did not come in at all.

He followed the creek where it wound toward the river and he stayed in the woods for days. He came out in a long stretch of bottomland at Riverside across from which was a country store. He bought candy bars and when he spoke his voice felt rusty and unused, it fell on his ears in a harsh croaking. Such folks as he saw had begun to look at him oddly. With the candy bars he returned to the woods and went on toward the river. He thought when he reached it he might follow to see where it led then follow that. Storms seemed to be following the streams as well and from the shelter of a cave he watched lightning sear the night sky like something irreparably wrong in the vaulted dome of the world itself and walked on over hailstones that lay gleaming like pearls.

He ate the candy bars and when they were gone speared fish in clearwater pools or ate nothing. He seemed to be drawing inward toward some point at which he would be reduced to the fundamental essence of himself. Finally he turned back. He'd reached a border beyond which lay a world he wanted no dealings with. He left the river and went back over hills and ridges he'd never seen but which had a comfortable familiarity about them nonetheless so that they led him without a misstep to the head of Grinders Creek.

Going up the long spine of ridges below Dee Hixson's he remembered a childhood haunt and descended into a deep hollow wickered in greengold light and followed it past an old whiskey still of which remained only twisted copper tubing and broken jugs and rusted fifty-gallon drums chopped with axes. Past an ancient springbox hewn or chiseled out of the limestone itself and to the ruins of a log cabin almost drowned in riotous honeysuckle and mimosa. The roof was halfcaved and virid with a thick growth of moss.

He stooped to pass beneath a tilted lintel and entered the house. It was curiously cold, perpetually shaded, profoundly abandoned save for a blacksnake that dropped from a ceiling beam and flowed like a moving inkslash through a floorboard and gone. He climbed a steep narrow stairway to the upper floor. The drone of dirtdaubers at their labors was all there was to break the silence. He looked about. Through the missing shakes the harsh trees and unreal sky looked intense and oversaturated, color bleeding into color. In the shadows of a wall an old work shoe cured hard as stone, like some piece of art sculpted from an alien material. Old newspapers pasted to the boxed walls. He crossed and read what he could as if to see was there news posted here for him but the paper was foxed and crumbling and such sentences as he could decipher seemed to be cryptic references to violent deeds splintered from some larger and more violent whole and they bore so little relationship to his life they might have been strange oral accounts filtered down from some older order or just ravings leaked through madhouse walls.

For this place as well was steeped in old violence. Folks called this place haunted, felt the emanations of an unspeakable act moving outward like ripples on water. Long ago, he did not know the year, a sharecropper named Parnell had come in from the fields after laying his crops by. Perhaps he had drunk at the spring, washed his face in the cold water. He had come into this shaded cabin and at some uncharted point had killed his wife and three children then turned the shotgun on himself.

Young Fleming Bloodworth sat for a time on the top stairstep trying to divine answers to this old lost mystery, the inevitable why of it, the event that permitted a previously forbidden thought, the impulse that transformed thought back to deed. In the charged gloom he heard the rattle of trace chains, a horse's hooves click on stone, heavy footsteps on the porch, the soft laughter of children at play.

He descended the staircase and went with some haste into the hot white light. He hurried through walls of flickering greenery. He had begun to fear for his sanity, felt that madness tracked him like a homeless dog, needed only a kind word or gesture to throw its lot with him forever.

It was a season of violent storms. He would be jarred out of sleep by an enormous concussion of thunder, open his eyes to a room of photoelectric light so intense all the color had been drained away. The thunder would go rolling across the bottomland in diminishing intensity, and wrapped in a blanket he'd go onto the porch and watch the storm blowing in from the southwest, the dome of light faulted by lightning so that the wild unfolding landscape of agitated trees and wet black stone was shuttered light to dark and back again like a series of snapshots that bore no relation one to the other. The wind would be stiff and cool on his face and in his hair and before it the pale undersides of maple leaves ran like quicksilver. Save for the wind in the trees and the thunder the night would be silent, holding its breath. The wind bore sticks and chaff and stripped leaves, the feel and smell of rain and ozone. The lightning wrought everything in bold relief, brought images leaping out of the dark in surreal clarity, and in its glare he would see like some release from tension the first wave of rain approaching, swinging slant and silver in the light, distorted by the wind, and behind it Hixson's house and the hills that framed it blurring then vanishing. The rain would be in the trees now and the first heavy drops striking the roof like stones.

FLEMING WAS passing the Snowwhite Cafe when a voice hailed him. He halted in midstep and turned. An English teacher named

Kenneth Spivey was holding the door open and motioning at him with his crippled arm.

Come in and drink a Coke with me.

I need to get on, Fleming said. I'm late already.

Late for what? Spivey asked.

In fact Fleming was late for nothing and bound nowhere in particular and he figured Spivey knew it. Trapped, he crossed the sidewalk to the cafe and went in. I guess I have time to drink a Coke, he said.

Spivey was sitting in a booth by the plateglass window and Fleming seated himself across from him with the width of the red Formica table between them. He sat crouched on the edge of the seat like one who only has a moment and must soon be off.

A waitress in a white uniform stood at his elbow. Let me have a lemon Coke, Fleming said, and she wrote it on a pad.

Don't you speak anymore, Fleming?

He looked up. A girl he remembered from school and for a dizzy moment no name came to mind. I didn't even know you worked here, he said.

Just on the weekends. I'm still in school.

Fleming doesn't know us anymore, Spivey said, leaning to his cherry Coke, his girlish mouth pursed, like a leech or a slug clamped about the straw. He's gone on to other things.

When the Coke came it was in a tall glass of shaved ice with a wedge of lemon floating atop. He sat sipping it and studying the scratched tabletop. B.C. loves E.M. Elise loves Warren Bloodworth.

Have you dropped out of school, Fleming? Spivey asked.

Well, I don't know. I guess not. I just haven't been going lately.

No. Not for quite a while. It would be a shame if you did drop out. It's always a shame when a young person gives up but even more so when it's you. You're the most promising student I ever had. I had high hopes for you, and I would hate to lose you.

Fleming was absentmindedly nibbling the slice of lemon. I don't know anything about any of that, he said.

You don't have to know it. That's my job. I'm the teacher. What do you plan to do? Somehow I don't see you working in the shoe factory.

Sharecropping. Perhaps you want to offbear at the sawmill and go home to a little country wife and a bunch of little Flemings running around.

He was leant across the table with his protuberant brown eyes fixed upon Bloodworth. Fleming was always uncomfortable in his presence and he was acutely so now. The soft bulging eyes were leaning an almost unbearable weight on him. Spivey's eyes were naked peepholes into his soul and whatever emotion he felt, pain, anger, frustration, was there for the world to read. This was knowledge Fleming had no use for and he looked away. Across the street in front of the poolroom a man and a woman were arguing in silence. Their mouths moved but Fleming could hear no sound. They spoke in gestures like angry mimes. Finally the man gave a contemptuous gesture of dismissal and walked back through the poolroom door. The woman stood there for a time and then she went on down the street.

What did you think of that book I gave you?

It's the best book I ever read.

There's another book, a sort of sequel to it called *Of Time and the River*. It continues the story of Eugene Gant. There's a very powerful scene where old man Gant dies. Would you like me to bring it to you?

Well. I'd like to read it. I could pick it up somewhere.

No, I'd like to bring it. I have a lot of books and books are better if you can share them.

Spivey's withered arm looked like the arm of a deformed child, the drawn fingers the talons of some grotesque sort of bird. The tiny hand fished in a shirt pocket and drew out a pack of Camels as if it were performing a trick it had been trained to do. Spivey took the cigarettes with his good hand and tipped one out and placed it between his meaty lips. By this time the withered hand had produced a lighter. As he lit the cigarette his eyes were still fixed on Bloodworth.

I'd like to help you, he said. I'm in a position to help you. I know something of the situation you're in.

The what?

The situation you're in. Your home life. I'd like to do something about it.

There's not a damned thing wrong with my home life, Fleming said.

Spivey smiled a sad onecornered smile. His wet eyes looked hurt, bruised. You southerners, he said. I've been here for fifteen years and I'll never understand you.

We do just fine on our own, Fleming said.

I live in this enormous farmhouse down on Catheys Creek. I used to live with my sister but she passed away a few years back and I'm alone in it. I just rattle around that old house. There's plenty of room. You'd have your own quarters, the use of my library. I know how lonely life can get.

I'm not lonely at all, Fleming said, and suddenly realized that he was speaking the truth.

Perhaps not, Spivey said. You're so young. You're so well read I sometimes forget you're practically a child. I wonder if I was ever that young.

By now Fleming had drained his glass and was standing. He felt like the character in a comic strip who suddenly has an enormous lightbulb appear over his head. The feeling was so intense that he could feel the hot knowledge on his face.

Spivey smiled his worn threadbare smile. It's not what you're thinking, he said.

I'm not thinking anything at all.

I'd like to believe that. Spivey looked away, past the sunwashed glass to the streets where there was nothing at all to see. I'll bring the book anyway, he said.

FROM THE SHADE of the ivy-covered end of Itchy Mama Baker's porch the old men in ladderback chairs and tilting Coke crates watched the hot blacktop that snaked up the grade toward Ackerman's Field three miles away. They'd sit daylong and wait for something to happen, anything to happen, waiting for the road to entertain them.

These were old men in clean chambray shirts and suspenders and pants so roomy they could have held another oldtimer entire and shoes split down the sides for comfort. They'd sit ruminatively, building their Country Gentleman cigarettes and leaning birdlike to spit their snuff-juice past the edge of the floorboards into the yard. Talking about old lost times and looking back over their lives as dispassionately as though these events were something they'd read about or something that had happened to somebody else.

The screen door opened, slapped loudly shut. An enormous woman had come onto the porch, a woman with a fierce turtlelike face and wild frizzy carrotcolored hair. She was wearing a bright yellow tentsize dress with dark halfmoons of sweat fanning out from the armpits.

One of you loafers spits on my porch you're cleaning it off, she said. She studied them in a kind of mock anger that they were so accustomed to they deemed it threatless and so paid her little mind.

I'm spittin in the yard, Ferris Walker said.

When one of you gets kindly caught up on his spittin I need some wood busted up.

I might could handle that, Walker said. What's in it for me?

Well, I ain't chargin you rent on this porch.

How about a little drink?

There might be a halfpint hid back up there in the holler somewhere.

I might could bust up a little wood, Walker said. He rose and ambled off toward the woodpile looking for the chopping axe.

Who's that rollin that car tire? one of the old men asked.

They turned to see. He had just appeared on the periphery of their vision, a gangling young man with a halo of wild white hair, slowly rolling a carwheel up the grade.

That's that Albright boy, Itchy Mama said.

He's lost his automobile, one of the men said. All but one wheel.

No, he's always doin that, another said. His casin's flat and he's rollin her to town to get it fixed. Nobody's ever told him about some folks havin a extra one they haul around in the trunk of their car in case one goes flat.

It wouldn't take many trips up that grade for me to figure it out, the first one observed.

That boy's opinion of himself don't match the one everybody else has got. He thinks he's all aces but he's mostly sevens and eights.

He may be a little slow but he ain't a patch on his daddy for crazy. That was the one rewritin the Bible. Old man Tut Albright. He was rewritin her start to finish, takin out all the begats and the therefores and writin it where what he called the common man could make sense out of it. He read me some of it one time. You ort to heard it. It was a part about some angels of heaven layin with the daughters of men and he took out that part about layin with and just put in they screwed the daughters of men. It was the damnedest thing I ever heard.

He used to cause carwrecks back when he was a young man, the first oldtimer said.

He what?

Used to cause carwrecks. He had this long blond wig he'd put on and this little red shortwaisted dress. He lived on this real sharp curve out by Horseshoe Bend and he'd put that mess on and go set in a lawn chair there by the bank of the road with his legs spraddled out. He caused I don't know how many bad wrecks. A whole carload of drunks run off out there one Saturday and two of em finally died. There was some said he wore red drawers when he done it but I ain't fool enough to know about that.

You can hush about some red drawers, the second man said. The thought of Tut Albright pullin on a pair of women's underwear is more than I want to deal with this early in the day.

JUNIOR ALBRIGHT WAS on the schoolhouse construction site long before seven o'clock, his battered Dodge pulled into the graveled parking lot and the door cocked open for what coolness remained. The sun had come up red and smoking and malign over the spiky treeline, instantly sucking the dew from the leaves and driving it into the parched earth and he judged it was going to be another hot one. He sat with a leg extended over the open car door, sipping the last of his coffee. He glanced occasionally at his wrist as if he'd check the time though he wore no watch there. There was just a band of paler flesh, like the ghost of a watch. His watch resided in a cigar box beneath the bar at the poolroom with similar timepieces where he'd pawned it for two sixpacks of Falstaff beer, and he resolved that the first thing he was going to do when he got a paycheck was redeem the watch.

After a while he got out of the car with his lunch box and seated himself on a pile of treetrunks a dozer had pushed into windrows. The bladescarred trees were lush with honeysuckle vines and the air was heady with the scent of their blossoms. He opened the lunch box and selected a sandwich and unwrapped it and took a bite. Occasionally he'd glance up the cherted road and cock his head attentively and listen but all he could hear was doves calling mournful as lost souls from some smoky hollow still locked in sleep.

He turned at a sudden whicker in the air and watched a humming-bird suck the drop of nectar from the throat of a honeysuckle. Curious creature, no bigger than his thumb. Its blurred wings, tiny sesame eyes. He stopped chewing and watched it. He studied it with a bemused intensity as if he'd learn its secrets. As if this might be a talent he ought to acquire. When he heard the first pickup truck he rewrapped the uneaten portion of his sandwich and restored it to the lunch box and fastened the clasps and stood up.

The truck pulled nearer the unfinished structure and stopped and two men got out. Doors slammed. They stood studying the schoolhouse as if to see did it meet their specifications.

Bout time you all got here, Albright sang out. I'd about give you out.

They didn't even look at him. They'd seen this fool before. This was the third day he'd been perched on the windrowed trees, drawing no salary, waiting like a vulture for somebody to burn out, not show up, die.

You reckon they'll be hirin today?

You'd have to ask Woodall about that, one of the men said.

The other man lit a cigarette. He glanced at Albright through the smoke. It gets any hotter than it was yesterday you can have my job.

I'd take it, Albright said.

The man looked at him. You wouldn't know what the fuck to do with it, he said.

Supposed to be a hundred in the shade and shade hard to come by, Albright said.

Other workers arrived in beatup trucks and rattletrap cars and even one man walking, angling across a field of kneehigh sedgegrass, his lunch bucket swinging along in his hand. The men fell to getting out tools and stringing power cords. Someone cranked a concrete mixer and began to hose water into it. Another to remove plastic sheeting from pallets of bagged mortar mix.

When the white truck with WOODALL CONSTRUCTION painted on the side arrived Albright was already sauntering toward the office. The office was a tiny metal trailer with the wheels removed shored up on concrete blocks. A set of steps of raw lumber led to the door. The truck halted before the trailer and a man got out. Heavyset man wearing khakis and a broadbrimmed gray cowboy hat. He removed the hat and laid it carefully in the seat of the truck and put on a white hardhat and adjusted it over one sleepylooking gray eye. He seemed not to have noticed Albright.

Albright cleared his throat. I was wonderin about a job, he said.

I don't reckon I need nobody today, Woodall said. He was studying the working men, looking all about as if to see was everyone accounted for.

Albright played his hole card. They locked up Clyde Edmonds last night.

They did?

Cleve Garrison arrested him last night in Baxter's on a drunk and disorderly. He was drunk as a fiddler's bitch. He'd of needed a seein eye dog to find his way across the street.

He was running the crimper, Woodall said bemusedly.

He won't be runnin it today unless it's got a hell of a cord on it. That's why I thought you might need somebody.

I don't need just anybody. I need somebody that can operate a crimper.

Hellfire. I can pick it up. I was drivin a tractor when I was ten year old. Runnin a haybaler. A crimper's a plaything next to a haybaler.

Woodall was thinking. His left eye had a cast to it as if he'd see a wider range of things than other men and Albright was never quite certain which eye was watching him.

There's not much to it for a fact, he finally said. I don't have anybody I can spare to put on it, so I'm going to have to give you a shot at it.

I won't let you down.

We'll get you a hardhat out of the trailer here. We'll have to fill out some papers anyway. This here is a government job and everything has to be wrote down five or six times.

He had ascended the steps and was unlocking the office door. Albright was glancing about to see was anybody watching him get hired. They went in. The air in the trailer was hot and stifling and Albright felt sweat break out instantly all over his body. Woodall set him to filling out forms and began rummaging through a wooden box of hardhats and rubber boots. He laid a blue hardhat upon the desk.

You have to wear this hardhat all the time you're on the work site.

Have you not got another white one like you got? Albright was licking the point of his pencil, studying Woodall's hat.

These blue hardhats are laborer's hats. This one I got is a superintendent's hat. It might be a little early in the day for one of them. I been here twenty years and I own the company.

Oh. Well. Blue's all right. One of them blue ones'd suit me just fine, I reckon.

Listen to me about this hat. You got to wear it all the time. This is a government job and the sons of bitches keep sending inspectors around trying to catch me fucking up. They catch a man working without a hat it'd be a hellatious fine on me and no telling what else. You got it?

Albright signed his name with a flourish. I got it, he said.

Let's get going then.

Woodall was already going down the steps, striding off toward the tall brick building. Hey, Albright called after him. Where's this crimper at?

Woodall turned. It's on the roof, where did you reckon it was at? Do you not know what we're talking about here?

Course I know. I just didn't know if it was already up there or if we'd have to carry it.

They stood before a ladder leading to the roof. Albright looked up. The sheer brick wall, the ladder telescoping into the nothingness of a hot brassy sky. He judged it forty or fifty feet.

That ladder sure is one long son of a bitch, he said.

It don't go but from the bottom to the top, Woodall pointed out. Let's be for going up it. Time's wasting and there's a world of metal waiting up there to be crimped.

Albright took a deep breath and squared his shoulders and laid a hand to each side of the ladder. He started up. The ladder swayed gently and disquietingly with his progress. He could hear it grating against the brick parapet high above him. He could feel Woodall coming up behind him. Halfway up he stopped. His hands gripping the rung of the ladder were bloodless and white. His knees began to jerk spasmodically nor could he make them stop. The ladder began to shake.

Hey, Woodall called.

Albright didn't say anything. He was staring through a window opening into a room where men were hanging drywall. He was imagining what the solidlooking floor felt like beneath their feet.

This ladder's tied off up there. It's not going anywhere.

I was thinking more in the line of me going somewhere without it, Albright said. Is there not any other way up?

No there's not. We've not put the elevator in yet and the helicopter's out on some other job. Why didn't you tell me you were afraid of heights?

I didn't know. I ain't ever been on em before.

Just go up one step at a time and don't be looking down. Look at the wall.

Albright rested his face on his clenched knuckles. He closed his eyes. After a time he began to ascend again.

When he reached the top he stepped over the parapet onto an enormous expanse of metal roofing. The roof was enclosed front and sides by the brick wall capped with stone but open on the rear and Albright's feet sensed a slight pitch toward the open area. The roof felt solid and substantial beneath his feet when he stamped it tentatively remnants of his normal cockiness began to accrue about him now that he was safe.

The crimper was a squat metal device built close to the floor with four short appendages each ending in a roller. There was a handle on its back not unlike a harness and to Albright it looked for all the world like a fullgrown dachshund. To complete this illusion it was powered by an electrical cord wound about the handle like a leash.

This metal is all laid out and screwed to the lathing, Woodall said. It's not going anywhere. But where the joints are there are two L-shaped edges and this crimper just rides down the joint and crimps the longer edge over the short one. You see? That makes it watertight. Here, I'll show you.

Woodall hoisted the crimper and set it astride one of the seams. Albright watched. Woodall flipped a toggle switch and the crimper sprang to life and began a loud clacketyclack and commenced pulling itself along the crimped edge, its little rollered feet gliding smoothly on the metal. Woodall paid out cord from the roll across his arm and when he'd crimped six or eight feet leaned and grasped the handle on the machine's back and lifting it and reversing its direction set it on the next seam facing and began crimping it. He cut the toggle switch.

You see? I just turned it to show you how. You let it crimp clear to the end of a seam then just pick it up and flip it onto the next one and go back the other way. You don't need to shut her off unless you quit crimping. Just keep your power cord feeding and let her roll. Watch her on that back side where there's not any parapet. Turn her two feet or so back from the edge. That's been handcrimped already to keep a man from having to lean out over the edge and turn the crimper. You got any questions?

Whose airplane is that? Albright asked.

What?

Albright was gazing over the brick parapet into a level green expanse of field. In the distance a one-engine plane was tethered and the sun glinted off guywires securing the wings. Cows like tiny ceramic cows from a knickknack shelf grazed placidly in the weight of the sun.

Whose airplane is that?

It's mine, Woodall said. Were you listening to what I said about that crimper?

Sure. I got it.

I had to fly all the way to North Carolina to get it. If there's one in the state of Tennessee I couldn't find it. Try it a seam or two.

Albright flipped the switch and walked alongside the crimper feeding it cord. When the crimped edge ended he flipped the crimper around and followed it back. Woodall nodded grudgingly. He laid a hand atop his head. Keep that hardhat on, he yelled above the din of clacketyclack. He turned and went back down the ladder.

I'm walkin the dog, Albright sang, paying out leash. Easy money, he was thinking, making up a shopping list as he sang, adding up prices.

By ten o'clock the heat on the roof was horrific. It danced off the metal in miasmic emanation like steam rising from a swamp and the sun off the mirrorlike tin was blinding. Albright was wringing wet with sweat. Son of a bitch, he said. It was like the basement to hell, like the furnace room to hell. He was constantly wiping sweat out of his eyes with a shirt-sleeve and when he glanced over the wall toward the horizon the land-scape warped and ran like a landscape viewed through melting glass. He felt lightheaded and so weightless he might go drifting aloft into the hot blue firmament and he divined that the only thing keeping him earth-bound was the length of leash he kept paying out, reeling in, paying out.

He cut off the crimper. Goddamn it's hot, he said. I'd give a five-dollar bill for a good cold drink of water.

But there was no water here cold or otherwise and the thought of negotiating the ladder again seemed not to appeal to him. He looked about for shade. There wasn't any. He took off his shirt and folded it and laid it on the roof and laid the hardhat atop it. Fucker draws heat like iron draws lightning, he said. He shook the water out of his spungold curls and wiped his eyes again and took a pack of Camels out of his pocket but he'd sweated them through and he tossed them over the edge. He stood for a moment catching his breath. The air was so hot it seemed to sear his lungs. He turned the crimper back on.

He was crimping away when he heard someone yelling at him. He seemed to have been hearing it subliminally for some time and when he finally turned Woodall was standing on the roof screaming at him. Woodall pounded the top of his hardhat and pointed a finger at Al-bright's bare head until finally comprehending but momentarily con-fused Albright dropped the cord and went to get his hardhat.

The crimper crimped on toward the sloping edge of the roof. Albright positioned the blue hat on his head and whirled to chase the crimper. Woodall was shrieking at him soundlessly. The crimper was at the edge of the roof when Albright grasped the cord. There was too much slack and the crimper tilted over the edge like a diver and just went on crimping sheer air and vanished from sight. Come back, Albright cried. The cord grew taut in his hands then went slack. The clacketyclack fell silent and something slammed against the concrete far below and Albright could hear the startled cries of the workers.

He raised a hand to calm Woodall, a placating hand of casual assur-ance, don't worry, just a minute, I'll go get it.

He made for the ladder. He went down it hand over hand without a thought for heights and dropped the last six or eight feet and was up immediately and headed for the Dodge. He went past crimper parts and oddments of metal strewn over an unlikely area of concrete and past where men were circled about the remains of the crimper standing hands on knees peering down at it like soldiers gathered about a comrade fallen in battle. By the time he reached the Dodge he was going at a dead run with his left arm already extended to open the car door he wasn't even at yet and his right hand was fumbling out the ignition keys.

Inside he cranked the car and shifted and popped the clutch in one smooth liquid motion and slewed spinning out of the gravel into the road. He went down it with the speedometer in a slow steady climb and a slipstream of pale dust rising behind him.

ON A FINE WARM MORNING in May Fleming Bloodworth carrying a string of sunperch rounded a bend in the creek and came upon a blondhaired girl about to heave a rock at a huge gray hornets' nest suspended from the branch of a sycamore.

Hey, he yelled.

The girl looked at him in wildeyed surprise but heaved the rock anyway and tore out a fistsize chunk of the nest. Instantly the air was full of hornets and they seemed in little doubt about where the rock had come from. Bloodworth dropped the fish and began to run. Batting away hornets onehanded he grasped the girl about the waist and dragged her upstream in a silver sluice of water. He was stung on the neck and he could feel them in his shirt and buzzing madly in his hair and the girl was fighting him with one hand and trying to slap away hornets with the other. The hornets were coming at his face like divebombers and the girl had clawed his left cheek and she kept trying to slap him away.

She was halfcrying. Get the hell away from me, she said.

Where the creekbed fell away to a thighdeep pool Fleming went under and when he came up pulled the girl under with him. He opened his eyes underwater and she had a wildeyed look of panic on her face as if she were drowning. She was frantically trying to unbutton her blouse.

She surfaced sputtering and choking. She gagged and spat a mouthful of water. She was still trying to undo the blouse but her hands were shaking. When Fleming grasped both sides of the collar and jerked the buttons spun away and she shrugged out of it and reached behind her back to unhook her brassiere. There was a coppery glint of stubble in her armpits, red welts already swelling on her sides.

She went over to the bank of the creek and sat down. She began to cry. The hornets seemed to have departed but he could see them downstream circling their ruined home and the air was vibratory with an angry hum.

She stopped crying and glared at him. You could at least turn your head, she said.

He looked away and when he looked back she had the bra off and was raking crushed hornets out of it. Her breasts were starkly white against the tanned flesh of her stomach and shoulders save the rosecolored nipples and the dark aureole surrounding them. His mouth felt dry and there was a faroff ringing in his ears.

I told you to look the other way.

How many times did they get you?

I don't know. A lot. I can't stand this, they stung me all over. She was dipping water in her cupped hands and rubbing it over her breasts.

You're not allergic, are you?

How the hell would I know? I don't even know what kind of bugs those were.

They're not bugs, they're hornets. Why on earth would you slam a rock into a hornets' nest?

I told you I didn't know what they were. It was just a big gray paper thing and I wondered what would happen if I hit it with a rock.

That's what happens.

Well. I'm from Michigan. They don't have the things hanging from lampposts in Detroit.

The girl had covered herself as best she could with the blouse and beneath it she sat hunched and miserable. Fleming's stings hurt as well but the sheer fact of seeing the girl and talking with her seemed to diminish the pain. She had blond hair with auburn lights in it and eyes of clear guileless blue and light played on the angles of her face in an interesting way. There was a faint prettiness about her but also something vaguely familiar, and he kept wondering if he'd seen her before or just someone that looked like her.

She was wearing dungarees cut off into kneelength shorts. They didn't get down into your shorts, did they?

She gave him a catlike look of anger. Don't you wish, she said.

I've got to get my fish, he said. He went back down the creek with some caution but the hornets seemed preoccupied with assessing the damage to their home and they ignored him. He found the fish washed into a stand of cane in shallow water. Some of them had flopped off the forked stick and he gathered them up and threaded the stick through their gills and went back to where the girl was.

She had put the bra and blouse on and tied the blouse across her stomach and seemed to be making ready to go.

If you're from Michigan what are you doing wading up Grinders Creek?

We're on vacation down here. Daddy works at Ford in Detroit but my Grandpa Dee Hixson lives close to here.

I live right across from Dee. Up on that hill on the other side of the road.

I didn't know there was a house up there, you can't see it from the road. What's your name?

He told her. They had begun wading up the shallow water toward the roadbed. He knew now why she had seemed familiar. What's your name? he asked her.

Merle. Daddy named me after this movie star named Merle Oberon. You think I look like her?

For a minute I thought that was her drawing back that rock.

She poked him lightly in the ribs. What are you going to do with those fish?

I planned on having them for supper. You could come over tonight and help me eat them.

What, you mean with you and your folks?

I live by myself. My folks are in Detroit Michigan.

They are? Where in Detroit?

I don't know. They're looking for work.

You mean you live all by yourself?

All by myself.

God. I wish my family would go off somewhere looking for something and leave me alone.

Suddenly Fleming did not want them to go their separate ways. He did not want to go back to the still house and wait for Boyd or for any of the other things he seemed to spend his time waiting for. Come on over tonight, he said. We'll eat the fish and listen to the radio awhile.

I'm not much on radios. In Detroit we've got this big twenty-one-inch Crosley TV. It's like having a movie theater right in your house. Anyway, I don't like fish, I'm always afraid of choking on a bone.

I'll pick the bones out for you.

Are you a smooth talker or what, she said. I've had boys promise me a lot of things but you're the first one that ever offered to pick out fish bones.

The creek widened in a shoal before they came upon the bridge until it was no more than ankle deep near the bank and at the edge where a riot of cattails grew it was almost lukewarm. With his pocket knife he cut a handful of the reeds and gave them to her. These roses were just growing wild, he said.

First you tear my clothes off and then you bring me flowers. What a man.

Will you come?

I don't know. I might. There's sure nobody else to talk to around this Godforsaken place. We'll see.

I can do this, he was thinking. All I have to do is just be as normal as everyone else. All I have to do is just not blow apart like a two-dollar clock. Just pick words and put one of them after the other like a baby learning to walk, like a drunk carefully crossing the street.

He reached out suddenly and touched her arm. She jerked it away as if the touch had burned her then gave him a curious smile and linked an arm through his.

Why did you touch me like that?

I thought for a second you weren't real, he said.

HE HAD FRIED the fish and ate a plate of them leaned against the front wall of the house watching dusk descend and sipping a Coca-Cola chilled in the springbox. In the wintertime he could have seen the lights from Dee Hixson's house but the trees were riotous with summer growth and for all the lights he could see this might have been the only house in the world.

She might come and she might not but the later it grew the more he doubted she would. Would she come in the dark? Perhaps she was scared of the dark, they probably don't have dark in Detroit. They have twenty-one-inch Crosley TVs but they don't have hornets' nests hanging from the lampposts.

He thought how ludicrous he would be wandering the streets of Detroit. He smiled, thinking for a moment of the four of them, Boyd looking for his wife and him looking for Boyd and Merle, all of them moving through a maze of brick buildings and dark circuitous alleyways and everyone just half a beat out of sync with everyone else, wandering each alone in the electric dark and any destination reached one just quit by another.

He set the plate aside and leaned his head back against the wall. He felt a curious solitary contentment. The world he'd heard rumored seemed enormous, roads led everywhere free for the taking, any one you chose had a destination at its end.

In the west a star winked on like a pinprick through the faulted dusk to a greater light beyond. Another. Bats came veering out of the murky purple twilight and one hollow over a whippoorwill called to him, brother calling to brother.

IN THE TWO DAYS following Junior Albright's destruction of the crimper the white company truck stopped in front of the small frame house he lived in three times. Each time Junior froze, hardly daring to breathe. Each time the horn honked three loud blasts, waited. A truck door slammed and Albright was mousequiet and mousestill, hearing in his constricted heart the heavy tread onto the doorstep, the measured hammering that shook the door on its hinges, rattled the glass in its unglazed sash.

The third time Albright was crouched in the kitchen and heard Woodall trying to turn the doorknob that Albright had had the foresight to thumbbolt, heard him yell in frustration, You're just making it harder on yourself, Goddamn you, ain't you man enough to even open the door? I'll catch you out sometime.

Which he did. Albright was sprawled in a chair in the poolroom watching Clyde Sharp clean out Big Shaw at straight pool. He was drinking a can of Falstaff with salt sprinkled on the can's top. He had just taken a swallow of beer and licked the salt when he felt a heavy arm settle about his shoulders.

You a hard man to find, Woodall said.

I didn't know I was lost.

Well you was. I've been out to your place three times but I can't ever seem to catch you at home.

I was out back there once when I seen your truck leave. I hollered at you but you just drove on off.

Well. No matter. We're both here now.

I figured you just brought my check out, you know for that day I worked. I just decided to let it slide on account of that crimper actin up the way it done.

No, Woodall said. It wasn't quite that. As a matter of fact I have a receipt in my pocket where I paid the rental company for the very crimper you're speaking of. Eight hundred and sixty dollars. That's the amount you owe me. So you see it's not something I can let slide, the way you can.

Big Shaw stooped and sighted drunkenly down the length of his pool cue, looking directly into Albright's face, one eye closed as if in a conspiratorial wink, and Albright leaned to the side in case the ball went wild. On the break Shaw had once laid out a man named Jess Cotham colder than a wedge so that he had to be lain on the concrete floor and water poured on his face. This time the cue ball just kissed gently off the seven and scratched in a corner pocket, but when Big Shaw stepped back Albright suddenly saw a folded twenty-dollar bill that had been hidden by Shaw's polished dress shoe. The little engraved two and zero were clearly visible at the corners and powerful as some occult or Masonic symbol, and Junior looked about to see if anyone else had noticed. He sat trying to devise some plan to recover this windfall without Clyde Sharp falling upon him with a pool cue.

Are you listening to me?

Mmmm?

I've got a note fixed up at my office trailer. I never thought that you would have eight hundred and sixty dollars. I never thought that you would ever have eight hundred and sixty dollars at one time so the note says that you will pay me thirty dollars a month for twenty-eight months then twenty dollars for the last month.

They Godamighty damn. That's nearly three years.

Well, if you wanted to pay sixty a month we could shave that time nearly in half.

Some months I don't have thirty dollars. Besides, there was somethin wrong with that damn crimper to make it behave that way. Runnin off the way it done. I believe the throttle hung on it or somethin. Anyway I don't believe it's my place to pay for it.

You are going to pay me that eight hundred and sixty dollars. We're not even discussing that. What we're talking about is how. You need to drive by tomorrow early and sign that paper so we can get it notarized and make it official.

I ain't signin shit, Albright said. And how about gettin your arm off my shoulder.

If you're not there by quitting time I'm lawing you, Woodall said. I'll take you before a judge and get a judgment against you. If you've got anything I'll take it. If you ever get anything I'll get that. You'll wind up losing your car. If you work I'll garnishee your check. You'll pay it one way or you'll pay it another. I'll see you tomorrow.

Albright closed his eyes and listened to Woodall's footsteps fade away. He was in bondage for three years, in debt with nothing to show for it. Here his life had never properly gotten up to speed and now Woodall was holding a mortgage on the next three years of it.

He rose and stretched, elaborately casual. He sauntered off toward the toilet at the back of the poolroom. As he passed the table he dropped his lighter and watched it fall within six inches of the twenty-dollar bill, stooped and gracefully scooped them both up. The bathroom reeked of urine and stale vomit but he paid it no mind, studied the bill minutely in the light of the bare ceiling bulb and rubbed it between thumb and forefinger as if he'd ascertain its authenticity. It had a rich crinkly texture and seemed official enough, coin of the realm, minted in Washington, D.C. He slid it into a pocket and went out.

At the bar he unpocketed it again and smoothed it onto the Formica countertop. I'm buying a round for the house, he said.

The house? the barkeep said. Hellfire, there's nobody in here but you and Sharp and Big Shaw.

Then I'm buyin a round for us, Albright told him.

SHE DID NOT COME the first night or the second and by then Fleming had given up on her but the third night a step on the porch brought him back from the edge of sleep. He waited for a knock but the door was simply opened without this formality and a warped rectangle of moonlight fell into the room.

Fleming?

Who is it?

Then he could see the dark outline of her body against the paler dark outside. She stood with a hand still holding the doorknob, leaning to peer about the room. Then she stepped out of the moonlight and he could hear soft footsteps approaching the bed. He was sitting on its side feeling about for his shoes when he felt her weight settle onto the opposite side of the bed.

Are you getting up?

Well. I thought I'd get up and talk to you a while.

It's kind of dark in here. Cool, too. We can just talk here.

It is dark. I've got some matches here somewhere and I'll just light the lamp.

Let the lamp go. This is nice, and my eyes are sort of getting used to the dark.

By now she had crawled into bed and settled herself against him. I thought they'd never go to sleep, she said. I tried to slip off over here for the last couple of nights but they watch me like a hawk. Finally tonight Daddy got drunk and passed out on the couch and I just headed out.

Fleming had thought about this at some length. He had made tentative plans that in their wildest fruition might achieve her presence in a bed beside him but to have this happen as the first card dealt rendered his scenario worthless. He lay silently beside her trying to think of something to say. Don't talk then, she said. He could feel her warm breath on his cheek and the cool weight of her hand on his bare shoulder. Then she pressed her face to his and kissed his mouth, gently at first and then harder, opening her mouth so that he could feel her tongue and sharp little teeth. Her breath and her flesh felt hot against his. She slid a hand down his side to his hip and then she jerked away.

You've got your pants on. What are you doing sleeping in your clothes?

Well. You never know who'll show up in the middle of the night.

Get them off. Here, I'll do it. She was unbuttoning his jeans and when he raised his hips to chuck them off he heard the soft sound of a zipper.

Wait, he said.

Wait? For what?

Stand over in the light and take them off.

Why not, she said. What the hell. You've seen about everything I've got anyway.

In the oblong area of light she posed for a moment like a parodic ballerina then pulled the dress over her head and dropped it to the floor. She slid her panties down holding them momentarily with a toe to step out of them then turned breasts bobbing to close the door. She vanished. He heard the thumbbolt click. It seemed to take her an eternity to cross from the doorway to the bed, in its span folks were born and lived their lives and died, whole generations passed away.

When she slid against him he had decided to remain calm and save all these moments for bleaker times, each instant a snapshot, a flower pressed in the pages of a Bible. But when she grasped his hand and placed it on her sex his mind reeled away and images shuttled like unsequenced frames in a film. He was unaccustomed to such urgency and he thought that perhaps girls from Michigan were different, perhaps this was the way things were done in Detroit. She was pulling him onto her, saying, here baby, I'll do this, and he felt himself sliding into her and she was whispering against his ear, No, baby, take it easy, slow down, we've got all night to do this.

Have you got a girlfriend?

No. I sort of had one last year but she took up with a football player.

Have you ever done this before?

Sure. Lots of times.

You liar.

Have you?

No. Find those matches, I've got a cigarette here. Do you want one?

No.

How come?

I just never took it up.

You just never took it up, she said. You talk funny. Sort of like a hill-billy and sort of not. You sound so serious. So solemn. What makes you so solemn, is the world going to end in the next few minutes? You act like you're always thinking about something. Were you taking notes?

He had found the matches and struck one on the iron headboard of the bed and lit her cigarette.

I never think about anything, she said through the smoke. I just do whatever comes next, whatever the next thing is.

What's the next thing right now?

Well, I've got to get home before he wakes up. Unless you wanted to try this again. I've been here almost two weeks and we've just got to-gether. Look at all the time we've wasted.

When he walked her within sight of Dee Hixson's house he didn't even suspect what time it was. She walked close beside him in fading moonlight, holding his hand. He could hear her feet in the gravel, her breathing, hear his own breathing adjusting to hers. When they separated at the rise before Hixson's cocks were crowing from Hixson's barnlot. He stood awkwardly for a moment then leaned and kissed her. He didn't know if he ought to say he loved her and he didn't know if he did and in the end he followed her lead and said nothing at all.

When he got back to the creek he had no desire to go back to bed so he sat for a time on the bridge, his feet swinging idly over the dark water. After a while a bird off in the woods somewhere began to sing and another took up the call. Before he knew it blue dawn light was fading out and the day began to gather itself out of the darkness. In the east a reef of salmoncolored clouds was rimlit by a bright metallic color he had no name for.

In old books he'd read the heroes were seized in the throes of self-denunciation when they'd finally yielded to temptations of the flesh, when they'd let carnality corrupt the spiritual. He felt that perhaps he ought to feel this way too, but all he felt was alive, as if his senses had been turned so that colors looked brighter, the tiniest sound had been given a bell-like clarity. He felt his fingertips could have read the words of a book as easily as if it had been printed in braille. He had been permitted brief access to a world of softer and warmer senses, and he was already planning how he could go there again.

SHE CAME for two more nights and then the following night she didn't. Finally he went to bed but he kept getting up and going outside and standing on the top step listening. He imagined her feet clinking the stones climbing the hill, when a cloud shuttled from beneath the moon he thought he saw her crossing the bridge. At last he went to bed but it was a long time before he slept.

The next morning he was about early and he crossed up through a stony sedgefield and a growth of halfgrown cedars. Dee Hixson's house sat at the mouth of a hollow, its tin roof rusted to a warm umber. The only vehicle parked in Dee's yard was his pickup truck. Dee himself was sitting on the edge of the porch shelling fresh garden peas into a bowl.

Come up, young Bloodworth. What you up to?

Fleming seated himself on the edge of the porch. I was headed down around the old McNally place. Thought I'd see if ginseng was up yet.

It's up. Starroot too. Blackroot, there's a world of that back in there.

I'm about to run out of money. I thought I might make a few dollars that way.

Dee was a wiry little man wrinkled and dark as a shriveled apple. In his younger days he was supposed to have been mean but to Fleming he didn't look big enough to have accumulated the reputation that mantled him. Yet his face was a roadmap of old violence. A knife cut on his cheek had been crudely stitched so that the healed scar and the dots where the stitches had been looked like a pale fleshy centipede crawling toward his hairline. Long ago a man named Scrapiron Steel had held him down and cut off the end of his nose with a pocket knife. A week later Steel had disappeared, never to be seen again in Ackerman's Field or anywhere else. The way Fleming had heard the story he was at the bottom of a cistern covered by the stones that Dee had rolled in to cover him, but studying this old man shelling peas he had trouble believing it.

Fleming unfolded himself from the porch. Well, I guess I better start looking if I aim to dig any.

Well. You'll need you a sack. Get one of them tow sacks out of that corncrib back there.

All right. Say, what happened to your company?

They've loaded up and headed out. Gone back north.

I'll see you, Mr. Hixson.

You come back anytime.

CAME THEN plague days of desolation when loss ravaged him like a fever. The house was empty and dead without her. A place of ice, of perpetual winds. He heard her voice at odd times, echoes of things she'd said. He awoke once in the night and her soft laughter had just faded into silence. Once he distinctly felt her hand lie on his shoulder. Before she'd shared his bed, life had been pointless, but now it had become unbearable. She had appeared from nowhere and returned to it, but she'd taken over his life, left with a lien on his body, a mortgage on his soul.

He tried to remember what she had said about writing, about

Christmas vacation. To replay it word for word. I'll snow you under in letters, she said. You'll dread to see the mailman coming. He heard the clipped Yankee cadence of her speech tell him how much she loved him. He'd been haunting the mailbox since Boyd left but now he redoubled his efforts. The barren mailbox mocked him. He wasted long hours computing distances, estimating the length of time it took a letter to travel from Detroit, Michigan, to Ackerman's Field, Tennessee.

In the final throes of desperation he began to check Dee's mailbox as well, sorting through the letters for one with a Michigan postmark, a firm girlish hand filled with curlicues, the *i*'s dotted with little circles.

Then one day as he approached Dee himself was coming down his driveway toward his mailbox. Fleming fell in with him, as if they'd check the mail together.

You ever hear from Merle since she went back north? he asked casually.

Who? Oh, no, Merle ain't never been much of a letter writer. Tell you the truth I'm sort of glad that bunch is gone. I reckon I've lived by myself so long I got used to the peace and quiet. Leastways her and that Randy got back together before they left.

Who?

Randy. Her husband. Big old redheaded boy. They set into fightin like cats and dogs for about a week there. Then she laid out on him somewheres a night or two and I reckon it taught him a lesson. They couldn't keep their hands off each other by the time they left. It would about turn your stomach.

Fleming had simply walked away. He was crossing the bridge before he even knew where he was. He turned and Dee was standing by the mailbox staring after him.

Why that undermining little bitch, he said aloud. There would be no letters, no Christmas vacation. *O lost, and by the wind grieved, ghost, come back again!* But by the time he had reached the foot of the hill he was feeling better and his face was a curious mixture of anger and rueful amusement. He took a small and bitter comfort in knowing that Randy was at least as big a fool as he was.

NO GOOD ever comes of having a police cruiser pull into your yard and park. This was not something that Albright had to learn, it had been bred into generations of Albrights all the way back to the days when the law rode up on horseback. It was part of his genetic makeup.

If in addition to parking a khakiclad deputy gets out with a paper in his hand and compares the name on the mailbox with the name on the warrant then everything is simply compounded, trouble multiplied by itself to an incalculable power.

By the time the curtain fell against the glass Albright was lightfooting it toward the kitchen, by the time he heard the official step at his hearth and the first peremptory rapping he was out the back door and gone, past the hogpen and the woodlot in a desperate stretch for the woods, the jagged line of pines bobbing in his vision with the pounding of his feet, the darkness beyond their trunks a land that offered its own kind of absolution, a land of timber and hollows so deep they threatened no extradition.

YOUNG FLEMING BLOODWORTH, with the proceeds of two weeks of herb gathering folded in the toe of his right front pocket, stood before Breece's Variety Store staring at a huge old Remington typewriter enshrined behind plateglass. After a while he went in past rows of hangered clothing and bins of toys and shelved cosmetics to where a salesgirl was marking prices on tiny white tags and stapling them to the sleeves of blouses.

How much is that typewriter in the window? There's no price on it.

I don't know how much he wants for it, you'd have to ask Mr. Breece. He's never said anything about it to me.

Is he not here?

He's somewhere there in the back. The storeroom. Just go to that door and holler at him.

Breece was a tall cadaverous man in wire-rimmed glasses and thinning gray hair worn long in the back and combed carefully forward in the forlorn hope it would cover his baldness. He was unpacking glassware from a cardboard carton filled with shredded paper and when

Fleming told him what he wanted he nodded and pulled on a gray sweater and buttoned it and clipped a black bowtie to the collar of his shirt. Let's go up to the front and look at it, he said.

I've learned there's not much call for typewriters here in Ackerman's Field, he said. If one tears up over at the courthouse they get a new one through some wholesale office supply. Same thing up at the school.

How much is it?

I'm asking sixty dollars. It's a eighty-dollar machine but I've had it too long and I'd like to move it. It's a top of the line machine. Crafted like a Swiss watch.

He popped the top and lifted it free and set it aside. See that? Like an expensive watch.

Fleming looked and he couldn't help but agree. Gleaming copper gears and steel springs and the bright hinged levers that worked the keys. There was an efficient businesslike manner to the machine that said it would brook no nonsense. It was not a toy. To Fleming it seemed some alchemical device out of a long-lost civilization founded on magic, capable of transmuting life into neatly stacked manuscripts. It looked as if it had a thousand tales to tell and needed only his complicity to begin the telling.

You wouldn't put it on layaway, would you?

Why Lord yes. It's been on layaway two years without a nickel paid on it. How much did you want to put down?

I could pay fifteen today.

I'll just put a sold tag on it and put it in the storeroom. You can come in and pay on it any time you want to.

He exited the store back onto sidewalks thronged with Saturday revelers. They seemed to have come from everywhere seeking some rumored carnival. Some from so far back in Godforsaken hollows the owls and chickens bedded down together just for the company. Out of tarpaper shacks that smelled of greasy smoke and kerosene. Young sharecroppers with their stoic calm faces and their childwives with querulous eyes that looked at him then darted away. Whole families, old women chewing their snuffsticks and old men in clean overalls listening to the sound of sand diminish in the glass. Babes in arms with wonderstruck eyes. Ribald whores from the countyline jukejoints and smooth country

Romeos with brilliantined hair and knives in their pockets or straight-razors worn under their shirts like necklaces on leather thongs. Splo whiskey on their breath and a taste for mindless violence and an affinity for finding it before Saturday night is gone. They will awake in alleys with the sun in their eyes, in jail, in places they don't remember going to and don't want to be. Every few Sunday mornings one of them wouldn't wake up at all.

Saturday drew these folk as a magnet aligns iron filings. They had come in pickup trucks or old rattletrap cars held together by some perverse suspension of the laws of physics, in sedans seemingly hacked into trucks with chopping axes and beds cobbled up out of sawmill slabs, in wagons drawn by mules, on foot, strung out on the road like refugees.

Mad streetcorner prophets ranted their own unhinged interpretation of the gospel so far removed from its source it might have been a garbled folktale handed down by word of mouth. Or homemade scriptures they'd written in Big Chief tablets by coal-oil light the night before. One had drawn a small crowd of stragglers and Fleming paused to listen. This preacher wore a guitar roped about his neck which he used not as you'd expect but as a sort of discordant punctuation at the end of his phrases.

The Bible says the hairs on a man's head is numbered, he raved. But listen, brother, where does that leave the baldheaded man? Is he shut out? Is he not even kept up with? Is he cut loose adrift without his name put down in the great book of records? The good book says His eye is on the sparrow, is a hairless man not as deserving of His eye as the fowls of the air?

He was full of such questions but like the rest he seemed to have no answers and Fleming soon drifted away.

In the poolhall he drank a Coca-Cola so cold it turned to slush when the cap was popped and watched Junior Albright put the last of his money in the pinball machine. He kept feeding it nickels until the odds were raised nigh off the scale then tilted it on the third ball.

It tilts real easy when the odds get high, Fleming said.

Albright looked at him. I notice the son of a bitch does, he said. He kicked it so hard it slammed against the wall and balls clanged hollowly in its bowels and Carlton Baxter came from behind the bar and fixed Albright with an angry scowl.

Keep your feet off that machine unless you plan on payin for it and takin it home with you, he said.

I've paid for the rotten whore ten times over, Albright said. He turned to Fleming. Let's walk down to the show and watch the girls come out, he said.

Passing the Snowwhite Cafe Fleming said, You want to go in and get a cheeseburger?

No, Albright said. I can't go in there. I saw a deputy in there this mornin through the glass and he might still be in there waiting for me. I'm keeping a lower profile than a snake. I fully expect another set of papers to come down on me.

I saw your picture down at the post office, Fleming said.

It ain't funny. To me it's not. I've got to where I dream about the damned cops. Once you do something to draw their attention you might as well hand it up.

I thought he already took you to court.

I didn't go. I never showed up and they went ahead and had it without me. They say I got to pay that eight hundred and sixty dollars and Woodall's lawyer. Somethin for the court. I think the judge's gone off down to Florida on a vacation and is sendin me the bill for it.

Why didn't you go to court and explain what happened?

I didn't have a legal leg to stand on so I just let her roll. There was about forty people seen the fucker blow up like it had a stick of dynamite in it. There wasn't much way of lyin out of it.

He was silent a time. They had approached the Strand Theater and stood before it studying the black and white stills of Rex Allen and the Durango Kid. Fleming could smell the greasy odor of buttered popcorn and hear the sound of distant gunfire.

Look at them duded-up outfits, Albright said. I seen one one time when this stagecoach was runnin away and he climbed out on the traces and worked his way all the way to the front. They was goin about ninety mile an hour and his fuckin hat didn't even blow off. They kept goin by the same rock too.

He fell silent again. Finally he said, I've got to get that damned Woodall off my back. He's goin to hound me all my life. If I ever get a decent job he'll garnishee me. If I ever get a car he'll take it. If I marry he'll be screwin my wife. My whole life is mortgaged.

Fleming grinned. Put a hex on him, he said.

Put a what?

A hex. A curse. Get my uncle Brady to voodoo him. He's got one on Harwood, the mail carrier, right now. Harwood run over one of Brady's dogs and now his insides are supposed to turn to concrete or something.

But does it work?

Does it work. Hellfire. Of course it doesn't work, Brady's as crazy as a shithouse mouse. He's got these widow women coming around to get their fortunes told. He tells them what they want to hear about their love life and they pay him five dollars. He's started believing it himself.

The wide double doors of the theater opened and folks began to string out into late afternoon light, first the kids, their eyes strange and disassociate from the visions they'd seen, brought back too abruptly from the purple sage and set down on these twentieth-century sidewalks. Young girls came out in giggling groups, bright as summer flowers. Albright was watching them with a kind of deranged hunger. One paused and studied Fleming with cool appraisal from a fringe of dark lashes then turned and caught up with her friends. Albright grasped him by the arm. He was staring after the girls in a kind of wonder.

Just think, Fleming, he said. They've all got one. Ever Goddamned one of them.

That's anatomy for you, Fleming agreed.

Going out toward home just before dark Fleming started up Park Avenue South and as he passed an office door it opened and a heavyset man in a dentist's smock hailed him.

What say, Young Bloodworth.

Hey Doc.

I saved a bunch of those magazines for you. You want them?

Sure.

Come in and I'll gather them up.

He went in the dentist's waiting room, bare of waiting patients. A pinepaneled room of wonders, a museum in miniature. While the dentist stacked copies of *True* and *Collier's* and *The American Magazine* Fleming made a slow tour of the room. He'd seen it all before but he looked again. Time caught like a fly in amber and displayed behind plateglass. Civil War swords, a Colt dragoon in a curio case. Old dentist's instruments so barbaric they looked like artifacts from a medieval torturer's toolbox. Arrowheads. A long lethal spearpoint chiseled with meticulous craftmanship from flint. The skull of some ancient Indian, the cranium shattered by a rifle ball in a concussion that still rolled wave on wave forever in this room.

Here you go. I don't have anything to put them in. Can you carry them under your arm?

That'll work fine. Thanks a lot, Doc.

Don't mention it. You take care, Speedo.

He went out and up the street but the stack of magazines kept slipping and sliding and he knew they'd wear him out before he'd walked the miles he had to go. He crossed the street and went down an alley toward the railroad where the feedstore was and behind it found a pile of burlap bags. He took up one and shook the loose grains of feed out of it and loaded the magazines into it and left with the bag slung across his shoulder.

He was no more than on the highway when he got a ride, a felt-hatted oldtimer in a pickup stacked with bags of corn. They rode in silence listening to the Grand Ole Opry on the radio. A country comedian was telling a story about a rube outfoxing a city slicker. In the west the sun had gone and the point where sun and horizon met burned in a blur like some cosmic conflagration.

Ain't that Rod somethin? That Minnie too. Don't they beat anythin you ever heard?

They're pretty funny, the boy agreed, and grinned weakly as if he'd prove it.

What's a young feller like you doin goin in this time of day? The night ain't even got wound out yet.

I guess I just ran out of anything to do.

I was your age they wasn't no runnin out. These warm nights you couldn't of held me down with a log chain. I'd do anything. I'd wake up in Alaska hungover with my beard froze to the ground.

The boy didn't reply. Beyond the dark glass fields and trees and houses slipped past, so blurred they were like ghosts of a landscape, just symbols that stood for a world. The truck had turned off and now they were going downhill, the wornout brake shoes skirling metal on metal.

I'd hang around that show and pick me up one of them young girls wanders around. Take her down by the tieyard and throw a tool to her.

I get off anywhere along here.

What?

I get off here.

The driver stopped. He looked. There ain't nothin here, he said.

There's a road across that branch. A log road. I live back across that ridge.

Well. You'd better get across it. It's about slapdab dark.

He went down an embankment and crossed a swift narrow stream that went noisily over the stones and followed a footpath through a thicket of elderberry and sumac and came out on an old log road that wound toward the timbered ridge. Everything was sinking in indigo dark save the road which seemed to exude a faint phosphorescence like an enchanted road in a witch's wood orphans might follow to the cottage at its end.

He trudged woodenly on, the bag slung across his left shoulder. He seemed to move in a pocket of silence, nightbirds and insects falling silent at his arrival, taking up the cry after he'd passed. He wondered how many times he'd walked this road with Boyd, how many times dark fell on them before they made the crossroads. Boyd in front, the burlap bag of groceries on his shoulder. The boy behind, folded comic books in his hip pocket. Landmarks rose out of memory. A stump, a tree. The way a horizon held against the heavens. Here we lost my shoes one time, had to backtrack a mile and a half to find them. The pale shoe box against the drifted leaves. I was beginnin to think we dropped them comin out of the drygood store, Boyd had said.

The feeling that off somewhere in the bracken man and boy still walked rose in him nor would it abate. With their steps locked in sync with his they paced him in the silent black wood, passed through the boles of trees like revenants. A moon the color of yellowed ivory cradled up out of the dark and he could see them moving through the trees transparent as water, insubstantial as a handful of smoke.

He went on. When he reached the crossroads the moon was well up and the intersecting roads lay dusted with silver until they faded into the velvet trees. He sat for a time and rested. He was uncertain as to which way to go. If he bore left he would wind up at his grandmother's. Straight ahead followed the spine of the ridge to his home. There was something mystic about crossroads, they doubled the options, confused both pursuer and pursued. He didn't know which he was, and after a while he made a pillow of the magazines and slept this night at the crossroads.

BOOK TWO

B OYD LIVED in a rooming house with other men whose lives he understood better perhaps than he understood his own. He did not know their names or their faces except to nod to when they met on the worn carpet of the hallway yet he had known them all his days, had known them as thoroughly as if he'd been an invisible listener to their every conversation, read their mail, hitchhiked through the burnt landscape of their troubled dreams. They were all men like him, gone north for something better, and finding there the trouble they'd fled was somehow augmented, their lives multiplied by themselves.

Nights he'd come out of the house to the electric neon streets and walk down to a strip of gaudy bars and find hundreds of others wearying themselves toward dreamless sleep. He watched drunken men pound themselves senseless in alleys, in bars, he kept to himself and he kept his mouth shut and he skirted barroom brawls that were just masses of men and whores and flailing cuesticks with a sort of amused contempt.

And so into the night. The rainy streets echoed the flickering neon as if the ghosts of revelry continued silently on at some subterranean level. The air was electric with sound: jukeboxes and the click of pool balls and the sluice of tires through the rain and police sirens, the wail of fire engines. Folks were always wounded, dying, burning alive. They died on roadhouse floors of gunshot wounds, of being flung through the windshields of automobiles that had been suddenly halted by utility poles, trees, concrete underpass abutments, they died of knife cuts you could just not get to stop bleeding.

He wondered at the jobs folks had, these curious restorers of order. There were people who moved in as if they homed on violence, they towed away the crumpled wrecks, others swept up the glass, others mopped up the blood. Together they knitted whole the fabric of night where violence had rent it. Everything was always changing and everything was always the same.

On the way back to his room there was a dog that would bark at him every night. Run down the length of a concrete sidewalk between box elders that were glossy black in the streetlights. There was a gate of wrought iron hung between two concrete posts. The posts were surmounted by gargoyle's heads. The German shepherd would come padding down the concrete barking furiously, halt at the closed gate and watch him, his eyes fierce and alert, the skin of his nose and upper lip wrinkling with its short, angry barks.

One night the gate was standing open and the dog paused as if undecided whether to come into the street. Boyd watched it. He'd halted when he saw the unexpectedly open gate. He fumbled out the hawkbill knife, knowing if he ran the dog would be upon him. The dog seemed uncertain, watching Boyd, watching the gate.

Boyd showed it the knife. Get away from me, you son of a bitch, he told it.

Something stirred on the porch. Here, Jack, a man's voice called. You there, what are you doing to that dog?

I'm just before cuttin the son of a bitch's head off, Boyd said.

He could see the man standing on the top step, just a dark shape against the paler shape of the house.

You do and I'll pound your hillbilly ass right into that sidewalk, the man said.

Why don't you do it first and brag about it later, Boyd said.

Something had been growing for weeks inside him and he felt it burst, the tissues rupture and a richly corrupt and violent liquid spread warmly through him. Are you the one? he thought. I could practice on you. Get my moves down. I could start on you and work up to that drummer.

I see that knife but it doesn't bother me, the shape said. I have a gun in the house.

In the house? Go get it. I don't know why you people think Winchester made one Goddamned gun and then went out of business.

A silence fell. It elongated, spun out, frayed.

After a while the shape turned and went into the house. The door closed. Boyd waited but the door stayed closed. Finally he looked once at the dog then backed down the street. Not even the dog would follow him.

FOR DAYS Fleming had been seeing smoke that lay perpetually on the southern horizon, and when the wind was right he could smell it, faintly acrid, sometimes with the scent of burning cedar and pine. A haze hung over the treeline, somewhere back toward the river.

Late in the day he went with a blanket and a coffeepot and ground coffee folded in a paper bag and climbed a tall bluff that ascended from the creek. At its summit the cliff formed a rough dome that seemed to overlook the world itself and all that grew there was one enormous cedar leaning and windformed, its roots finding only precarious purchase in the fissured stone.

When dusk fell he built a fire and set the coffee in the coals to make. He sat against the trunk of the cedar and watched bats come veering up out of the twilight on isobars sheer and plumb as if they'd had courses plotted for them. In deeper darkness an owl crossed above him, its wings beating heavily and almost invisible, just a pale shape shifting against the dark heavens.

It had grown cooler with the fall of night and when the coffee was made he sat with the blanket drawn about his shoulders and drank a cup watching a glowing line of fire that was the southern horizon, a faint line that ebbed and throbbed like a length of redhot wire. In the unstable dark it seemed to advance and retreat, tremble and flare brighter under the fanning of winds he did not feel. As night deepened all he could see was the shifting line of fire, like some malfunction in the wiring of the world itself, as if the very night had combusted and was creeping incrementally toward him.

He branched off the Grinders Creek road and walked back toward the river. This road was just a log road but recent and heavy traffic had smoothed it and widened it and turned the hard white clay to a pale thick dust that rose and subsided with his footfalls and the passage of vehicles had talcumed the sawbriars and honeysuckle that shrouded the roadside. The road seemed to ascend all the way to the river and he stopped once to rest where he'd remembered a spring that flowed out of a hollow. He raked the wet black leaves away and let the water clear and drank from his cupped hands. The water was sweet and cold.

After a while he began to hear the sounds of machinery, trucks and what sounded like bulldozers, the stuttering whine of chainsaws. Still the timber held steady, a thick wall of green, but he could smell smoke strongly now and he could see it. He'd reached the summit of the long grade and here the world flattened out and the walking was easier. He'd forgotten how far away the river lay.

In late afternoon the road wound through an area being decimated by saw and dozer. Trees lay felled in all directions with dozers shaping them into smoking windrows and the blue haze shifted over everything as far as the eye could see. This was the spine of the ridge and here the earth sloped away toward the river and the hills and hollows seemed to be just blackened ash. Alongside the road trucks and lowboys had been parked and he could see men fanned out like an army of ants. He followed the road a time past all this destruction until the road itself vanished in a field of quaking ash. He hunkered for a time and studied the countryside in a kind of wonder. Not a sapling, not a twig or flower seemed to have survived. Everything past this point was ashes.

When he passed the trucks going back the way he'd come in a man was filling a Coke bottle with water from a five-gallon cooler set on a stump. When he drank he set the bottle back and took up a yellow chainsaw and set it atop a stump and began to file the chain.

How about a shot of this water?

The man turned and looked up. He wore a yellow hardhat and he appeared not much older than Fleming. Help yourself, good buddy, he said.

Fleming filled the bottle and drank then filled it again and walked with it to where the man was filing the saw.

What's going on back in here?

We're clearing off a hell of a new ground, the man said. You better drink up and go before a foreman sees you. Not supposed to be any civilians back in here. Have they not got those no trespassing signs up yet?

I didn't see any.

There'd be a hell of a lawsuit if somebody got a tree cut on him. The TVA's got a thing about avoidin lawsuits.

There's nothing back there. Not a bush or a sprout. Why are you clearing it out so clean?

Do you not know sure enough?

No.

There's goin to be a dam and a lake back in here. A hell of a lake, what they tell me. We're clearing it clean enough to eat off of. I thought everybody knowed about it. Course nobody lives back in here, this is all company land. But we're spreadin that way. Where do you live?

Fleming pointed with the empty bottle. How far does this lake go that way?

I don't know, the man said. I just cut what trees they tell me. But it's goin to be a hell of a lake. You might give some thought toward movin or learnin to swim.

FOR THREE DAYS the mail carrier had been a person unknown to Junior Albright and he had observed all this with a more than casual interest. On the fourth morning he sauntered down to the blacktop and idled there by the mailbox until the dustcolored Plymouth came around the curve.

This mail carrier was a woman, a heavyset woman with a bulldog jaw and short hacked-off hair. Albright had his three pennies ready. I need a stamp, he said.

She carefully tore a single stamp from a book and slid it into a small glassine envelope and exchanged it for the pennies.

Say, what's happened to Harwood? he asked.

Mr. Harwood's sick, she told him. They got me substitutin for him. He's in a Nashville hospital.

You don't say. What's his trouble?

They don't even know yet, the woman said. They keep runnin tests on him, callin in more specialists. Somethin to do with his stomach.

You don't say, Albright said bemusedly.

OBLIQUE YELLOW LIGHT moved in waves across the broomstraw and early morning crows called from the cedar row where the cool still held and the dew lingered. When they set out it was just after seven o'clock but already a bloodred sun hung poised like a threat and the sky was a serene cloudless blue.

Fleming had expected they'd follow the road but the truck was bouncing across a field Brady had chosen as a shortcut. The furrows jarred Fleming so hard his teeth clattered. He was holding the water jug and a bucket of food his grandmother had packed and he was hard put to hang onto it and stay in the truck, for there was no righthand door. In fact the truck looked like a truck cobbled up by someone who'd heard trucks rumored but had never actually seen one, a funhouse mirror reflection of a truck. It served most of the time as a cutoff saw, one rear wheel removed and a belt and pulley mounted on the axle. The hood and front fenders were missing and on the driver's side door someone had painted the legend JOLIE BLON in faded freehand script.

The flat wooden bed of the truck was loaded with concrete blocks and shovels and picks and jacks and all the tools they might need to set up the old man's trailer. Fleming had been conscripted to help and he was curious to see how this job might be accomplished.

Where the field ended they lurched out onto a roadbed and turned right. After some distance Fleming caught the glint of the sun on metal and then he could see it, a short cigar stub of a trailer with two rounded ends. Brady parked before it and cut the switch. Home sweet home, he said.

Fleming got out trying to rub feeling into his backside. Where's the rest of it? he asked.

What?

There doesn't seem to be much to it.

Well, he's not but one old man. Likely he won't live long anyway. Beggars can't be choosers, can they?

How's he begging? I thought you said he sent you the money to buy him a trailer.

And you see it before you, Brady said. Let's get this stuff unloaded. I've got more to do than set up this mess. Find a shady spot somewhere for that water jug.

Shade seemed hard come by here, and he wondered, but did not ask, why Brady had chosen this spot. There were no trees surrounding the trailer, nothing but chesthigh blackjack scrub.

Why don't we clear some of this brush and move it back in there where the trees are?

Move it? Pick it up and set it back there?

We could maybe move it back in there with the truck.

Maybe. Or maybe turn it over and bust it like an egg. Don't worry about it. Maybe the Lord will take mercy on a sinner and miracle an air conditioner into that front window yonder.

Brady set him to digging a hole for a makeshift septic tank and positioned a jack at the low end of the trailer and began to raise it, shoring up with concrete blocks as he went, checking the underside of the trailer from time to time with a spirit level. After he'd dug through the top layer of clay and chopped out the tree roots Fleming found the going easier and actually began to enjoy the work, loosening the earth with a mattock and throwing the dirt out with a shovel. By midmorning he had an enormous amount of earth mounded on the rim above him and he was standing chestdeep in a hole he could have buried a horse in.

Hey.

Brady came over to look.

How deep does this thing have to be?

Some deeper than that. We can't have a worldfamous musician doing his business in the woods like a heathen.

Where's he going to get water?

I guess I'll have to haul his water. Unless you want to fly in when you're through with that hole and dig him a well.

Fleming wiped sweat out of his eyes and stood leaning on the shovel. He could think of nothing worse than being trapped in this eggshaped tin can dropped down in the boiling sun and dependent on Brady to haul his drinking water.

That old man is going to singe and draw like a spider, he said. He went back to shoveling.

At noon the heat felt malefic and they walked through the brush behind the trailer into the shade and ate the lunch the old woman had prepared, roast beef sandwiches and hardboiled eggs. The boy finished with a fried apple pie he washed down with tepid coffee from a Mason jar.

How come you're so down on the old man, Brady?

If you'd ever been around him you wouldn't need to ask me that.

Well, I wasn't, so I do. None of you talks about him, or none of the family anyway.

Boyd and Warren ain't so down on him. Let him come on back, they said. You'll notice Warren's in Alabama and Boyd's traipsed off God knows where and I'm the one out here sweatin over this mess.

I've learned more about him from listening to other old men talk than I ever did from you or Pa, Fleming said. You act like he just stepped through a hole in the ground and vanished.

Well, Brady said, that's about what happened. Except now he wants to crawl back out of the hole. If it was left up to me I'd stand on the edge of the hole and stomp his fingers ever time he tried to get a handhold. He just left Ma settin and walked off. Just walked. Not havin a car never stopped him. He'd rather ride but he'd walk if he had to. He always had these trashy people he could turn to. He had all the company he wanted, of one kind or another. But blood is never left up to you, blood will call to blood. You can't deny your own kin.

He was silent for some time, his sharp intent face locked in concentration. I expect it was mainly that music, he finally said. I've thought about it a lot, and for a while I thought it was the whiskey. But I've come to see it was them old songs. They was real to him in a way they wasn't real to nobody else. Whenever he'd take that old banjo out of the case and go off by himself, you'd know in a few days he'd be gone. Like a man goin on a drunk, except it'd be them old songs he'd be drunk on. That old lonesome-soundin banjo. His voice sounded like a fingernail on a blackboard. They say he's made some money at it but Lord I'd like to know who spent it. It never sounded worth fifteen cents to me.

The boy sat and listened in silence. He tipped the last of his coffee onto the ground. The earth was dry and baked white and fissured with cracks like miniature faults in the earth. Like the embryonic beginnings of some ultimate cataclysm. It sucked the coffee instantly into itself and left no trace. He thought about what Brady had said. He felt instinctively that every coin had two sides and that this was only one of them. In the poolhall and on Itchy Mama Baker's front porch he'd heard another story. Once people knew who he was they always had a story to tell him about his grandfather. They seemed to regard him as somehow larger than life. As if in living life on a larger scale than they were permitted or perhaps permitted themselves he had somehow redeemed them. He'd heard stories of a man who'd sometimes lived outside the law but had forded a swollen river on horseback to pay back a two-dollar loan. But, the man amended, it might have been that E.F. just wanted to see if he could swim the river. He was a man who had had trouble adjusting himself to the expectations that other people, particularly people in authority, had for him. He seemed to have some difficulty playing the role that life had cast him.

The last time he left, Brady said, he had just got out of the pen. He was making whiskey then and he wound up shootin a deputy sheriff. I wasn't there but he must have just walked in the front door and out the back. And then that was that.

He sat for a time without speaking. He seemed to be studying his shoes. He was studying them intently, as though they were some make of shoe he had never encountered before.

I ought never to have let you get me started on this line of talk, he finally said. Things run along smooth when I don't think of him at all. My mind'll smooth off. Then I get started on him and it's like somebody jabbed a stick down inside my head and stirred everything up. My mind's like muddy water. There's times I could have killed him like a copperhead I seen in the woods and just walked off and left him. Let's get this mess done and get out of here.

There's not going to be any electricity?

Not unless you want to box it up and tote it to him. Do you see any wires run in here? Then let's get to work. We can run them septic tank lines and cover the tank over without it.

They stood up. You reckon you could really find water around here? Fleming asked.

I could if it's here. Back on a dry ridge like this here it'd be a long way down if you did find it.

Let's see you try.

Why? You wouldn't know anymore if you watched than you do right now. It ain't somethin you see. You feel the fork jerk and tremble in your hands. If the stream's strong enough it'll draw it straight down, like a magnet draws iron. I've seen it twist the bark off.

I never saw anybody witch for water before. If it wasn't too far down me and Junior Albright might dig him a shallow well.

I'd almost pay money to see a well you and Junior Albright dug, Brady said. In fact I'd see it if I had to borrow the money to get in.

He walked about the clearing, stooped and cut a forked sprout. Folks'll tell you it has to be a peachtree sprout. Or a willow, or some such. That's rubbish. It ain't the stick, it's you. If you've got the gift you could find it with a jack handle just as easy.

He walked about the clearing, the stick held before him by the forks. Once at the corner of the trailer it jerked spasmodically, as if a slight current of electricity had coursed through it. He walked away, began covering the area in a gridlike pattern. When he approached the same corner of the trailer the forked stick trembled again.

You mind if I try?

Brady halted and offered him the stick. This here's the only nibble I got, he said. And it's doubtful at best. You may do better. We may be just drownin in water a foot or two down.

Fleming held the stick in his hands as he'd seen Brady do. He crossed to the woods, back again. The fork held steady. But at the corner of the trailer it jerked in his hands, seemed almost to be vibrating. Brady was watching. He shook his head in amazement. We may have somethin here, he said. You may be on to somethin.

Fleming walked away. When he returned the stick twisted again. Brady had approached, was following along behind him. You may have the gift, he said. It shows up in ever generation of the family, I've run it back. You may be the one in this generation.

I may well be, the boy agreed.

He approached the deeper timber. At a clump of sweetgum the witching fork seemed taken with some kind of fit. It jerked and struggled, seemed to be trying to wrest itself from his hands. Then the point sprang earthward.

The boy tossed it aside. He stood and withdrew the water jug from the thick shaded greenery. Not too far to this, he said. Brady was watching balefully. Fleming unscrewed the lid and drank. He lowered the jug. Pretty fair water too, he said.

You're a cruelhearted little shitass, Brady told him. It's no wonder your whole family moved off without tellin you where they were goin.

ON HIS WAY to the bus station E. F. Bloodworth was caught up in a surging tide of humanity that had turned out for some sort of festivities. He had gone only a few blocks from Cora's boarding house when he found himself borne along whether he wanted to go or not, so dense were the folk here. Every strata of Little Rock's society seemed represented, from sharecroppers to prosperous farmers in Panama hats. Even the jaded merchants themselves were standing in the doorways of their shops, fondling their watch chains and watching the streets expectantly as if something of enormous significance was on the verge of happening.

He finally made the shelter of an awning that shaded the front of a jewelry store, a pocket of calm backwaters eddied in the lee of swift water. He leaned on his walking stick, a handcarved length of hickory emblazoned with stars and moons and enigmatic hieroglyphs and the carved handhold carved to represent the neck and head of a serpent. The old man stood at least a head taller than anyone in the crowd milling about him and with his ferocious eyes and irritated demeanor he looked like a weary old bear beleaguered by a pack of hounds. He took out a handkerchief and wiped the perspiration off his neck and folded the handkerchief carefully and slid it into the pocket of his black suitcoat. Aside from this coat he wore a baggy pair of biglegged gray slacks and a starched white dress shirt. He wore an enormous maroon tie with the likeness of a longhorn bull adorning it. He wore the pearlgray fedora with the brim slightly rolled and cocked at a jaunty angle, and with his height and demeanor and the Stetson he would have been an imposing figure anywhere but in this sweating throng of humanity.

A short ducklike woman had been swept into the shelter of the awning. She was hanging on to three wildeyed children like survivors she'd snatched from floodwaters.

The old man had begun to hear music, the brassy strident sound of a marching band. He searched his mind for some holiday this might be that would call for a parade but could not think of one.

I was as tall as you I might be able to see something, the ducklike woman said irritably to the old man, as if she held him responsible for the disparity in their height. What do you see out there?

The tops of folk's heads, mostly, Bloodworth said. What is this mess?

Can you not see any mules yet?

Mules? he asked in disbelief.

Yes, mules. This is Arkansas Mule Day and I'm tryin to get these kids closer so they can see better.

Why anybody would want to see a mule closer is a mystery to me, Bloodworth said.

These is all champion mules, she said dismissively, as if he'd taken leave of his senses.

A champion mule ain't nothin but a mule with a ribbon tied on it.

You walk behind as many turnin plows as I have you'd be well satisfied to never see a mule again. Or even know there's one left in the world.

But she had no ears for such heresy and she jerked the children back into the packed wall of humanity and began to struggle toward the street.

Mules had indeed now swung into sight, a trio of them decked out in red, white and blue bunting, ridden by girls in sequined swimsuits that glittered in the sun. Behind them a phalanx of baton twirlers and a band playing a just-recognizable version of *Stars and Stripes Forever* and behind the band cavorting clowns on tricycles and even one riding a unicycle and waving bothhanded at the crowd. Then mules and more mules like some vast migratory herd headed westward into Oklahoma. Bloodworth ignored the mules and watched bemusedly the smooth tanned thighs of the strutting baton twirlers, his leathery face impassive and sleepy eyelids blinking occasionally like some ancient turtle basking on a rock in the sun.

When the main battery of mules had passed the crowd straggled after it as if loathe to lose this magic and after a time the old man was able to continue up the street. He had set out this day for the Trailways bus station to inquire as to ticket prices but as he reached for the door and was about to enter something caught his eye and he released the door and went on down the street. What had drawn his attention was a truck parked in an alley, not actually the truck but its license plate, a Tennessee license plate shaped like the state itself. He stood for a time studying it, leaning on the stick and lost in the geography of the shape as if it were a map, the chart of some landscape he'd crossed long ago and left his mark on.

He walked about the truck examining it intently as if it were some purchase he was contemplating making. It was a red Diamond-T truck of recent vintage and lettered in white on the doors was the legend COBLE CATTLE COMPANY, MEMPHIS TENNESSEE. The truck was sideboarded with a framework of black lathing, floored with straw and cow dung.

Bloodworth looked about. The nearest business was a long stucco building with a sign that said WILD BILL'S BILLIARDS. Next door was a diner. One or the other but I'd give odds on the poolhall, the old man thought and turned and limped back to the Trailways station.

Inside he drank thirstily from a drinking fountain and with the water an icy bulb swinging inside him he strode toward the counter where a young woman sat reading a paperback book.

How much is it to Ackerman's Field, Tennessee?

The girl laid the book face up on the counter. The cover showed a nearly naked woman being shot in the abdomen by an enormous .45 caliber automatic held in a gloved and disembodied hand. The girl glanced up at the old man and unconsciously smoothed her hair and began to search through a list of cities on a schedule.

I don't show it, she finally said. What is it close to? Maybe we can figure it out from there.

It's close to Schubert, the old man said. But I doubt you show that either. Have you got Nashville?

Of course, she said, a red fingernail tracing a column of figures down a sheet. It's seven-eighty. Did you want one way or round trip?

Let me think about it a minute, he said.

She looked up and smiled at him. Of course, she said. There's seats over there where you can rest in the cool.

There was a curious quality to the old man, a sort of courtly dignity that made people treat him with a certain unconscious deference. He had long grown accustomed to it and it sometimes amused him that he had been mistaken for someone of importance.

He tipped his hat to the girl and went over to a row of seats that looked like church pews and chose one and sat next to a sleeping soldier. He leaned the back of his head against the hard back of the seat. The girl had taken up her book and begun to read but occasionally she glanced over the top of the pages at Bloodworth. He closed his eyes. She thinks I ain't got no money, he thought, feeling the lowgrade heat from the folded greenbacks in his front pocket. I got plenty of money. I got enough money to burn a wet mule. Even a champion mule, he smiled to himself. He thought of returning to the boarding house to pick up the rest of his belongings, but it was a thought he immediately discarded. When Bloodworth was ready to go he was just ready to go, and when he itemized his possessions he came up with nothing that could not be discarded, carried in a pocket, or worn.

In truth the old man did not trust bus stations. He had once had a Gibson Mastertone banjo stolen out of a bus station in Shreveport, Louisiana, and he had been in a rage monumental even for him. He had haunted the bus station for weeks demanding the return of the banjo until folks dreaded to see him coming; with any advance notice at all the help went out the back as he came in the front. He had been a banjo picker all his life and banjo tunes still ran through his head like brightly colored threads.

He rose and put on his hat. He raised a hand politely to the girl and went out into the sun and struck out for the poolhall. After a time he could hear raucous laughter, the click of pool balls. When he entered he was inundated in a cool gloom like the deepest of summer shade. He seated himself in the cloistral calm at the bar and placed his hat before him, first wiping the counter with a coatsleeve should there be an errant beerstain.

What'll it be, the barkeep said.

Give me a draft, the old man said. Just whatever you got that's cold.

The man took up an enormous schooner and filled it from a siphon and tipped off the foam and slid it across. He rang up Bloodworth's dollar and slapped three quarters on the bar. Them fools off the street? he asked.

Mostly, Bloodworth said, watching bubbles rise in his beer. I never realized that mules was that well regarded. It may be that I never gave them their proper due.

He took up the schooner and drank, his adam's apple pumping the beer down. When he set the schooner down empty his eyes were slightly unfocused and his upper lip was coated with mustaches of pale thick foam. He wiped them off with a coatsleeve and turned to survey the room: two pool players and a heavyset man in a broadbrimmed white straw hat watching them. This would be Coble Cattle Company, Memphis Tennessee. While he was debating the best way of approaching Coble the problem solved itself. The man in the straw hat leaned and whispered something to the pool player on the bench beside him then rose and crossed the painted concrete floor toward Bloodworth and seated himself on the next stool over.

Watch this, oldtimer, he said. We may see us a little action here.

He tilted the brim of the white straw hat toward the pool players: some sort of confrontation seemed to be shaping up. Pills had been shaken out onto the pool table and accounted for and one of the men was shaking his finger in the other's face. When the hand was slapped away the tall man swung from the ground up and knocked the other into a rack that exploded with pool cues and armed with one of them the fallen man struggled up shaking his head as if to clear cloudy vision.

Coble had ordered two beers and he pressed one onto Bloodworth. They had swiveled their stools the better to see the fight.

They fightin over pills, Coble volunteered. The one and sixteen come up missin and turned up in thatn with the pool cue's pocket. They wasn't playin for but a dollar a game but I reckon that's where honor come into it.

You mean he was holdin out pills?

He was after I slipped em in his pocket and told the other one he was hidin em. Coble chuckled to himself, not a pleasant sound.

The gangling man was trying to get to the pool cues but he was kept busy dodging swipes from the stick the fat boy was using and finally he grabbed up a handful of pool balls and began firing them like baseballs.

Here, Goddamn it, the barkeep yelled.

You mean you started that mess yourself and then eased out?

Didn't cost me a red cent and it passes the time, Coble said.

One of them pool balls upside the head would pass a right smart of it, Bloodworth mused.

I don't know but what I'd watch out, oldtimer, Coble said. His aim don't appear to be the best in the world.

Even as he spoke a ball whizzed past Bloodworth and smashed the mirror behind the bar. Hellfire, the old man said. He grasped up his hat from the bar and sat cradling it in his lap.

I said by God stop it, the barkeep was screaming. He had jerked up the telephone and was dialing numbers as fast as he could work his fingers.

A pool ball had struck the fat boy squarely in the middle of the forehead and he dropped his cue stick and clasped his face in both hands and swayed gently from the knees up and slowly settled to the floor. The tall man had begun to hurl balls in a kind of random malevolence. The door opened and a man made to enter but when a ball shot past and halted the jukebox in midsong he just grinned and shook his head and eased back out the door and through the glass Bloodworth could see him hurrying away.

They get a right lively trade in here, don't they? Bloodworth asked.

The barkeep snatched a cigar box from beneath the counter and withdrew a small black pistol and by the time he had fired one shot into the ceiling Bloodworth was up pulling on his hat then taking up the walking stick and limping toward the door.

I just might join you, oldtimer, Coble said. It's gettin a little close in here, ain't it?

Outside they could hear a siren's whooping down through the hot vibratory air. Let's just move our patronage over to this diner, Coble said. I believe I can hear a fan blowin in there.

When they were settled into a booth with a cold beer before them Coble said, That's a mighty fine hat you got, oldtimer.

It is that, Bloodworth admitted. I paid too much for it but I wanted it. I ordered this hat from Miller Stockman out of Wyoming.

I figured you for a cattleman right off, Coble said.

The old man studied Coble. His face was round and vapid, the small piglike eyes holding a kind of self-satisfied stupidity, the result, the old man figured, of the fight he had caused. Why is a fool such a hard thing to resist? he asked himself in a kind of wonder.

I'm about out of it, Bloodworth said. I'm about ready to sell my cows off for next to nothin and settle up a bunch of medical expenses I've run up.

I noticed you went with a sort of limp but you appear healthy enough.

Oh, it ain't me, Bloodworth said, and he felt almost a physical dividing of himself, so that momentarily there seemed two Bloodworths, one trying to divine how big a lie Coble would swallow and another, a tiny cynical Bloodworth, standing aside with its head cocked attentively as if this was all news to him too.

What's your name, oldtimer? Coble asked.

Rutgers, Bloodworth said without hesitation, wondering immediately where the name came from. After a time he seemed to remember seeing it on a seed catalog.

What kind of cattle you fool with?

Black Angus, Bloodworth said. But let me tell you. Back in the winter we was buildin a new silo and a section of scaffoldin come loose and that boy of mine fell. He never fell more than eight or ten feet but there was a walkboard swingin on a rope and it caught him right square in the head and knocked him coldern a wedge.

They Lord, Coble said.

Bloodworth nodded. That wasn't the worst of it. He never had been right but this plumb addled him. He drug around like a chicken with the limberneck for a week or two and then one Sunday he decided he was goin to church. He never had been to church much, we never was big on churchgoin. Anyway he put on a suit and went, and what they tell me he cut a shine. Jumpin pews and rollin around foamin at the mouth like a maddog. Took some kind of Jesus fit and went to talkin in tongues. After that he went to preachin. He'd preach to just whatever. It didn't matter whether folks'd listen to him or not. He'd preach to cows or stumps or just whatever was in front of him. Chickens. He baptized nigh every chicken I had on the place, drowned a bunch of Allen Roundhead fightin cocks I had.

Course I was laid up with a stroke of paralysis with this left leg stiff as a preacher's pecker and I couldn't do much about it. Then the doctor sent me to Hot Springs for the baths and that's where I been.

Bloodworth paused, drank from the amber beerbottle. He glanced covertly at Coble to see how he was taking all this. He thought he might have been ladling it on a trifle heavy. But Coble's porcine face showed no sign of disbelief, just a thin veneer of spurious commiseration masking opportunism, and Bloodworth took heart. He did not feel that Coble was overburdened with brains, and he was seized with a perverse desire to see how far he could go without Coble realizing the old man was making a fool of him: in addition to this, the old man had not taken any alcohol since his stroke, and he could feel a pleasant buzzing in his head that seemed to be in some manner lubricating his tongue. He pressed on, and felt free to let his imagination soar.

I was layin up there in Hot Springs takin the waters when I got a telegram about that boy. He'd gone plumb off the deep end. He'd started tryin to keep my cattle from breedin. Called it fornicatin. He couldn't stop it so he started marryin em. Performin these ceremonies on em, reading out of the Bible. He was pairin em off a bull to a cow but there was more cows than there was bulls and what was worse he couldn't keep em lined up the way he'd married em. They kept committin what he called adultery with cows they wasn't married to and he couldn't manage em. It was wearin him out. He was slippin around at night watchin em. When he couldn't stand it no more he got a gun and shot four of my best bulls. He was tryin to drag a little Texas bull I had off a cow with his bare hands and that bull just figured I reckon he'd by God had enough and come off that cow and gored him. He's layin up there in Vanderbilt opened up stem to stem and them doctors don't hold out much hope for him. He'd have to improve some to be a vegetable, what they tell me.

Good God, Coble said. That's the damnedest thing I ever heard, old-timer.

It's been the ruin of me. I don't even want to think about the doctor bills.

Where do you live, Mr. Rutgers?

I live about seventy miles back from Nashville.

I'm out of Memphis myself. I might just take them cows off your hands. That's what I do, buy and sell cattle. You didn't know that, did you? How's that for a coincidence? I got caught in that mess of a parade and just had to wait it out.

If that don't beat all, Bloodworth said. He took out a thin gold pocketwatch and popped the case on it. I got a bus to catch, he said. You call me up and we might work up a trade on them cows, if I ain't done sold them.

Why we'll go right now, Coble said. You'll ride in my truck. We'll drive straight through and if the cows suit me and the money suits you we might just strike up a deal. How's that sound to you?

Why I hadn't thought of it like that, Bloodworth said. That's the very ticket.

I'm about ready to kiss this place goodbye anyway, Coble said. Mule parades and folks warpin one another with pool cues. I never seen such a place for foolishness.

The day was further progressed than Bloodworth had thought and by the time Coble was assisting him into the high cab of the truck evening shadows were lengthening and a fireball of sun lay low in the west. Coble turned the truck eastward and drove fast toward the open highway with Little Rock kaleidoscoping dizzily past the windows on either side and the road lying in wait like a promise someone had made them. When at length they were rolling toward the Tennessee line the old man was touched by a rising tide of exhilaration. Coble as well seemed touched by it for he began to sing. *T for Texas,* he sang loudly as the big truck strung the curves. *T for Tennessee.*

HE WAS COMING up the spring path carrying a bucket of water when he heard a car engine shut off at the foot of the hill. A car door closed and then nothing. Fleming set the pail down and waited. He knew it wasn't Boyd. If a taxicab had let Boyd out the driver wouldn't even have shut off the engine. He guessed it was Brady, and Brady had nothing to say that he wanted to hear. He approached nearer to the house, watching the rocky ledge of hill through the cedars.

A head appeared, a smooth oiled wing of auburn hair. Spivey. Spivey in a shortsleeved nylon shirt, a brown paper bag tucked under his deformed arm. Goddamn it, the boy said. He sat down to wait.

He could hear Spivey knocking at the front door. Fleming, Spivey called. Hellfire, just go away, the boy thought. He wondered how persistent Spivey was, how stubborn. He was caught in a freezeout here without supplies or weapons, some hunter would kick his bleached bones out of the leaves some winter to come.

He looked. Spivey was standing on the porch silhouetted against a harsh cobalt sky, an electric sky in a failed painting. He wasn't holding the bag. He stood a time as if undecided. Then he turned and went back down the hill. As if expecting a trap the boy waited not only until the car had started up but until it had turned at the mailbox and its sound had diminished down the road. Then he took up the water and went on.

The bag was on the doorsill tilted against the door itself. Three books. A book called *Nine Stories* by J. D. Salinger, *Other Voices, Other Rooms* by Truman Capote, a huge volume by Thomas Wolfe, *Of Time and the River*. When he opened the Wolfe novel there was a thin sheaf of bills, two twenties and a ten, stuck to page one with a piece of transparent tape.

ALBRIGHT PARKED the car where a chainlink fence stopped him and followed the fence by touch until he found a gate. He'd commenced hearing the dogs when he cut the switch and they had grown louder, a cacophony of barks and howls and long plaintive moans such as wolves were told to call one to the other. He didn't know if the dogs were walled in or walled out but there was a wild sound to their voices that stayed him with caution. So far he was trespassing, he hadn't been asked in, he hadn't even made it to a door to knock on. He guessed he should have come in the daytime but he had felt instinctively that this was a thing best done at night. He glanced about, picking out an escape route, a back door out of here, imagining himself levitating the chainlink fence with a dog's teeth clamped in the tail of his shirt.

The house sat yellowlit beyond the inked shadow of the great pine and he strode on toward it, the hot pungent smell washing over him as he passed beneath it.

Who are you? a voice asked out of the darkness.

Albright leapt at the sound and turned in its direction. A man was sitting in a metal glider watching him, barely visible in the darkness. Albright had thought he was walking past an empty glider.

My name's Junior Albright. I'm lookin for Brady Bloodworth.

I thought that was who you was. I've seen you around town and out on the roads. What did you want with Brady Bloodworth?

I need to talk to him, Albright said.

You are talkin to him. Get that other chair, set a while. I like to set out here in the early part of the night and settle my mind. I got a restless mind, it don't always do what I want it to. What can I help you with? If you're sellin somethin I won't buy it and if you're runnin for some office I probably won't vote for you.

It ain't nothin like that. I need to hire you for somethin.

I don't work out much anymore. Did you want the cards read?

Albright had seated himself in the other glider. The night was warm and balmy but the metal was already wet with dew and it felt cool against his skin. I don't want my fortune told, he said, perhaps feeling that all of his future at once might overwhelm him, he'd rather learn it a piece at a time.

Well, I can see things but you have to run out the cards for me to see them. You may as well break down and tell me what it is you want.

Harwood ain't carryin the mail no more, Albright said tentatively.

No, he ain't.

Albright was noticing that the dogs had fallen silent. It seemed to him that they had grown quiet at the moment that Brady had said *Who are you?* out of the darkness, as if they had been waiting for him to speak and so right the world.

There's a fellow, Albright began, and while Brady listened in respectful silence and his voice took on an aggrieved quality he told the story of the crimper's destruction. He was remembering the heat dancing off the metal roof, the weight of Woodall's arm on his shoulder in the pool room, his own name typed so neatly on the official-looking papers he had been served with.

He's holdin a mortgage on the rest of my life. I won't never have eight hundred and sixty dollars at one time, and he's chargin me interest on that that keeps mountin up. They've probably had to take on extra hands over at the courthouse to handle all the paperwork, and they'll likely be wantin me to pay that. I want him off my back. I don't want him took with no cancer or nothin like that but I want him to let me alone. Maybe he could just wake up some mornin and realize it was all a bad mistake.

Come on in the house and drink a cup of coffee, Brady said.

They sat at a kitchen table covered with oilcloth so faded and worn he could see the weave of the cloth at the corners of the table, faintly discern lithographed coffee grinders and spice mills on the slick cloth. Once a tiny old woman who looked like an Indian passed through the room but she did not speak, just nodded once birdlike at Albright and went into the front room.

Brady took from a purple chamois bag a deck of cards. He shuffled them. His fingers were long and delicately formed as a woman's, the nails pink and smooth as if he manicured them. They moved the cards with a liquid dexterity, placed them with a slap on the oilcloth before Albright.

Cut them, he said.

I don't want my fortune told.

Then I won't tell it. You've got to cut the cards anyway.

Albright cut the deck and slid it back to Brady. Brady rifled the cards into three stacks then fanned each section and sat in bemused concentration. It took him a long time. Albright sat in a strained silence, like a man in a doctor's office waiting to find out just what it is he's got. He studied the fading flowers climbing the wallpaper, the windows that instead of showing the world outside turned the room back at him in a tense claustrophobic reflection.

At length Brady scooped them up and restacked them and restored them to their soft bag. He studied Albright in silence, his blue eyes focused and so intense that for a moment Albright felt that he was staring with clinical detachment into his very soul, turning to the back pages where his darkest and most shameful secrets were written in cryptic notation, and he turned slightly in his chair, as if he'd in some manner impede Brady's view.

It'll be tricky, Brady said.

What?

I said the cards when I run them out showed me it'd be tricky. When Harwood run over the dog he done it on purpose. He told me to put the dog up and I didn't and he run over it. That's black and white, left and right, up and down. Your situation is blurrier than that. You did break his whatchamacallit, his crimper, and he did pay money for it. Whether he paid eight hundred and sixty dollars for it I can't say. The cards are uncertain and I'm thinkin he's tryin to make money off you. He don't like you. I believe he's had it in for you for a long time.

Then you can't do it?

Oh, I can do it all right. I just said it'd be tricky.

Say, how come you can do things like this, anyway?

I don't know. I always had secondsight. I was born with a caul, I always knowed things. It seems natural to me, a better question might be how come you can't. I reckon I just see a wider range of things than most folks. Other people can just see the things, I can see the connection between them. Once when I was eight years old I was choppin cotton for a feller down on Grinder's Creek. This dog I had met me when I was halfway home and walked the rest of the way right beside me. I found out later he had been dead for two days, but what does that mean? He was as real as me or you. He was a collie and had long hair and there was cockleburs in it. I stopped on the way home and pulled them out, I can still see them comin off with long strands of his hair wound up in the burrs. Does that make any sense to you? It don't to me. All I can do is take it and go on. I can witch for water. Pa dug out a hole forty feet deep and five feet in diameter because I told him there was no water where he was diggin. When he finally moved to where I said he hit water at eighteen feet and that's the well we're usin to this day.

His voice had taken on the curious singsong quality of a fundamentalist preacher. It made Albright nervous and kept reminding him of his crazy father but he didn't get up to leave. He had begun to believe for the first time that Brady might actually do such a thing.

What do you mean by tricky?

I can't control what'll happen. I had a picture in my mind of Harwood clutchin at his bowels and cryin but this don't give me no clear picture. Just somethin about a machine. I guess because you say that thing you broke was a machine. It's like . . . it's like there's a wall, but my hand'll go through the wood, and on the other side are all these things that can happen but ain't happened yet. They're just swirlin around. Might never happen. But when I get hold of one I can't always see what I'm gettin. You see? When I haul it out through the wall into this world I may not know what it is, but it's goin to happen, and you can take that to the bank.

Albright sat in silence. Brady was watching him. The silence went on until it honed itself to a thin wire so taut it gave off a faint humming. Brady's eyes had fixed him where he sat. Albright thought of taking out a cigarette and lighting it, just to have something to do, but he sat without moving.

You want me to hex him?

Yes. I got to get him off my back, get some relief. He's drivin me crazy, I think he's gettin a kick out of it. Do it.

Then let it be on your head. Have you got fifty dollars?

Albright had it in his front pocket, five folded tens, and he laid it atop the table. Brady did not pick it up, as if now that its existence was confirmed it was of no moment, as if it was the willing exchange rather than possession that mattered.

I'll need somethin of his. Somethin he touched.

Albright rose and went through the front room. The old woman was peering at an unfolded newspaper through a pair of spectacles and she did not look up. Outside the yard was dappled with shadow and light, the moon was out now and curdled clouds ran before it as if in the keep of some enormous lunar wind.

He took the blue hardhat out of the back floorboard and for a moment just stood holding it, wondering how Brady could use it, trying to feel something of Woodall in its sleek metal surface. He put the hat on his head and stood remembering the hot metal through his shoes, the clicketyclack of the crimper. He tried to think as Woodall might think. Then in a moment of insight he saw himself as a fraction of the fool he was. He felt a tremendous compulsion to just get in the Dodge and drive away without looking back. Then he took off the hardhat and went slinging it along in his hand toward the house.

THERE WAS a hollow booming sound that he dreamed he went from room to room looking for, but it was always in the wall he'd just left or the one he was bound for. Then it fell silent. His eyes opened. He looked at the phosphorescent hands of the clock.

You want to open the Goddamned door?

Fleming raised up and felt around for his shoes.

The pounding commenced again. I know you're in there, a voice said.

All right, all right, I'm coming, he called.

When he opened the door his uncle Warren Bloodworth was regarding him with a kind of bland patience that belied the intensity of the pounding. He was standing in the moonlight with his handsome dissipated face showing only a benign placidity, blinking occasionally as if waiting for the boy to do something he had already been instructed to do.

You're a sound sleeper, ain't you?

Well. It's two o'clock in the morning. I'm usually abed by then. Are you drunk?

I probably am. That's not my problem though, I've managed somehow to run off the road down there and I can't seem to get back on it. You reckon you could give me a hand?

Sure, I guess so. What do you want me to do?

Anything would be an improvement over what I've managed. You don't have a mule or anything like that in there do you?

I don't have a mule or anything like a mule.

I guess Boyd gave up on farming.

I guess.

Well come on anyway. Maybe we can figure something out.

They cut through the woods with Warren falling twice before they reached the embankment that shouldered the road. Fleming could see the car tilted off the road in a stand of sumac that followed a three-strand barbed wire fence.

Can you drive? Warren had halfslid and halffallen down the embankment and now he was struggling up onto the roadbed.

Brady lets me drive his tractor. Junior Albright let me drive his car once, but I wasn't very good at it.

Hellfire, it sounds to me like you're qualified for a chauffeur's license. Get in and see if you can do anything with it.

He tried rocking the car, shifting from low to reverse and popping the clutch and back again but the right rear wheel seemed to have no purchase and spun impotently until he could smell thick acrid smoke from the burning rubber. He cut the switch off and then the lights and got out.

He found a stack of fencepost inside Dee's field and threw three of them over the fence and climbed through the strands of wire. He jammed a post as far as it would go under the rear wheel and wedged the others beneath it and got back into the car. The car smelled like new leather and whiskey and perfume and some other odor, musky and somehow unpleasant.

He cranked the car and when he popped the clutch he felt the rear end shift and come off the post but when it did it caught solid chert and sent the car spinning onto the roadbed with the barbed wire breaking and whanging away into the darkness and him whipping the steering wheel impotently this way and that and the red chert bank looming enormous in the headlights. He slammed the brakes as hard as he could and slid lockwheeled to the side of the ditch with something slamming hard against the seat and knocking him into the steering wheel and thumping solidly into the rear floorboard. When he looked back over the seat a woman in bra and panties was struggling up out of the floorboard ranking lank strands of hair out of her eyes like someone struggling up through deep foliage.

You little bastard, she said. I'll claw your eyes out. What have you done with Warn?

Fleming rolled down the glass. Warren, he called.

Warren came up beside the car. This thing's got a tendency to take to the air, he said. You need to lighten your foot a little.

Who is that?

I don't know, Warren said. Crack the door so we can see.

When he opened the door the dome light came on and the woman had subsided back onto the seat and perhaps she slept. Her mouth was open and she had one arm folded beneath her head for a pillow.

Oh. That's just my accountant, Hazel. You want some of that?

What?

You want some of it?

Fleming looked. He could smell the rank fishy odor of her and a line of spittle had escaped the corner of her slack mouth and was tracking down her throat. He noticed that there was a handful of wadded money stuffed into her panties, the corner of a twenty-dollar bill showing above the elastic.

Not right now.

No matter. I expect you're used to adding up your figures all by yourself anyway.

Accountant?

I came up here to, let's see, I came up here to sell two lots in town and pay the taxes on something somebody was fixing to foreclose on. I picked Hazel up in the poolroom to help me keep up with everything.

Abruptly he stood very still and then he sat down in the moonlit roadbed and began to empty his pockets one by one and to hold slips of paper close to his face. I wonder if I paid those damn taxes? he asked.

I think you ought to come up to the house and sleep it off and wait till morning to drive anywhere. You can bring your accountant. It's getting cold down here and besides, somebody's bound to come by sooner or later and call the law.

Fuck that. I've got to be in Alabama immediately. I was supposed to have been there this morning. Yesterday would have been better. You'll have to drive. They've probably got a search party out by now and I've got to get Neal's car back.

He struggled up out of the roadbed. Let's see if we've done any damage to it.

They walked around the car and Warren took out a packet of matches and kept trying to strike them until finally reaching them to Fleming. See if you can make these son of a bitches work, he said.

Fleming lit a match but he hadn't needed it. Moonlight had shown three scratches deep as if three steel claws had hooked at the headlight and raked viciously down the length of the car. Something, a fencepost perhaps, had struck the passenger side door hard enough to knock a fist-size dent in it.

Little soap and water and a good coat of wax and he won't even notice it, Warren said. He removed a huge roll of greenbacks with a rubberband containing them from a pocket and handed it to Fleming. Stick this in your pocket and keep up with it, he said.

Good God, I don't want to carry that. I might lose it or something.

You can't lose it at the rate I can. Everywhere I've been tonight folks've been glad to see me coming and sorry to see me go. I've bought and paid for enough friends tonight to hold a Baptist footwashin and I doubt I'll ever see any of them again. You reckon you can get me to Alabama?

I don't have a driver's license.

I'm drivin on a revolted, a revoked driver's license myself and if they catch me it's my ass. I'll pay your fine if you get caught. You're not drunk are you?

No.

That's a start then. You furnish the sobriety and I'll furnish the car and the money and we might just get organized here.

What about the accountant?

Well, yeah, I'm furnishin her too.

No. I mean what are we supposed to do with her?

I don't know but we've by God got to do something. She almost got me killed over at the Knob tonight. Started something with some big logger off Beech Creek. I'd have to be drove with a shotgun to ever set foot in that part of the county again.

When they were underway Warren leaned back across the seat and shook the woman awake. Where do you need to go, he asked.

I need a cheeseburger. Go by the DariDip.

There won't be no more cheeseburgers in here this night, Warren said. You've done puked all over the whole Goddamned car.

Take me down to Early's then, she said. We can get a halfpint and he'll let me stay there.

Take the Dial Holler Road, Warren said, and leaned his face against the glass and closed his eyes.

With the night coming at him in tatters of groundfog that streaked across the hood and broke on the windshield and his confidence in being able to handle the big car growing Fleming began to realize the enormity of his situation and to appreciate the curious curves and switchbacks that lay along the road of life. An hour ago he had been asleep in his bed. He couldn't even drive. Now he was barreling through the night in an eight cylinder Buick, a roll of money in his pocket and a carload of drunk folks. On top of that he was headed to Alabama, a place he'd never been.

Warren had opened his eyes and was watching the yellowlit night roll at him. You know where Early lives?

Yeah.

Let her out there.

Early lived in a little clapboard house on the bank of the road at the head of Dial Hollow. He parked before the house. The woman got out unsteadily and stood swaying in the yard pulling a dress over her head. When her head cleared the neck she looked the very caricature of a mad harridan and she fixed Fleming with a fierce look of parodic outrage. When you get your eyes full open your mouth and load it up too, she told him. Fleming had always thought that Warren's wife, Juanita, was fairly attractive and he wondered why he'd wound up with Hazel the accountant.

Give me some money, she told Warren.

Make change out of your drawers, Warren said. Don't come at me with that poormouth shit.

She staggered up the sloped yard and climbed the steps to the porch. Warren leaned his head back against the seat. Damned if it ain't a long road to Alabama, he said.

The boy studied him. He looked like an aging film star out of the forties, the cropped mustache, the smooth brown hair. His clean Roman profile was beginning to slacken from liquor and accountants and too many nights driving highpowered cars through barbed wire fences. Fleming guessed that if the war had gone on forever or until Warren died in it he would have been all right but it had not. When he came home with his medals and shrapnel scars he had found a different world than the one he had sailed away from.

The accountant had gone in the front door but almost immediately she was ejected back onto the porch and the door slammed in her face. She stood on the porch cursing the door and shaking her fist at it. She kicked the door then gestured viciously toward it with an upraised middle finger.

Ahh, Lord, Warren said. I've always held there was nothing in this world as sacred as southern womanhood.

When she was back in the car she said, Early won't let me stay. Take me to my ex-husband's out on Drake's Lane.

Look, Warren said. I'm willin to take you wherever you need to go but I can't be takin the scenic route all over the midsouth. I've got to be in Alabama. We've got to get on some kind of a schedule here.

Take me to Drake's Lane.

Where in hell is Drake's Lane? the boy asked.

They were halfway back to the highway when the boy fell to thinking about Warren's drive-in theater. He had suddenly remembered that Warren owned a movie theater in Alabama and he was thinking he might be invited to remain a few days and watch the movies and he was trying to think of any recent movies that might be playing when he came into a lethal hairpin curve and straightened it by leaving the road through a spinney of alders. The alders were whipping the car like triphammers and the boy was fighting the wheel desperately and wondering where the blacktop had gone. Great God, Warren said. The accountant had been asleep with her face against the glass and when she awoke she awoke clawing bothhanded at the shrubbery flailing the glass and she began to scream. The alders had thinned and he was going sixty miles an hour through a waving sedgefield. The woman was beating him about the head and shoulders with her fists and Warren was shouting, The brakes, the brakes.

The car lurched back onto the roadbed where the curve straightened and the boy remembered the brakes and applied them. The car came to a halt crossways in the road with the headlights outlining trees stark against the sky. The boy was shaking and he could feel icy sweat tracking down his ribcage. The motor idled smoothly and a disc jockey on the radio said, Now friends, I'd like to send this out to all the sick and the shut-ins, and a gospel quartet began to sing.

Now you're catchin on, Warren said. This flat black thing, I think that's what we're supposed to be drivin on. These woods and shit, I believe I'd just try to stay out of them as much as I could.

We turned over in the woods three or four times and I'm alive, the woman said in an awed voice.

Fleming slid his hands under his thighs to halt their shaking. We never turned over, he said.

The hell we didn't, she said. You blackhearted little liar. You tried to kill us. We turned over three or four times in the bushes and I seen every bit of it through the glass. I've wet all over myself and I ain't ridin with you crazy son of a bitches one more foot.

Warren got out and yanked the back door open. The woman sat there a moment then she climbed out into the roadbed. Warren climbed into the back seat and kicked out a hail of clothing and purses and empty whiskey bottles that rattled hollowly on the macadam. He got out and climbed back into the front seat. Let's roll, he said.

Fleming backed the car onto the shoulder of the road and straightened the wheels and drove cautiously away. He looked once in the rearview mirror but all was darkness where the taillights faded out and he couldn't see Hazel. He resolved to attend to his driving and when the speedometer hovered at forty-five he eased up on the gas. Warren settled himself against the seat and closed his eyes but he did not sleep. He seemed to be sobering up.

Fleming turned the radio off. You want to drive?

No, you're doin fine. I'm just dreadin goin home. Juanita's goin to pitch a bitch of a fit and I'm just too tired to handle it. I don't know what's the matter with women anyway. Now you take Juanita. I took her out of a situation where she was living with cracks in the floors where you could keep an eye on the chickens and flour gravy to eat three times a day, and put carpet under her feet and electric heat to sit by and T-bone steaks, and do you think she's grateful? Why hell no. I'll probably sleep in the concession stand tonight, if I sleep at all.

He fumbled out a cigarette and lit it. He offered the pack to Fleming but it was waved away.

I don't know. A couch ain't the worse place I ever slept. I've slept in graveyards and cottonfields and hayricks. Graveyards are the best. Folks'll leave you alone in a graveyard. When I was bummin around them first few years after the war I'd always try to find me a graveyard if night caught me on the road.

Where's the worst place you ever slept?

In a jail in Meridian Mississippi, Warren said. Second worst was a jail in Sicorro New Mexico. You may see a pattern beginnin to emerge here. A young man like yourself just startin out in life would do well to stay out of jails as much as possible. Cops love you when you're up and they love to kick a man when he's down. They had me in jail as a vag one time in Arizona. Had me and a bunch of us, mostly Mexicans, cuttin lettuce on a big lettuce farm. When my time was up they let me out and damned if they didn't pick me up again before I made the city limits. I reckon I'd made too good a hand. Had me right back in there cuttin lettuce. I can't eat lettuce till this day. Now if I wanted to I could buy me a motor home and cruise around out there lookin at the country. But I don't guess I will. Things like that sort of sours you on a place.

The boy drove in silence, early predawn fog white by the roadside, rising out of the wet brush like a community of ghosts turned out to watch his passage. He was headed south now on U.S. 43 and the eastern sky lay on his left hand, the sky above the horizon already mottled with red. He thought of Warren storming a German bunker or whatever he had done, flailing through waistdeep water toward the Normandy beaches. He had never asked Warren what he had done to earn his medals, but he knew they did not hand them out just for showing up. He thought of Warren with his medal swung about his neck, leaning to slice heads of lettuce in Arizona.

Ma said Boyd headed out north. You ever heard from him?

No.

Damned if I ain't beginnin to believe he's geared the way Pa is.

What do you mean?

I always wondered what made Pa do some of the things he did. He'd head out, turn up again. But it was the damnedest thing, you couldn't stay mad at him. He was always glad to see you and it was like he never left. It was like somethin he had to do. There was just somethin about a road, he never could let a road alone. Then he left that time and never turned up. Playin that music. I finally just figured out he was geared in a higher gear than other folks. Had to have more goin on, things movin faster. After I figured that out I never worried about it again.

He was supposed to write. Pa was. But I've about given up on him. I'm sick of blaming everything on the U.S. Mail.

Warren lit a cigarette off the butt of its predecessor, cranked down the glass and threw the stub out in a slipstream of sparks. Boyd'll turn up when he's old and broke down and needs you to help him across the street, he said. Piss on him. Get on some kind of schedule. What do you plan to do?

The boy grinned. Right now my plans are just contingencies, he said. They all seem to hinge on other folk's plans. It's like everything's in motion and I'm just waiting for it to settle down. Waiting for the glass to clear so I can see what I'm doing.

No move is the wrong move.

What?

Sometimes any move at all is better than nothin. If you're right you're one up. If you're wrong you start over. This sittin and waiting for somebody else to make up their mind is for the Goddamned birds. You have to take control of your own life.

Day was coming in broad shields of light that spread over the eastern world, breaking over the smoking fields, and a crescent of bloodred sun burned through the trees. He had crossed the Alabama line into a world foreign to him, the hills and hollows were behind now and he was driving into a flat featureless land planted with cotton fields that paced the highway for improbable distances, driving past happenstantial tenant shacks side by side with great brick mansions with iron gates and alabaster columns, plantations so grand their squires might not have heard that the Old South had fallen long ago, had moved from slaves to sharecroppers with hardly a wasted motion.

I never could figure Pa out, Warren said. You never could figure why he'd do somethin. He never would tell you anything. Either he figured you could read his mind or he figured it was none of your business. I remember one time these two old boys come up to the house lookin for me and I wasn't there. They had planned to beat hell out of me. I was just a boy and they were grown men, thirty years old or better. It was something about their sister, I don't remember what. Pa asked them what they wanted with me. There's just a feller down the road wants to meet Warren, they said. Wait and let me get my hat, Pa said. I just might want to meet this feller myself. He had this old gray felt hat he wore all the time. He always had to get his hat. He got his hat and they walked off down the road and he kicked the holy bejesus out of the whole bunch. I never could figure whether he done it for me or he just wanted to kick somebody's ass. Probably a little of both, most everything is.

Who's Elise?

Who?

Elise. I saw your name cut in a table in the Snowwhite Cafe. Elise loves Warren Bloodworth. It looked old, like it had been cut in there a long time ago.

I'll be damned. I went to school with a girl named Elise Warf. Never went with her though, we was just schoolmates. She was pretty, too. Never let on she liked me. Why didn't she say so? Shit. You reckon the offer's still good?

Coming into a town just big enough to have a post office and a cafe Fleming parked before the restaurant. Traffic had increased with the day's advent and there were a few cars and trucks on the road and two or three beatup pickups parked before the diner.

You want a sandwich?

I don't believe I could go it. Get you one. You've got that money. Get me a glass of tomato juice if they've got it. Bout half a bottle of hot sauce in it.

At the counter he ordered a bacon and egg sandwich and a cup of coffee to go and the tomato juice for Warren. Standing by the cash register awaiting his order he noticed he had forgotten in his haste to wear socks but such folk as were in the diner looked sleepnumbed and in dread of whatever the day held for them and no one seemed to notice this deficiency. He kept glancing at the gleaming car through the plateglass. Warren was slumped with a hand shading his eyes from the sun. Fleming wondered if these folk had seen him climb casually out of the white Buick Roadmaster. If they thought it was his. If they wondered where he was bound bareankled and with a pocketful of money this fine summer morning.

He paid and went out with the bag the waitress handed him and in the driver's seat unwrapped the greasylooking sandwich and took a bite. Warren looked away, rolled down the glass and sat staring out the window, sipping his tomato juice.

Can you drive and eat at the same time?

Sure.

Let's roll, then.

No move is the wrong move.

Damn right.

Driving into a country so monotonous and flat an enormous spirit level laid across it would have shown no deviation, something metallic formed shapeless and elongated far down the sunwarped highway and shot toward him, coalesced into a green sedan moving so fast the speedometer must have been pegged, a blur of a face he recognized instantly as his cousin Neal. Watching in the mirror he saw brakelights come on and the sedan fishtail crazily down the road in a haze of smoking rubber. Instead of backing around in the highway as anyone else would have done Neal simply drove out into a cottonfield and came back paralleling the road in a rising cloud of red dust.

Fleming had pulled the Buick onto the shoulder of the road and cut the switch. Warren had been dozing and he came awake instantly. He opened one bleary eye. What is it?

It's Neal, the boy said.

Oh hell. Is Juanita with him?

It looked like just Neal. Fleming was fumbling out the roll of rubberbanded money. Here, you'd better take this.

Slip you some of it off. Everybody else has, and you've earned it.

I don't need it.

Warren shoved the money into a shirt pocket as if it were a thing of no importance and closed his eyes. Neal had pulled the Ford back onto the road behind the Buick like a highway patrolman apprehending a miscreant and he got slowly out of the car. Fleming cranked down the window and the warm day rolled in, the smell of the fields, the distant woods. The fields were arsenical green and they seemed to roll on forever with no change perceptible to the naked eye.

Neal laid his hands on the roof and leaned to look inside the car. He was wearing sunglasses and Fleming couldn't see his eyes but he seemed to be studying Warren where he lay huddled against the glass with his eyes closed.

Hello, cousin. You and the old man been on a drunk?

Something like that.

Where'd you run up with him?

He just sort of turned up in the middle of the night.

Neal took a pack of Luckies out of his shirt pocket and tipped one out and lit it. Fleming could smell him, the scent of aftershave and mouthwash and the pomade he used on his hair. Neal's sandy hair was brushcut flat on top but the sides were worn long and waved smoothly back over his ears in a ducktail.

Mama's just climbing the Goddamned walls. He was supposed to be back two days ago. First she thought he was in jail and then she decided he was dead in a carwreck. The more she thought the madder she got and she's about worked herself up to a killing spree. Did he have a woman with him?

Fleming uncapped the cardboard cup of coffee he'd forgotten about and drank from it. All I saw was Warren, he said.

Neal was five years older than Fleming and a good halffoot taller. He was said to be wild and it was told that he had been kicked out of every college foolhardy enough to enroll him in the first place. He had turned and walked around the car, inspecting it critically as he went. When he came up on the passenger side Fleming looked away across the field to the sky. The sky was absolutely cloudless and so blue it looked transparent and against it a wave of blackbirds shifted shapeless as smoke.

Goddamnit, Neal said, and kicked the door so hard the car rocked on its springs till the shocks froze it. He came around the front of the car inspecting the grill and headlights.

I guess that was him instead of you?

Warren had roused himself. I run into a fence. Somebody had built a barbed wire fence right across a public road. People in Tennessee, I don't know, strange folks.

Hellfire, why didn't you take your car? Mine won't clean out ditch-runs any better than yours will. This was a brand new car.

Well. I paid for both of them. I guess I can pay for fixin it.

I guess you can. Come on, Dad, Jesus, what's the matter with you? Why do you do this shit? Mama's wound tightern a two-dollar clock and set to go off the minute we drive up. I believe I'll just let you out at the mailbox and ease on down the line.

We'll take Fleming, Warren said hopefully. She's always liked him. Maybe a little company will placate her.

I don't believe we need to put Fleming through that, Neal said. There may be things bouncing off the walls and I expect he'd rather be somewhere else.

He turned to Fleming. You drive my car back to Tennessee. Leave it at Brady's and I'll pick it up there. Try to keep my car out of as many fencerows as you possibly can.

All right.

You don't have a beer in that other car do you? Warren asked.

No I don't.

Warren was climbing out of the Buick. Oh well, he said. At least Elise loves me.

Whoever Elise is you better be grateful for her, Neal said. Elise may be the only person this mornin that gives a damn whether you live or die.

They got into the green Ford. Warren, rueful and resigned behind the glass, smiled and raised a hand at Fleming. They drove away. Fleming sat for a time just soaking up the warm sun then he backed the car around in the highway and drove back the way he'd come. He turned on the radio. Coming in sight of Wheeler Dam he met a car from the Alabama Highway Patrol, but the cop just threw up a hand, good morning, and kept on freewheeling south.

WITHIN THE OLD MAN'S DREAM Brady dreamed as well, talking in his sleep to phantom mules, his hands moving against the quilt snapping plowlines that he did not hold. In his dream the old man leaned to him and shook him awake so that Brady roused startled and disoriented, looking wildly about the bedroom, the old man saying hush, laying a calming hand on his naked shoulder, you hush, boy, you're not plowing, you're here in your bed, I just worked you too hard in that bottom today. Go back to sleep now. You've plumb wore yourself out.

Bloodworth awoke thinking for a dislocated moment that Brady had woke as well to the eerie green light of the truck's instrument panel. All he could make out was Coble's dark bulk humped against an invisible sleepfast countryside, his cigarette pulsing as he drew on it. He glanced about and there was no one in the truck save Coble and himself, but the dream would not release him. It was of such strength and clarity that it had dislocated him in time, moved him into the past so that a Brady who was just a boy worn out from plowing was more concrete than the seat his head rested against, truer than the yellowlit road the headlights were sucking up. He had felt Brady's heart hammering under his hand, seen his chest rise and fall with his breathing.

You wakin up oldtimer?

These hours before first light were merciless. You could not go back to sleep and it was too early to get up and the things you had done or not done lay in your mind immovable as misshapen things you'd erected from stone. There was no give to these hours. They took no prisoners, made no compromises, and the things you had done could not be rationalized into anything save things you had done. The past was bitter and dry and ashes in his mouth, its bone arms clasped him like some old desiccated lover he could not be shut of.

Say, oldtimer, this place we're goin to, this Ackerman's Field. How come it's named that?

I don't know. Seems like the first courthouse or the first jail was built in a field that belonged to a man named Ackerman.

He was wishing the past was a place you could backtrack to, take a sideroad you'd walked hurriedly past, wake somebody from a bad dream he was having.

How big a place is it?

It wasn't much when I left, he said, coming wide awake instantly and thinking, Goddamn, Bloodworth, what's the matter with you.

Hellfire, oldtimer, how long you been gone?

The old man chuckled smoothly. Folks are runnin off in wholesale lots to go to Detroit and make cars, he said. You never know who'll be gone from one day to the next.

Don't I know it. It's the same where I live. What in the world do you reckon they're doin with all them hillbillies and niggers up there?

The old man remained silent and tried to regather the threads of the dream but the intensity of it was lost to him now. He guessed seeing all those championship mules had made him remember Brady plowing the mules so long ago. He sat and watched the dark glass, houses rearing up out of the night and subsiding like houses constructed on floodwaters, lonely houses set like sentinels against the black hills, once a town constructed on a mountain with lights strewn earthward as if something enormous and full of light had broken there and spilled down the mountainside.

NEAL TURNED UP with a tale about being kidnapped off a Greyhound bus. He showed up about seven o'clock in the morning while Fleming was sitting on the doorstep in the sun drinking a cup of morning coffee. He went in and filled another cup and brought it out and Neal stood in the yard drinking it.

Neal was wearing a black T-shirt with his deck of Luckies rolled up in the sleeve and he was wearing mirrored shades that turned the world back from him and in whose lenses Fleming could see his own grinning reflection as Neal told the story of the kidnapping.

I met these four girls on the bus, Neal said. Nice girls they acted like, friendly. Coming home from a Baptist youth camp, they told me. They were getting off in Iron City and talked me into getting off too; said we was going on a Sunday school picnic. Well, you know me, I was all for that. One of them had a car there in Iron City, and we all piled in and rode out to this big place where a limestone quarry was. A big hole in the side of a hill, a cave, like. I wondered that there wasn't no picnic basket. One of them had a sixpack. Well, to make a long story short they raped me. They held a switchblade knife on me and one by one they had their way with me. I felt defiled. Humiliated. It wouldn't surprise me if I developed some kind of a trauma.

The boy just shook his head and grinned and turned away.

You still writing up those stories and sending them out?

I've about quit until I get a typewriter.

I was thinking we might team up and make a few dollars that way. I could do the thinking, get all the ideas for us. It ain't nothing for me to have two or three ideas in a day. You could write them up for us.

I don't think it's that easy, the boy grinned.

We could write up the story of my rape by them Baptists. It would be painful but I'm willing to sacrifice my dignity. I need the money now that I'm out in the cruel world on my own. Some magazine would buy it. *Sports Afield,* it'd be right down their alley.

Hellfire, Neal, are you not ever serious?

Not unless I have to be.

How come you're out in the world on your own?

It got too damn squally around the house. All that damn fighting and carrying on, you couldn't sleep, I figured fuck it, I'd come up here and help with your education. I don't know what'll happen to Mom and Dad, I guess they're quits. They're both crazy, I can't see after them anymore.

Help with my education?

Initiate you into the world. Get you out of this Nat King Cole Nature Boy shit and take you out into the world and get you laid.

I can do just fine on my own.

Neal set his empty coffee cup on the edge of the porch. He climbed the steps onto the porch. He stood looking around. Turned and peered into the interior of the house.

You call this doing just fine? What have you done, took some kind of vows of poverty? A sharecropper would curl his lip at this place.

I don't believe in putting up much of a front, the boy said.

Well, come on, let's go. Get your town clothes on and let's get out amongst em.

I don't think so.

Come on, keep me company. I'll let you in on this plan I've got to make a few bucks. Didn't you say you needed a typewriter? Let me tell you about this.

Oh, all right. Wait up a minute.

Out amongst em, Neal said again.

They had hidden Neal's car in a sideroad two hollows down from Early Dial's house and gone up the hollow to its head and followed the spine of the ridge and came down through the wooded hillside almost to Early's house. It was a morning that suited their purpose very well. It was raining, a slow dawn drizzle from an invisible sky, fog rolling up out of the hollow so blue and dense the dripping cedars looked spectral and insubstantial, the oaks and hickories penitent and without detail, just dark slashes of trunks rearing up out of the mist.

They came down the hillside like conspirators, Neal with a finger to his lips, easing down the slope as close to the house as they dared come, each carryin a length of stick to prod the earth for faults. Under the sodden leaves the sticks prodded for stumpholes, for holes spaded and refilled with leaves. Neal found a jug almost immediately, the stick sliding into the leaves and glancing off the slick glass surface. He fell to his knees, hauling away wet black leaves bothhanded and lifting from the hole a gallon jug of clear whiskey. Soon he had two in each hand, carrying them by the fingerholds in their necks, dancing gleefully about the hillside. It's like an Easter egg hunt, he whispered. We're sittin on a fuckin gold mine here. Let's carry them up to the ridge and put them all together.

They had six gallons cached at the top of the slope and were searching for more when Fleming froze in an attitude of listening. Someone was coming up from the house: a screen door slapped, there was a whisper of footsteps through the sodden leaves. Almost immediately a man appeared out of the fog like a ghost. Fleming and Neal sank to the earth, faded back past a huge pine the winds had taken and crouched in the hole the roots had excavated. Fleming peered cautiously through the roots.

A long skinny man swinging a shotgun along in his hand came up through the scrub brush. He wore checked pants too big for him and a black derby hat canted over one eye and he was talking to himself.

If he sees us rush him, Neal said. We'll coldcock the motherfucker and head up the hillside.

The boy nodded. The man passed very near to him, Fleming could see the weave of his trousers, the veins in his bony ankles. He was wearing bedroom slippers. He seemed to be telling himself some story, recounting some kind of confrontation. I told that bitch, I said, bitch, he was mumbling as he passed, then the monologue grew vague and incoherent.

The man paused and prodded the ground with the barrel of the shotgun, knelt and raked the leaves away from a fallow hole. He grunted. He rose and kicked the leaves back in and looked about. He went eight or ten feet up the slope, poking the earth at random until he found a jug and went back toward the house cradling it up in his arms like some strange baby he'd found.

Neal flung imaginary beads of sweat from his forehead. I'm glad that's over, he said softly. I'd hate to kill a man this early in the day. Let's get four or five more and get the hell out of here.

Ultimately they had twelve gallon jugs and they carried them back across the ridge to the Buick. It took them two trips. They sat down to rest and Neal unscrewed one of the metal caps and drank a mouthful. He spat it out in a fine volatile mist that looked explosive. He shook the jug and watched the bead, greasy grapeshots of nitroglycerin shifting in its smoky depths.

This stuff is very nearly undrinkable, he said. It tastes like doublestrength rubbing alcohol would if you chased it with carbolic acid.

He rose and from the trunk of his car brought forth a quart of black viscous liquid.

What's that?

Caramel coloring. I got it off this old bootlegger in Hickman County. It won't do much for the taste but it'll pretty it up some. Give it sort of an official look.

Neal had unscrewed the lids from the gallon jugs and with a judicious eye gauging quantity was pouring coloring into each jug. He set the jar aside and took up a jug and shook it, watching the tarry coloring swirl into the alcohol, a cloudy spectra like ink in water. He was satisfied when the whiskey was a warm amber. Look at that, he said. All I need is some federal stamps to slap on and you'd swear this stuff was bonded.

What do you plan on doing with it? Fleming asked again.

I aim to resell it to Early.

Don't that seem a little risky? We could sell it out of the poolhall a halfpint at the time. Sell it to Itchy Mama.

I got nothing against Itchy Mama, she never done anything to me. Early run me off from down here the other night. Said he was calling the law on me. Can you imagine that? A Goddamned bootlegger with a lifestyle a hop skip and a jump from the federal penitentiary and he's calling the law on me. I was outraged. I don't even know why I went. Well, actually, he had a gun throwed on me at the time and he was looking so crazy out of his eyes I thought he'd use it.

Why did he run you off?

You know that crazy whore he married? That little Mathis girl? I was down here drinking homebrew and playing poker. Everything was copacetic till she started giving me the eye. Standing behind me rubbing on me and looking at my cards. Before you know it we were in the back room with her drawers off and Early throwed down on me. Run me off. Hell, it ain't been six months since I give her ten dollars there in the alley behind Baxter's. I told Early that. That's my wife you're talking about, he said. Well does that mean the price's gone up, or down? I asked him.

Neal raised the trunklid with a flourish, gestured in a manner curiously theatrical, a carnival barker presenting his show perhaps, a salesman his apothecary of exotic drugs.

Where'd you get it? Early peered into the trunk, leaning precariously on the wooden leg he'd never gotten used to. They stood grouped about the trunk in the drizzling rain, the boy wiping water out of his eyes with the tail of his shirt. The aforementioned whore stood in the dry on the porch and watched Neal sullenly, slateyed and enigmatic as a cat.

The yard where they'd parked the Buick was full of all manner of fowl, ducks and gamecocks and guinea fowl, all alike sodden and disconsolate in the rain. An arrogant guinea hen kept fluttering to the roof of the Buick as if to roost there and Neal kept slapping it off.

This whiskey came out of keg county itself, Neal said. Hickman County. I'm running some for a fellow over there, Herman Tiptoe, and last night he was a little short and paid me in whiskey. I got no use for this much whiskey, but I can always use money.

Early rubbed the gray stubble on his jaw. I expect you're going to tell me it was chartered in oak kegs.

I am not. I don't know where it's been, but I doubt seriously if it's ever seen an oak keg. I do know it's a lot better than that popskull shit you peddle. Try a little knock of it.

Fleming watched Early tilt a jug back and drink. Early's neck was skinny and stringy as a turkey gobbler's, his fistsize adam's apple pumping the whiskey down. His eyes looked wide and wild as some startled animal's. Fleming turned away and looked at the girl. Her face had the stunned vacuous look you'd see in a mental hospital, as if life had dealt up a card so high and wild she could not handle it, that had caused her mind to reel away in shock.

Early lowered the jug. His eyes looked slightly out of sync. It's not so bad, he said grudgingly. Neal rolled his eyes up at Fleming and turned away laughing. What was you askin for it, Early asked.

Neal assumed an expression of businesslike sobriety. Twelve dollars, he said.

Early lowered the trunklid. I can't use it, he said. I sell it for seventy-five cents a half, you know that.

I might go down to ten. Sell it to them for a dollar, tell them it's bonded, they won't know the difference.

They settled at ten and even helped Early carry the jugs to the edge of the slope. I'll take it from here, Early said. I'd ask you in but I don't never want you in my house again. I wasn't speakin about you, young feller, he said to Fleming. You perfectly welcome to come in and visit a while.

Fleming didn't know what to say to this so he said nothing at all. When they were halfway to the car Early called to Neal, you watch them chickens. You run over a duck when you hauled out from here the other night. People ain't got no respect. People do a onelegged man's chickens anyway.

COMING INTO the county from the west you drop off a long hill that slopes toward the river, where lush black bottomland leads you down to the swift yellow waters of Buffalo. You cross on a high steel span of bridge rusted to a warm orangebrown, and almost immediately the blacktop begins to ascend again into steep broken hills. Sometimes there will be a boat on the river or kids fishing from the banks with cane poles.

The day E. F. Bloodworth returned an old man had oared a skiff into the calm water away from the current and was casting near a bed of cattails. Old man in a straw hat, light off his glasses when he looked up at the cattle truck and raised a friendly hand. Bloodworth waved back, and the old man was gone somewhere beneath the beams and girders, but Bloodworth took the wave as an omen and felt in some obscure way that he'd been welcomed back from exile.

They were climbing now, Coble gearing down for a road that not only climbed steeply but curved hard to the right. They were climbing the highest spot in the county, and Bloodworth turned in his seat to study the countryside out the back glass: it fell gracefully away in soft green folded hills, the river wending its way through it, and looking west the horizon diminished into other horizons layered behind it as far as the eye could see.

Bloodworth was almost home and he was touched by exhilaration so sharp it was almost pain. For the last fifty miles the country had had a familiar look to it that gave him a calm feeling of comfort that almost succeeded in allowing him to forget that in the next thirty minutes or so he was going to have to come up with a herd of Black Angus cattle.

He looked back at the road, glanced at Coble beside him. He was sorry he had not simply ridden the bus. For hundreds of miles he had listened to Coble's autobiography until he felt he knew Coble and his genealogy better than Coble did himself. Coble loved to talk and no subject suited him better than Coble. He had come up from nothing and made a small fortune by using his head and keeping his eye on the ball. Nobody ever got up early enough in the morning to put one over on him. He was well thought of in his hometown. Without actually saying so he left the impression that everywhere he went in town he was carried on the shoulders of cheering compatriots. That when he left town things shut down and stores did not even bother to open until his return. Women found him wellnigh irresistible. Women began flinging off their clothing at the faintest rumor that he was even within screwing distance, and would not settle for second best. Had the old man possessed so much as a jackhandle he would have leapt upon Coble sometime during the night and beaten him into unconsciousness, let the truck go where it might.

Up here on the left is a place I need to stop a minute, Bloodworth said, thinking: up here on the left twenty years ago is a place I need to stop. It may be blackened ruins, ground scraped by a bulldozer, a Baptist church.

Stop why? We need to roll, oldtimer. I need to get them cattle loaded and get gone.

There's a beerjoint right up here got the coldest beer in the county. I been nursin a thirst for the last fifty miles.

We'll pick up a sixpack when we get to town and drink it on the way to your farm.

I got to take a leak anyhow, Bloodworth said. Less you want to float the rest of the way into town.

The high wood gallery of Goblin's Knob rolled into view through a stand of loblolly pines, and the old man felt almost dizzy with relief.

Hellfire, Coble said. He pulled the truck onto the cherted parking lot. There were no other vehicles on the lot and the old man was trying to see was the place open. Or even in business anymore. The gray clapboard building looked in a poor state of repair but it had looked that way twenty years ago when the old man rolled past it outward bound.

He fumbled up his stick and climbed out, looking about to see was there anything he was forgetting. There was not. Travel light, travel fast.

Bring me one of them beers you was braggin about, Coble called.

Bloodworth nodded and struck out toward the Knob. It may not even be Sharp anymore, he cautioned himself. But inside he knew it was Sharp. He could always tell when he was on a roll.

Sharp looked up from the worn *Outdoor Life* magazine he was reading when the door opened. He glanced back at the magazine then at Bloodworth in a doubletake of amazed recognition. Son of a bitch, he said. Where'd you come from?

Off the porch, Bloodworth said. He laid a five-dollar bill atop the bar. Gimme two bottles of beer.

What kind? Sharp asked, turning to slide back the lid of the cooler.

Cold, Bloodworth said. Listen. I don't have time to explain all this right now, I'll tell you later. But you ain't seen me. I never come in the front and I ain't goin out the back. All right?

Sharp set two brown longnecked bottles on the bar. I guess you're back all right, he said. It don't take long for things to get back to normal.

Bloodworth took up the beer and crossed the room and went down a narrow hall to the back door. He went out the door and down the steps and was immediately in the woods themselves, a thick growth of pine that had over the years carpeted the ground with two or three inches of coppery needles. He did not tarry, hurrying on into the trees, bemusedly remembering other times when the patrons of the Knob had emptied out the back as the law came in the front, men and women alike fleeing madly into the dark maze of trees where they'd not track you down unless they'd brought along a bloodhound in the back seat. Though once, he remembered, grinning to himself, they'd stationed a deputy at the back door to head off these fleeing miscreants and he fell to handcuffing or blackjacking at his discretion.

He went carefully over a debris of bottles, cans, rotting condoms, to where the woods were clean and denser still, picked his way down a hillside where a spring branch ran and following it away into summer greenery, filling his lungs with the smells: the hot crisp smell of the pines, the delicate odor of mimosa that had gone wild and taken the hillside.

He paused to rest, breathing hard. Sweat had broken out over him, he could feel it beneath his shirt but it did not bother him. It felt good. He seated himself against the trunk of a pine and worked out his pocketknife and pried off the bottlecaps.

Sharp was halfway through an article about a man being mauled by a polar bear when the door opened again. He'd been glancing up occasionally and eyeing the truck through the window and he'd thought whoever was out there must be the most patient of men or else he'd fallen asleep.

Hey, good buddy, where's that old man at?

Sharp looked around. Nobody in here but me, he said. Not countin you. What old man?

He said he was a Rutgers.

I don't recall ever knowin anybody by that name.

You don't have to know him. Where'd he go?

Who go?

That old man that come in here. Coble was peering all about the room. Old man with a walkin stick carved like a snake and wearin a gray Stetson hat.

I ain't seen him, Sharp said. He went back to his story.

It was silent for a long time. Coble seemed to be thinking all this over. Sharp finished the page he was reading and turned to another.

Finally Coble said, Let me get this straight. I watched him open that green door there and go through it and shut it behind him. You was on this side of the door and you never saw him. Well what the hell happened to him? Did he step through a hole in the fuckin world? He was a goodsized man, way over six feet tall. I don't believe you could of missed him.

Sharp closed the magazine, slid it behind the bar. Look, he said. I don't have time to argue with you. Maybe it was some other green door, in some other beerjoint. Why don't you go see?

Beneath the brim of the white straw hat Coble's face had gone a deep brickred. Why don't I just haul your skinny baldheaded ass over that bar and mop the floor up with you?

Because that's just quarterinch paneling on the front of that bar, Sharp said. And because on this side of it I'm holdin a sawedoff loaded with doubleought buckshot. You might want to give some thought to where you are. You're in my place of business, and as far as the law's concerned you just tried to rob me and I wouldn't agree to be robbed.

Coble dropped his arms back to his side and retreated from the bar a step or two. I don't know what kind of number you people are trying to run on me, he said. But I want you to know you fucked with the wrong man. If you think I drove over four hundred miles out of my way just to deliver an old man to a honkytonk you're badly mistaken. I aim to get to the bottom of this.

Sharp brought the shotgun up from the bar and laid it on the counter. I'm all for that, he said. But I'm tired of hearin about it.

Coble wiped a hand across his mouth. You tell that old man he's goin to regret this the rest of his days, he said. He turned and went out. The door creaked to behind him.

Sharp shook his head. What is that old man up to now, he asked himself.

ALBRIGHT HAD BEEN WORKING at the stave mill for three days when the boss came down to the shed where he was stacking bundles of handlelength staves and called him off to the side.

That Woodall fellow is trying to attach your paycheck, the foreman said. He's got some kind of legal paper where he can garnishee you. I thought I'd tell you so you'd know what was coming Friday when we pay off.

Albright filled a paper cup from a cooler of ice water. How much is comin? he asked.

Very damn little, the foreman said.

Albright left in the middle of the day without even looking back. This was the second job in as many weeks he'd lost because of Woodall's sheaf of legal papers. He felt that Woodall had taken to following him around, sleeping only when he slept, up at a moment's notice to follow him again. He caught himself glancing constantly over his shoulder, setting an extra plate for Woodall at the supper table.

At the hardware store he bought a gallon of yellow paint and a pint of red and he bought a brush. He drove home and parked in the shade of the chinaberry tree in his front yard. After he'd taken a bath and made a pot of coffee he came back out and opened the gallon bucket of paint and found a stick to stir it with. He dipped the brush into the paint and began to paint the car yellow.

When the nighflourescent yellow was dry to the touch he took up a roll of tape and masked off the word TAXI on each of the front doors carefully then stepped back to look at it. Satisfied he cleaned the brush and uncapped the pint and painted in the letters in red.

The car was still tacky at nightfall and he was forced to wait until the next day to go into business. Even then nothing much happened, but Saturday was another story. Few of the sawmill hands and sharecroppers around the county owned their own car and he was kept busy hauling families and their week's supply of groceries from Long's store out to the various hills and hollows where they lived. He hauled drunks to Goblin's Knob, picked up other drunks there and drove them wherever they were inclined to be. At the end of the day he had a fistsize chunk of quarters and halfdollars and wadded ones in the toe of his pocket. Garnishee this, motherfucker, he said aloud.

Weekdays he'd lounge around the front of the Snowwhite Cafe for the occasional fare. He knew a waitress who worked there and sometimes she'd take phone calls for him or refer customers his way. He was sitting out front on Tuesday reading a funny book when she came out the door with an agey-looking fellow wearing a gray hat and a black suitcoat in all this heat. The waitress's foot was malformed in some way and she went with a limp and they looked like a matched set of cripples coming down the sidewalk.

Junior, this is Mr. Bloodworth. He was wantin to talk to you.

Albright wondered why she hadn't just sent the old man out to the car without limping out with him. A bright yellow car with red lettering on the side was not what you'd call inconspicuous. Then he looked again and saw that Doris seemed taken with the old gentleman. She was normally foulmouthed and sharptongued but she seemed to be deferring to him as if he was the president or something or other.

The old man was looking the cab up and down. I reckon you're the proprietor of the yellow cab company, he said. He'd swapped hands with his walking stick and was holding his right out stiffly for Albright to shake. Albright grasped it and pumped it a time or two briskly as you might a hand pump.

I believe I knowed your daddy, the old man said. Ain't you Tut Albright's boy?

That's me, Albright said. I don't see him much anymore since he run me off. Daddy's a little crazy.

We're all a little crazy to various degrees, Bloodworth nodded. What I need don't require a great deal of sanity. I just need to go down to the freight office and pick some stuff up and then I want took out to where my people live. The Bloodworths.

You any kin to Fleming and them?

I couldn't say. What's his daddy's name?

He's Boyd Bloodworth's boy.

I reckon that'd make him a pretty close relative then since Boyd's a son of mine.

He had taken out two one-dollar bills and turned and handed them to the gimplegged waitress. I thank you for your help, young lady, he said, tipping the brim of his hat. You buy yourself somethin pretty with this.

She protested but the old man waved her protests away and after a moment she limped reluctantly away toward the restaurant.

I thought for a minute she was goin with us, Albright said. You wantin to go out to where Brady's set up that housetrailer?

For starters I do, the old man said. We'll ride out and look it over. The old man had opened the rear door of the Dodge and was climbing in. He had trouble getting his left leg in and finally he just picked it up bothhanded and set it inside. I'm about wore out, he said. I've walked a little more than I meant to today. Cattle farmin's hard on a man my age.

Albright drove slowly down toward the railroad where the freight depot was. He kept stealing covert looks at the old man in the rearview mirror. All his life he'd heard people talk about E. F. Bloodworth. Bloodworth would kill you if he had to, Bloodworth would kick your ass even faster than that. He could make a banjo talk, he had served time in the Brushy Mountain state pen, he had once shot a deputy while the deputy was using Bloodworth's wife as a shield when the laws had come to arrest him. His reflection in the rearview mirror did not look like any of this. Bloodworth had taken off the Stetson and closed his eyes and leaned his head back. He just looked like an old man who'd finally found a soft spot to rest his head.

Fleming had not seen Albright's Dodge since its transformation into a taxicab and he was somewhat surprised to see a bright yellow car pull into the yard and Albright alight and go around and open the door for an old man. The old man got out with no more luggage than a walking stick and approached a step or two favoring his left leg and halted and pushed a gray fedora back from his forehead and stood regarding the boy.

Fleming had been sitting on the doorstep to the trailer reading a book and now he closed it and arose and approached the car. Albright had unlocked the trunk and was at unloading what appeared to be a trunkload of musical instruments.

Steadying himself with the stick, Bloodworth turned about in the yard, as if he'd get his bearings, a fix on where he was. Then he told the boy, the house'd be about a quartermile up that road then across that long field where the cedar row is.

Fleming nodded. The old man was bigger than he had expected, and less of a cripple. In the back of his mind he had pictured a wizened little man twisted by a stroke of paralysis, but Bloodworth struck him as something of an imposing presence. He had fierce black eyes that looked right at you, or through you to whatever you were standing in front of, and the hair that lay on the collar of the white shirt was as black as a crow's wing. He wondered if Bloodworth dyed it, decided after a moment that he did not. Somehow the old man just didn't look like a man who dyed his hair.

The old man had jabbed a big weathered hand out and seemed to expect it to be shaken. He took the hand and shook it. The old man had a hard grip for a cripple.

My name's E. F. Bloodworth. From the looks of you I take you to be a grandson of mine.

How'd you know that?

I ain't always looked like this. You favor some the way I looked when I was a young man. You'd be Boyd's boy.

Fleming nodded. Albright had come around with the guitar case in one hand and the banjo in the other and seemed to be awaiting instructions.

Just put them in the trailer there, Bloodworth said. Let's just all go in and get acquainted. The old man halted and stood regarding the trailer, his face showing the first intimation of misgivings. It's not real big, is it?

No, the boy said. And it's hot in there. Brady left a key and I went in there this mornin and brought some water. But it's about too hot to stay in there until the day cools down some.

Along about October, the old man nodded, and fell silent, studying the silver trailer with the sun hammering off its roof, the absence of any sort of electrical wires running to it. Brought some water, he mused, as if the implications of this phrase had just sunken in. Well, we can't stand here in the yard all day. Let's go in, I ain't put off by hardship. I could live in a brush arbor if I had to. And have, once or twice. I can have it real homey in a week or so.

Fleming sat on the couch in the living room and studied the old man. Bloodworth seemed ill-prepared to stay so much as a night here. He had brought no food, and there was nothing to cook it on if he had. Dark was already seeping out of the woods and there was not so much as a kerosene lamp in the trailer. He was mulling over the idea of asking the old man to spend the night at his house when Albright spoke.

You could bunk with me, he said. As long as you're not too particular. We could fly in on this thing tomorrow and maybe shape it up in a day or two.

The old man appeared to think this over. Finally he said, I thank you for the offer, but I ain't never been much at movin in on nobody. Anyway this place is where I aim to live, around here where I was raised. But I've got to have a bath, seems like I been livin in a cattle truck a week. Has this place got a motel? It didn't when I moved off.

Yeah, the Cozy Court's right on the north side of town.

Well, that sounds like my best bet for a bath. Let's lock this place up and find somebody willin to sell us some supper.

In the cab Bloodworth asked Fleming about Warren and Boyd, and the boy figured he'd been expecting them to meet him. If he was he never said so, and he did not ask about Brady at all.

I reckon it's worked down to me and you then, he told the boy.

Within a week the old man, with the help of Albright and Fleming, had wrought a considerable change in his holdings. Albright fell into the role of chauffeur and general handyman as easily as he had assumed the mantle of cabdriver. Fleming found the old man's company agreeable and improvements on the trailer a way to use up time, a commodity this summer he seemed to possess too much of.

Bloodworth learned of a man at Beaver Dam who had benefited from the rural electrification program to the extent that he had a Delco unit for sale cheap. This Delco was a system of storage batteries and a generator that charged them. It furnished direct current for lights and small appliances and since the farmer had no further use for them he sold Bloodworth as well a fan and a refrigerator and a small stove designed to operate on direct current.

The old man said his pockets weren't deep enough yet for a well but he was mulling over plans for a cistern and pump. In the meantime they found a steel tank that had done service on a dairy farm and laboriously mounted it on poles so that Albright could juryrig a gravity flow of water to the plumbing of the trailer. A county truck with a water tank was hired to fill it and with water in the pipes and lights to defray the darkness the trailer was approaching the comforts of home.

The first night there his sleep was broken and chancy as an old man's often is and sometime in the night he dreamed of wolves. The dream was so vivid it was almost tactile, he could have brushed the silver ruff at the wolf's throat with his fingers. He was looking across an expanse of ice and snow toward a huge wolf baying at the moon. The wolf was silhouetted against the moon which was full and hung low in an indigo sky strewn with curdled clouds the color of foam on seagreen water and the wolf's breath smoked coldly in the air.

He woke knowing that something had slammed against the front door, a sound that vanished the instant he was awake to hear it. Dogs were howling. They seemed to be all about the trailer and he rose and turned on the light. The cacophony of howls and barks did not diminish with the light and the old man crossed the room and opened the front door. A dog sprang from the doorstep into the yard. You hush that up, the old man yelled. There was no moon and all he could see was the vague shape of dogs like revenantial dogs cobbled up out of night and shadow crossing and recrossing the yard. Now I'm not about to put up with this mess all night, he said to himself.

He pulled the guitar case from beneath his bed and opened it and removed the guitar and from the storage compartment meant for picks and extra strings withdrew a shortbarreled .38 Smith & Wesson revolver. He crossed back to the doorsill and stood on the top step with the pistol held beside his leg. The dogs were still milling about the yard and at the edge of the woods he could just discern a spectral human figure, a vague paleness against an indecipherable darkness, perhaps a man wearing a lightcolored shirt.

Who's out there? he called.

He could hear the soft almost furtive sounds of the dogs fading toward the woods. No one answered him and even as he watched the figure vanished, not abruptly but like something sinking slowly backward into deep blue water, like a light dimming down until finally there is nothing there at all.

Brady? he called.

SHE HAD BEEN brought up hard but not that hard. Not as hard as it was to live in an uncertain state of fear, knowing each day that the law would sooner or later come with government warrants and going to bed at night with that knowledge somehow intensified because it seemed even more apt for them to come at night. Even E.F. had to sleep sometime.

Not as hard as the door being kicked from its hinges behind her as she crossed from the stove to the table, a hot pan clutched bothhanded before her, the door caving inward and the room abruptly filling with stumbling men, Julia halfturning, the pan tilting, and she remembered the hot bright spatters of scalding soup on her ankles.

Julia sat in the shade of the pine in the metal chaise lounge. A broom stood tilted against her knee and there were fresh broommarks on the earth where the straw had gone. The air was winey with the smell of the sun in the hot pineneedles, a breeze arose and the smell intensified, a dust devil spun lazily down from the barnlot like a ghost and across the driveway and passed over her, her clothes rustling, the whirling wind cool against the drying sweat on her face.

She took off the goldrimmed glasses she wore and polished them on the hem of her apron, old feedsack material so often laundered it had gone patternless and soft as chamois. A catbird called from the tree but the bird's cry had no more reality than the sounds of deputies in her kitchen long ago, a raincrow called from a distant field but what she heard was the castiron kettle striking the hardwood floor, tomato soup spattering the wall like blood.

E.F. was sitting at a wide pine trestle table that bisected him above the waist and cut from view the pistol shoved into his trousers. All this was caught in a moment, etched her memory like acid filigrees on steel: there was a bowl of milk before Bloodworth, he was holding cornbread he was in the act of crumbling into the milk. His eyes widened but only momentarily, then narrowed to slits, the face gone at once sleepylooking and intent, and she knew him so well his thoughts were almost audible to her, what to do, what to do.

She was grabbed hard from behind, her throat and head caught in the crook of an elbow, she could see part of a blued rifle barrel extending into the upper corner of her vision, feel the rough serge overcoat sleeve against her throat. She clawed at the arm but it was strong and adrenalinecrazed, it was like struggling against a steel band. She felt her throat close, she was gasping for one more breath.

E.F. rose, facing the men, his hands raised, turning suddenly to kick away the chair behind him. The chair slammed into the wall, careened impotently across the floor.

Suddenly she slid downward toward the floor, the serge scraping across her cheek, felt her face distort against the clamped arm, eyelid stretched and distended until the eye opened against her will, the sandpaper of serge across the ball of the eye itself. The floor seemed somewhere she had to be. Her hair was caught in the buttons of the man's overcoat then he seized her hair in his fist trying to haul her back up to shield him.

She was no more than halfway down the man's body, descending him like a ladder, when E.F. fired. The hollow boom was enormous and the concussion came wave on palpable wave and the fist released her with her hair stringing away and she could feel strands of it plucked from her scalp. Her head slapped the floor and when she rolled over onto her back the man loomed above her, enormous but wounded, like a stricken god. He clutched himself where neck and shoulder joined then moved the hand away and stared at his bloody palm in a kind of wonder. A haze of smoke drifted.

She now saw that there were three of the men. She'd thought the number greater and she wondered were there more outside. The deputies seemed frozen, the rifles at port arms across their chests. She could read in their faces that they had just wanted to arrest him without killing or being killed and the faces showed how unlikely that possibility had become. E.F.'s face just showed that he didn't care if he killed them or not and maybe he'd a little rather kill them. He had the pistol pointed at the man's head and she watched the cylinder's slow turn and the hammer go to halfcock.

Lean them pieces against the wall, E.F. said. No, throw them out that door into the yard.

They did.

Get over in that corner, he said, or one at a time I'll punch three tickets to hell.

He was helping her up, leading her through the doorway into the bright sun. A wind had risen and shadows moved across the yard like something the wind was blowing before it.

No, she said, tugging against his arm, wondering what he was thinking. Fight one man off and there's always another one, she thought. The boys were in school, they'd be along. To an empty house that smelled like gunpowder, blood on the walls, blood on the floor.

No, she said, I can't live like this no more, I won't do it. Go on and go wherever it is you want to.

I can't leave you, he said.

You left me a long time ago, she told him.

He released the cock on the hammer of the revolver and shoved it into the waistband of his trousers. It's none of my doin, he said.

It's all your doin, she said. And always has been.

She stood leaning against the wall. Her throat felt raw and her right eye hurt. She felt she might faint. The world shimmered, flickered like something halfway between reality and dream. She slid down the wall, sat on legs that had miraculously folded beneath her.

When the engine cranked she looked up. E.F. was turning the old truck in the yard. An old model-T cut into a pickup truck, the likeness of a woman brushed in white on the door, Jolie Blon. The truck bucked and jumped and died when he popped the clutch and he restarted it, his face focused and intent, the eyes already prepared to see whatever it was the road wanted to show him.

She sat on her legs. Light through an intricate wickerwork of branches moved and swayed, moved and swayed. Light and shadow latticed together moved endlessly on the earth and she stared at it, thinking for a time that she could divine pattern there, order. But it moved with the sun and it moved with the wind and ultimately it was as random and unordered as life and she gave up on it and closed her eyes.

She thought she'd just dozed a moment with her head against the wall and the sun on her eyelids but when she opened them the metal of the chaise lounge was hard against the bun of hair on the back of her head and the sun had gone and looking upward into the thick pine branches was like staring down a tunnel into night itself.

She rose stiffly, still caught in the memory, touched for a moment the sagging crepe of her throat as if she'd expected to feel there the flesh of a girl. She took up the broom and went on toward the house. She wondered where Brady was and why the lights were not on.

On the porch she turned, hand already reaching for the doorknob, at some sound. Banjo music came drifting across the barren field, down through the cedar row, soft and then more defined, louder then almost fading out, as if during its passage through the cedars the trees were performing this alchemy upon it. *Oh my whiskey bill is due, and my board bill is too,* the music said, *and my last gold dollar's done and gone. And my last gold dollar's done and gone,* and she was suddenly touched with terror. She didn't know if the music was in the world or in her head.

Feeding bats crisscrossed in the deep blue dusk. The last of the light throbbed like a distant fire above the treeline. She suddenly heard a wave of sound, cicadas and whippoorwills and crickets that just abruptly assailed her, and she wondered if they'd just begun or if they had already been calling and all she'd heard was the banjo music, ancient and myth-laden and somehow enticing, like sound seeping through the cracks of a place you couldn't get to anymore.

ALBRIGHT HAD LEARNED of the widow with the barn roof that needed painting at Patton's store and had gone immediately to her farm across the river, to the edge of a wild area called the Harrikin. He was hired. The husband had died sometime back leaving three five-gallon buckets of vilelooking green paint but the roofs untouched. When Albright was through with the barn she looked at the level of the paint remaining and decided to paint the other outbuildings as well and she waited until the last of the paint was used and Albright was cleaning his brushes in a bucket of kerosene to tell him that she had no money and had planned on paying him with a halfgrown hog.

Albright was outraged. I need my money, he said. I don't have any use for a hog.

Well. I don't have any money.

He suspected she was lying but short of falling upon her bodily he did not know what to do about it. Why didn't you tell me ahead of time, he asked. I don't know what in the world I'd do with a hog. I don't even have any way of haulin a hog.

I figured you knew, she said. It was known all up and down this creek I wanted to trade that shoat for work. That hog's worth every penny of thirty dollars, and they'll buy him down at the store.

In the end it was take the hog or take nothing and they went out to look at it.

The hog was lying in a dry mudhole in the shade of a fence encumbered with virulentlooking poison oak. When Albright climbed over the fence the hog fixed him with a look of unalloyed malevolence and scrambled upright. The hog had a razorous mouth and a frayed ear and malignant little piggy eyes.

A dog done that to his ear, the old woman said. Just clamped down and hung on while that hog drug it over half the county.

How do I get him in the car? he asked. I don't know anything about hogs.

Well, she said. She gave him what was almost but not quite a shrug. I guess you could do it ever how you want to. He's your hog now.

He sat down on his heels and thought about it a while.

I believe there's an old dog collar and a leash in that stable back there, she said. I'll go look. Or you might try tollin him.

Tollin him?

Leadin him with an ear of corn or somethin. Callin him.

Let's try all of it, Albright said.

She came around and opened a gap in the fence Albright hadn't seen. It would be a sight easier if you brought your automobile down here, she said. I don't know much about automobiles but I do know they got wheels and hogs don't.

He gave her a sharp glance. A different tone seemed to have entered her voice since the last roof was painted. That's a good idea, he said. I was just about to do that.

He went and got the taxicab and backed it to the edge of the gap and got out and opened one of the rear doors. She had the leash and collar in one hand and an ear of corn in the other and she was waiting on him.

He finally managed to get the collar on the hog but it bit him once in the calf of the leg and once on the forearm. Collared and leashed like some degenerate breed of dog the shoat lay down in the dusty mudhole and put its chin on its paws and watched him arrogantly. He pulled as hard as he could on the leash but all it did was draw the hog upright. It positioned its sharp little hooves and leant against the leash and Albright couldn't budge him. It didn't want the corn, either.

Maybe you could push on him or somethin, he said. You push and I'll pull and maybe he'll get the idea.

She just shook her head. I believe he's already got the idea, she said. Anyway I never liked that hog. It had the worst turn of any shoat I ever raised.

He threw the ear of corn as hard as he could at the hog and walked around behind it and encircled its chest with both arms and heaved with all his might. The hog lurched upon its hind legs and began to squeal. He waltzed it toward the car this way and that and with his arms about the hog and both upright they looked like two lascivious drunks trying some new kind of crazy dance. Bemused perhaps by this approach the hog allowed itself to be pushed to the car and Albright put a heavy foot against its haunch and kicked. The hog went scrambling over the seat and Albright slammed the door and stood against the Dodge breathing hard. He could hear the hog squalling in outrage and lurching about inside the car. He was wishing he'd left shoatless half an hour ago, wishing he'd never heard about the old woman at Patton's store.

He didn't even look at the old woman. He got into the car and started back toward the river. He looked back once and the hog was studying him with something akin to speculation. Halfway across the railroad trestle over the river the hog seemed taken with some sort of fit. It began to whirl about and slam against the doors and leap from seat to floorboard and back again then it made a razorous slash in the upholstery and dragged out a mouthful of stuffing. Shit, Albright said. He slammed on the brakes and turned in the seat and began to beat the hog about the head and shoulders with his fists. Quit it, he yelled. He climbed out of the car and opened the rear door but when he did the hog leapt against it desperately. The flung door caught Albright on the temple and he fell as the hog bolted across him and struck out for the end of the trestle. Albright scrambled up and managed to grasp the end of the leash. He ran fulltilt after the hog trying to get slack in the leash then slid in the gravel at the trestle's end. Somehow he managed to hang on to the leash. The hog dragged him six or eight feet then turned in the roadbed facing him and just stood there gasping.

He closed on it. They fell together in the road like the very essence of degeneracy and struggled up with Albright cursing and the shoat grunting in short explosive bursts and upholstery gummed hydrophobically around its mouth. Albright had a long slanting cut on his bicep and man and hog alike were crazed with dust and blood.

That trestle ain't but one lane wide, a voice said. You was to move your car I'd get on out of your way and let you go about your business.

Albright whirled. An old farmer in faded overalls and a baseball cap was looking down at him. Perhaps slight amusement in his craggy face.

What the hell do you mean by that? Albright asked. The hog seemed to sense this moment of indecision and jerked hard on the leash and streaked desperately toward the line of woods bordering the road.

If that's your hog, and I got no reason to suspect it ain't, then you can do whatever you want to, he said. But you're holdin up traffic here.

My hog is gettin away, Albright said. If we wasn't standin here arguin you could be helpin me run that hog. It got out of my car back there.

I'm a little too old and brittle to be runnin hogs through the woods, the old man said. I never knowed anybody to hogfarm out of a taxicab anyway.

He hunted the hog for what must have been hours, letting time get away from him, pausing at last to study the sun through the trees and get some sort of fix on the time. The sun stood past its zenith, perhaps halfway down the western quadrant. He didn't know how far he'd come or for sure in what direction but he knew where the river was and he felt that ought to be enough.

The hog seemed to be playing with him, drawing him ever deeper into the lush riverbottom undergrowth. Just when the realization of how crazy this all was began to sink in the hog would show itself or slow tantalizingly and permit him to almost but not quite catch it. Once in a stand of wild cane it had completely stopped, not even breathing hard, and waited for Albright to get his own breath back, Albright resting hands on knees watching beads of sweat drip off his nose and listening to the harsh rasp of his breathing. When he'd judged the hog off guard he sprang forward and got two hands on the hog's haunches but the hog just squealed and leapt away into the cane.

He had come to hate the hog. He had come to loathe it and the old woman who foisted it upon him. He began to think of the hog as the old woman's bastard offspring, the result of a misbegotten crossroads alliance between her and some porcine representative pushing the devil's wares.

He wandered about the cane looking for the left shoe he had lost in the sucking mud and envisioned posting a reward, a thousand dollars for the shoat or its head, dead or alive, pictured armed bounty hunters stamping through the vines and greenery, the hog's face leering at him fullface and profile from a flyer on the postoffice wall.

Right shoe on and left shoe gone he consulted the mental compass he used for a guide and struggled through the briars and creepers toward where he judged the roadbed to be. He imagined the hog following him through the brush, and considered driving back to the old woman's farm and strangling her, laboriously scraping off all the paint he'd so carefully applied.

When he staggered onto the roadbed he was strung with briars and spiderwebs and slathered with blood and mud and he was lightheaded and halfcrazy. He looked about and had reason to question his sanity, to suspect dimensional displacement. There was nothing familiar in the landscape, he was somewhere he had never been. Far across the roadbed the country tended away in a soft green tapestry, just before the limit of his vision faded out was a farmhouse, tilled fields, a column of smoke from burning brush. A bucolic scene from a feedstore calendar. Nothing looked familiar. Gradually he realized that the hog had drawn him so far into the riverbottom that he had come out on another road, and from all appearances one that he had never been on before. He looked up the road and down the road and was undecided which way to go.

Everything looked like just more of the same. He tried to remember which way west lay from the river but he was in country unfamiliar to him and a cointoss would have made as much sense as anything else.

He was sitting on the shoulder of the road smoking his last cigarette when a white Buick Roadmaster came up the hill and slowed, came to a stop parallel with him. It was on his tongue to inquire as to directions when he saw a grinning Fleming Bloodworth peering out the passenger window at him. He pinched out the cigarette and tossed the butt away and scrambled up brushing dried mud off his jeans. Lord God, he said. Homefolks.

Fleming had been taking in Albright's bedraggled appearance. His muddy clothing, the missing shoe. Wild unstrung albino hair. Were you in a carwreck? he asked.

No.

Are you lost?

Hell no, I know where I'm at, I'm sittin right here on this bank. It's my car and the bridge and the rest of the fuckin world that's wandered off.

Neal leant across to ask, What went with your shoe?

Albright started to speak, paused. He took a deep breath, let it out. I lost it runnin a hog, he finally said.

Neal looked at Fleming. He pushed his sunglasses up with a forefinger and nodded. It makes sense to me, he said. That's the way I always run my hog, one on and one off. That way you've got speed on one foot and traction on the other. Just whichever one is called for you've got it right there.

It sounds to me like something that would have a story connected with it somewhere, Fleming said.

Neal reached into the back seat. There was a foottub of ice and the water it was melting into in the floorboard and he fumbled around in it and withdrew a can of Falstaff beer and tossed it out the window at Albright. Here, he said. Albright caught the can onehanded and sat looking at the icy water tracking down its side. Almighty God, he said in wonder. He worked an opener out of his front pocket and punctured the can on opposing sides of the top and raised it to his mouth.

Damned if he don't go prepared, Neal said. His own opener and everything.

When the can was empty Albright folded it in half and tossed it over his left shoulder into the honeysuckle. That thing don't have a brother livin in there anywhere, does it?

This one he sipped slowly then set it on a level spot he'd scooped out with the heel of his lone shoe. I really need some help catchin that hog, he said. I need to sell it. You all wouldn't help me run it, would you? I believe the three of us could hem it up without any trouble.

I believe I'll pass, Neal said. We've run hogs since before good daylight and I believe it's about quitting time.

Where'd you get a hog? Fleming asked.

It's kind of a long story. I needed some money to get to Clifton so I worked for this old woman over by the Harrikin. She seen me comin a mile off. She worked me like a dog and come settlin up time turned out she didn't have no fuckin money. It was either take that shoat or take nothin. Now by God I guess it's nothin after all. She had that little son of a bitch trained or somethin. No tellin how many times she's traded it for work. It wouldn't surprise me to learn that the damned thing's swum the river and is back scratchin at her screen door right now. It's my intention to strangle her and burn her house, after I've drunk this beer and rested a while.

Fleming opened the car door for the breeze. What there was of it came looping up from the riverbottom, hot and steamy with the smell of the river, the heady essence of honeysuckle.

Your car's setting down by the trestle where you left it, he said. Looks like you could have noticed which way the water was flowing.

I was huntin a hog, not a river, Albright said. That shoat's worth thirty dollars, what she told me. I need to court this lady I know over in Clifton and I always take her a present.

What sort of present? the boy asked.

Well. Generally I take her twenty dollars.

Old Mrs. Halfacre, Neal said.

Who? the boy asked.

She ain't old, Albright said.

Hellfire, she's older than you and me put together. She must be getting on toward fifty years old. That's old from where I'm sitting.

She keeps herself up, though, Albright said.

Well. If stumbling around drunk on blackberry wine is keeping in shape, I guess she does.

Albright looked as though he was about to defend Mrs. Halfacre's various attributes so the boy said hastily, We're just driving around looking for some place that'll let us in long enough to sit down. Neal here's about got us barred from everywhere. We may have to go clean out of the county.

Barred from where?

Hellfire. Everywhere. The Snip, the poolhall. About two weeks ago they barred us from the Knob. They barred me for being underage and Neal for being Neal.

I never heard of anybody bein barred from the Knob, Albright said in disbelief. They'd let the devil hisself set there as long as he had the price of one more beer.

Not Neal. He started a fight in there that day and they just about tore the place down to the foundation. Broke all the chairs. Somebody tore a piece of boxing off the wall to use for a club and a rat the size of a fice dog run out of the wall. Neal was about halfdrunk and he was trying to go with this woman that was with somebody else. Finally the guy told Neal to get lost and Neal told him the girl was playing with his dick the night before. The guy knocked Neal across the room and it just spread from there.

It was the gospel truth, what I said, Neal said.

He emptied a pistol at us, Fleming said. Neal tried to run him down. Did run over the doorstep.

They Lord, Albright said, as if this was something he deeply regretted missing. You all can go with me, he said. We'll catch that hog and sell it and head out for Clifton. Mrs. Halfacre'll let you in, she don't bar nobody.

I pass again, Neal said.

That daughter of hers, that Raven Lee, she's about the prettiest girl in a three-county area, Albright said. You ought to come with us.

Fleming thought this an odd way to describe the girl's beauty, wondered how the three-county area had been canvassed. What the criteria were.

I won't argue with that, Neal said. He raised a wrist and tilted the dial of his watch to the sun. I know Miss Halfacre well. But I've got a date with a redhead from Beaver Dam tonight and I believe I've seen all I ever need to see of Raven Lee Halfacre.

Albright glanced at him curiously but didn't reply. He turned to Fleming. What about you, young Bloodworth? Want to ride over to the Tennessee River? Makes this one look like a spring branch.

Well, I don't have a date with a redhead. I expect I need to get home, though.

I expect you do, Neal said contemptuously. You've got to feed all them stock. Cook supper. Change all them doilies on the coffee table. Why do you remind me of some eighty year old woman?

I wouldn't mind ridin down there, Fleming told Albright.

All right then. We'll need my car though. You could ride down and drive it back up here. I doubt Neal'd let me in his car, muddy as I am.

Hell, crawl in here, Neal said. Daddy's about ruined it. Raised chickens out of it and everything else. Another few trips to the woods up above Early Dial's and I may just buy me a new one.

They got out at the railroad trestle. You want some of this beer? Neal asked.

Albright was already loading up his pockets. I might take three or four, he said.

I might could take one, Fleming said.

You've got the makings of a hell of a Bloodworth, Neal told him. Might could take one. You don't watch your step you're going to get drummed out of the whole damned family. Sip on two beers all day long.

They returned to the top of the hill in Albright's Dodge. Albright got out studying the undergrowth as if the hog might be lurking there awaiting his return. Now let's round up that shoat, he said. We can't sell him we'll stick a apple in his mouth and roast him on a spit.

Fleming gave it a halfhearted attempt but could not get fully caught up in the search for the missing hog. The undergrowth was hot and stifling and absolutely breezeless. Sweat immediately popped out over his entire body and clots of gnats plagued his eyes as if seeking ingress to the skull itself. Mosquitoes buzzed about his ears and he kept slapping at them bothhanded. He stood for a time before the river. It was slow-moving and turgid, viscous as a river of mud easing along. A cotton-mouth dropped from a branch and undulated sluggishly away.

Something was crawling up his leg. He hauled up his breeches legs and he'd been beset by an army of seedticks. Barely visible. His legs were already itching. He shucked off his shoes and socks and waded into the river and began to scrub them off with handfuls of sand.

Hey, he yelled.

After a while Albright came shoatless out of the undergrowth.

I've got a little money, Fleming said. How about if I just loan you the twenty?

Where'd you get twenty dollars?

I came into some money. How about it? Does that suit you?

It suits me right down to the ground, Albright said. We'll go back to town where I can get me a bath and some clean clothes and we'll head out.

They had been following the Tennessee River for miles, losing it behind enormous stone tablets black as ebony in the darkness, regaining it in the breaks and switchbacks, the car paced by a pale moon that hung over the river, its luminous abstract reflection shattered in the hammered water. The river was wider than Fleming had expected, more of a presence than the road they drove on, it kept drawing your eyes back to it, it refused to be ignored.

The road to Clifton had been long and varied, had consisted of side-trips and dead ends. Albright had been hot and tired and he hadn't eaten that day and the beer seemed to hit him hard and immediate. He fell to concocting other entertainments as a prelude to the visit to Mrs. Halfacre. Fleming made no protest, he had made a conscious decision to roll with the current, go where the night might take him.

It took him first to Waynesboro, where Albright had heard of a dance. The women were wild there, he said, especially if you came from another county and were therefore foreign to them. He described various acts of intimacy at which these women had no peer. Degrees of abandon to which the women of Ackerman's Field could only aspire. Fleming doubted all this but he listened anyway and thought with a kind of sardonic amusement that before the night was over life itself might grasp him by the scruff of the neck and jerk him out of the doldrums he seemed grounded in and into its swifter currents. One of these wild women might spring upon him and perform an act so abandoned his life would be altered forever.

Their way was barred at the door of the dancehall by a muscular arm stretched in front of Albright's chest, a fist clamped on the doorjamb. The man jerked his head toward a handlettered sign nailed to the wall. NO STAGS ALLOWED, the sign said. COUPLES ONLY.

Albright took offense at this. I'll give you to understand I'm not no Goddamned Staggs, he said. I been a Albright all my life and I got a driver's license to prove it.

He bought a pint of bootleg whiskey at Goblin's Knob, sipped it driving while he grew morose and regretful, remembering old wrongs and new done to him as if fate had a dark sense of humor and amused itself at Albright's expense with every toss of the dice. Fleming rode silently, awash in the raw reek of whiskey that seemed to be rising out of the floorboards, out of the very upholstery itself. While the headlights rolled up scenes he'd never viewed, new configurations of trees and houses and bluffs as if the shifting of their arrangement in the tableau made them new things altogether. A world forever restructuring itself. Strange country rearing up out of the night and subsiding off the dark glass like one of those books whose rapidly flipped pages give the illusion of motion.

It wasn't so far back I'd go check on that hog, Albright said. Roust that old woman out of bed. I'm thinkin she probably sleeps with that shoat, I'd get em both together.

Fleming leaned his head against the glass and closed his eyes. He'd about decided they'd just drive in circles until daylight then go home. There were no wild women, no Mrs. Halfacre in whom he had invested twenty dollars. Certainly there was no Raven Lee Halfacre, prettiest girl in a three-county area. Likely there was no Clifton, all he'd seen so far was the Tennessee River.

I ought to hex her, Albright said. But I done got one workin, and I don't know how many they allow to a customer.

Slow down a minute, Fleming said. Are you tellin me that you actually hired Brady to put a hex on Woodall?

I damn sure did. She's simmerin on the back burner now, waitin to come to a boil.

You paid him.

Yeah. It must of been the top of the line hex, too. It cost fifty dollars.

Where on earth did you come up with fifty dollars?

I borrowed it at the bank.

You what?

I borrowed it at the First National Bank.

You mean you just waltzed in there and told them you needed fifty dollars to put a curse on a man and they counted it out?

Hell no, what do you think I am, crazy? I told them it was for house repairs. He took a mortgage on my car. It don't matter anyway, unless this thing pays off pretty quick Woodall's goin to be drivin it anyway. What do you think about that?

I think you've just about cornered the market on craziness, Fleming said.

The broken cliffs had fallen away now and they were descending toward the lights of a little town strewn between the hills. On his right hand the river lay shimmering as far as the eye could see. Fleming watching could see the lights of a ferry working its way across, a searchlight arcing through the fog like an acetylene torch. They drove down the main drag of town, a few stores and cafes. Albright turned down a steep incline to a sidestreet and they were following the river again. Fleming saw a marina where boats rocked at their lines, a lighted barge so long it seemed to pass forever, a huge monolith nighshapeless in the starblown dark, like a city slipped its moorings and was drifting toward parts unknown.

Albright parked the car before a small steep-roofed pink house. The windows were ablaze with light and when Albright cut off the engine Fleming could hear the low gutbucket thump of guitar music.

Let me have just a sip of that bottle, Fleming said. When Albright reached it to him Fleming unscrewed the cap.

Don't smell of it, Albright cautioned. Just get you a good horn of it and when you swallow kind of clamp down on it. Get you a good hold.

Fleming did but he had to swallow a time or two to ensure that it would stay where he put it. He shook his head. His eyes were watering. Hellfire, he said.

Every bit of it, Albright agreed. Now listen, Fleming. Just talk up to them and you'll be all right. Don't start talkin about books or quotin poems at them. These is good folks but they ain't real crazy about readin books. Just do what I do and you'll be all right.

Fleming was irritated. I do what you do and I'll wind up in the penitentiary or the crazyhouse one, he said. Don't worry about it. I'll try not to slobber or wet myself.

Albright slapped his shoulder. That's all that a man can expect, Youngblood. Now let's check em out.

Out amongst em, Fleming said.

The outside light was turned off but coming onto the porch Fleming saw a swing that seemed to be drowning in ivy or honeysuckle suspended from the ceiling on the shadowed end of the porch. A slim dark presence was lying in it but that was the sum of what he could see. Albright turned to face the swing and tipped an imaginary hat. Miss Raven, he said. Is your mama in the house?

The girl if girl was what she was did not reply and Albright rapped the screen door smartly against the sash. Apparently he was recognized from within for a woman's voice cried out, Junior, Sweetie, and Albright entered with Fleming practically stepping on his heels.

Fleming stood for a moment blinking in the harsh light. He was in a small front room, low-ceiled, the room papered with wallpaper so loud the walls seemed to be shimmering with a constant vibratory motion. A vinyl couch shoved against one wall, a tall console radio tuned to the Grand Ole Opry. A ratty green armchair set facing out of the corner in which sat a shirtless man clutching a guitar. His eyes were focused with a fierce dark intensity on these newcomers as if he'd immediately know their business here but the woman had embraced Albright with her left arm and was running her right hand through his wild stand of curls and she wasn't paying the man in the chair any mind.

A woman would kill for a head of hair like that, she said, stepping back to look. Albright was standing directly beneath the hot white glare of the ceiling bulb and with his hair uplifted from the ministrations of the woman's fingers he looked as if his head was afire.

Wouldn't they? she turned and demanded of the man in the corner chair. The man was drinking from a snuff glass a dark liquid so opaque it might have been India ink. He appeared to be thinking this over. Wouldn't they? she demanded again but the man would not go on record as to whether they would or wouldn't. There was a five-gallon jug of clear scalloped glass set before the chair halffull of the same dark liquid he was drinking and he had his feet propped atop it possessively as if it was something he was charged with guarding with his life.

Fleming figured the woman had been pretty in her youth but by the impartial glare of the light there was scarcely any of it left. He judged her not yet forty-five but the flesh of her upper arms sagged and her face looked curiously as if it was formed of melting wax and gravity itself was undoing her a little at a time. She seemed a little drunk. She hung onto Albright and swayed as if they were dancing though no feet were moving.

Abruptly the man in the chair got up and leant the guitar against the wall. He went out the screen door. It fell to behind him. Something's goin to tote you off settin here by yourself, Fleming heard him say. Nobody answered him and his footsteps receded down the doorstep and faded out in the yard.

For lack of anything better to do Fleming crossed the room and sat on the couch beside the radio. Now folks I've got a little lady here I really want you to put your hands together for, Ernest Tubb said. The woman had turned to study Fleming. He's a finelookin thing, she said to Albright. Are there any more like him at home except bigger and closer to my age?

If there was you wouldn't hear it from me, Albright said. That's Fleming. We out amongst em tonight.

Get you a glass of that wine, the woman told Fleming. It's blackberry, it's good. What's went with Albert?

If that was him in the chair he left, Fleming said. He crossed to the jug and unscrewed the lid. The wine had the fruity smell of summer to it, a curious hot undercurrent of alcohol. There seemed to be nothing to drink it from.

Guitar music's nice but money's something a person has an actual use for, she said obscurely. There's glasses in the kitchen yonder.

They were upended on a clean towel on the counter beside the sink. Fleming couldn't seem to get rid of the smell of the drink of bootleg whiskey he'd taken. It seemed to have soaked into his clothing, his hair. Between his teeth. He filled a glass from the tap and stood drinking it, facing his reflection in the window behind the sink. He could hear affectionate noises from the front room. He'd scarcely walked through the doorway and already they were groping each other. Squeals, giggles, throaty little growls ensued. All this just from Albright. He couldn't fathom why he'd gotten talked into this. I'd sooner be in hell with my back broke, he told his disgusted reflection in the windowglass. He emptied the remaining water into the sink and went through the doorway with the glass and halffilled it from the enormous jug. He sipped from it. It was sweet, almost treacly, with a sour burning aftertaste.

Just make yourself at home, the woman told Fleming. You can go talk to Raven Lee out on the porch or just sit here and listen to the radio. Fleming noticed that she was holding the twenty-dollar bill he had lent Albright. Abruptly she crossed the room and laid an arm about his shoulders. She leaned and kissed him noisily on the jaw. She showed him a corner of the folded bill. He watched it disappear into the depths of her bosom with some regret. Don't you wish you had something that would make you twenty dollars this easy? she asked.

Some reply seemed called for but none came immediately to mind. While he was mulling it over she linked an arm through Albright's and they went into a hall and toward the back of the house. On the radio Uncle Dave Macon was frailing a banjo. Keep your skillet good and greasy all the time, time, time, he sang. After a while he could hear the woman's throaty laughter through the gaudy walls. He arose and with the glass of wine went out onto the porch in the cool night air and sat on the doorstep. He could smell the river, a rank weedy smell of ripening summer, honeysuckle so overpowering it almost made him dizzy. Somewhere behind him off in the dark the horn of a barge came in sporadic bursts.

He was staring out toward Albright's car and past it to where the shapeless buildings of town reared against the night sky when the presence in the swing rose and crossed the porch and sat beside him on the floorboards. Though there were several inches of space between them he could smell her and the fragrance cleared up all questions of gender but he could not have said exactly why this was. It was not perfume. Perhaps it was the smell of her hair.

You favor Neal Bloodworth. Are you kin to him?

He's my first cousin. How come you know Neal?

Everybody knows Neal. I went with him a few times. Why are you not drunk? I'd hardly expect Neal to have a sober relative at all, let alone a first cousin.

Fleming judged it a flippant question but he tried to frame a serious answer for it. I tried it a few times, he said. But I don't much care for what it does to me. It does something to your attention, the way you see and hear things. You miss things. I don't know, that's not what I mean. I can't say exactly what I mean.

You mean it dulls your senses?

Yes. It dulls my senses. That's exactly what I mean.

Why didn't you just say that then?

I don't know, he said. He turned to face her for the first time and something about her, her face or perhaps her total presence, hit him like a blow to the abdomen. She was the prettiest girl in a three-county area, Albright had said, but Fleming would have moved the boundaries outward to encompass considerably more geography than that. She was small and dark, hair the color of her namesake, eyes black as sloe. Her features were as delicate as if she were a scaled-down and infinitely complex model of some coarser and larger being, as if she were the very essence of herself. There was something subtly foreign about her but he could not define or even isolate it. Indian, Hispanic, Oriental. And something was coming off her, exuded from the pores perhaps, that made him feel heavy and tongue-tied and simpleminded.

I don't know, he said. I believe you've addled me.

Addled you? You'll know for sure when I addle you. I never did anything to you.

Maybe you've accidentally addled me, he said.

You mean I've vamped you, like those old silent movie stars with the long black eyelashes? Hypnotized you? What do you think I am, one of those highpriced callgirls?

No. Lord no.

You think I'm a cheap callgirl then?

Hellfire, Fleming said. I don't think anything at all. I'm going to quit thinking. Kick it like a bad habit.

She seemed obscurely satisfied. Maybe I have addled you, she said. Maybe I'm turned up too high. Or your resistance is just too low. I'll turn myself down a notch or two.

I wish you would, he said, thinking, Raven Lee Halfacre, I've got to watch myself here, this may be getting out of hand. And I believe I'm helping it along.

What's your name?

Fleming. I know yours, Junior Albright was raving about how pretty Raven Lee Halfacre was.

The girl was studying him. I said you looked like Neal but now I'm not so sure. You favor him but not that much. You know how Neal's got that sort of smartass look.

Yes I do.

You don't have that. You look nice.

Fleming was silent. He'd been given the kiss of death. He did not want to be nice. He wanted to be wild and reckless, a rake and a rambling man, the highwayman who came riding, riding up to the old inn door.

You're not as good a talker as Neal is, either. Neal would have had a girl's blouse talked off by now. You haven't even tried.

He didn't reply. He'd only been sitting by her for a bare ten minutes but already the idea of Neal talking her blouse off held little appeal for him. He wondered if Neal talked it off. He remembered Neal saying he'd seen about all he wanted to of Raven Lee Halfacre. Perhaps he'd tried and failed.

You want to walk up town and get a Coke or something? she asked.

I guess. Is anything open?

The cafe. Maybe the drugstore, we can look at the magazines.

We could just ride up there in Albright's car.

I'd rather walk, it's nice out. That yellow he painted it is a little wild for me.

Clifton seemed to have been constructed on hillsides. They walked up, they walked down. Folk here seemed to suffer some aversion to level ground. He could hear the lapping of water, you were always aware of the river.

She walked easily along beside him, swinging her arms, once she hooked an arm in his and something coursed through him like electricity, like the immediate onset of some rare and powerful drug.

At the drugstore they drank vanilla Cokes and she sorted through the movie magazines and selected a copy of *Modern Screen* with Montgomery Clift on the cover. They drank their Cokes at a table by the window while she thumbed through the magazine. He watched her. Her profile new and bright as a newlystruck coin. She twisted a curl around a finger as she read.

Fleming noticed the countergirl watching them with open irritation. After a while she came around the corner and approached their table.

This ain't no library, she said. You can look through them and pick one out but you can't just set and read one then put it back.

Raven Lee laid the magazine on the table. Take it then, she said.

Fleming picked up the magazine. Twenty-five cents, the price was stated. He laid a halfdollar on the counter and slid the magazine back toward Raven Lee. The countergirl picked up the money and walked away. After a time she came back and laid a quarter down on the red Formica tabletop.

A big spender, Raven Lee said. What's that going to cost me?

What?

Boys always expect something back when they do something for you, she said. What do you expect?

Hellfire. If I did I wouldn't expect much of it for a quarter. I doubt you'd even miss a quarter's worth. Besides, I don't want anything from you.

That's what he heard himself saying but it did not even come close to being the truth. What he wanted, he had realized in the last few minutes, was everything. He wanted the rest of her life, and failing that, he wanted permission to walk along beside her while she lived it. As dying men are told to have their past unreel before them Fleming had been gainsaid a kaleidoscopic view of his future. In the space of seconds whole sequences unspooled before him. They stood before a Bible-holding preacher. Hand in hand they stood before a crib where lay their firstborn. They stood shoulder to shoulder against a world that did its utmost to drive them to their knees and they prevailed. She knelt before his grave, tousled gray curls swinging, and imbedded into the clay a single white rose. There was a mist of tears in her eyes. He saw all this instantly, not as a future cast in stone but as a swirling maelstrom of events that could be mastered and controlled. It was a future to aspire to. Fleming considered himself a fairly stubborn and persistent person, and he planned to aspire as hard as he could.

As long as you understand that I'm not some watered-down version of my mama. We're two different people, so don't go getting us confused. She don't tell me how to live my life and I don't tell her how to live hers. I've already changed my name from Evelyn and I expect before long I'll be changing the Halfacre too.

You planning on getting married?

You don't have to get married to change your name. Besides, I'm sixteen years old, way too young to be married. Not too young to get married, just to be married. Mama thinks I'm pretty enough to get into some line of show business. Maybe not a movie star, or anything like that, but something. Really Mama sees me as her best shot to get out of Clifton. Out of Tennessee. She hates Tennessee, says it's full of hillbillies.

Where's she from?

Tennessee, the girl said, grinning, then leant to suck the last of her Coke through the straw.

We closing up in here, a woman at the counter called, proving it by crossing the room to a panel box on the wall and flipping a switch that killed the exterior lights.

They rose from the table, Raven Lee rolling up her magazine. That woman just hates me, she said. And I've never done a thing to her.

Fleming suspected that before time eventually did whatever it was going to do to Raven Lee Halfacre a lot of women were going to just hate her, but he didn't say so. He followed her out the pneumatic door onto the sidewalk where enormous moths and candleflies fluttered about in confusion as if they'd ascertain where the light had gone. One entrapped itself in the girl's hair and after slapping at it unsuccessfully she allowed Fleming to extricate it. He released it and it flew away.

I hate those things, Raven Lee said. Let's walk up by the cafe and see if it's still open.

They had gone scarcely a block and a half past dark stores shuttered and barred when they came upon Fleming Bloodworth's worst nightmare.

He was lounging against the front of the Eat and Run Cafe. The cafe was closed and dark. This nightmare was wearing engineer boots with straps and buckles, one of them on the sidewalk and the other propped back against the brick facade of the cafe. He was wearing jeans turned up one turn at the cuffs and a white T-shirt with a pack of unfiltered cigarettes rolled into a turned up sleeve. A pair of aviator sunglasses hung by an earpiece from the neck of the shirt. His hair was as flat on top as if it had been barbered with the aid of a spirit level and the sides were worn long and brilliantined back into a gleaming ducktail. A cigarette drooped from the corner of his mouth in a studied manner, as if he'd practiced it before a mirror.

Hellfire, Fleming was thinking.

Raven Lee Halfacre, the boy-man said.

Just walk on by and don't answer, the girl hissed.

They did. Fleming didn't look back but the boots had toe and heel taps on them and he could hear them clicking along behind them. Clicking faster.

When you goin to give me a shot at that stuff, Raven Lee, the man called. I believe it's about my time.

Fleming stopped. She jerked his arm. Are you crazy? she demanded.

I may well be, he was thinking. He felt called upon to say something. Do something. Defend her honor in some manner. At length he allowed himself to be propelled along but by this time the man had approached, passed, and halted in front of them.

When you goin out with me?

When hell freezes over, she said.

Looks like you down to scrapin the bottom of the barrel, he observed. What'd you do, decide to get you a young one and bring him up right?

We're not bothering you, the girl said. Why don't you just let us alone and go about your business?

Right now you are my business, the man said. I heard you had some excellent stuff.

I heard you didn't, the girl said. I heard you got that no account Sheila Brewer in the bedroom with none of her folks at home and couldn't even get it up.

You lyin little slut, he said. He slapped her openhanded hard and then whirled on Fleming. The girl clasped her face bothhanded and stood for a moment with her head down and her hair fallen over her hands. The man spun his cigarette into the street in a spiral of sparks. His face was flat and angry. What do you have to say about this? he asked Fleming.

I heard—Fleming tried to swallow but there was insufficient spit in his mouth. He could feel cold clammy sweat in his armpits, tracking down his ribcage—you couldn't get it up till her brother came in the room.

He knew he was going to be hit and he threw up both hands in a kind of clumsy guard, with the result that he was hit not only with the man's fist but by his own as well. His own hands slammed nose and mouth and a larger fist connected with his lower jaw and his knees just seemed to liquefy. He struck out as hard as he could aiming at the man's face but felt glass break under his right hand. His left connected to something with more flesh to it but then a blow caught him in the solar plexus and the air exploded out of his lungs like a bellows someone had closed. He sat down hard with his hands splayed out behind him to break his fall and the man kicked him in the thigh with an engineer boot then whirled and ran.

You cowardly son of a bitch, the girl cried. She was looking about wildly for something to throw but could find not so much as a Coke bottle. She made as if to throw the magazine then thought better of it and turned and caught Fleming by the hand.

Can you get up?

He stood but his left leg wouldn't work. The muscles in his thigh felt as if they had cramped themselves into a series of knots, one atop the other. He made it to the curb and sat down and massaged his leg hard. The muscle in it was jumping like something alive but separate from him and he rubbed it until he could feel some of the tension easing out of it. Blood kept dripping on his jeans and he reached and felt his face and worked his jaw back and forth with his hand then leant and spat a tooth into the street.

Let's go, the girl said. We need to be out of these streetlights before the law drives by. They'll lock you up.

He spat a mouthful of blood. I haven't done anything.

That makes no nevermind. You're from out of town and you've got blood all over you. They'll lock you up.

He staggered up out of the street. Then by all means, he said.

They went down a narrow sloping alley between the Eat and Run Cafe and a feed store past broken crates and garbage cans and an inkblack cat that vanished into nothing at all in the darkness. They came out on a street near the river and struck out down it, the boy pausing now and again to raise his left foot and kick the leg as if some delicate mechanism had become misaligned and he might jar it back into place. After a while he noticed his right hand was aching and when he raised it to the light there were streaks of blood coursing down his fingers. He just shook his head and went on.

Abruptly the girl stopped in the middle of the street and began to laugh. She grasped his arm. Why did you say that about Sheila Brewer's brother? she asked.

Hellfire, he said. You were the one that came up with that crazy shit about that no account Sheila Brewer. I'll bet there's not even such a person.

After a moment she began to laugh again. It was a throaty halfmusical sound and Fleming for a crazy moment thought that if he hurried he might be able to catch his assailant and get beaten up again and she'd go on doing it.

Anyway I thought I'd make him mad enough to charge me, and if he was out of control I might be able to handle him. It may be that I've seen too many movies.

He was out of control, all right, the girl said. I believe that I've misjudged you. I believe you're something of a smartass after all.

I just never can learn when to keep my mouth shut, he said.

I'm sorry about your tooth, I swear. But I never expected you to set him off like that.

He smiled a rueful smile. He was picking shards of broken glass out of his knuckles. He's going to have a mighty sore pair of sunglasses in the morning, he said.

They left the street under the girl's lead and ascended a slope to its smoothly mown summit where trees stood about as if landscaped and benches were aligned under their branches. He saw that they were overlooking the river where it passed thirty or forty feet below them. Lights were mounted here on poles and where the light pooled below the bluff the river was a swirling lurid yellow but this tended away toward the enormity of its width and there was not the slightest rumor of a farther shore, as if this was land's end, they stood with the earth at their backs and all there was left of the world was water.

Let me see your face, she said.

I'll show you mine if you'll show me yours.

She wiped his bloody face with the hem of her dress. He glimpsed the smooth brown expanse of her legs when she raised it but she saw the cast of his eyes and turned his face gently away and examined it critically. She raised the dress again and moistened a folded corner of the hem with her tongue and gently scrubbed the blood off his burst lip and the corners of his mouth. She grimaced. This is going to be a swollen-up mess in the morning, she said. You won't be so pretty then.

I wasn't much for pretty anyway.

They sat on a bench beneath an enormous maple. Well, she said. Do you suppose Junior and Mama are done yet?

He turned to look at her sharply. What? he asked.

He may be, what is that song they used to play on WLAC, a sixty-minute man. Do you think he's a sixty-minute man?

What I really think is that you're mighty blasé about all this, he finally said.

Her eyes widened slightly. Blasé? What kind of word is that? What does it mean?

I just read it somewhere and always wanted to use it in a sentence, he said. I never heard anybody say it. I guess it means that you don't seem to take what she's doing, what they're doing, very seriously. It's almost like you think it's funny.

She looked away, across the river into the darkness. I doubt if it's been thirty minutes since I warned you about getting me and Mama confused, she said. If we're going to be friends, if we're going to be anything at all to each other, you've got to get that straight. I'm just me, and I'm not taking responsibility for what anyone else in this round world does.

All right, he said. I'm sorry. It seems I'm a dumbass instead of a smartass.

They fell silent. The bench was cool and damp against the back of Fleming's neck. He closed his eyes. His tongue prodded the hole where lately his tooth had been. He wondered what time it was. It occurred to him that he was over forty miles from home, that Albright had already been drunk and would almost certainly be drunker, and that the road back to Ackerman's Field from Clifton held hairpin curves and switchbacks beyond his power to number. After a while the girl settled her head against his shoulder. He sat without moving for a long time. Scarcely breathing. It seemed to him that the universe had tilted slightly on its axis and come to rest against him and that the barely perceptible weight on his left shoulder was the only thing that kept the stars spinning on their mitered courses.

He opened his eyes. Fireflies had come out over the river, thousands of them, more. They seemed to have appeared inexplicably and simultaneously, so many of them that he could see the dark water moving below them. They'd shaped themselves to the contour of the river, shifting and darting and roiling like sparks thrown upward by a river of smoldering fire. As far as the eye could see, up the river, down, like some rite of nature he'd been called forth to witness. He watched until she rose and pulled him up by a hand and led him off toward town.

Where've you been? Mrs. Halfacre asked.

We walked uptown, the girl said.

Town's closed.

It's closed but it's still there, the girl said, as if that was that.

Fleming sat in the armchair in the corner of the room. Albright and

Mrs. Halfacre were on the couch. There was nowhere else to sit and Raven Lee poured Fleming half a glass of wine and gave it to him and settled herself on the arm of his chair.

Mrs. Halfacre seemed to have lost all the playful friendliness she'd exhibited earlier. She looked drunk, not like a raucous drunk or a happy-go-lucky drunk but a mean drunk, a drunk who is looking for trouble and knowing just where it's hidden. Every time Fleming glanced up she'd be watching him. Mean little eyes in the thickening flesh of her face.

What's happened to him? she finally asked.

He kept falling down, Raven Lee said. He's about the clumsiest boy I ever came across.

Albright bore evidence of what Fleming had feared. He seemed to be profoundly drunk. He'd spilled wine all down his front and he was holding a guitar in his lap like something he'd found somewhere and couldn't fathom the use of. He sat watching the tall radio cabinet with a fixed intensity as if he saw through the speaker cloth to where wires and condensers and tubes magically reconstructed images of folk picking guitars, sawing on fiddles, hawking barn paint.

I guess you know you've got blood all over the tail of that dress, Mrs. Halfacre said. It won't come out. I reckon you think dresses like that are just give away.

The girl didn't even reply.

Fleming was looking at Albright with a wary disgust, already dreading the long ride home. Something had changed during his absence, the very atmosphere had altered. Perhaps some shift in the magnetic field. Perhaps she'd asked Albright for more money, the twenty Fleming had given him was all he had. Spending the night here no longer seemed an option to be considered.

You know who he is, don't you? the woman suddenly asked.

A curl like a comma, like a question mark, had fallen over Raven Lee's eyes. She raked it away with a hand. Of course I know who he is.

He's a Bloodworth and I won't have one in the house after the way that cousin of his done.

What's this about? Fleming asked.

Never you mind what it's about, Mrs. Halfacre said.

Don't pay her any mind, the girl said. She's drunk.

Fleming laid a hand gently on the girl's back. He could feel the bone knobs of her vertebrae through the thin cloth of her dress. Then he dropped the hand and set the wine down and arose.

It's time to go, he said.

Albright turned. He laid the guitar in Mrs. Halfacre's lap. She jerked it up and tossed it into a corner. What? Albright asked.

It's time to go.

It's early yet.

It's time to go.

They went out into the yard. Moonlight through the branches made the yard black and silver, light and shadow, the clotted ivy was black as jet.

You're drunk as a dog, Fleming said. Drunker than a dog. You'll kill us both before we get to the city limits. I'd better drive and I don't trust my driving much more than I do yours.

I can drive, Albright said. He clasped Fleming's shoulder. I can drive better dog drunk than you can cold sober. Better asleep than you can awake. Trust me.

Raven Lee had followed them out. You better make him drive slow, she said.

Make him? You can't make him anything. That's like making the sun wait up because you need a few more minutes of daylight.

Albright was already in the car. The engine cranked, set idling. Albright was mopping condensation off the inside of the windshield with a wadded shirt.

Well, Raven Lee said. It was certainly interesting drinking a Coke with you. Thanks for the magazine. Do you reckon you'll ever make it back down here?

I was just going to ask you about that. How about going to the show with me next weekend?

She nodded her head toward the house. You heard her opinion of Bloodworths.

I also heard you say you don't tell her how to live her life and she don't tell you how to live yours.

Well. She smiled. I guess you've got me there. You could try and see. It's a long way down here just to try and see.

Don't you think I'm worth it?

Yes. I know you're worth it. I'll try and see.

Have you got a car?

Of course I've got a car, he said, wondering where he'd get one. But such minor details could be worked out later.

She suddenly placed both hands on his forearm as if she'd use it for leverage to raise herself higher and tiptoed and kissed him on the mouth. He turned to hold her but she'd pulled away and she was already going up the walk toward the house.

A mile or so out of Clifton Albright pulled onto the shoulder of the road. Maybe you'd better do this, he said. The road keeps fadin in and out like. I don't know what's the matter with it.

Fleming got out and came around and slid under the wheel. Albright had scooted over and was resting his face against the glass.

I might as well, Fleming said. If I'm goin to get killed I may as well have some control over it.

What would it matter if you got killed, Albright said. You was kissed on the mouth by Raven Lee Halfacre. What in the world did you do to her to make her do that?

Fleming didn't reply. After a while he looked over and Albright was asleep with his head against the window. He drove on. The thought of her hands on his forearm as she'd tiptoed to kiss his mouth lessened the ache in his thigh, straightened the curves in the road toward Ackerman's Field. The weight of her head on his shoulder as he watched the fireflies.

There was something oddly restful about the fireflies. He couldn't put his finger on it but he drew comfort from it anyway. The way they'd seemed not separate entities but a single being, a moving river of light that flowed above the dark water like its negative image and attained a transient and fragile dominion over the provinces of night.

BOOK THREE

I N DETROIT Boyd had worked for a time in a steel mill, stoking furnaces in an atmosphere so charged with fire and noise and molten metal he seemed constantly to toil in the eye of an electrical storm, a place if not hell then certainly the room across the hall from it, a foundry that he felt might be more aptly occupied by scaleyskinned demons or other of the devil's toadies. Then he got a job in a factory loading huge rolls of corrugated cardboard onto a machine that sucked the cardboard off the roll into itself and spat it out in cardboard boxes.

He was a man much to himself. He asked no questions, and in turn was asked few himself. He seemed to be descending into a well of silence so deep the hammering of machinery was as impotent to defray it as the discordant jangling jukeboxes that furnished the hillbilly bars he haunted at night. He'd eat his meager supper and bathe and put on clean clothes that were just like the clothes he'd taken off except laundered and go into the nighttime bars where other hillbillies crossed and re-crossed in tangents of random violence as if they were all looking for something they'd lost.

These folk from Arkansas, Tennessee, Missouri did not seem to melt into the common culture of the city. They seemed to have changed only in the matter of geography. They were who they were. Drop them into a beaker of acid and they would list down and rest unchanged on the bottom, unassimilated, unrepentant, unreconstructed. All these folk seemed to have more past than future and it was a common past of failure and loss and they seemed to recognize each other on sight as Masons were told to do.

So he never doubted that he would find them. The peddler was much given to drink and Boyd had only to haunt the bars in the hillbilly section of Detroit. Trash always settles to the bottom, he had told himself, drifting downward himself. The wonder was not that he found them, but that it took so long. They must have been moving through the gaudy neon half a beat out of sync, coming when he was going, arriving when he'd just left.

He saw them once crossing the street where Delancey intersected 114th. He saw them first from the back, but he knew them instantly, as if something had been encoded into him so that he would have known them from the ghost of a reflected gesture, from a scuffmark on the sidewalk. Boyd's wife had said something and the man had turned to hear. Something grinning and obsequious in his manner gave Boyd a moment of unease, perhaps he was killing the wrong half of this couple. The peddler seemed deferential and indecisive. Yet something ran through Boyd tangible as a seismic tremor, he felt an actual altering of his heartbeat, a change in the speed of the blood coursing through his body.

He was stopped from killing the peddler not by any compunction at violence or even by the fear of getting caught in so public a place under the eyes of scores of witnesses but by the sheer and abrupt realization that it would be the end of something. It was less a jumping off place than a denouement. He had not thought beyond it. He did not know what came next. He was at the point on an ancient map beyond which the old cartographers had drawn dragons.

He went back to his room at the boarding house and lay on his bed atop the covers with all his clothes on. He lay on the sweaty sheets with arms outflung in an attitude of crucifixion. He looked like a man who had fallen from an enormous height. There was a ceiling fan turning above him and he lay watching light play on the revolving blade. His life had honed itself down to a finite number of revolutions of a metal blade through dead air.

They came into a bar on Twenty-sixth Street. He watched them cross the room to a table near the back. The man came to the bar to order drinks. He stood at Boyd's elbow unbeknownst as he did it. Like a man asking the Reaper if the seat next to him was taken. He ordered Boyd's wife a whiskey sour. She used to be down on drinking but he guessed not so much anymore. He pondered how all good resolve is sanded away by the attrition of time and circumstance. The man paid for the drinks and left the bar. Boyd finished his bourbon and water and set the glass back. He ordered another. He drank it slowly, tasting the smooth whiskey on the back of his tongue. When he set the glass back empty he raked his change off the bar and pocketed it.

He was halfway across the room when the woman saw him. She sprang up, her chair fell behind her unnoticed. She had the peddler by the arm saying something harsh and peremptory to him. Instead of running the peddler jerked up the woman's purse, and for a surreal instant Boyd thought that was funny; grabbing up a purse ought to be the last thing you'd do when someone was bearing down upon you with a hawkbill knife. But the man had opened the purse and was dumping its contents on the table. Coins went cartwheeling, lipsticks and bottles rolled off the table. A small chromeplated automatic pistol tilted onto the black Formica.

When the woman slapped the pistol away there was a moment when things could have gone either way. But Boyd was upon him now, there had been too many nights of absolute solitude, things had just gone too far, too far. The knife sank itself so deeply into the peddler's viscera he thought his fist would go too, he jerked the knife upward with such force it wedged itself in the breastbone.

He rocked the knife free and turned and fled in what appeared one smooth motion, a movement so graceful it might have been rehearsed, choreographed. He came out on the street and then into it a dead run, horns blowing and tires squalling and then he was crossing on the hoods and trunks of automobiles, leaping from one to the other, the outraged faces behind the windshields like the appalled faces beyond footlights of a stage where a play has gone horribly wrong.

He leapt onto the sidewalk still holding the knife and without slackening his speed. He went down a narrow alley between buildings that rose on either side like the limestone bluffs rising from the banks of Grinders Creek where he'd been raised, and the concrete he ran full tilt on, arms pumping, seemed to be a creekbed. He dreamed a fan of water that rose before him, that diminished behind his churning feet. He could see light at the canyon's mouth, pale green diffused light like a May sun in willows, and he ran on toward it.

ON AN EARLY Sunday morning Fleming left the street and went up a driveway toward a white stucco house set back in a grove of pecan trees. The house was flatroofed and low and the windows had ornate shutters of wrought iron painted black that made the windows look barred when they were closed. He went up wide concrete steps to a patio where from a chaise lounge a great marmalade cat lying in an oblique square of yellow sunlight watched him with disinterested and insolent eyes.

He opened a storm door constructed of the same iron as the shutters and knocked on a dark wooden door. After a while it opened and an old man stood regarding him with a friendly quizzical expression. He came onto the patio and closed the door behind him.

Could I help you this morning, young man?

I'm Fleming Bloodworth, Mr. Marbet.

Ah. Boyd's son.

Yes sir. We live down on the creek on that place you own.

Marbet took off his glasses and began wiping the lenses on a handkerchief he took from his jacket pocket. He seemed dressed for church. His cheeks were ruddy and shiny from being freshly shaven and he was wearing a white shirt and a necktie. The tie was maroon silk figured with tiny regal lions rampant across it.

How is Boyd getting along these days?

I don't really know. He's up north, working up there making cars or something.

Well. It's a shame when a man has to leave his home to find a way of making a living. Is there something I could do for you? Would you come in and have a cup of coffee with us?

No, thank you. I just wanted to ask you something. I was back toward the river the other day talking to a man cutting timber and he was telling me something about the TVA planning to build a lake back in there.

Oh yes. They plan to build a dam on the river, they tell me for flood control. It's going to be a huge lake, enormous. Most everything not underwater they'll use for a recreation area. Camping, and so forth.

Will it affect your property down there?

It's not going to be my property much longer, Marbet said wryly. As soon as we come to terms it'll all belong to the TVA. No papers have been signed, but it's just a matter of time. The way it was put to me, it's not something I have a choice in. Not my decision at all. If I don't sell they'll just pay me what they consider a fair market price and take it.

Can they do that?

Oh yes. Certainly. They've done it a lot in the past, and I expect they'll do it a lot more in the future.

Where does it come to?

Where does what come to?

The land they're taking, or buying up. My grandmother lives back across the ridge there and I was wondering if she would be affected.

Oh, I know that place well. No. It's a long way back through those woods. As I understand it, the TVA line will be on my property somewhere about that old crossroads. Do you know that place?

Yes.

I should have driven down there and had a talk with you, but to tell the truth I had forgotten about that house even being there. I never charged Boyd any rent, in all honesty I never considered that house worth renting. I have so much to look after, and that place just slipped my mind.

Well. I guess I'll get on, then.

You've probably got a few months, but I'd certainly be making other arrangements. That's all going to be underwater. If you need a place to live come see me. I've got a farm down there on Cane Creek I could use another cropper on. There's an empty tenant house on it, and we'll find something for you to do.

Well, I'll think about it.

You're well spoken and you look as if you'd make me a good man. Don't think too long, I've got people asking about houses all the time.

All right, Fleming said. He turned to go.

We'd be glad to have you out at the church this morning, Marbet called.

Fleming raised a hand and went on.

THE DOG DAY HEAT held into the tag end of August, and there were days when they'd just head out in the communal taxicab with no destination in mind save sufficient speed to engender a breeze through the rolled-down windows. Albright and Fleming would pick up the old man at the trailer, Bloodworth coming out wildeyed with the heat and fanning himself with the Stetson, reeling on his stiff leg like some casualty of the malevolent heat itself, a celluloid man left in the heat too long.

They might sit in the shade of itchy Mama's front porch with others like them but not quite, old men who treated Bloodworth with the sort of deference they might accord exiled royalty or a man living under the edict of death. The old man holding one warming beer for hours and listening to the tales the old men told, telling some himself. Fleming and Albright sitting among these garrulous old sots like acolytes or apprentices, as if they were picking up the fine points of being old.

You need to let your chauffeur there take you deer huntin, E.F., Cater Hensley said.

Who's that, young Albright here?

When they first started bringin deer into this part of the country Junior took it into his head he had to kill him one.

Hellfire, Albright said. I've heard this till I'm sick of it.

He just lived in the woods there for a while, Hensley went on. But he never did come up on one. Then he was drivin up Riverside one day and there was a eight-point buck standin right in a fencerow. Junior got his rifle out and took a rest on the trunk and cut down on it. It never so much as blinked. He shot again. It didn't even look around. Junior couldn't figure how in the world he'd missed it. Clyde Tennison was with him and Clyde said it looked for all the world like that deer had heard how bad Junior wanted to kill one and was offerin itself up for a sacrifice. Clyde had done seen what it was but he said Junior shot up a whole box of 30-30 cartridges and that deer just wouldn't fall. Junior kept sayin his sights was off. Shot off one of its horns and it never moved a muscle. Finally they walked out there to the fencerow and somebody had skinned one out for the meat and hung the head and hide over that fence. Clyde said that hide looked like it had been stood up before a firin squad.

Clyde Tennison is as black a liar as ever drawed a breath, Albright said. I never shot up nowhere near a whole box of shells. It could of happened to anybody.

It could happen to anybody one or two times, Hensley said. How many shells is in a box, twenty? It could only happen twenty times to you.

He killed two concrete deer off old Judge Humphreys's front yard, old man Breece said. Humphreys shoveled them deer up and rolled em off in a wheelbarrow.

Or they'd late in the day head out in the cooling air for a breath of the river, sit hours on the high gallery of Goblin's Knob where you could look out across the river and mingle with the revenants of men who'd been knifed there or shot or simply clubbed to death with the hickory truncheons the men of Beech Creek were told to carry. A place of almost mythic violence, the haunt of men so confident in their ability to push things past their limits they could empty a lesser bar by coming through the door and sizing up the clientele. Men who killed each other over being called a son of a bitch with the inflection of the voice a shade wrong or over looking at the wrong woman the wrong way.

Men who would for a kind of twisted honor kill each other over a woman who did not care which lived and which died and would before the matter was settled have taken up with another man altogether.

To Fleming's bemusement Bloodworth and Sharp and the other old men remembered all this with something like nostalgia, as if this violent history was something you'd save bloody mementos from and place between the pages of a Bible like faded flowers. The old man himself, Sharp said, able and better to hold his own. When he was in his prime, Sharp said, the old man used to sweep the place out on Saturday nights like a longhandled broom.

You ever tell your runnin mates there about that shootout you had with the deputies?

The old man gave Sharp an almost imperceptible shake of the head. Sharp hushed. Bloodworth sat watching bubbles rise in the glass of beer on the table before him. Some things is better in the ground with the dirt throwed over them, he said.

Like deputies that use your wife for a shield and cut down on you with a .44 Special, Sharp grinned.

The old Dodge had idiosyncrasies peculiar to it and was subject to innumerable malfunctions and you might see it halted on the shoulder of the road with the hood raised, Albright blowing trash out of a fuel line or cleaning the points with a piece of sandpaper, Fleming looking on and the old man ensconced in the back seat, fanning himself and waiting with the ingrained patience of the old.

They might have been on their way back to Itchy Mama's, and they might make it yet, where some nights they had vicious cutthroat games of Rook where millions of conjectural dollars rode on the fall of a single card, Itchy Mama and the old man teamed against Fleming and Albright, Itchy Mama watching Albright's dealing with a hawklike intensity and describing the serious bodily damage that would ensure if she caught him palming the Rook or red one.

In these early days with the old man it seemed to Fleming that he was already changing, though he had never known his grandfather before and could not have said what he was changing from: from the protagonist of other men's stories, perhaps, for he no longer looked like a man given to gunfights with deputies, this benign old man watching whatever moved with his wry ironic eyes did not seem the type to clean out Saturday night honkytonks, to be waylaid on Indian Creek by men who rose out of the sage like sepia men of another century who sighted down the barrels of their rifles and blew him off the wagonseat into the bloody weeds.

Even when he'd arrived he'd had restless eyes, eyes that were always looking about as if he might notice some place he'd rather be and head out for it immediately. Fleming had heard him tell Albright once that he had come back to make peace with his family. But as far as Fleming knew he had made peace with nobody. After a while it occurred to him that without even knowing it the old man was making peace with himself, and that that had probably been a good part of the trouble all along.

THE OLD MAN rolled six lemons on the countertop until they were soft and full of juice. The hot air in the tiny trailer took on their astringent, citrusy smell. He cut the ends off them one by one and one by one squeezed them into a widemouth glass jug and sliced them into chunks with his pocketknife and dropped them in as well. He poured in sugar gauging the amount with an eye instead of a measuring cup and added water from the tap.

Chunk us off some of that ice, he said.

The refrigerator had refused to freeze more ice and Albright had brought out a fifty-pound block the day before from the ice plant. What remained the old man had wrapped in a quilt and stored beneath the sink. Fleming unwrapped it and with a clawhammer knocked off several fistsize chunks. He handed them to the old man. Bloodworth folded one of them into a clean towel and pounded it with the clawhammer and dumped the shaved ice into a snuffglass. He took down from a doorless cabinet a bottle of Early Times and poured an inch or two over the ice.

He held the tumbler to the sunwashed window and then held it to his face and breathed in deeply. Early Times, he said. I always liked the name better than the whiskey. Early Times are the best times there is.

I believe we'll drink these in the sitting room, he said, filling a glass with lemonade and reaching it to the boy. I believe I can smell my hair starting to singe.

He had supervised construction of this sitting room himself. What it consisted of was a clearing perhaps twenty feet by twenty feet hacked out of the undergrowth behind the trailer. Junior Albright and Fleming with briarblades and brushhooks and axes had cleared the smaller saplings and honeysuckle vines and brush then raked the earth clean as if swept with a broom. Above them a tangle of summer leaves and grape and muscadine vines interlaced so tightly they formed a virtual ceiling, so that the sitting room was always in shade save the early morning hours and just before dusk. The old man had bought three lawn chairs and he and Fleming and Albright would sit about the glade at their leisure as if they were quality folk taking the air from the balcony of a columned mansion.

This place is all right with me, Bloodworth said. I could live in a brush arbor. I could live in a groundhog den.

The old man did not actually drink the whiskey anymore. He had a bad stomach and a bad liver even aside from the stroke and he'd sit hourlong with a glass of bourbon in his hand as if he were absorbing it into his blood by osmosis. He'd occasionally take a birdlike sip or wet his lips with it, sometimes he'd raise the glass and just smell, taking in the odor of icy whiskey and mint like a connoisseur of fine wine inhaling the bouquet from a crystal goblet.

I've drunk good whiskey and I've drunk bad, the old man told Fleming. I've drunk whiskey so good you could smell the leaves in the woods where it was made and I've drunk it so bad you could strip the paint off a barn door with it. I'm inclined to believe it was the paintstrippin kind that left my stomach in the shape it's in.

The boy tilted back in the lawnchair and drank down half the glass of lemonade. It was so cold it made his throat ache, strong with the sour taste of lemons, sweet with the sugar the old man had dumped in. The old man always used too much of everything, too many lemons, too much sugar, as if halfmeasures at anything were beneath him. He tipped too high in restaurants, exhorted Albright to drive faster, was wide awake and ready to roll in the small hours of the morning when Fleming and Albright folded on him.

Fleming was finding E. F. Bloodworth strange past any expectation of him. Much accustomed to only the company of himself the old man might complacently sit half a day without saying a word. Or he might, under the boy's gentle prodding, begin to talk, telling little by little sections of his life. At some point it began to seem like a story telling itself, and finally a narrative the old man was telling for his own benefit. As if he'd make some order out of these chunks of personal history, some sense. Like shifting about the pieces of a puzzle on a table until the edges dovetail.

Studying him where he sat Fleming tried to match the old man to the photograph he'd found in his grandmother's picture box. No pictures of him hung on the walls of the house. Fleming had seen family portraits with the old man neatly scissored out and only the blank man-shaped space he'd occupied remaining, as if the old man had been there a moment ago and you'd looked away then back and he'd vanished. Vanished so thoroughly all you could see of him was the newsprint or fabric you were holding the picture against. The air itself. Now you see me, now you don't, the old man seemed to say. Wink and I'm gone, cross me or badger me and I'm down the line.

This photograph had somehow escaped, and Fleming suspected the old woman had hidden it away. It was perhaps four inches by six, darkened to varying stages of sepia, from the palest beige to a brown almost darkened to umber. It had a thick crumbly texture as if it had been fired in a kiln. A man stood before a board wall. Rough sawmill planks, you could see the circular marks where the saw had gone, the nailheads where they'd been hammered together. The man wore what looked like part of a dark serge suit, pants that looked oversized suspendered over a collarless white shirt. The man wore a dark fedora and beneath its brim the fierce empty eyes looked out as if they were coming from a thousand miles away, and were off immediately another thousand in some other direction. The eyes were just dark holes, he'd thought as a child if you canted the photograph to the light he could have seen through them like pinpricks charred through the cardboard.

He held a banjo that was slung by a strap across his shoulders, and the banjo was what the photograph was about. I'm not so much, the re- served young man in the photograph seemed to be saying. But look what I've got here. The left hand formed a chord on the neck, the right loosely clasped the head of the banjo, as if he were proffering it slightly for the camera's inspection. The face was intense and slightly ill at ease, as if the young man was on his way elsewhere and only had a moment to pose for this picture.

Music had been his undoing, he told the boy in an ironic self-deprecation. His bane and his salvation. It had gotten him through times that would have otherwise been unbearable and it had made everything else he had gone at twice as hard.

A cold glass of lemonade in his hand, the air full of the winey ferment from the curing vegetation they had cut, Fleming began to learn something of the old man's life.

When he had gone courting Julia Bradshaw he had managed to have six hundred dollars that he carried folded in the pocket of his pants. Six hundred dollars at that time and place was an enormous amount of money. It had taken a long time and a lot of work and stinting to save it. He had a place lined up to crop. He had a wagon and a team of horses. He had a house spoken for should the need arise. Julia's father did not care for him and he knew better than to go courting a girl as pretty as Julia with no prospects.

Saul Bradshaw liked him no better with six hundred dollars in his pocket than he had liked him when Bloodworth was a penniless banjo picker uncasing his instrument at any gathering he heard rumored.

E. F. Bloodworth was a layabout, a drunkard, a seducer of innocent young women and a patron of whores. When Bradshaw looked into his eyes all he saw was horizons receding fold on fold until the last one faded into a transparency of the palest blue. He will not stay put, he told Julia.

Julia Bradshaw was part Cherokee Indian. She was small and dark and the inscrutability of her eyes hinted at enigmas a man might unravel would he take the time to try. Bloodworth was to learn that it is the nature of an enigma to remain unsolved, and that inscrutability means just what it says.

It had come down finally to a choice between Bloodworth and her father and she hesitated only a moment before she climbed onto the wagonseat with Bloodworth. Another man might have noted only that she chose the wagon, which was already turned in the yard and pointed outward bound but Bloodworth saw the hesitation. He saw it as a lack of commitment, and while realizing how absurd this was, nevertheless wore it the rest of his life like a scar.

What he told Fleming was a shorthand version and there were things he kept to himself not because they painted a picture or told a story he did not want told but because they were things he could not articulate.

He could tell Fleming he was a musician but he could not communicate what the music said to him or said to the people he played it for. The music told itself, it made some obscure connection for which there were no words. The music was its own story, but a man could dip into the vast reservoir of folk and blues lines and phrases and images and construct his own story: though upon performing it and without it losing any relevance to his own life it now belonged to the audience as well. It was something he could not fathom. The old songs with juryrigged verses like bodies cobbled up out of bones from a thousand skeletons. Songs about death and lost love and rambling down the line because sometimes down the line was the only place left. Songs that treated the most desperate of loss with a dark sardonic humor. *I'm goin where the climate suits my clothes,* the song said, not saying the frustration and despair that created it, saying that in the sheer lonesomeness of the sound, in the old man's driving banjo. There was an eerie timelessness about it that said it could have been written a thousand years ago, or it could have been an unfinished song about events that had not yet played themselves out.

So quick it would jerk your breath away I went from bein a man with six hundred dollars in his pocket to a man twelve hundred dollars in debt, the old man said. You couldn't see over the top of twelve hundred dollars, it was just too big. Julia had a bad sickness and before I knowed it I owed what was then a small fortune to doctors and hospitals. A man might make two or three hundred dollars cash money a year sharecroppin. I said hundred, and I said year.

Then I had a fallin out with the landlord and he took the crop. Lookin back on it I can see it was as much my fault as it was his. I was always quick to get mad and slow to get over it. The way I saw it he cheated me, not just me but everybody that scooted a chair up to my table. I beat hell out of him, and there we went with all our plunder roped to the wagon. Winter not too far off. Not just one winter to get through, I could see that, but a long line of winters. One winter after another. I went to makin whiskey. Julia thought banjo playin was the road to hell but with whiskey makin she figured I was off the back roads and on the blacktop highway.

He fitted shells into the cylinder of the gun watching through moted glass Bradshaw sitting the wagon seat erect and proud as a deacon sitting a church pew. Look at the old son of a bitch, he thought, spinning the cylinder as smoothly as a barrel whirling in water. Let's see if he sets that straight when I clip his spine, let's see if he keeps that head cocked to hear whatever it is Jesus is whisperin in his ear.

He's here because I sent for him, Julia said.

I don't know why anybody would send for a dead man, he told her.

He had to fight her and he had to do it without hurting her. He could have killed Bradshaws, fathers and brothers, all day long like ducks popping up in a shooting gallery but he could not hurt her. He held her finally back to his chest and the soapy smell of her hair in his face and clamped in arms that would not constrain her urgency.

If you do you'll have to kill me too, she finally said, and he knew that she was telling him the truth.

Did I ever hurt you? he asked.

You hurt me ever breath I draw, she told him.

He laid the pistol aside and watched the door close behind her and watched her climb aboard the wagon and watched the old man speak not to her but to the mules, popping the lines and turning the wagon into the dusty roadbed, watched the wagon diminish into the white dust until there was nothing to see but dust settling, and watching even that.

You hurt me ever breath I draw.

The house was so silent it gave off a faint humming, like a banjo string turned relentlessly toward the breaking point. Madness and self-loathing hung over him like a plague, violence moved in him like another sinister self moving *under his skin, trying to adjust itself to the shape of Bloodworth's body or adjust the body to itself.*

All right, he thought, if they can't quit tolling her off I will kill them all. If she can't quit going when they toll her I'll kill her too. I'll stretch out Bradshaws till they hold each other up like trees felled in a thick woods, Bradshaws hung up in each other's tops. They ain't quit makin shells. They ain't quit makin caskets. I'll stretch out Bradshaws from the biggest to the least, till they have to import caskets out of other states, till they run dry on that and bury them without caskets, till they finally throw up their hands and let em lay where they fall.

When did you quit?

What? Quit what?

Quit making whiskey.

Oh Lord, I never quit. Well, I guess I've quit now. I quit a thousand times. I'd quit when anything else come along. One time I got a shot at makin some records. Another time I'd make a cotton crop and do all right with that. A few times I got caught. You'll damn sure quit when they send you to the penitentiary. A few times I quit to get Julia to come back.

When she left word at the store for him to come get her he rode there with a pistol shoved down in the waistband of his trousers and the grip and hammer exposed and handy. The Bradshaws had told around what they were going to do to him. Shoot him and let him lay where he fell, just a windfall for the undertaker.

The house lay like a house in a dream, empty and silent, utterly devoid of motion. Not even light moved on the windowpanes. A hawk hung in the cloudless blue like a hawk frozen forever by the eye of a camera.

He waited. When the door opened inward he could feel the checks on the pistol grip against his palm. It was her. No one else showed a face, no hand drew back a curtain. Lifting her onto the wagon seat she had seemed weightless, he could have set her down on the moon just as easy.

She saw the pistol stuck in the waist of his pants. You never needed that, she said.

I had it if I did, he told her.

You started in again when you got out of the pen? Fleming asked.

I always started in again, the old man said. You couldn't tell me anything. Couldn't beat sense into me with a log chain. I was shot at more than I was hit, I guess that made me think I was ahead of the game. I couldn't run off a few gallons like everybody else. I had to make more of it, sell it over a wider territory. It had to be the best, I had to make good whiskey. Once they laid for me on Indian Creek, hid out in the bushes. Never showed theirselves, or anyway not where I could see them. Just shot through the weeds and brush. The air was full of little chopped-up green weeds. Killed both my horses and shot me four times and left me for dead. Shot me clean off the wagon. I was layin there and I was half in and half out and I could hear the glass jars rattlin when they unloaded my wagon. I could smell their horses, and I was layin in bitterweed, I could smell that, I just couldn't open my eyes. I thought I was dead.

It was awkward for the old man to chord a banjo anymore but he'd tune an old Martin double-F guitar into an open E and fret it with a pocket knife, the guitar laying across his lap, the music he made was strange and marvelous and so fragile Fleming would fall silent so the spell would hold.

Here, the old man would say, handing him the glass of whiskey, drink this before I forget and drink it myself. Get something on your stomach before that lemonade makes you sick.

The guitar would be the lonesome wail of a lost train climbing through Georgia pinewoods. Fleming could see the raw earth red as a wound through the trees, see the boxcars flickering in and out of sight. *The longest train that ever I saw,* the old man sang, *went down that Georgia line . . .* Or, *Clouded up and lookin like rain, round the curve come a passenger train . . .*

Fleming would take tiny sips of the whiskey and let it dilute in his mouth while the guitar faded the old man out, took him down that long lonesome road, to where the climate suited his clothes, to where the water tasted like cherry wine.

ALBRIGHT ORDERED a Falstaff and rang his thirty cents down on the countertop. He was sprinkling salt onto the top of the can when he noticed three highbinders downbar huddled over a newspaper they'd unfolded on the countertop. He drank deeply from the can then rose with it and walked past the jukebox to see what was so interesting in the paper. When I'm drinking, I'm nobody's friend, Webb Pierce sang from the jukebox.

What's the big news? he asked, leaning down in the poor light to read for himself, but already seeing it all. LOCAL BUSINESSMAN KILLED IN PRIVATE PLANE CRASH, the black headlines read.

Woodall run over a mountain, one of the men said with some satisfaction. I reckon the son of a bitch thought Sand Mountain would just duck its head and let him go by.

I heard there wasn't a piece of that plane you couldn't have toted off in a shoe box, another said.

He felt lightheaded, his body went weightless, he had to grasp the bar to keep from floating off. Son of a bitch, he said.

He was that, the men agreed.

Albright was halfway down the street before he realized he was still holding the beer. He drank it off and tossed the can into the street without even looking around for the law. Somehow being a coldblooded murderer put the open container law into a different perspective.

He'd walked past his car without seeing it and he had to retrace his steps. He got in and sat behind the wheel. Traffic passed in the street without his hearing it. Dimly he realized that he was free, Woodall would never again knock on his door, he would never swear out another paper. But the ramifications of what he had done were enormous. That Goddamned Bloodworth, he said aloud. He had killed a man as surely as if he had held a pistol against his head and discharged it.

He leaned his head onto the steering wheel. He could feel the hot plastic against his face. He felt like weeping.

GENE WOODALL HAD BEEN on his way to Valdosta, Georgia, to look over a potential job and prepare a bid on it. He was somewhere over the mountains on the Tennessee-Georgia line when the engine sputtered the first time. A palpable shock of anger ran through him and he thought, Oh, that son of a bitching mechanic is going to hear from me.

He was flying alone but not really alone, because for the last hundred miles he had been thinking of his new girlfriend, Carolyn Spiess, so intently that she was almost a tangible presence in the cockpit. He had only just met Carolyn, but he had big plans for her. She was twenty years younger than his wife, and at least that many times as pretty and when she had opened her mouth under his before he boarded the plane she tasted like Juicy Fruit gum.

He'd lost a little altitude and he adjusted the throttle and tilted the yoke to climb and the pitch of the engine increased and smoothed out momentarily then began to sputter. It misfired, hard, caught again, and when it misfired this time the engine seized.

Almighty God, Woodall said. He began to struggle impotently with the instruments and then ceased, drifting in an eerie silence save the rushing of the wind.

He thought of Carolyn. Within hours she would be on her way to the Maury County airport to meet him. There would be a bag in the floorboard containing two bottles of wine. They would spend the night in the Dixieland Motel and the thought of his frogfaced wife would be far away.

Below he could see moonlight on the rocks, the fleeing shadows of clouds tracking darkly across the pale limestone, the strewn lights of a mountain town like spilled jewelry. The wall of the mountain rising to meet him looked as pale and smooth as a granite headstone.

The plane was spinning now like a carousel that had slipped its moorings and it went through the tops of the firs and cedars like a mowing machine, the air full of chopped greenery and the smell of the pines. He thought very hard of Carolyn, her sharp insistent tongue, the way she'd opened her thighs as she kissed him, the feel of her sharp pelvic bone against the fleshy heel of his hand. The tail section struck first and sheared away and the white stone rising to meet the fuselage looked like something surfacing with dread inevitability from calm clear water and he flung an arm across his eyes.

When the plane exploded fire went streaking down the wall of night like trails of phosphorous from a firework of unreckonable magnitude and cascaded away in a shower of falling stars, touching the velvet balsams with a profound and eerie beauty.

IT HAD NOT rained for some time and the road lay thick with a dust pale and fine as talcum. It rose light as smoke with the old man's footfalls and hung suspended and weightless in the air, whitened the cuffs of his trousers and pressed itself covertly into their folds and into the webbing of his shoelaces. It was early but already hot. The sun lay over the eastern horizon and burned its way toward him through the trees with a bluegold light. When he crossed from the road into the edge of the fallow field the earth beneath the trees where the wild oats did not grow was pale and baked hard as clay from a kiln, faulted with cracks and crosshatched lines like defects in the surface structure of the earth itself.

Forty years ago he had set out a row of cedars that extended for over a quarter of a mile, that ran from the road he'd just left and crossed the wide field to the fencerow that had enclosed his garden. He thought for an amused moment that if he was ever remembered for anything it would likely be the cedar row. His wife had finally had enough of his sinful ways and doings and his sons' lives had followed strange and destructive bents but the cedar row was as straight as if they'd been set to a staked line, and he stood for a moment leaned on the stick and staring down the row cedar on cedar until they diminished before the house he'd built, bluelooking and cool in the deep morning shade of the woods.

He heard a screen door slap to, though he could see no one, and the sound seemed to have a curious quality of timelessness about it, something that had happened years ago with the sound just now reaching his ears.

If she came out, if she came out.

He stood, leaned on the stick, watching. A hawk circled the field in lowering revolutions, its feathers trembling in the sun like light flickering on water, shrill cries falling to earth bright as broken bottleglass.

He remembered the man who had come looking for Warren with such dire intent.

There was the cedar the man had been standing beneath, looking up and batting his eyes in surprise, expecting a seventeen-year-old Warren but encountering instead the old man himself, bad news that morning, hungover and violence moiling about his feet like a vicious watchdog.

He'd sent his emissary to the house and waited with his two brothers.

It's a man by the cedar row wants to see Warren, the boy said.

What's he want?

The boy looked away. He just wants to see Warren.

Well just let me get my hat, the old man said. It may be that it's me he needed to see all along.

The man stood with his cap cocked over one eye, a fistsize chew of tobacco in his jaw, a hawkbill knife printed against his leg in thin worn denim.

The man was on the ground before he could even get the knife out and after a while he forgot all about it. He might just as well have left it at the house.

Motion drew his eye back to the house. A figure crossed the porch. He was so far away he could discern little. The vague illusion of a blue dress, that was all, but what he was had been gone for fifty years, frozen in his mind as if it happened yesterday, a young woman coming onto a porch, a door slapping to behind her, a pan of dishwater slung into the yard. Just that, but the woman, who had been his wife, was so vibrant and alive that she seemed a symbol representing life itself, and the dishwater she threw glittered in the sun like quicksilver.

At length he turned back the way he'd come. Brady seemed to be avoiding him and he thought that perhaps he might catch him out around the house. But dogs had begun to bark somewhere below the house, and he wondered if maybe they'd caught his scent. The dogs he'd seen around the trailer that night had a distinctly dangerous look. Now the dogs barked on and on dementedly as if they would never shut up. The old man had never been much for barking dogs and he wondered how they stood the racket. The dogs were company, Brady had always said, but company like that he would have long ago put on the road.

He was halfway back across the field when something happened that he had never seen before or heard tell of. A rattlesnake fell out of the sky and thudded onto the path six or eight feet in front of him. This so stunned Bloodworth that he froze and just stood staring at it in a kind of slackjawed disbelief. Then finally he looked up as if to see were more on the way. A huge hawk drifted on the updrafts, the white undersides of the wings like polished chrome in the sun.

Got somethin you couldn't handle, didn't you? the old man asked, then added, or decided you didn't want no part of.

He wondered if the hawk had been snakebit but he guessed not for after a moment it began to ascend until it was just a black dot printing itself on the blue void and ultimately vanishing as if he'd just been imagining it all along.

The snake was a diamondback rattler, thick as the old man's arm. He approached it with caution, brandishing the stick like a club. The rattler was stunned but it was not dead. Its tail moved sluggishly, like a snake caught out in wintertime. He tried to count the rattles but could get no precise count. The snake was making no attempt either to escape or bite him, and he figured it was so addled it couldn't fathom where it had gotten itself to.

Damned if you won't have a story to tell the rest of them when you get home, he told it. But nobody is going to believe a word you say.

Copperbrown and black, the snake looked atavistic and evil, its ancient eyes cold and heartless as time itself. Its coils moved on themselves sluggishly, thick and heavy with poison. It seemed to be recovering itself but it still wasn't crawling away.

He leaned and placed the tip of the carved stick lightly on the rattlesnake's head, serpent to serpent. He was going to grind it into the earth then he stopped. Somehow it didn't seem fair. Something flies down and hooks its claws into your flesh and soars away with you, high into the thin blue air, the comforting earth miles away and no more than a remembered dream. Then it drops you, and you slam into the ground and you lay there with your senses knocked out. After you finally start to get at yourself, and marvel at your incredible escape, an old man limps up and shreds your head into the clay with a hickory stick.

All right, he told the snake. I'll tell you what I'm goin to do. I'm fixin to let you go. But the only people you can go into the world and bite are my enemies. Folks with guns and badges, khaki britches. Prison guards with shotguns. Lawyers, no limit on them. Maybe an undertaker or a insurance salesman every now and then. But no kids. No kids and no folks just tryin to scratch out a livin. You bite one of them, just one, and it's me and you, I'll be on your ass like a plague, I'll finish what I started.

He moved the stick. After a while the snake began to crawl slowly away. It went into the cedars, finally vanished as if it had been no more than the coppery cedar needles and a trick of the light.

The old man went on, glancing skyward every now and then. He was no believer in signs and portents, but if the Almighty was going to rain serpents on him out of a clear blue sky he figured he might as well be indoors.

WE PULLED INTO Blythesville, Arkansas, one time, Sharp told Fleming. He opened the bottle of Coca-Cola and slid it across the bar to him. We was flat broke, he went on. Not a cryin dime between us. Hadn't eat in nearly two days. We run out of gas right past the city limits sign and had to get out and roll the car out of the street.

It was on a Saturday mornin and there was a lot of folks stirrin about. People haulin cotton into town on wagons to the gin. Folks come in on Saturday to trade. Saturday was a big day back then. Saturday was what got you through the week. What do we do now? I asked E.F.

He got his banjo out of the trunk and by the time we got up to the square we had folks followin us. Kids, everybody. We looked like a parade. He had folks hollerin at him, Hey E.F, and as far as I know he'd never been in Blythesville, Arkansas, before. I played fiddle for him then, and I know I hadn't. How about a tune, E.F, they was hollerin. Play a little for us.

By then we was on the courthouse square. E.F. set his banjo down but he never took it out of the case. I'll tell you how it is, he told them. Our car's out of gas and we are too. We ain't eat since yesterday mornin. I don't mind pickin, but it's goin to cost you a little change. By then somebody was passin a bottle around and E.F. took a good horn of it. I may have too, I was bad to drink back then. I passed the hat around before E.F. ever uncased his banjo. Passed it around again while he was tunin up. It beat everything I ever saw. We'd took up over ten dollars before he ever commenced the first song. Hell, it plumb put workin in the shade. A man might make a dollar a day back then, if you could find anything to do.

By the time he was through with *Goin Down the Road Feelin Bad* he had em in his hip pocket. They would have followed him off a steep bluff, into a house on fire. The cops come and was goin to break up the crowd cause it was blocking traffic and before you know it they was just like anybody else. I seen one take a drink out of a bottle somebody handed him. Time we went down to the cafe to eat E.F. could have run for mayor and been elected hands down. They thought he ought to be on the Grand Ole Opry.

The old man drank beer and wiped the foam off his upper lip. He laughed. I did try out for the Opry one time, he said. And they was goin to hire me. But by the time they sent a man around I'd got caught makin whiskey and done been in Brushy Mountain penitentiary three months.

Bloodworth was already forty years old when he heard that a man from a New York company was auditioning performers in Knoxville. He rode there on a bus, a pint of his own whiskey in his coat pocket, the cased banjo held upright between his feet because he did not trust the bus company to keep up with it. Watching the countryside ascend into mountains he'd never seen he tried not to think of the crop that needed laying by, Julia's eyes that looked through him or around him when he came into a room. There was a hunger in him that he did not trust and could not even come close to explaining.

In Knoxville he played on streetcorners and passed his hat. It always came back with money in it. After a while he'd grow cocky and pass the hat before he'd even uncased the banjo. There would still be money in it. Even then there was something about him. He had a tale to tell. He made you believe it was your tale as well. Police came to tell him to move it along and stayed to listen. Sometimes they even dropped their own half-dollars into the hat. Bloodworth sang songs he'd heard and songs he'd stolen from other singers and songs he'd made up. He sang about death and empty beds and songs that sounded like invitations until you thought about them a while and then they began to sound like threats. Violence ran through them like heat lightning, winter winds whistled them along like paper cups turning hollowly down frozen streets.

The auditions were held in the Norton Hotel and it was full of pickers and singers from all over the south. From North Carolina, Tennessee,

Arkansas. The old man sized them up. Even with a halfpint of his own whiskey comforting him he felt intimidated. Here were folk who played and sang for a living. They had bands, they toured and played county fairs, dances, church functions. They were professionals. Bloodworth was a sharecropper, a whiskey runner, whatever fell handy. A man named A. P. Carter was there. He failed the audition. Bloodworth did not.

He rode a train to New York City and cut eight sides, four 78 rpm records. All the way to New York what he wanted to do most in the world seemed to follow above him just out of reach. I can do this or I can do that, he thought. There seemed to be no way he could do them both.

He seemed to be betting his life on the fall of the next card and even if he won he'd lose.

The record company wanted more sides cut but E.F. put them off. We'll see how these do, he said. He had the countryman's fear of being taken by these city slickers. He did not become famous but the records sold well enough so that he was asked to cut four more. By then he was part of a band called the Fruitjar Drinkers and they were touring the rural south in a Model A Ford. A fiddle player, a guitar player, Bloodworth and his Gibson banjo. Playing little towns that were hardly more than a grocery store and a couple of churches, shotgun sharecropper shacks, red roads that did not seem to go anywhere anyone in his right mind would want to be.

They'd set up on the long porches of country stores, stores that might have all been constructed from the selfsame blueprint. There'd be electric lights strung up and moths drifting in and out of their arc so thick they seemed some curious by-product of the electricity itself. Before Bloodworth had finished tuning up folks would be drifting toward the lights, at the first driving notes of the banjo, the old man squaring his shoulders and leaning into the din of noise like a boxer coming out of his corner, folks would have clustered the porch as if they'd risen out of the dusty red clay itself.

Tubercular revenants in overalls and a week's beard, their wives and stairstep children, old men on canes and ole women in pokebonnets hanging on to them and boldeyed women staring up at him out of the hot electric dark who seemed to be hanging on to nothing save the night itself.

Oh, Death, he began to sing, a song that in its various incarnations predated even his forebears' presence on the continent, his smoky sardonic voice half defiance, half entreaty. Get out of the graveyard, E.F., Sharp the fiddle player would call, grinning his gaptoothed grin above the sawing bow. These folks don't want to hear about the graveyard.

But Bloodworth was not fooled, he had these folks' number, he'd been reading their mail, walking a lifetime in their shoes. Beyond the mothriddled light their faces were rapt and transfixed, he sang about death as if it was the only kept promise out of all life's false starts and switchbacks, all there was at the end of the dusty road, his voice told them about calm and quiet and eternal rest. No landlord, no cotton to chop, no ticket at the company store growing like a cancer. Just time itself frozen like leaves in winter ice and nothing in the round world to worry about or dread.

They sold records out of the trunk of the Model A. They sold them with no trouble at all, folks digging up change out of their purses so worn the faces denominating it looked spectral, mere ghosts of themselves. They sold them to folks who did not even own phonographs, who had no prospects for owning one, folks who seemed to regard the records as talismans. Who handled them reverently and turned them to the light and studied the spiraling grooves as if they'd find there some physical evidence of their own provisional existence, as if their very lives were somehow encoded there.

I sure would like to have one of them records, the woman said.

I'll sell them to most anybody, Bloodworth said.

I don't have any money.

Money has always been one of the requirements for buying something, he pointed out.

The woman had huge dark eyes that did not look away when he studied her face. They held his own eyes locked to hers and seemed to communicate on some whole other level. The black hair like a shadow down her back was as straight as if she'd taken a flatiron to it. She stood so close he could feel the heat of her.

We could maybe walk down by the levee and talk about it, she said.

Likely we could, he agreed.

They walked along the side of the road. Between the black honeysuckle and sawbriars the road was white as mica. She carried the record against her breasts as a young girl might carry her schoolbooks. Somewhere out there in the dark beyond the levee the Mississippi rolled like something larger than life, like a myth, like a dream the world was having. Here the land was flat and the stars swung so close to earth they seemed foreign, in configurations he'd imagined but never quite seen. A whippoorwill called out of the musky dark in some language he'd never heard. Sin seemed so evil, so sweet.

You got a drink on you, Mr. Bloodworth?

Of course he had a drink. What would a Fruitjar Drinker be without a drink?

Is anybody goin to be lookin for you? he asked.

Just you, I hope, she said, turning to him.

All this was a negation of death. The taste of her mouth, the feel of her breast, so soft that the feel of a naked breast always surprised him. Her quickened breath was the very affirmation of life.

Death in those days had a tendency to walk past his house at night, cross the yard and peer in his window, bone hand raised to shade black eyeholes that were just night augmenting itself, death fought him every night for the covers, tried to crawl into the very bed with him.

Not tonight, he'd think, hands gentle at the buttons of her dress. Death, you'll sleep at the foot of the bed tonight.

WARREN SAT awkwardly in the old man's lawn chair, his car parked at the edge of the road. There was a blondhaired woman sitting in the passenger seat drinking something from a paper cup and glancing occasionally toward the trailer.

How you makin it, Pa?

I reckon I'm scrapin by, Bloodworth said. It's good to be back here.

Seems like it's peaceful, just bein in a country that lays the way you remember it layin.

Warren was wearing dress pants and a white shirt and his slippers were shined. He took a flat pint bottle out of the side pocket of his coat and offered it to the old man.

I reckon I'll pass, Bloodworth said. It don't agree with me anymore.

Then I don't reckon you'll mind if I take a drink.

You're well past the age where what I think about anything matters, Bloodworth said. He sat studying Warren. It was not yet ten o'clock in the morning yet Warren already seemed unsteady on his feet. Perhaps he'd started drinking when the sun came up, perhaps he'd not waited for the sun. The old man was touched by something in Warren's face and he wished he could make things right. Pick him up out of his tracks and set him down in other tracks going another direction. He could not think of anything to say to him, and since his own life did not lend itself to example he would not have said it anyway.

Warren drank from the bottle and screwed the cap back on and returned it to his pocket. Brady come around much? he asked.

No, he kindly seems to be avoidin me. The time or two I've talked to him he's mostly just raved and ranted about me goin to hell. I reckon him and God Almighty's got together and worked it all out.

There's somethin the matter with Brady. I hate to say it but I believe he gets worse ever time I see him. He's got all that crazy mess about fortunes and hexes on his mind and I don't think he can think about anything else anymore.

I blame myself some, Bloodworth said. But you can't walk back to where you was twenty years ago and start over.

There was somethin wrong with him twenty years ago, too, Warren said. You just never noticed it. Does that boy of mine come by much?

No, I've not seen him. That boy of Boyd's speaks of him a lot.

I've about give up on Neal. Just throwed up my hands and said let him roll. He'll probably wind up in the pen. All he studies is pussy and whiskey and I can't seem to get him interested in anything else.

Reckon how in the world he wound up like that, the old man grinned. Many preachers and Sunday School teachers as this family has turned out.

I reckon he's a throwback to olden times or somethin. Say that boy of Boyd's comes by and keeps you company? He seems all right.

He's around here a right smart. And he is all right. He's about as peculiar a young feller as I ever seen, but he's all right. He's goodhearted. Mostly keeps his mouth shut but he looks like he's watchin and listenin all the time. Hard to figure what he's studying about.

Warren we need to go, the woman called from the car. I'm just melting down out here.

Warren stood up. He seemed obscurely relieved to be getting underway. Well. You're sure you're all right, Pa?

I'll make it. That's not Juanita out there, is it?

Warren turned. The woman was studying her face in a tortoiseshell compact, reworking her lipstick. No, I reckon me and Juanita has come to the parting of the ways. Me and Modine there's goin down to Florida and walk barefooted in the sand.

He withdrew a moneyclip from his pocket and handed the old man some folded bills. If you need anything just get it, he said. You got any way of gettin to town?

Young Albright hauls me around a lot. I don't want this money.

Keep it. It'd make me feel better if you'd take it.

Bloodworth slid it into his pocket. I don't want the responsibility of makin you feel bad, he said.

Well, let's go where the palm trees grow, Warren said, turning for a moment and shaking the old man's hand.

You be careful, Bloodworth said, still clasping the hand, not knowing what he wanted Warren to be careful of, but aware suddenly that the road Warren was headed down was fraught with a thousand kinds of peril and it saddened him that he had only noticed this long after it was too late to do anything about it.

It's too late for that, Warren said in an eerie echo of what the old man had been thinking.

HALFWAY DOWN the row of cedars was a tree fairly taken over by muscadine vines and Bloodworth stood for a time beneath it picking muscadines one by one off the lower branches and eating them. It seemed early for muscadines to ripen but he figured the hot dry summer had caused it. But the muscadines were of a good size and full of juice, he liked the hot winey smell of them and the sharp evocative taste that made him think of wine he had made and drunk fifty years ago.

He was watching the house. It set still and depthless against the blue border of woods, the white weight of the sun thrown on it like a floodlight. The top branches of the great pine stirred with a breeze that never touched the earth and in his mind he smelled pine needles in the hot windless calm.

He filled his shirt pocket with the black fruit and went on down the cedar row, from time to time unpocketing one and breaking the tough skin with his teeth. Well, let's pay a call on the family, he told himself, something that was almost dread swinging in him like a pendulumed weight.

He was coming out of the cedar row almost at the garden fence when Brady saw him. Brady was coming up from the kennels with a fifty-pound sack of dog food across his shoulder. The old man raised an arm just as Brady saw him and immediately Brady dropped the bag and began to hurry toward him, loping crookedly along on his bad leg. The old man turned to look about as if to see was there some imminent danger Brady was running to rescue him from, a bear stepped out of the woods perhaps but there was nothing, it was Bloodworth himself Brady was closing on.

When Brady grasped his shoulder it was so unexpected he staggered and dropped the muscadines he was holding and stabbed wildly at the ground with the stick to recover his balance. When he did he stood for a moment with the stick held like a weapon he was brandishing.

What's the matter with you? Are you crazy?

Brady's red curls had tumbled across his forehead. You got no business over here, Pa. Don't you know enough to stay where you're put?

I've always been accustomed to puttin myself pretty much where I wanted to be, Bloodworth said.

I don't want you around Ma, I thought you understood that. Now go back across that field the way you come. No, wait right where you're at. I'll get the car and drive you, that'd be faster.

Wait a minute, what do you think I'm goin to do, hurt somebody? Do you think I aim to hurt her?

You done that long ago and I'm not about to stand by and let it happen again. She's old and her mind's gettin bad and as far as I know you've been forgot. It's my plan to see you stay that way.

Boy, you've got me all wrong. I just walked across here to see what you was up to.

You wait right where you're at till I get the car, Brady said. I don't want her seein you and me havin to explain all this mess and I don't ever want you back over here again.

I don't recall ever signin this place over to anybody, Bloodworth said. You got a deed to it in your shirt pocket?

Wait right where I told you, Brady said.

For reasons he could not understand the old man waited until Brady brought the car. There was something in Brady's face that did not brook argument, something in his congested eyes that scared the old man a little. He looked for something of the boy Brady had been twenty years ago in the pale freckled face but if any of the boy remained he could not find it.

When Bloodworth was seated awkwardly in the front seat by Brady instead of driving up the road the way a normal driver would go Brady drove along the cedar row through the wild oats and broomstraw, the car lurching wildly on its shocks, Brady peering at the house in the rearview mirror. He kept raking his hair out of his eyes with his long freckled fingers. The old man watched him, thinking for a surreal moment that Brady might not even stop at the trailer, just put the pedal to the floor and drive him farther than he ever meant to be, drive him deep into the Harrikin and shove him out like a man dropping an unwanted dog.

Let me ask you something, Bloodworth said. Why did you ever agree for me to come back here? Why didn't you just pocket the money and forget it, or just refuse to talk about it in the first place? I never pushed it on you. I had a place to be, and somebody that would have looked after me.

Blood is blood, Brady said. You can't deny your own blood askin for help.

I believe blood needs a little more acknowledgment than that, Bloodworth said dryly. Here's what I think. I think you liked the idea of me settin over there in that oven with no water and no lights and you knowin where I was ever minute. I think you can't stand it because me and that boy and young Albright scuffled around and made it livable. You wanted to make it hard on me. But I've got news for you. Hard's what I'm used to. I've always been able to make do. I can live in a brush arbor. I could live set out on a flat rock in the sun.

They had reached the edge of the road. Driving onto it the car bottomed out and the rockerpanels scraped the shoulder but Brady seemed not to notice. He drove slowly until they had reached the trailer. Brady parked and wordlessly climbed out and opened the passenger side door. Bloodworth got out.

You told me what you think, Brady said. Now here's what I think. I think when you went wherever it was you took off to it was like we never was. We wasn't real to you. You was wherever you wanted to be, doin whatever you wanted to do. Tunin your banjo, maybe. But I was here. I had to see her them first few years. You never. We didn't even exist to you. You was in Arkansas, tunin your banjo.

The old man shook his head, stood leaning on the stick. I never felt the need to explain my actions to any man, he said. But I will say this. There's two sides to everything. That's all I'll say. But I will give you some free advice. You keep tryin to live a life somebody else has already lived and it'll drive you crazier that you already are.

Just don't come around her no more. Brady got into the car and closed the door. If you do I'll make it hard on you.

I told you I was raised on hard, the old man said. But if you're goin to be so damn unsociable I may bring somebody in over here for a little company. That wouldn't bother you, would it?

Brady cranked the car. He jerked it into gear, held it with the brake. His mouth worked and he leaned and spat onto the hard white clay. You bring some Arkansas whore on this place and I'll kill you myself, he said.

BY THE TIME half the hay was loaded out of the field onto the flatbed truck and hauled to the barn the sun was at its whitehot zenith and it seemed to hang there pulsing malevolently. Fleming had sweated so much into his eyes the edge of things he looked at had a blurred provisional look to them. The field sloping away with its hundreds of neat rectangles of hay seemed to roll on forever until it faded out in a green smear. His arms were scraped raw from handling the bales and latticed with bleeding scratches and the flesh around his midsection where the waistband of his jeans chafed felt parboiled. He wiped his eyes on his forearm and stood staring down at the foreshortened shadow beneath his feet and wondered how much longer this day could be.

He couldn't fathom how Albright did it so effortlessly. Albright looked all arms and legs and was skinny as a carpenter's rule but he'd heft up the bales by the seagrass twine and thrust them with his left arm onto the truck with a sort of offhand grace.

Fleming watched the sideboarded truck diminish down the rolling hillside, the stackers atop the hay clutching the sideboards and swaying and bouncing toward the barn.

Fleming's mouth was parched and dry. He turned and spat a cottony mass onto the field. Next time you get one of these highdollar jobs with the work all picked out of it you can leave me out of it, he said.

Hell, I never told you it was a candy-pullin. You're a country boy, you know what a bale of hay looks like. See that shade yonder? Look how blue it looks. Go set in it, and I'll tell the old man I burnt your gimlet ass out.

Piss on you. I never said I was burnt out.

You're showin a whole lot of the signs. Let's hit that water jug while they're unloadin the truck.

I wish I had about a gallon of the old man's lemonade.

I wish I had a beer about the size of a fifty-gallon oil drum. I'd just lay down and roll it on top of me. I aim to have one tonight, too, if they make such a thing.

They started toward the line of shade at the woods. The cured hay they walked through smelled as if it were smoldering, Fleming could feel the heat of it through his shoes. The skin on his back felt tight and drawn, as if the sun was shrinking it, and he figured it was too late to put his shirt on. The cooler sat on a stump in the edge of the woods. Albright rinsed a bottle and poured and out the water and filled it with ice water. He drank and hunkered on his heels, sat holding the bottle as if he'd forgotten it, his face screwed up in a sort of bemused perplexity.

If you're not going to drink that don't tie up the bottle. I'm about sweated down here.

Albright reached him the bottle. Ever time I get still that Woodall business comes back on me, he said. I can't for the life of me figure what I'm goin to do.

Do? Do about what?

Do for Woodall.

Say a prayer for him or put flowers on his grave. That's about all you can do for a dead man.

That's a hell of a way to look at it, Bloodworth. I the same as killed him. Like I held a pistol against his chest and pulled the trigger. I took him out of this world, or hired it done, and somehow I've got to make it right.

Well. You could borrow another fifty dollars at the bank and hire Brady to unhex him. He'd probably come flying right up out of the ground like it was the rapture or something. Dirt flying everywhere.

Shitfire, don't talk like that, ain't you got no respect? Anyway I done talked to Brady.

What'd he say?

It took him twenty minutes to say it but what it boiled down to was tough shit. He said let it be on my head.

You sound as crazy as he is. Who do you think you are, God Almighty? You think you can grab an airplane out of the sky and slam it against a mountain? Seems to me you and Brady have sort of an in-flated idea of what you can do.

You're lookin at it all wrong. If I had laid for him and shot him, would that mean I was God Almighty? If I had wired a stick of dyna-mite to his ignition? It would not. It would just mean I killed him. And that's what this means. If I was God Almighty I'd be plannin on how to bring him back. Or makin it to where it had never been.

Just shut up about it. You're giving me a hellatious headache.

I've got to make it up to his wife. Or whatever family he's got.

Maybe you could just pay back the money. Rebuild that crimper. That's what it all come up about.

Maybe.

You could take all this hayhauling money and endow some sort of charity in his name. The Gene Woodall Foundation. The Busted Crimper Society. Give out college scholarships or something. Send missionaries amongst the heathen to save souls in his name.

Just shut the fuck up, Bloodworth. I'm sorry I ever mentioned it to you.

Donate crimpers to the underprivileged.

Yonder comes that truck and I'm damn glad to see it. When I'm slingin them bales I don't hardly think of him at all. That fucker's just as worrisome dead as he was when he was swearin out all them papers.

COBLE IN THE red Diamond-T cattle truck circled the courthouse twice before he found a parking place. He'd had to wait until Saturday and he might have known the town would be overrun with woolhats and rednecks buying their flour and bacon. Such town as it was. He climbed out of the truck and locked the doors and stood looking about Ackerman's Field with a sort of bemused contempt. To a man from Memphis this place looked like a wide place in the road, a hog wallow, less than that.

The courthouse was a red brick two-storied building centered on a neat city block of closecropped grass. Benches set beneath huge old elms and on them old men sat in clusters whittling and telling lies and unraveling the mysteries of the universe. An American flag and the Tennessee state flag hung devoid of motion from a flagpole. On this hot morning even the leaves on the trees seemed frozen. By the time he got to the courthouse steps and opened the door sweat was already darkening the armpits and across the shoulders of his khaki shirt.

The sheriff's office when he found it was in the basement but the door was locked and he could not see through the pebbled glass. Probably sitting in there asleep, he told himself. A sign hung from the doorknob. Back in thirty minutes. Thirty minutes from when? he asked it.

He went back up the stairwell and stood for a time beneath a slowly revolving ceiling fan. He kept glancing at his watch. At last he went out the door and down the steps and across the street to the General Cafe. A sign on the wall behind the counter said that the special of the day was meatloaf and three vegetables. He ordered the special and sat down in a booth by the window.

The waitress who brought it was young and pretty. It was hot in the restaurant and she was filmed with a sheen of perspiration. He tried twice to get a glimpse of her breasts, once when she placed his plate before him and again when she leaned to lay his check on the table. All he saw was a stubbled armpit, a worn pink bra.

I'm lookin for a feller named Rutgers, he told her.

He ain't down the front of my dress, she said. She slapped his tea onto the red Formica table and walked away.

Everything on his plate seemed drenched in grease but he ate it anyway then wiped the plate clean with a slice of lightbread. He sat sipping the tea and watching out across the lawn where a huge red sun flared behind the courthouse. When thirty-five minutes had passed he arose and paid the check. He didn't leave any tip. He went back to the sheriff's office. The sign hung on the doorknob as before. You're a lyin son of a bitch, he told the sign.

He was lounging against a limegreen wall of stippled plaster picking his teeth with a sharpened kitchen match when the sheriff appeared. He looked pointedly at his watch but Bellwether did not seem to notice. Bellwether fumbled out a large ring of keys and selected one and unlocked the door. When he went into the office Coble followed him.

Bellwether crossed the room to a coffeepot that sat on a corner shelf. He poured a cup of coffee and drank from it and spat into a wastepaper basket then cranked the window out and poured the coffee out the opening and hung the cup back on its peg. What could I do for you? he asked. He went behind a scarred blond desk and seated himself in a swivel chair.

Coble had told his story twice before on the telephone, with no result, and it didn't take him long to tell it again. When he was through

Bellwether shook his head. You say you drove two hundred and seventy miles? This sounds like something that could have been handled over the telephone.

Well, a man would think so, but I guess not. I called twice, and both times I got the same shit-for-brains deputy. You know what he told me? There's nobody in this country named Rutgers.

Do you know why he told you that? Because there's nobody in this county named Rutgers. Bellwether picked up a thin telephone directory and tossed it to Coble. It struck him lightly in the chest then dropped to his lap. There's also a county census you could check, among other things, Bellwether said. And speaking frankly, Mr. Coble, I don't care to hear my deputies categorized in that manner.

Coble straightened in his chair. Categorized in that manner, he echoed. Hellfire. Now I let this old son of a bitch out in your county. I know he's from here. He talked about this place like he was born and raised here. Like he come over on the fuckin *Mayflower* or somethin and discovered it. Now by God I traded for a herd of Black Angus cattle and drove four or five hundred miles out of my way to get them. That old man owes me a herd of cows.

He owes you a herd of cows? You paid him sight unseen for a herd of cows?

Hell no, I never paid him. You know what I mean. My only reason for even bein in this Godforsaken place at all was to pick up them cows. I'm either going to have a herd of Black Angus at a substantial discount or that old man's goin to tell me the reason why.

Bellwether tapped a Lucky Strike against a thumbnail and scratched a match and lit the cigarette. I'll tell you the reason why myself, he said. There's not a Black Angus in this county. Look, Mr. Coble, it's obvious his name wasn't Rutgers. What did he look like?

He was a right presentable old gentleman, Coble said. Big man, held hisself kind of straight. Went with a stick, told he'd had a stroke of paralysis. That was likely a lie too. Had kindly long black hair, dyed, I figured, and a gray Stetson hat he wore. Had these real black, kind of meanlookin eyes.

For a moment he thought he saw something flicker in Bellwether's eyes but he wasn't sure. If he did it was gone almost before it registered. I'll keep an eye out for him, Bellwether said.

You'll keep an eye out for him. All right. What do you people do in this county, watch each other's backs? Sweep one another's tracks out? I'll tell you what I'm goin to do. I'm goin to find him, and when I do he's goin to rue the day he made a fool out of me.

Bellwether stood up. He stabbed his cigarette out in an ashtray. Well, he said, I rue the day he made a fool out of you too, because I don't see much I can do about it. What do you want me to do if I could find him, lock him up? What crime is that? I don't know, extortion? It looks to me like he owes you for your time, or mileage, or something, but that's about all.

All the time he'd been talking Bellwether had been crossing to the door. I don't mean to be abrupt with you, he said. But I've been over on the Hickman County line where we had a head-on carwreck. Three killed outright, two of them kids, and another little boy that opened his eyes and looked at me while I was helping get him loaded into the ambulance. All the time I was listening to you complain I was thinking about calling Vanderbilt Hospital in Nashville. To see if he made it, or he didn't make it. That's why I couldn't give the proper attention to your little story about some cows.

He opened the door and made a sort of sweeping gesture, as if he meant for Coble to go through the doorway.

Coble was fumbling for his cowboy hat. He squared it on his head and went through the doorway without speaking.

LET ME show you something, the old man said one day. He rose and set the tumbler of whiskey on an orange crate he was using for a coffee table. From beneath the bed he drew a suitcase, scuffed and battered black leather with brass plates at the corners. He unlocked the clasp and opened it. Inside there was a sort of leather satchel, and the old man opened that too. Like a Chinese box, Fleming was thinking. Inside there'll be another one. Instead there were four 78 rpm records with squares of cardboard placed between them for packing. They looked new, their sleeves crisp and clean, as if the old man had just run them off a few minutes before. He withdrew one from its thin paper housing and handed it to Fleming. He was hunkered on his knees on the floor of the trailer and a long strand of his thin black hair had fallen across his forehead.

Fleming studied the record. Okeh Records, the label said. Race Records. The name of the song was *James Alley Blues.* E. F. Bloodworth, the name below the title said. He turned the record over. *I Wish I Was a Mole in the Ground* was the title on this side.

I don't guess you've got any way of playing these, Fleming said.

I'm afraid not. The old man arose with some effort and seated himself on the side of his iron cot. He raked his hair back with his fingers. That's four I saved back, he said. They ain't never been played. Never had a needle set on them.

What's this mean, Race Records? What's a Race Record?

The old man laughed. Back then they made records for different races of folks, he said. They made Okeh and then they made Okeh Race Records. They was for the colored. Blues singers, that kind of stuff. I reckon there was some kind of confusion about me, I was long gone when they pressed the records and made up the labels. Somebody I reckon thought my voice sounded colored. Or maybe the way I picked a banjo, I didn't frail a banjo the way most of them oldtime pickers did. I picked the notes, in a different key than most of them songs was in.

The old man took a tiny sip from the whiskey, set it aside. He took up the guitar, held it loosely across his lap. It never bothered me to be taken for a colored singer, he said. To tell the truth, it kind of tickled me. I never liked them old ballads a lot of the white singers used to sing. Somebody grieves theirself to death for love and a rose grows up through their ribbones. I never cared for that. But them old blues songs cut right to the quick. Says it all in very few words. Like it was . . . like it was boiled down, concentrated. All that feeling. One says, *Sometimes I think you just too sweet to die, another time I think you oughta be buried alive.* That's *James Alley Blues,* and it's old, old. Always been here ever since the first man set on the side of the bed with a halfpint of whiskey in his hand wondering where his old lady was.

You mind if I take these somewhere sometime and play them?

You do what you want with them. Play them or throw rocks at them. I'm giving them to you.

I can't take them. You kept them for souvenirs.

I don't need souvenirs, the old man said. I remember everything I ever done, I don't need keepsakes to remind me. I kept them because I figured someday I might run up on somebody that was interested in all that old stuff. Them old times.

I'll keep them then. I'll take care of them.

Give them to your kids. You don't have any kids yet do you?

No.

You got you a girlfriend?

I guess not.

What's the matter with you? You look tolerable presentable.

I just don't get out much, the boy grinned. I met this girl back in the spring because she busted a hornet's nest with a rock. Dee Hixson's granddaughter. She turned out to be already married though.

The old man laughed, sat staring at the floor for a moment as if lost in memory. That Hixson family was wilder than a bunch of cats in heat. Every one of them acted like they was on some kind of medicine that kept them crazy. Come to think of it, though, I remember haulin some of it to them in gallon jugs. What I started to say, though, about four or five of them Hixson girls come in about the same time and it was high times twenty-four hours a day. If they couldn't sell it they'd give it away. If they couldn't give it away they'd pay you to take it. Saturday nights there'd be so many wagons and cars they'd run out of yard to park them in. They'd be strung out on the road. I never heard of anybody bein turned away. They'd take anything. Sometimes Dee'd go out in the front yard and fire off his shotgun a time or two just to calm things to a manageable level.

The boy sat holding the records. He wondered how much was left out of the old man's stories, he wondered if his grandfather had been observer or participant at these mad revels.

Then the babies started comin, the old man went on. They never heard of rubbers, I reckon, or maybe they figured that that would be cheatin. One of the youngest of them girls told me one time, she was drinkin a little or she never would have told it, she said her sisters would bury them babies in widemouth Mason fruit jars.

In what?

In fruit jars. I reckon she meant the ones was born dead. Or maybe if they wasn't dead they'd help them along. Said they never wanted them. She told me there was several buried on that bank up from the creek below Hixson's garden spot, where they had a cat cemetery when they was little girls. I never asked if the cats was buried in fruit jars or not.

God, the boy said. Do you suppose it was so?

I've often wondered. I'd hate to think it was. I don't know why she would have made it up, though. Or even how, how would she think of that, a fruit jar? Back at that time there was no place for meanness like Hixson's farm. That bunch of men would take to fightin each other like dogs fightin over a bitch. Which was about what it amounted to. Likely it's folks buried on Hixson's place you never could of fitted into a fruit jar. They had everything from killins on down. The devil had to let things slide elsewhere to keep an eye on that place. Take on an extra demon or two. Oh things run on overtime for a while around there.

Whatever happened, then? I don't remember any of that from the time I was a kid.

There's a balance to things, things got their own way of balancin out. What happened this time was that two of them girls, one of them was the youngest one I spoke of, that told me about the fruit jars, she was pretty as a China doll, she was in the car with a couple of wild boys off Beech Creek and they straightened out some of the curves over by Riverside. They had a Packard wound out as far as she'd wind and took to the air comin down that long grade. Just flew off. I can take you to where the mark's still on the whiteoak that Packard hit. Higher off the ground than you'd believe, too. It throwed folks everywhere. Killed all four of them and froze that Packard on the peg, it was like that old song, whiskey and blood run together. Then one of the girls got married and the others went north. But it was that Packard that shut it down. Like flippin a lightswitch. That quick.

FLEMING CAME DOWN through a tangle of elderberry and sumac, wild pokeroot taller than his head, its poisonous-looking berries a deep virulent purple. Blackberry briars that latticed the hot windless cage of dying greenery. Nothing moved. He looked up, the sky was just broken shards of blue bottleglass glittering through the sumac berries. He could hear the creek trilling over the stones. He came out of the thicket where the earth sloped itself toward the creekbed.

He studied the earth here, curious young archaeologist appraising the shape of the earth, looking for folks buried among the cats. Timeless glass coffins amongst the rotted shoe boxes of cat bones. Here were the juryrigged gravestones of a children's pet cemetery. Small depressions in the ground long grown over with weeds, tall virile pigweed thrusting through the tilted husks of summers past. He sat for a time on the roots of a beech. Gnats had come to trouble his eyes and he kept trying to slap them away.

If he closed his eyes he could imagine them coming down the slope with the cardboard box, solemn, perhaps tears in their eyes. Here was a hole Dee had spaded in the black loam. They came single file, the first in line carrying the box before her, the other three following like acolytes at some ritual they'd not mastered yet. Their thin legs browned by the sun and crisscrossed with the pale scratches from sawbriars, their hair plaited into pigtails. Imbued with a Sunday decorum, playing at being adults, something of ceremony about them.

He could not imagine one of them covertly interring a fruit jar and its bloody freight into the earth. How did you get from one burial to the other, there was too much distance between, windy gulfs of darkness that lay between the child with the shoe box and the woman with the glass jar in her hand. Surely it could not happen by accident or even by a multitude of wrong choices, you'd think it would take an act of sheer will to plummet so far.

When the sun tracked behind a cloud the light turned strange and green like light through smoked glass and the air felt dense and oppressive, too thick to breathe. He rose and descended the bank into the creek. The sun came back out and the shadows of the clouds moved about his feet like vague shapes moving beneath the surface of the water. Where the creek deepened he lay down in it, the sudden cold like a jolt of electricity coursing through him. He lay on his back and felt the gentle tug of the current, closed his eyes and let the water rise above his face, his hair fanned out in the moving water like a drowned man's. The creek felt cold and clean, and he stayed beneath the surface until his lungs felt like fire in his chest and lights like fireflies drifted gently across the black expanse of the underside of his eyelids and he came up gasping and sucking air into his lungs.

FLEMING PARKED the yellow cab in Itchy Mama's yard and climbed the steps to the front porch under the jaded eyes of the old men aligned in canebottom chairs. Lord God, one of the old men said. It's somebody lost, lookin for Hollywood, California.

No, another said. It's one of them Chicago white slavers, down here after another load of women.

Fleming was wearing brown gabardine slacks and loafers with pennies in the slots. He had on a blowsy Hawaiian shirt with huge yellow pineapples imaged upon it. His dark hair was parted smoothly and combed to the side, and you could smell aftershave from some distance away. He crossed to the dopebox and lifted a dripping Coca-Cola from the ice water.

I'd shut them socks off when I wasn't usin em, one of the old men said. You'll run the batteries down and a man might need a little light after dark.

Cater Hensley was studying the car. I don't know if I've ever seen a better match between man and automobile, he said.

Fleming popped the lid off the Coke on the edge of the cooler. The screen door opened and Itchy Mama came onto the porch.

You old highbinders shut up, she said. Let me look at this boy. I believe he's shaved. She ran a workroughened hand the length of his jaw. Lord God. He has shaved.

She had an arm about his shoulders, bumped him with an enormous hip. If things don't work out for you just show up here about ten o'clock, she said. I'll fix you right up.

The old men whooped with laughter. She can do it, too, Hensley said. Or could a few years back. Where's that old man at?

He's at home. Him and Albright's playing rummy. Junior let me use the car.

Likely he's hopin you'll elope with it and not bring it back, Hensley said. I was just tryin to think if I've ever seen a uglier automobile. I don't believe I have.

Fleming drained the bottle and set it in the Coke crate. Well, he said, it's better than walking.

Hensley seemed to ponder this. I guess it would depend on how far you had to go, he said.

I've got to go a long way, he said, starting down the steps. I'm going off down to Clifton.

Stay and play some Rook with us tonight, Youngblood.

I got to get on.

Ten o'clock and not a minute past it, Itchy Mama called after him.

He drove on into a late afternoon countryside that might have been a Halloween autumn scene from a calendar, some old proletarian mural come to life. When he reached the stretch of riverbottom farms before Clifton the fields were shocked with corn and pumpkins and once he saw folk gathering corn into a muledrawn wagon like some old print from Currier and Ives. He drove with the windows down for the smell of the air, crisp and clean and sere with the scent of drying leaves.

When he came over the last hill overlooking Clifton the car started to overheat but he told himself it was nothing to be concerned about. Still he cut the switch and took the Dodge out of gear and coasted down the long stretch of hill to the city limit. He popped the clutch at the bottom to restart the engine and when he cut the switch in Raven Lee Halfacre's front yard the temperature gauge was out of the red by a comfortable margin.

Raven Lee was lounging in the swing, the same place she'd been the first time he saw her. She laid a book facedown on the porch and sat up. He was coming up the walk when she stepped off the porch into the yard.

Lord God.

He couldn't tell if she meant him or the car. That's what they said the last place I stopped, he said.

What is that thing? she asked.

He guessed she meant the car. It's Albright's taxi, he said. You've seen it before. Right now it's the car that's going to take you into Ackerman's Field to the drive-in movie.

Mmm, she said. I don't think so.

Why not? It'll be night when we get there, nobody'll see it.

She had a hand upraised to shade her eyes from the slanting sun. A curl had come undone and laid across her forehead like a question mark, her left eye the dot that completed it. I believe that thing would glow in the dark, she said. Anyway I can't go. Mama's drunk and she's pitched one fit after another all day.

Well. You sort of talked like you might go.

God, that was a long time ago, she said. I figured you'd died. Or run away to become a professional fighter.

Who is that? a voice yelled from inside the house.

It's the Watkins man, Mama.

Get me a bottle of vanilla flavoring, the woman said drunkenly.

Give me a bottle of vanilla flavoring, Raven Lee said.

We'll stop and pick one up. Are you going or not?

I guess I am. Anything's better than listening to a drunk woman yell about vanilla flavoring. But get a move on, she'll be out here in a minute.

The screen door opened and Mother stood peering into the yard. She swayed gently from side to side and seemed to be holding herself up by hanging onto the door.

Who is that? Her speech was loose and slurred. Who's that you're traipsin off with?

By this time they were in the car. Raven Lee rolled down the glass on her side. I'm taking a taxi uptown to get a magazine.

Oh no you're not, Mother said. She had released the door and staggered across the porch and into the yard. You little whore, she screamed.

Go, go, Raven Lee said. Unless your plan was to take Mama with us.

He released the clutch and drove into the street. Raven Lee had turned in the seat, facing him, her back to the door. She was wearing white shorts and there seemed an enormous expanse of smooth brown legs.

Stop by the hardware store a minute, she said.

The hell you say. Is that not right next to the Eat and Run Cafe?

When she grinned her teeth were very white.

I meant to bring a gun and I clearlight forgot it, he said.

At the hardware store she bought a small can of yellow paint and a small brush. While Fleming sat in the car and watched gulls forage over the river and blue twilight seep out of its timbered farther shore the girl painted out TAXI on one door and went around and painted it out on the other. She stamped the lid on the paint with the heel of her shoe and threw the brush away and climbed back into the car. I just put Junior out of the taxi business, she said.

By the time they reached the city limits she had slid across the seat and put her left arm about his shoulders. You look good tonight, she told him. Smell good enough to eat, too. What is that aftershave, vanilla flavoring?

Two miles more and he felt so lightheaded he fully expected to drift car and all a few feet off the road. She had lain her face against his and kissed his cheek then twisted his mouth to hers. The car was drifting all over the road and finally he wrenched himself away from her and where the road widened above the river he drove onto the shoulder and cut the switch. When he turned to her she slid into his arms like one piece of a puzzle interlocking with another. He held her face against his throat. When he raised her face to his and kissed her her mouth opened under his and he could feel her tongue. He opened his eyes and hers were open as well and it seemed strange to see two enormous dark eyes so close to his own. When he cupped her breast she turned slightly on the seat to accommodate him but then he slid the hand inside her blouse and she twisted away from him.

My God, we're parked right in the road. What's happened to you? Did you take one of those correspondence courses on girls or something?

Me? What's happened to me? What's happened to you might be a better question.

She laughed against his throat. I believe it's this car, she said. How could a girl resist a guy with a car like this? She straightened and adjusted her clothing, smoothed back her hair with her fingers. Beyond the glass night had fallen, and he could barely see her.

No, she said, I suspect my life's in for some major changes and I don't know how everything'll work out. I just decided to have fun while I can.

What do you mean your life is changing?

Nevermind. It's more of a feeling I have than anything else. Maybe I'm psychic, aren't Indians supposed to be? Are you ready to go?

I'm ready for anything, he said. Just whatever. But why don't we just stay here?

He could see the flash of her teeth. You are ready for anything, but we're here in the middle of the highway. You promised me a movie and I want a cherry Coke. Take me there. This is a taxi, isn't it?

It was before you attacked it with a paint brush, he said.

From a high point of cupping the breast of the prettiest girl in a three-county area things could only go downhill and almost immediately they began to do so. Before they were halfway to Ackerman's Field the temperature gauge began a slow and inexorable climb into the red and the engine had begun to miss. By the time they were part of a long line of cars waiting to pass the ticket booth and enter the drive-in the previews were already flickering on the screen and the needle had pegged into the red as far as it would go. The engine wheezed and loped like a washing machine.

Hey, *Showboat*'s playing, Raven Lee said. That's all right. I love musi-cals. He scarcely heard her. He was wringing wet with sweat. He was willing the car to go a few more feet. There were cars in front of him and cars behind and he was able to progress only a few feet at a time. In order to keep the engine running he had to knock the car out of gear and hold the accelerator halfway to the floor. A shifting blue haze of oilsmoke hung over everything and folks in the other cars regarded them with interest.

When he was pulling up the banked tier of earth where the speaker posts were aligned the engine died and it would not start back. A sinis-ter thumping sound was coming from under the hood and hot waves of steam rolled from beneath it. The car was roughly parallel with the last row of speakers and it was facing the concession stand. They sat for a time staring at it. It was a square whitewashed building. A multitude of moths fluttered in the hot beam of light from the projector.

Well, anyway we made it, he said.

Made it? This isn't making it. We can't even see the screen.

If we turn sort of this way and look out the side we can see, he said. I'll let you next to the glass.

On the screen small Technicolor animals smashed each other into oblivion, resurrected themselves with the marvelous recuperative powers peculiar to their species.

What do you think is the matter with it?

I don't know. It's never done that before.

Well, it's done it now, and picked a fine time to do it. Will the speaker reach?

He got out to see. If it was about eight feet longer it almost would, he said.

Oh well. Why don't you go get us a cherry Coke?

At the concession stand he bought two large cherry Cokes and two enormous tubs of buttered popcorn and returned with them to the car. She lay down in the seat with her feet in his lap and her back against the passenger side door. She ate popcorn and took sips from her Coke.

I may have to rethink my whole philosophy of life after going out with you, she said.

What are you talking about? He turned and watched the screen. Some sort of chorus line had formed, folks with walking sticks and straw boaters were singing and dancing, all in silence.

I was thinking about all the guys I've gone with. I had about decided men were the worst kind of trash on earth. I didn't want anything else to do with them. They use you and drop you, slap you around a little every now and then to keep you in line. Kiss you and slobber around on you. Take Neal, for example.

You take him if you want him. I believe I've about figured Neal out.

If Neal brought me to the drive-in, which he wouldn't, he never took me anywhere, and the car had died like this one did, which it wouldn't, Neal has a new Buick, it wouldn't have bothered him a bit.

Tough shit, Neal would have said. Likely he would have just walked off or got a ride somewhere. You were really bothered by it, I could tell. It embarrassed you. Not only did you get us drinks and popcorn, you bought the giant economy size. Maybe I got to you in time and I can shape you just the way I want you. Make my own little man.

He was silent a time. He was no good at these kinds of conversations. Words would not come to him as easily as they did to her. Words carried weight, some more than others, and it seemed to him that once you'd arranged them into phrases they stayed that way like bricks you'd laid in a wall and went on meaning what they said no matter what happened. Finally he said, I'd just as soon not talk about Neal. If you think I drove all the way to Clifton and back in this garbed up piece of crap to talk about Neal Bloodworth you're sorely mistaken.

What's the matter with Neal? Aside from the stuff I already mentioned.

Neal's crazy. Sometimes I think my whole damned family is crazy except me. Maybe me too. Come to think of it, especially me.

She bit a chunk of ice with her clean even teeth. Why did you drive all the way to Clifton in this garbed up piece of crap?

Because I had to see you, he said.

She pulled her feet back off his lap and straightened in the seat. Let's go sit on the grass by the speaker post where we can hear, she said.

In the trunk he found a folded blanket Albright had been using for a dropcloth and spread it on the speaker ramp. He turned the speaker up and the girl became engrossed in the movie. It did not interest him. His mind would not focus on it, he could make no sense of it, as if the reels of film were being shown in random order. She was too close to him, leant against his shoulder. He'd begin to get some grasp on the plot of the movie and when he turned toward her her coinclean profile roiled his mind into a jumble of colored images. And the blanket they were sitting on seemed as public as the movie screen and did not lend itself to any sort of intimacy. On the way to town he'd kept his eyes open for any sort of likely-looking sideroads and he thought that on the way back he might talk her into parking for a while. He had a crazy feeling that time was running out for him. He felt that he'd crossed some line and everything on this side of it was represented by Raven Lee Halfacre.

Let's go sit in the car, he said. What happened to having your fun while you could?

She just shook her head without taking her eyes from the screen but after a while the mosquitoes found them. He was kept busy slapping his arms and neck. The things are the size of bats and they're eating me alive, he said. You can sit out here it you want to.

She slapped one and left a bloody smear on her cheek. If you leave me here they'll probably fly off with me, she said. We'd better get somewhere.

She would not get into the back seat but after they'd kissed heatedly for a time her shirt was unbuttoned and her brassiere around her waist and he had managed to get her into a semireclining position half in the front seat and half against the passenger side door. Quit, she kept saying, but she kept raising her mouth to his and she still had her arms tightly about his neck. He was in some confusion about interpreting these conflicting signals and he was nearing a state almost ecstatic, his entire body tumescent. He was crouched on his knees above her trying to work her shorts down when the door she was leaning against sprang open. The dome light came on as she toppled backward, arms outflung and a wild look on her face and her bare breasts white in the disinterested glow of the light. Hellfire, Fleming said. He turned in the seat and kicked the dome so hard the plastic cover smashed. Darkness fell. You crazy shitass, she said. She climbed back in the car and adjusted her clothing. She slammed the door with such force that the glass rattled. He put a tentative arm about her shoulders but the moment seemed to have passed.

On the way back to Clifton he listened to every tick and tremor of the engine with the concentration of a doctor holding a stethoscope to the chest of a dying patient. He had refilled the radiator with water from the concession stand but upon getting underway the car began to overheat immediately. The engine labored and wheezed and even on level ground seemed to be ascending some almost insurmountable grade, on hills it came to a near standstill. He had decided the car was dying and was determined to roll over every foot of ground it was capable of covering.

The girl seemed oblivious to all this. Why are you driving so slow? she asked.

He didn't reply. His hands were whiteknuckled on the steering wheel, and he was listening to a new sound, a sinister muffled knocking that seemed to be coming from beneath the hood, as if something was trapped inside the engine and was trying to pound its way out with methodical blows from a sledgehammer. They had started up a long grade five or six miles out of Clifton, he was locked in concentration deep as prayer, when there was a final blow from the engine, then an explosion of steam from beneath the hood and the car stopped.

He shoved the emergency brake down and got out and raised the hood. A radiator hose had burst but he suspected that was the least of his problems. He wondered what the old man would do in this situation. What Junior Albright would do. Thomas Wolfe. *O lost, and by the wind grieved . . .* All the poems he'd read seemed of little benefit here.

He went back and climbed behind the wheel. Now let's just see, he said.

Did you fix it?

We'll try her and see, he said. All he got was a clicking, a dead telegrapher tapping along wires with nobody at the other end.

What do you think is the matter with it?

To tell you the truth I think I blew a head gasket and just kept driving it till I broke a piston or threw a rod or something.

You don't have another one? A spare gasket?

He looked at her. No, he said. And I don't have a pair of pliers to put it on with if I did.

Well, what do I know, I'm not a mechanic. What do we do now?

I guess we'll walk. He was already climbing out of the car, trying to get a fix on where he was, trying to remember how far it was to Clifton. Was it five miles, six? More in all likelihood.

She made no move to climb out. That's crazy, she said. Shit. I'm not walking anywhere.

Well you'd better make up your mind. If you're staying here there's no point in me heading toward Clifton. All that's waiting for me in Clifton is that thug who kicked hell out of me and your mama. And we don't even have her flavoring.

Oh well. She climbed out. Neal could fix it, you know. Or one of his buddies would just happen along with a backseat full of tools and a headgasket that would just happen to be for this make of car. He's the luckiest thing I ever saw, Neal is.

If I hear the word Neal one more time I'm going to run off and leave your ass, he said. Let something carry you off.

She wound an arm through his. Anything that grabbed me would turn me loose when morning came, she said.

Not me, he said. If I caught you I wouldn't ever turn you loose.

Anyway I was just teasing you. It's like waving a red flag at a bull, you bite every time. You don't much like Neal, do you?

There's not much there to either like or dislike, he said. I think I finally figured out how he looks at things. He thinks the world is his front yard, and everything else, people or whatever, that's just stuff left lying around for him to play with. Are you in love with him or something?

No, I guess I'm not. I thought I was there for a while, but it's over now. It was just that he was goodlooking, and he had that new car, Neal always had women running after him. But you're right. When Neal don't need you, he just don't need you. Like that old blues song, Neal don't know you when you're down and out.

You don't seem so down and out to me.

I'm laughing on the outside, crying on the inside.

They had finally topped out on the hill. The blacktop spooled away in the moonlight, an ungodly amount of it. The landscape was all indigo and silver, a few scattered yellow lights from houses in the bottomland. He could see the bluffs along the river, clumps of ebony trees that were just indecipherable shapes.

They rested a moment, standing close together, her hand still clasping his. He suddenly realized that he felt comfortable with her. Most of his life seemed to pass in a lurch of nervous anxiety about things he had no control over, a rush to be in some undefined future events had not even shaped yet. She was like peaceful waters, like a calming hand laid on his shoulder.

I've got this crazy uncle if he was here he could just pass a hand over it and miracle it back on the road. Heal that blown headgasket. Just a curse with a little reverse spin on it.

What's your father like?

He was silent so long she looked up at him, her eyes darkened further by the shadow of her lashes. He realized that Boyd was a cipher to him. I'll be damned if I know, he said finally, and wondered for a moment where Boyd was, if he was ever coming back, if even now he might be climbing the rocky path that led through the cedars, a paperback book in his hip pocket, his eyes already set to the point where the unlighted house would come into view.

They descended the long hill toward the bridge. The night was cool but not uncomfortably so, a good October night for walking. A wind they had not felt on the other side of the hill went scuttling through the trees, sent clouds streaking across the face of the moon, intent and purposeful, as if they knew just where they were going and were in a hurry to get there. He thought of Alfred Noyes, looked about the night in a kind of wonder; the wind really was a torrent of darkness, the moon a ghostly galleon tossed upon stormy seas.

When I was a little girl I used to slip off up town and go around asking grown men if they knew my daddy. If any of them did I'd make them tell me everything they knew about him. Most of it wasn't very good, he'd beat a lot of them out of money. He was a con man from somewhere, supposed to be half Indian. Or a full-blooded Cherokee, depending on who was doing the talking. He came in here with some kind of oil scam, he was going to make everybody rich. I probably oughtn't be telling you this. I should have told you he was a Baptist preacher, who got killed on a mission somewhere saving souls.

I was never much on preachers anyway.

He was supposed to be a sharp dresser, Daddy was. And a slick talker, too, he had a bunch of papers saying he represented some big oil company. I don't know exactly how it worked, but he got a land lease and a bunch of heavy equipment from somewhere and started setting up to drill a well. He had reports on the soil, all that. I reckon folks were just tripping over each other to hand him money. It went on a while and then one morning all the investors showed up to watch the drilling start and Daddy never showed up. He was longgone, and the money was too. Everybody talked big, they say, telling what they were going to do when they caught him, but he was just gone. Nobody knew where he came from, nobody knew where he went. He just faded out. I guess he was always conning everybody, he for sure conned Mama. She always used to say he'd come back and get us, but I said the hell with that. Why would you come back to a place where they were going to tar and feather you? That's crazy. Clifton's a mean place, they'd skin him alive.

They walked on in silence. Then she said, see how you men are? Mama might have been a schoolteacher instead of a drunk. You men are always breaking things you don't know how to fix.

Below them the river wound through lowering trees that seemed to be adrift on pale shoals of mist and past the bridge the world simply faded out as if everything beyond that point had merged together, water and tree and sky become some combinent and alien element. For a moment nothing existed save himself and Raven Lee, then voices came out of the fog sourceless yet with a bell-like clarity. They seemed to be simply appearing out of thin air.

Clyde. Clyde. They're out there runnin our trotlines, a woman's voice called.

You get away from them lines, a man shouted. I've got a gun over here and I'm fixin to shoot.

Laughter, the lapping of oars in the water. Oh, no, he's got a gun over there and he's fixin to shoot.

Raven Lee pulled off her shoes and inspected her heels. God, she said. Blisters. You tote these, I believe I'll try it barefoot for a while.

They trudged on, Fleming carrying the shoes. We seem to do a lot of walking on our little get-togethers, she said. In the unlikely event that we ever go out again, how about if we do something different?

We could sit on a porch somewhere and rock.

I believe I'd just sit, she said. I'm too tired to rock.

They began to pass farmhouses set back from the road in lush tactile fields, manicured-looking pastures kept by wooden fences painted white. All these houses seemed well supplied with watchdogs that sensed these interlopers' presence and passed the word down the line dog to dog until the entire valley was beset by barking and howling dogs. They began to be accompanied by dogs that followed barking at them from the shadows, their slitted eyes aglow as if from some internal malevolence. Goddamn a bunch of dogs anyway, he said. He handed her the shoes and gathered an armful of rocks and began to hurl them one by one into the dark at the yellow eyes. Behind them porchlights clicked on as if they'd inadvertently triggered some obscure alarm.

Far down the road behind them headlights appeared, streaked toward them out of the silver mist. He could hear the fullthroated roar of a gutted muffler.

Let's get off the road, she said. That could be anybody.

It could be a ride into Clifton, he said. I'm going to thumb it.

He was standing by the roadside with his thumb in the air when the car passed, only slackening speed for someone to roll down the passenger side window and lob a halffull beer bottle at him. It struck his shoulder so hard it spun him sideways and onto his knees. His left hand was still full of rocks and before he even considered what he was doing he'd changed hands with them and aimed carefully and hurled one at the fleeing car with all his might.

The rock with its freight of anger-drenched adrenaline deadcentered the rear windshield. It disappeared in a dull whumpf of collapsing safety glass, the brakelights came on instantly, and the car slewed crazily onto the shoulder of the road. Yellow backup lights came on and the car lurched drunkenly toward them with the rear tires smoking.

Shit, the girl said.

She went down the sloping shoulder of the road at a dead run and into a field, half falling over a fence. He caught her by the time they reached a thin stand of willows and they ran on into them. He could hear angry shouting from the highway. They sat crouched in the darkness, breathing hard, the dew soaking their knees.

Come out and fight like a man, you coward, you chickenshit son of a bitch. She clasped a hand over his mouth and collapsed giggling against his back. A drunken ranting ensued, four or five different voices, elaborate and inventive namecalling. What future he had was going to be painful and extremely brief, the voices informed him. He'd be emasculated, his bloody testes pounded past broken teeth with a ballbat. God, she whispered. He twisted her hand off his mouth. I don't need that, he said. At least I know when to keep my mouth shut.

I doubt it, she said. I keep telling you things not to do and you keep right on doing them. Nobody but you could thumb a car and have it be the only carload of drunk escapees from a lunatic asylum in the state of Tennessee.

After a few moments of sitting in silence they heard the car crank and drive away, tires squalling on the macadam. She rose but he pulled her back down beside him.

That's only the driver, he said. The ones with the knives and baseball bats are there waiting for us to come walking up out of the bushes.

How do you know?

I just do.

Oh well. Thank God for the bushes anyway. I've been about to pee for an hour. You won't look will you?

Go back in there wherever you want. Just watch for cottonmouths.

Watch? I can't even see the ground. I'm not going out of sight of you. Just don't look, all right?

He lay on his back in the grass with his hands clasped behind his head. Through the roof of branches a three-quarter moon fled at breakneck speed into endless reefs of clouds that it illuminated briefly then shuttled past. She came back and lay beside him, an arm thrown across his chest.

How long do we have to wait?

I have no idea.

Life with you is so interesting. Is this the way you always meet girls?

Look, he said. I'd like to tell you I'm sorry for all this, but if I did I'd be lying. I am sorry that you're having to walk, and I'm sorry you won't ever go with me again. But I'd rather be here with you, with all that blacktop in front of us, than what I'd be doing at home.

What would you be doing?

I don't know. Reading, sleeping. Nothing. Listening to my cells break down and die. What would you?

Listening to the radio probably. There's this radio station in Nashville, WLAC. Nights they don't play anything but blues. Old blues, songs you never heard of. Songs by Blind Lemon Jefferson, Robert Johnson. You ever listen to it?

My grandpa gave me some records he made a long time ago. He said whoever labeled the records thought he was a colored blues singer. They say Race Records on them.

What were the songs?

One I remember was *James Alley Blues*. One named *Sugar Baby*. I wish you could hear him play and sing. He sounds . . . he just sounds strange. Like nothing I ever heard on the radio.

Maybe I can hear him sometime. Can you not play the records?

I don't have a record player.

I do. Bring them the next time you come.

By the time we get to your house you probably won't allow a next time, he said.

It seemed a long wait. They fell silent and after a time he could feel her steady breathing against his throat and when he looked at her her eyes were closed and she was asleep. When the car returned it lingered only long enough for a few drunken threats then it left again. He shook her gently awake. She awoke reluctantly, as if into a world she wanted no part of.

I think they're gone.

She was rubbing her eyes. Oh God. Do we have to? I was dreaming I was in the swing on the front porch.

We could just stay here. Set up housekeeping here by the river. Move us in a bed and a cookstove.

Trust a man not to forget a bed. Or a stove. Food and sex, that about covers it, don't it?

After a while she rose and reached an arm to pull him up. If another car comes we get off the road, right?

We get off the road immediately.

It was after four o'clock when they reeled drunkenly up onto the front porch. Somewhere a cock crowed mockingly. She turned at the door and kissed him. Goodnight, Fleming.

Goodnight hell, he said. What am I supposed to do? I'm looking for a place to lie down.

Well you can't sleep here. Mama wouldn't let me have a boy here all night.

The night's about shot, he said. She's probably passed out anyway.

She opened the door. Wait here, she whispered. She crossed the room quietly, disappeared through the bedroom door. The house seemed full of the woman's breathing and he was already sitting on the couch pulling off his shoes when she returned.

You have to be out of here before Mama wakes up, she whispered.

All right. He tried to pull her onto the couch with him but she came reluctantly and only for a moment. She kissed him and when she pulled away he was too tired to make more than a token protest. She's asleep, he said.

She gave him a sharp annoyed look. Let's save something, all right?

Save it for when?

For sometime I'm not dead on my blistered feet, she said. Just be gone when she wakes up. She wakes up mean sometimes.

He covered the couch with the blanket she brought and turned out the light. He tried to go to sleep but the couch exuded the sour reek of years of dried vomit and finally he got up and made a pallet on the floor. He kept thinking that after he rested a minute he might crawl into Raven Lee's room and talk her into letting him into her bed but he was too tired and he guessed she was already asleep. He was still thinking about it when he drifted into sleep and when he slept he dreamed that he had in fact been welcomed into her bed. She had grasped him with waiting arms and clasped him into her and he was approaching a moment almost apocalyptic in its intensity when the broom slammed into him the first time.

He leapt up wildeyed and disoriented. The room was full of daylight and Mother was trying to kill him with a broom, screaming at him all the while. And then just lay up and sleep in my own Goddamned house, she screamed. The broom caught him a solid blow alongside the head.

Hellfire, Fleming said. He wrestled this mad harridan for the broom and threw it against the wall and made for the door. She recovered the broom and came through the doorway swinging it and he retreated off the porch into the yard.

And don't come back, she yelled at him. She threw the broom at him then went back in and slammed the door. He stood in the dewey grass a time wishing he'd slept with his shoes on. Then the door opened partway and a shoe came sailing into the yard. Another. When the door slammed again he picked them up but he waited until he was safely into the street to put them on.

BOOK FOUR

O UT OF ALL the infinite destinations the night held Boyd had just the sound of music he was moving toward and he had been following it for some time. It waxed and waned and at times ceased entirely and he'd thought at first it was just folks playing music, maybe grouped on a porch somewhere, but as he drew nearer he could sometimes hear brass instruments and a female chorus singing harmony and once even an entire orchestra playing big band swing, *In the Mood,* and the idea of all these phantasmagoric folk crowded onto someone's porch and jostling for room made him grin wryly and he judged it a roadhouse jukebox.

He was following a road that wound through heavy timber, dark trunks like inkstains seeping down a page, velvet pine foliage against the sky. After a while a three-quarter moon eased up over the treeline and the dusty road went white as milk, Rorshach patches of grass bleeding through the white dust that rose and subsided with Boyd's footfalls.

When the honkytonk came first into view he could see it through the trees, or the light from it, a bright outside light mounted on a utility pole. He climbed an embankment and cut through thinning scrub pine and came out in a graveled parking lot.

The building was set back from the road on earth so bare it looked bulldozed. It was a white stucco building in a mock Spanish style and blue neon script read WRIGHT'S PLACE. Everything looked stark and bare in the light from the highwattage bulb and even the air was bluelooking and cold. The door to the honkytonk was closed but yellow light spilled out the windows and the chimney smoked and music drifted out like something dangerous seeping from an imperfect container.

Boyd squatted on his heels and studied the dozen or so cars on the parking lot. He fished a cigarette pack from a shirt pocket and felt it between thumb and forefinger to ascertain the number of smokes left: two. He tilted one out and lit it and just squatted, halfhidden by the pines, studying the cars. After a few minutes he rose and walked among them, still dragging deeply on the cigarette, studying the license plates.

A green Hudson Hornet bore a Tennessee license plate. The doors were locked and the windows frosted over and even leaning and peering in he could make out nothing inside. He turned and glanced at the warm yellow light from the honkytonk and fingered the change in his pocket but after a moment he climbed onto the turtledeck of the Hudson and lay back against the windshield and closed his eyes. He could hear the wind worrying the tree branches, a paper cup scuttling across the parking lot. When the cigarette burned his fingers he tossed it away.

The sound of a door closing opened his eyes but it was only a man and woman coming out of the roadhouse door. He could hear the man's voice, but not what he said, he could hear the woman's soft laughter. They moved hand in hand around the darker side of the building and embraced and parted and eased along the building until shadows took them save the flash of the woman's thighs when she raised her dress then the man's leaning torso blotted even that. In the world but not of it, Boyd watched them couple with a bemused disinterest.

He was weary and he dozed off a time or two but it was so cold he'd shake himself awake and the icy metal was freezing him through his thin clothes and finally he rose and slid off the car and stamped about just to get his blood circulating. Goddamn a bunch of Missouri winter, he said aloud. When the hell's closin time around here? He noticed the man and woman had gone back inside and he guessed it was too cold even for that.

He was on the trunklid again when the doors of the honkytonk opened and folks strung out toward the cars. A fat man in a gray gabardine suit came weaving his way toward the Hudson. When he saw Boyd he stopped and gaped at him.

That's my automobile you're sitting on, he said.

I was sort of hoping it was, Boyd said.

How about sliding your ass off it, the man said. That's a new car and I paid two hundred dollars extra for that paint job.

Boyd slid off it. I need a ride to Tennessee, he said. I got sick folks there.

I'm not going to Tennessee, the man said.

You're wearin Tennessee plates.

They let me run them in other states, the man said dryly. They work coming or going. I'm out of Nashville on my way to Indiana. I'm a traveling salesman.

What do you sell?

The man studied Boyd with sour amusement. Was you fixing to buy some of it? he asked.

I might.

I'm in women's undergarments.

Boyd allowed himself a slight smile. I don't know if I'd be advertisin that around, he said.

The drunk man had a thick head of wavy black hair brushed up in a pompadour and he kept smoothing a hand across it as if he'd feel was it combed right.

You hear the one about the dumb country boy ordered him a girl out of the Sears and Roebuck catalog?

No, Boyd said.

When it come all it was was this brassiere and a pair of stepins. The old boy just raised holy hell. Wrote them a letter threatening to sue. All I got was the harness, he said. Where's the rest of her at?

Boyd grinned a tight mirthless grin and looked away across the trees. They were just a jagged ironlooking blur rising from the pale gravel. The cars were gone now save one other. The moon was well up now and the parking lot looked purposeless and desolate.

The fat man had his car keys out. He came around to the driver's side of the Hudson. I'm sorry you got sick folks but I'm not going to Tennessee, he said. I wouldn't go to Tennessee on a bet. I wouldn't go to Tennessee if you deeded the son of a bitch to me.

All at once he got a peculiar look on his face. His eyes suddenly focused as if he was trying to see something very far away. Then he leaned toward the car and rested his forehead on the cold fender. Sick, he said. The car keys dangled from his right hand. He was wearing shiny wingtip shoes with little ventilating holes in them and abruptly he jerked convulsively and vomited on them. Arghh, he said. Oh, Jesus, I'm sick. He retched. A shudder ran across the tight gabardine fabric of the jacket.

Boyd hit him as hard as he could behind the left ear and the man's head rebounded and bonged the fender and he slid silent and slack onto the ground and halfturned then lay with his head in the gravel. Blood black as ink crept out of the fat man's nose and down his cheek.

Boyd kicked the car keys out of the puke and picked them up gingerly. Then he leaned and wiped them on the salesman's suit. As he was doing this he heard a door close and looked around to see and there was a man coming out of the darkened roadhouse. The man turned and locked the door. He'd started toward the remaining car when he glanced toward the Hudson then he paused and came on toward Boyd.

Come on, Boyd thought to himself. Nose in, why don't you? But he knew the man would have either a gun or a slapstick and he was wondering which and what pocket it would be in. What's the trouble here, he thought.

What's the trouble here? the man asked.

I believe you've overloaded him a little, Boyd said easily. He was all right then it looked like it hit him all at once. He took drunk and puked a while and then I reckon he just laid down to think things over.

It looks like his nose is bleedin, the man said.

He fell against the car, Boyd said. He's all right.

Where do you figure in this? I don't remember seein you inside.

I'm his cousin, Boyd said. His wife sent me to see about him.

Looks like she sent you a little late, the man said. Can you get cousin home?

Yeah. He done give me his car keys. Reckon you could help me get him laid out in the back there?

When that was done the man turned and went to his own car. He cranked it then Boyd started the Hudson. The cold motor turned over a few times and caught, set idling smoothly. Boyd backed around and followed the car out of the parking lot, red taillights winking through the exhaust. He drove onto the road, easing off the accelerator and letting the taillights pull farther ahead. When they vanished around a curve he slowed the car to a crawl, widening the distance, and when he judged it safe he pulled the Hudson onto the shoulder of the road, stopped and got out. He opened the back door. Last stop, he said. Everybody out, end of the line, everybody off the bus.

He grasped the fat man's feet and heaved. A shoe came off and Boyd slung it away. Goddamn you're heavy, he said. The man came sliding feetfirst across the seat and tilted and rolled slackly onto the road. Boyd took a leg beneath each arm and dragged him off the road into a thin stand of sassafras and stopped and stood breathing hard. Then he went through the salesman's pockets. He took his cigarettes and a Zippo lighter with the likeness of a naked woman on it and a wallet and a thin sheaf of bills from his right front pocket. He went through the wallet and removed the money without counting it and dropped the wallet onto the fat man's chest.

He stood looking down at the sleeping man. He lit one of the cigarettes with the Zippo lighter. The fat man was lying with his head in a bed of fistsize rocks and after a time Boyd leaned and worked the coat off the man, struggling to pull the tight sleeves off his arms. He rolled the coat into a pillow and grasped the fat man by the pompadour to raise his head. When he did the hair came away in his hands and Boyd stood staring for a moment at the crazylooking thing. It looked like a great hairy spider his hand was disappearing into. He shook the thing off his hand then wiped the hand on his jeans. Goddamn, he said. Then he raised the man's head and worked the coat under it. Looks like women's undergarments ain't the only thing you're in, he told the fat man.

HER HAIR WAS drawn thinly back on either side of her face, the line of scalp that showed where it was parted like old parchment. The face itself dark and corrugated as an old walnut kicked out of the leaves in the woods. Her eyes were near lashless and murky, like water that had once been clear and clean clotting up with seaweed and slime. Already the cataracts that would blind her created shifting islands of darkness, areas of whatever she was looking at that had simply been negated, did not exist anymore.

Have you not got anything to do that's better than settin and talkin to a old woman?

I guess not, Fleming said. Here I am doing it.

Well. You're in a sorry shape then. Leastways as long as you're here maybe you'll tell me the truth about somethin. You're not much of a liar are you?

I never was much good at it.

Sometimes I believe E.F.'s come back here, she said. You don't know anything about that, do you?

He'd been lying back with his eyes closed and his head against the metal of the lounge chair. Now he opened his eyes, saw to the composure of his face. What makes you say that?

I've been hearin banjo music sometimes in the evenins, she said. Long about dark. You ain't took up banjo playin, have you?

No.

Brady can barely play a radio so I know it's not him. Anyway he was settin right where you are one night when we heard it, so it couldn't be Brady. You know he looked me right in the eye and swore up and down he never heard it? Said my mind's gettin bad.

In fact Brady had told the boy the same thing, that the old woman was getting feebleminded, that time had shifted around her so that she didn't know if something happened fifty years ago or yesterday. That she might arise in the middle of the night and cook breakfast, running now on some time inside her head that was utterly dismissive of clocks and calendars. That she might then turn around and cook the identical meal again.

He said he had arisen at one o'clock in the morning to go to the bathroom and discovered the old woman taking a pan of biscuits out of the oven, turning to break eggs into a bowl for scrambling.

Fleming had always found information related to him by Brady chancy at best, it required a certain amount of consideration. Everything had to be factored in, the look on his face as he told you, the intensity of his voice, what he had to gain or lose in the telling. After all this had been considered you could arrive at some approximation of the truth. But when he'd told this what had been on his face and in his voice was a kind of quiet horror, and Fleming expected all or most of it was the truth.

Now she turned and studied his face intently. What about you? Do you think I'm goin crazy, or do you think I heard a banjo?

He thought about it a time. I'd say if you thought you heard a banjo you probably did, he said.

Anyway I knowed that song, she said, and fell silent, remembering not just the tune but the pattern of the fingers on the strings, the words to it floating into her head though there had been no words with the melody that came drifting across the field, the words had just risen unbidden from memory: *Got no use for a red rockin chair, I got no sugar baby now . . .*

It was one of E.F.'s songs and I've heard it a thousand times, she said. Do you know anything about this?

He sat for a time thinking about conflicting loyalties. You keep your mouth shut about this, Brady had told him. What's done is done, and there ain't no changin it. She's better off thinkin he's dead, or whatever it is she does think. She's hardly ever out of the house and there's no need for her to know he's even in this part of the country.

I guess that's why you set the trailer in the back corner of the place, he had said, but this was so self-evident it did not even require an answer. It seemed to Fleming that it was the old woman's business, hers and E.F.'s. It was not his, and if you came right down to it it wasn't Brady's, either. It went back further than either of them. He also didn't like being told to keep his mouth shut, and he liked even less being painted into a corner and having to tell the old woman a direct lie.

Grandpa bought a trailer, he finally said. Or sent the money and had Brady locate one and buy it. He had a stroke back in Little Rock, a mild one I reckon, it don't seem to have impaired him much.

Where's it at, this trailer? Back across that field somewheres? That's where the music was comin from.

Back up past it towards the blacktop. Me and Brady set it up for him.

That's the craziest thing I ever heard in my life, his grandmother said. If he had to live in a trailer why wasn't it set up over here where the power and water is? That's just about as crazy as you livin like a gypsy and sleepin wherever night catches up with you when you could have a warm bed ever night and a full plate three times a day. If sense was gunpowder ever one of you men put together wouldn't have enough to load a round of birdshot. And folks goin around sayin I'm losin my mind.

Look, he said, this was not my deal, I was just helping Brady set it up, and I was ordered to keep my mouth shut. If you say anything to Brady he'll wind up putting some kind of curse on me.

I'll keep you out of it. I aim to have the straight of it, though, I may put a few curses of my own, I ain't above it.

Well. I reckon I better get on. I guess I've done about all the damage I can do here for one day.

She looked at him fondly. You won't never make much of a liar, she said. I can see right through you like lookin down into still water. I expect law and politics is goin to be out of your reach.

She was silent a time, and he had already turned to go when she said, What's E.F. like these days?

I don't know what he was like any other days. I don't know what to tell you. He's just an old man, has to go with a stick. Kind of easygoing, talks about music all the time.

He must've calmed down with age some. Easygoin is not a word anybody would put to E.F. back when I knowed him. You tell him I said come by here some day. I done some talkin once a long time ago when I should've been keepin my mouth shut.

He turned to go. She would have told him more but he didn't want to hear it. All these old troubles were burdensome and hard to carry, folks would load you down if you'd let them. He had plenty of troubles of his own, old and new, and he did not want to be further encumbered.

FLEMING WITH a sharp putty knife was scraping calcified bits of gasket off the heads while Albright cleaned the block. Albright had been drunk the night before and had given himself a tan with a bottle of suntan lotion called Mantan that was supposed to darken the skin chemically but had succeeded only in giving him a curiously piebald appearance. He'd tanned the palms of his hands, between his fingers, most of his face save round areas about the eyes which remained albino white and gave him the startled look of a raccoon.

You put me in mind of a spotted horse I had one time, the old man said. Come out of north Mississippi, I named him Cisco. His pattern of spots was laid out a whole lot similar to yours. Course I doubt he could have rebuilt a automobile engine.

I doubt if he could drive one just into the ground, either, Albright said. Just down to the ground and then into it. You'd think a man would know when to pull a car over to the side of the road and just cut the switch off.

Well, Fleming said, you said it needed overhauling anyway, and I'm helping you do it. Plus I bought that rebuild kit with the last of my typewriter money.

You couldn't drive a typewriter to Clifton anyhow. Haul Miss Halfacre around on it.

That was my thinking exactly, Fleming said.

What I don't understand is how you broke the inside light out of it. Plastic cover and bulb and everything. What happened to it?

It was the beat of anything I ever saw, Fleming said. We were going up that long hill before you get to Clifton. The motor was knocking louder and louder. When it knocked that last time, the loudest lick of all, that light blew up and scattered little pieces of white plastic all over the car. I didn't understand it, not being a mechanic. I expect a mechanic could figure it right out. Probably something to do with the wiring.

Albright stopped scraping for a long moment and looked at him. I guess that explains why it don't say *Taxi* on the sides no more, he said.

SHE SET the tone arm carefully onto the spinning record, waited. It was as the old man had told, the record was unused, there was scarcely a hiss as the needle tracked the grooves. The banjo commenced so abruptly it must have been going full tilt when the recorder was switched on thirtyodd years before. The old man's voice, smoky and sardonic, almost mocking, but you couldn't tell if he was mocking you or mocking the song or perhaps mocking himself.

She glanced at Fleming sharply, as if the voice had startled her. She opened her mouth to speak, then remained silent. The voice cast out words and drew them back misshapen, twisted to the nihilistic thrust of the song; phrases foreshortened then elongated, drawn out in entreaty. *The last time I saw my woman, good people, she had a wineglass in her hand. She was drinking down her troubles with a nogood sorry man.* The banjo seemed at an odd counterpoint to the voice, the blues rushed and almost discordant, playing out of the melody and then back into it. The banjo at times sounded as if it were playing a different song entirely, a song you could barely hear seeping through the walls of time itself, the banjo and the voice each telling a separate story, the music an almost satiric comment on the words and on the singer who was singing them, reducing the disembodied singer to a specter you could see through, and all you saw when you looked was a swirling empty darkness.

God, she said. He sounds a hundred years old and terribly pissed off. What's he mad about? I don't get this at all.

But when the voice and the banjo ceased, halted abruptly as if the old man's pain or rage had spent itself, she set the needle back at the beginning and let it play through again. When it had played through a second time she turned the record over and played that, a driving raucous banjo, the voice so disaffected and distanced from everyday life it wanted completely gone, wished itself a mole in the ground. *Well, the railroad man, he'll kill you if he can, and drink up your blood like wine . . .*

Well, she said when the song ended, that's about as far from Bing

Crosby as you can get. He's strange. Strange but good. It leaves you feeling like you heard something important but you can't quite figure out what it was. What's your grandfather like?

I don't know. What anybody's like. I think he's just an old man who's about decided he misspent a good part of his life.

When was this made? Do you have others?

Back sometime in the twenties. I've got three more of them.

She closed the lid of the phonograph so that it looked like a small suitcase. It was checked in a red and white plaid, with white musical notes emblazoned on it, and its appearance formed an odd juxtaposition to the songs that it had just played.

He sounds black.

So what? You look like Pocahontas.

I've seen photographs of Pocahontas, and I'm much prettier. Seriously, when can I meet this old man?

Never, the boy said. He'd just take you away from me without even trying and head out to Arkansas or somewhere. Not, he added hurriedly, that you're mine to take.

I'm yours if I'm anybody's, nobody else wants me. Do you think he'd marry me? I always wanted to marry a real blues man. You're not one, are you?

I could learn.

She shook her head. You don't learn that, she said. It's just there. It sounds like he spent his whole life trying to unlearn it. Trying to forget it.

I don't see how you get all that just from listening to two songs.

Maybe I'm wrong. Maybe I think too much. I sit in this room, I listen to dead people singing and I read books dead people wrote. I read strange things into it. Or maybe I just need to get out more.

He had crossed to the window and held aside the curtain to peer into the back yard. A bleak day which held winter like an implicit threat. A wind scuttled leaves along; even as he watched leaves fell and drifted away. On a strung length of clothesline perched a temporary bird. A lean black cat paced beneath it, as if charged with guarding it from other less civilized cats. Its hypnotic eyes never left the bird. The bird flew and the cat sprang impotently, its paws batting empty air.

Down a concrete driveway a little girl was learning to ride a bicycle, her mother following, the mother's mouth calling anxious warnings Fleming couldn't hear.

He dropped the curtain and turned. I think I'm getting a little too fond of you, he said carefully.

She looked up at him from the iron cot she slept on. I don't think you can do that, she said. I think people need to be as fond of each other as they can.

Be serious for once.

Why? You're always serious enough for both of us. Besides, maybe I am serious.

I'm getting too dependent on you. Using you to get through the day. You need to tell me to just get away and leave you the hell alone.

Just get away and leave me the hell alone, she said.

He turned back to the window. The cat was playing with a leaf, rolling it over, slapping it intently. Fleming thought it might be practicing for the next bird.

She rose from the cot and came to stand beside him. She laced an arm about his waist and leaned her head against his shoulder. They stood staring at nothing. A cloud passed the sun and the light grew dense and somber.

This is no way to bring me to my senses, he said.

I don't want you at your senses, she said. You'd be even duller at your senses. Will you take me to meet that old man?

Sure. If you'll stand by me like this a day or two.

Make up your mind. I thought you wanted let alone.

He turned her to him and raised her face and leaned and kissed the hollow of her throat. She seemed all there was to life. He hoped obscurely that she could save him, but he did not even know from what.

LET ME TELL you this story, Neal said. Do you know Jimmy de Nicholais, that works in the post office?

I've seen him around the poolhall, Fleming said. I don't really know him.

He was staring through the car glass across a flat sweep of field, a bleak and wintry landscape. Trees were baring and already the sky had a look of immeasurable distances, the winds that morning had borne a trace of ice; cold was coming, cold hard on man and child, cold hard on old men in unheated rattletrap trailers.

Hey, he said. You want to come out tomorrow and help me rig up the old man some kind of heater? He bought one of these little sheet-iron jobs and I figured we might take that window out of the back and put in a piece of tin. We could elbow the pipe right through there.

I guess, Neal said. All right. Listen to this story though. Me and Albright was in the poolhall about halfdrunk thinkin about finding another drink of whiskey somewhere and we didn't have any money. Right off we thought of de Nicholais. He's always got a little drink hid away. We went over there, Jimmy was off that day, it was some kind of government holiday, Veterans Day or something, some such day. He wasn't home, though, but the door was standing about half open and we decided to just go in and wait. Jimmy lives by himself and he wouldn't mind, we'd done it before, or anyway I had. Anyway he didn't come and he didn't come and we got to looking for his bottle. We turned up the mattress, that's where he usually keeps it, but there wasn't no bottle there. Well, we turned that place upside down looking for whiskey and do you know what we found on the top shelf of his bedroom closet? Just guess.

What?

Well, are you going to guess or not?

Fleming was grinning. Just tell me, he said. Although I'm not sure I even want to know.

A sex doll, Neal said.

A what? A what doll?

One of them blowup sex dolls. It was the damnedest thing you ever saw. I'd always heard about them, but I sort of figured it was something folks made up, but there she was, and nothing would do Albright but he had to blow her up. We couldn't find no pump and Albright he huffed and puffed around on her. I wasn't about to blow that bitch up, no telling what you'd catch. Plastic clap or something. Pretty soon there she was. Big round titties, had these pink nipples on them. Had all these orfices, orifices, little round holes everywhere. Little round mouth. Had this like mop of steelwool-lookin hair. Albright like to fell in love.

Anyway at first we couldn't decide what to do with her. Finally carried her out by the mailbox in front of the house and stood her up. I found some bricks and piled them on her little feet so she wouldn't blow away. Taped her hand to the door of the mailbox and she looked for all the world like she'd just run out to see what the mailman had left her.

Probably something in a plain brown wrapper, Fleming grinned.

Probably. Anyway we parked down the street to wait on Jimmy. It was a while before he come. This woman come by walkin a little dog and neither one of them knew what to make of her. Finally Jimmy come and it looked like he seen her from a long way off cause he started loping. He was looking all around, like he was trying to see was anybody looking out the windows of the other houses. Then he just run by her and grabbed her under his arm like a football and run right up the steps and through the door without ever slowing down. You ought to have seen it. Hey, hand me that pack of Luckies out of the glove compartment.

Fleming popped open the glovebox and tossed the unopened package of cigarettes to Neal. Then he withdrew a pair of women's underwear and held them upraised by their elastic waistband. Pale blue watered silk, Tuesday embroidered in black thread. He regarded them with amusement.

I guess we've all got our secret side, he said.

That damned Raven Lee Halfacre, Neal said. For somebody that fought so hard to keep them she don't seem to put much value on them. They say Tuesday, but I believe it was along about Friday before I got her out of them.

The road was running parallel with a wire fence, beyond it dying grass, weeds the wind had tilted. When he looked up nameless birds were moving patternlessly against a gunmetal sky, like random markings on a slate. He studied them intently, as if they were leaving some message there for him to decipher. Suddenly he wanted to be anywhere else but here, desperately wanted to be somewhere Neal was not.

I believe I'll just walk, he said.

What?

Let me out.

Neal slammed the brakes and simultaneously slid the car toward the shoulder of the road. What the fuck's the matter with you?

There's nothing the matter with me, Fleming said.

He opened the door and climbed out. He stood for a moment leaning his left arm on the car and holding the door with his right.

Well there's sure as hell something the matter with you. It's three miles to the old man's place and coldern a bitch out there.

I'll see you, Neal.

You're about as crazy a person as I ever saw in my whole God-damned life.

I may be. You're not very subtle, are you?

What? Neal took a last drag off the cigarette and spun it past Fleming onto the roadbed. Fleming turned and toed it out in the dry weeds. I guess not, Neal said. I guess subtlety is not my strong suit, as they say. Or it could be I just wanted to tell you something.

Could be I didn't want to know it, Fleming said.

You need to know it.

I'd just as soon be the judge of what I need to know.

He was still holding the car door. It seemed to him for an absurd moment that closing the door would in some manner alter the rest of his life. Mark forever a line between what had been and what was yet to be. He slammed the door and started through the brittle weeds up the roadside.

Hey.

He turned and gave Neal the finger. He heard the door open. You crazy son of a bitch, Neal said. He heard Neal's feet in the gravel. Then the footsteps stopped and a car door slammed and the engine cranked. He could hear Neal laboriously turning the car in the roadbed. Pulling up, backing, pulling up again.

He looked down and saw that he was carrying the panties balled up in his fist. His expression was caught somewhere between a smile and a grimace. He tossed them away and the wind pressed them furtively into the clashing weeds like a dirty scrap of paper, old newsprint. He hunched his shoulders into the wind and went on up the roadbed.

THERE WERE three carloads of them, two county cars and a state car full of Tennessee Highway Patrolmen. They had search warrants and official looking papers but as they had been expected most of the day they hardly disrupted the old man taking the pale sun on Itchy Mama's front porch. Itchy Mama's sources were wellnigh infallible and the whiskey had been removed hours before to a safer and more distant location and the old men watched all the legal proceedings with a bemused interest.

Deputies fanned out into the woods with sharp metal rods to prod the ground for jugs of contraband. Others searched the house with thoroughness and a mounting frustration but the place might have been a Pentecostal church so free of alcohol it was.

Bellwether seemed bored and he did not even participate in the search. He leaned against a porch support and smoked a cigarette, glancing occasionally at an old man in a gray fedora who sat beside a boy with dark hair and sleepylooking eyes like the old man's. Bellwether knew the deputies wouldn't find anything. He knew that Itchy Mama had a connection in the judge's office, though he did not know who it was. Perhaps the judge himself, who knew. The moment a warrant was sworn out Itchy Mama would get a telephone call and everyone went into action. When the law had left and had time to get its collective mind on matters more pressing everyone would go into action again and move the whiskey back.

Finally the deputies strung emptyhanded out of the woods and made ready to go. Be a temperance meetin here at eight o'clock tonight, Garrison, one of the old men called to a deputy. Be testifyin and hymn singin. Everybody's invited.

Bellwether rose to go as well. Crossing the porch he laid a hand in passing on Bloodworth's shoulder.

Mr. Rutgers, I believe it is, he said.

THE DRIVEWAY was exposed aggregate concrete, long and winding, snaking sinuously up through enormous evergreens Albright had no name for but which he admired nonetheless. Finally the house came into view. Woodall had apparently done well for himself, for the house was huge, a long low ranchstyle dwelling shaped like the letter L. Before the house was parked a gray Lincoln Towncar and a white pickup truck; the truck immediately gave Albright a strong and unpleasant sense of déjà vu, and wrenched his insides with guilt. He remembered the truck idling in front of his house, he remembered Woodall taking off his cowboy hat and laying it carefully on the truck seat.

At closer range the house did not seem so opulent. There was an air of benign neglect about it. The paint was faded and peeling, the trim in places showed areas of bare wood. He was out of the Dodge and inspecting the cornice when the door opened and a middle-age woman came onto the porch. Albright couldn't help noticing the front door itself was in bad shape, weathered and dull, the dark stain leached off the wood and everything in general just needed a good scraping and sanding.

Albright was wearing a paintspotted painter's cap over his pale curls and he was studying the pocked and scaling fascia board with a professional eye.

What do you want here? the woman asked him.

Albright took off his cap and turned to inspect her. She was a squat ungainly woman with a hairdo that came down past her ears then curled abruptly outward. Her hair looked all of a piece, something sculpted from wood, a wig chopped carelessly out of dark mahogany and clapped onto her head. Albright judged her perhaps the ugliest woman he had ever seen.

Mr. Woodall told me to come out and look at the paint on this house, he said.

Mr. Woodall is dead.

I know he is. This was sometime back. This house needs paintin. It needs it about as bad as any I ever seen.

She didn't argue. Gene was so busy he let things go quite a bit around the house. You appear to be a painter. Do you want the job of painting all this woodwork?

I owe Mr. Woodall somethin, Albright said. I figure to work it out. Paintin this house might not square it, but it'd go a long way.

I know nothing about that, the woman said. That would have been between you and Gene and Gene's dead. I'll pay you for your work.

I'd rather just do it to settle up.

What do you owe him?

Albright thought about it. To begin with I guess I owe him a house paintin, he said.

He began the next day. There was an enormous amount of scraping and caulking to do before he could begin the actual painting. As the paint flakes flew his heart grew lighter. He felt his debt being whittled down to a manageable size. The second day she came out and watched him at work. He thought at first she was keeping an eye on him to see that he did the job right but this seemed not to be the case. Perhaps she just liked to watch folks work. These were warm golden days of Indian summer and sometimes she would bring a book out to the lounge chair she favored. She would read a while then watch him work for a time. She wore hornrimmed glasses when she read but when she watched him she would lay them aside on the arm of the chaise and study him with no look at all on her face.

Toward the end of his first week she asked him if he'd like to use Woodall's pickup truck to haul his ladders. It's just sitting there going to waste, she said. I've been thinking about selling it. Gene was very fond of that truck. I may give it away, or let some junkyard scrap it out for parts.

This made no sense to him but he had about quit looking for sense in things folks said to him and he drove the truck anyway. It was easier than using the Dodge with ladders jutting ten feet out behind the trunk. He couldn't help noticing that it handled a lot better than the Dodge, too. Sitting behind the wheel gave him an eerie sense of power, as if he were absorbing something of Woodall's essence from the cab of the truck. He caught himself wondering what had happened to Woodall's white superintendent's hat, and he decided that if an opportune moment ever presented itself he would inquire about it.

JUST AFTER dark the red cattletruck parked where the chainlink fence stopped it and Coble got out. He stood squaring the straw hat on his head, looking at the house, listening to the raucous barking of dogs. Brady rose from the lounge chair beneath the pine tree. Hush, he said. The dogs fell silent. Coble came through the gate and Brady crossed to meet him. Pools of shadow lay like dark water beneath the pine and Brady limped nimbly around them. Without an inkling of who Coble was or what he wanted Brady knew intuitively that this was someone he needed to know who possessed knowledge he needed to acquire.

THAT NIGHT E. F. Bloodworth had difficulty in falling asleep and he lay in bed for a time thinking about the horse named Cisco that he had once owned. A small spotted stallion gaudy as a circus poster that he had traded for in Mississippi. The night of Cisco's demise Bloodworth had been trying to keep a mare and the stallion apart. He had penned them in separate pens. Between the pens and joined to them on either end was a barn with a sloping tin roof.

Sometime in the night he woke to bedlam. He could hear a horse screaming, dogs barking madly. He jumped out of bed and ran into the moonlit yard. The stallion was screaming and thrashing about inside the barn. Bloodworth saw with a stunned disbelief that the stallion had climbed a stack of haybales at the end of the barn and somehow managed to clamber onto the roof; the tin and two-by-four lathing had not held, and the spotted horse had fallen in a jumble of tin and broken lumber. The horse looked like a unicorn struggling wildly to free itself from a snare and he saw with horror that a sharp section of rotten lumber had imbedded itself in one of the horse's eyes like a horn. He'd struggled in the darkness dementedly with Cisco trying to remove the splintered board until he finally noticed that one of the stallion's front legs was broken and he gave up and went to the house for his gun.

What the spotted horse had done awed him a little. He thought then and he thought now the cry of flesh calling to flesh must be the strongest thing in the world.

Finally he slept but woke to a din of barking dogs and for a moment he was caught in a deadfall he'd laid in time long ago himself and he knew he was going to have to struggle with the stricken horse again, sick at heart he was going to have to go on shooting it until it stayed dead. Then he remembered where he was and picked up the gold pocket watch from the table. It was just past two o'clock in the morning. He laid the watch back and closed his eyes and tried to go to sleep. It was useless. Hellfire, the old man said. He lay listening to the dogs and staring wide-eyed at the ceiling. One dog after another or the same dog repeating itself was running up the steps, barking furiously all the while, slamming against the door, running back down into the yard.

He got up and poured himself a shot of Early Times and stood looking at it for a while and then he drank it. He took the pistol out of the Martin's case and checked the loads and stood beside the door. He turned the doorknob but when he did the door was jerked roughly from his hand and he had a German shepherd in the trailer with him. He wasn't using his stick and when the door leapt backward he fell. He didn't even think. He fired three times as fast as he could squeeze the trigger and the dog was jerked backward and tumbled howling down the steps. He sat on his haunches holding the pistol bothhanded before him as if expecting the onslaught of other dogs.

He struggled up cautiously and peered into the yard. The dog lay by the doorstep, its legs working slowly as if it were swimming. He fired the gun at random into the yard until both gun and yard were empty. The dogs had fallen silent. They seemed to have vanished into the woods, slunk back up the road to the field. He reloaded the pistol and sat for a time on the doorstep. For no reason he could name he felt as if someone was watching him from the edge of the woods.

AFTER HE LOADED the dead German shepherd Brady sat hunkered by the side of his juryrigged pickup truck. His hand held a length of stick he'd sharpened with his pocket knife like a stylus and he was scrawling the earth with meaningless hieroglyphics, random scratchings. You ought never to have shot my dog, Brady had said by way of preamble. Bloodworth didn't ask him how he knew the dog was dead. He didn't want to know. He sat on the doorstep staring at the pickup truck, on whose side long ago he had painted JOLIE BLON in some other life-time.

I don't want to even be around you, Brady said. All I want to know is why you told all those lies on me.

The old man was dumbfounded. Hellfire, boy, I don't even know what you're talking about. Lies to who? I can't remember saying anything about you, truth or lies either one.

That's funny. That cattle buyer, Coble, he remembers it word for word. How crazy I am. Babtizin cows and chickens. Preachin to stumps. Where'd you come up with all that mess? I knew you were evil and worthless but I never knew you were totally insane.

The old man was silent a long time, hands on knees, stick propped against his leg. How to begin. Finally he said, Boy, that wasn't about you. That didn't have anything to do with you. I don't really know why I made that stuff up, but it wasn't even about me. It was about a man named Rutgers who wanted a ride to Tennessee.

All that crazy stuff about me marryin bulls and cows. Readin at them out of a Bible. Did that man really sit there and believe all that nonsense?

Bloodworth permitted himself a small smile. He eat ever bit of it and set there holdin his bowl and spoon wantin more, he said.

Well. I believe he's about had a bait of it now. He's makin trouble.

I figured after a while he'd just laugh it off.

No. For some strange reason he don't see the humor in it. You took him hundreds of miles out of his way and worse than that you made a fool out of him.

Hell, I didn't make him, Bloodworth said. He was a fool when I got there.

He thinks you're crazy and he's goin to do all he can to get you into trouble. He thinks you ought to be put away somewhere, and I agree with him. All the lies you told about me, then that remark the other day about company. I knew what kind of company you meant, you never needed but one kind. Women. Shooting off a pistol like you was doing last night. You are crazy.

I'll just pay him his ride bill and be done with him, the old man said.

That's not what he wants.

Then to hell with him. The only reason he done it to begin with was because he thought my back was against the wall so hard I was goin to practically give him a herd of Black Angus cows. Damn them cows anyway. I wish I'd never even thought of them.

In truth the old man felt a certain amount of guilt about the story he'd concocted. Long after telling it he'd remembered that Brady as a youngster used to preach funerals for runover dogs, writing sermons in tablets to read at them, said prayers over roadkill animals. He wondered if all this hadn't in some manner seeped up out of his memory and colored what he was saying to Coble. The hell with it anyway, he thought. If it did it did. It was just one more misstep in a long line of missteps and there was nothing he could do about it now.

His idea was for us to get a lawyer and have you declared incompetent. Have the court appoint somebody to see after your business.

I guess you'd be a fine candidate for that, the old man said. You couldn't see after the business a settin hen could accumulate.

None of it matters anyway, Brady said. You're fixin to die. You'd be dead before the ink could dry on the paperwork. I run it out in the cards. Worse yet, you're goin straight to hell. When I look at you settin there now it's like you're already on your way. Comin into the city limits of hell. Your hair's startin to singe and little blue flames are flickerin all over you. Smoke boilin out of your ears. Your blood'll boil and your brain snap and pop like grease in a hot pan. Your bones'll burn white-hot and just burn through your flesh.

The old man struggled up. Get away from me, he said, and although he tried to keep the contempt out of his voice he could not.

WITH THE SHIFT in the seasons Fleming brought saw and axe and began to cut the old man's winter wood. He felled blackjack and red oak and cut them to length with the bucksaw and split the cuts and ricked the wood behind the trailer. Working in the woods seemed to bring purpose to the days, a sense of order. He cut dead pine for kindling and a red cedar whose closegrained oily wood gave off a rich exotic odor that evoked some vague memory he could not get a fix on.

Finally the old man stopped him saying he'd never live long enough to burn such a pile of wood as the boy was accumulating. It was just as well for the rains of November began and the world turned bleak and somber, the woodsmoke from Bloodworth's heater clinging to the ground in the damp heavy air. It seemed to rain every day and the days shortened and seemed to be perpetually dimming so that it was impossible to tell the exact moment that night fell. There were days he sat in the house watching rain string off the eaves and he was touched with a desperate and growing unease. The rain fell with an unvarying intensity until it seemed that the weathers of his world had coalesced in this mode and it had become a rain without a proper beginning or end and crossing through it to check on Bloodworth he moved always with the rushing of rain in the unwinded trees like a dark unmetered poetry of the woods.

WHEN FLEMING got out of the cab in Itchy Mama's yard he closed the car door and stood for a moment staring past the hills toward the southwest. It was no more than midafternoon but the world had darkened save for a band of light that lay above the horizon. A bitter wind had swept the drunks from Itchy Mama's porch and it rattled beercans hollowly against the stone steps and blew scraps of paper like dirty snow. Birds alighting about the trees were soon off again restlessly as if they'd had word of ill weathers that had not reached the world at large.

He went up the steps and crossed the porch and rapped at the loose screen door. Come in here, Itchy Mama yelled. Everybody else has. When he went in he saw that the cold wind had blown the sots and derelicts not to homes if they had them but to Itchy Mama's front room, where they were ill-contained on ragged couches and easy chairs and even hunkered against the walls. He went past them acknowledging their greetings and comments about the falling temperature with an upraised hand and to the kitchen where Itchy Mama was slicing ham into an enormous iron skillet.

What are you doin out?

I'm just out, he said. Why wouldn't I be? I didn't know the world was coming to an end till I saw all those refugees camped out in there. Have they not ever been cold before?

Don't you listen to the radio? They got warnins out about a ice storm. Done hit Alabama.

It looks like it's hit your front room. That bunch looks ready to start breaking up chairs for firewood.

You better be checkin on your grandpa.

I just came from there. He said he's denned up like a badger and dragging the dirt in after him. And he didn't even need a radio.

You might ought to be huntin a hole yourself.

He smiled slightly at this and gestured toward the coffee pot. I thought I'd stop by a minute and see if you'd sell me a cup of coffee.

No, I'll give you one. Give you a cup of coffee or a drink of whiskey either one. Which do you want?

I guess I'll take the coffee, he said.

But she had produced from between her huge breasts a flat halfpint of clear whiskey. She tilted it to study the bead.

You don't have a cup of coffee down there, do you?

Here. Take a little dram of this. It's heated to body temperature already and it'll go down like sweet milk. I'd even put a nipple on it if you wanted.

He took the bottle she was proffering. It did indeed feel warm to his touch. He unscrewed the cap and drank and stood by the window looking out to where the wind blew the cold trees. All the monochromatic world seemed in motion.

What's the matter with you? You look like you've got the whole world's troubles to sort out and you're runnin behind already. Did somebody die?

No. I don't know. I guess they did somewhere, nobody I knew died. I guess I better be going. I thought I might drive off down to Clifton.

You took Albright's car away from him?

He's been driving that pickup truck Gene Woodall used to drive.

She grinned, turned to cap a lid over the popping grease. Ain't a fool a wonderful thing? she asked.

He wasn't sure who she meant by that, but he didn't ask. I'll see you, he said. I'm going before this ice storm or whatever spreads from your front room.

Pile up in there with that bunch of drunkards, she said. About midnight I'll come drag you off to my bed and show you how to stay warm. Goodlookin thing like you. I'd keep you for a goodluck charm.

You'd give that up soon enough, he said, reaching her the bottle.

She waved it away. Take it with you. You never know when a snake's goin to bite you.

When he went out the day was more chill yet but he drove off into it anyway. A bleak feeling lay in the pit of his stomach heavy as a stone. He knew this was purposeless and could come to no good end but any sort of end at all was better than his life. Time had been grinding to a halt and he no longer possessed the tools to set it to motion again. He kept thinking he ought to turn back but he drove on into the leaden day. The wind spun a few snowflakes against the windshield.

The closer he got to Clifton the stranger the weather grew and by the time he cut off the switch before the pink house it was snowing hard and the wind was blowing it in shifting windrows ephemeral as smoke. When he got out of the car bits of ice scoured his face like sand.

He knocked and waited a while. He kept glancing back at the car and at the street. So far the wind was whipping the blacktop clean but the Dodge's tires were slick and it was a long way back to Ackerman's Field.

The door opened, the screen was unlatched. He was expecting Raven Lee but it was the mother herself who stood aside and bade him enter. He went in and stood awkwardly in the small parlor, not quite knowing what to make of the civility he was being shown.

I was just looking for Raven Lee, he said.

Well, she ain't here. She's uptown somewheres. Maybe the drugstore, she sets in there and reads them old magazines.

I guess I'll go look.

You see her tell her to get herself home. They're callin for ice and freezin rain on the radio and from the looks of things it's already here.

I'll tell her. He turned to go. He already had the door in his hand when she spoke again and he paused.

You talk right up to her. I can tell you think a lot of her but she's a little pushy. A little overbearin. You speak up or she'll run right over you.

He didn't know what to make of this or even how to reply to it so he just nodded and pulled the door closed behind him.

She was not in the drugstore or in the Eat and Run Cafe. Nor about the snowy streets, which were as bare and bleak as if the town lay under an edict that shuttered its citizens inside. He sat with the Dodge parked at the curb and sipped at the whiskey and kept one eye out for the law but the law itself seemed denned up somewhere with the dirt pulled after. He drank and searched the streets as if he could conjure her appearance by sheer will. It was his intention to marry her on the spot or as close to it as possible. Or to launch himself into insane recriminations about Neal. He had no idea what his intentions were beyond the next sip of Itchy Mama's whiskey, which had now cooled far below 98.6, and watching the snow list and slide on the glass. The day was failing and down the street where the poolroom was the nightlight came on, the harsh blue neon bleeding into the frozen air like ink in water.

He cranked the car and drove around the city square, down sidestreets blown free of snow. Snow was sticking now on the uneven surfaces of folk's lawns and in the glow of the streetlights it had a bluish cast.

He was about to cut his losses and leave when he noticed a brick building with a brass plaque that said LIBRARY. He parked the car and went in. She was sitting at a table reading a book, her back to the door, and she did not turn toward the noise the door made opening or closing. She was alone at her table and he crossed and seated himself opposite her.

What are you reading?

She looked up from her book, her eyes lost for a moment in transit from the place the book had taken her to this room with its oaken tables and the intense young man sitting across from her. She looked for a moment as if she couldn't fathom who he was or why he might care what she was reading.

Then she said, What are you doing here?

It's snowing, he said, meaning to say anything but that.

You drove forty miles to give me a weather report? I could have got that from the radio. Or looked out the window.

You didn't tell me what you're reading.

Rebecca by Daphne du Maurier. It's about my favorite book, and I've probably read it a dozen times already. Is the snow really starting to stick?

Your mother said tell you to get home. What's the matter with her? She treated me very nearly as if I was human.

She's desperately searching for a bridegroom, Raven Lee said. She's measured you for a suit and tie and decided you're better than nothing.

I'm not sure I know what you mean.

She gave him a small cryptic smile. You will here in a minute, she said. Let me get this book checked out and if you're so set on driving me home I guess I'll let you.

When she rose with the book and her purse and crossed to a desk where a bluehaired woman sat he saw that what he had judged a blouse was in fact a maternity smock and that beneath it her waistline had thickened considerably since they had sat in her room listening to the old man's records. While he waited for the library card to be processed he crossed to the glass double doors and stood looking out. The night had darkened and all he could see was his reflection and snow drifting against it. Then Raven Lee's reflection turned with the book and approached him. Her reflection slid an arm through his. They went out.

Did you see that woman watching you? She was wondering if you're the proud father.

He opened the passenger door and she got in. He closed the door and came around and climbed in. It was very cold and he cranked the engine and sat for a time with a hand cupped over the heater vent and watching windshield wipers clear the snow.

It's starting to stick now, he said.

I'm showing pretty good, don't you think? she asked, laying a hand on her swollen abdomen. This is what they call showing, you've heard people say that, she's starting to show. I may be better at showing than I expected to.

To have something to do with his hands and to avoid answering her he eased the car in gear and pulled away from the curb. There seemed no other cars anywhere and he backed around and turned in the street and drove to the square where the traffic light went from red to green shuttling phantom cars through the windy snow. He did not speak until he had laboriously maneuvered off the twisting sidestreets and down the hill to Raven Lee's house.

What are you going to do?

Have you read *Rebecca*?

Yeah, I read it a long time ago. It's pretty good.

It's just about my favorite book.

He had left the engine running for such poor heat as the heater was pumping out but it was still cold in the car. You said that, he said. What are you going to do?

I'm going to read it again.

Beyond her clean profile the porchlight flared like a cheerless beacon. The door opened and he could dimly see the mother come onto the porch and stare at the car before the cold drove her back inside.

I guess it's Neal's baby?

You guess correctly. Neal's the only guy I ever got serious enough with for things to get to this point. And they sort of reached this point without me knowing what was going on. I guess you could say it's sort of out of my hands.

You never told me what you planned to do.

She turned to look at him. He thought she might have smiled but in the poor light he couldn't tell. I don't know how much you know about biology but this is something that's pretty much happening on its own. I'm not doing anything. Or planning on doing anything, except having a baby.

I meant like an operation. There are doctors who will perform abortions, for enough money.

Not in Clifton. Besides, I'm way too far along. It wouldn't matter anyway. I'm not going to kill this baby.

I reckon Neal knows.

Oh yes. He knows in no uncertain terms. Mama seen to that. She was trying to make him marry me, even with him denying right down to the ground that it was his baby. I said to hell with that. I'm sixteen years old, I'm not signing the rest of my life away to some jerk who'd lie about a thing like that and can't even keep his pants zipped. Anyway, he'd already quit coming around. I think he must have some sort of sixth sense that warns him when this happens.

That sorry son of a bitch. I'll kill him.

This time she did smile, and leaning toward him in the darkness, laid a hand on his arm.

If you're going to start in killing folks right and left you may as well start with me. He didn't waylay me in some dark alley and rape me. Club me over the head and drag me back to his cave. We did it, the both of us, I'd be lying if I blamed it all on him. He can just walk, and if I walk, it sort of goes with me.

God, he said.

I guess this is just my way of telling you to get the hell away from me and leave me alone, the way you asked me to do that time.

I must be the dumbest person in the world.

You're pretty dumb, all right.

Brady can see the future like a man reading a newspaper and Neal's got this fabulous sixth sense. All this shit just blindsides me out of a clear blue sky.

Oh stop feeling sorry for yourself. At least you don't get morning sickness. You'll get over it. You might even learn something from it. If it ever happens to you you'll know not to walk out from under it.

I'd know that without having to learn it, he said.

Little by little the windowglass had gone opaque. Rain had begun to mix with the snow and instead of tracking down the glass it was freezing in a thin translucent skim that made the streetlamps blurred and otherworldly. The interior of the car seemed the world's last outpost, these two the last two survivors.

I've got to go, he said. Likely I'll slide off the road and be walking in this mess and it won't be nearly as much fun as it was with you.

That was sort of fun, looking back on it. Probably because I'm comfortable with you. I was never comfortable with Neal, though I guess a look at me would make you doubt that.

Were you pregnant by then? That night by the river?

Of course I was. I was even a tiny bit pregnant that night you got the crap kicked out of you. I've never known you when I wasn't pregnant.

I haven't seen Neal since before that night Junior brought you over and we met. He doesn't even seem real to me anymore. Like I dreamed him or something. He just came to me in a dream and knocked me up and then I woke up.

You don't have to be so crude about it.

That was the least immaculate conception you could possibly imagine.

I've got to go.

Then go. No, wait, not yet. Anyway you don't have to go. Sleep on the couch, I doubt if Mama would say a word. By now she's probably thinking any Bloodworth is better than no Bloodworth.

Don't think I wouldn't like to. But it's getting slicker all the time and I've got to get back. Somebody has to make sure the old man has wood brought in and a fire kept up. He's sort of got to depending on me.

She had opened her purse and taken out a small wirebound notebook and a pen. She opened the notebook and wrote a number on a page and tore the page out. Here. Do something for me. When you get back to Ackerman's Field, I don't care what time it is, call this number. That's a girlfriend of mine and she'll tell me tomorrow.

Why on earth would you want me to do that?

I'm hooked on you. No, I don't guess I'll ever see you again but I don't want to spend the rest of my life thinking you're iced over in a ditch somewhere. Will you do it?

I guess I'd do about anything you asked me to.

Except leave me the hell alone.

Except that.

She couldn't get the door open and he had to reach across her and shove the door hard with the heel of his hand. It opened with a soft shriek of splintering ice and he slid across the seat after her and helped her to the door. The sidewalk was iced over and they walked in the grass beside it. At the door she squeezed his hand hard for a moment but there seemed nothing at all to be said and when he turned back toward the street the world glittered like an ornate world fashioned from ice.

In times to come he would decide he made it back simply because he didn't care if he made it back or not. The world came and went through the headlights, freezing rain blurred the road until it finally vanished and every so often he'd have to get out and scrape a porthole to see through. Then coming off the long hill before the river bridge the car went into a slow drift, the rear wheels spinning sidewise, the car drifting off the hill in eerie freefall, the headlights limning the steep dropoff into darkness, telephone poles strung with ice like strands of crystal, the topmost branches of trees that beckoned like a haven that promised a warm place to sleep, to rest forever. He took this foot off the brake and just let the wheels roll on their own. Little by little the car drifted around and righted itself, the black highway like a mitered track that slid toward the cold iron trestle of the bridge rising out of the dark like a tunnel's mouth. In his mind the unseen water below it was steelgray and choppy and hard as stone.

He drank the last of the whiskey and tossed the bottle into the floor-board. He did not know what time it was but he judged it late. He saw no other fool on the road save a highway patrolman he met who was paid to be there but he saw cars slid down embankments and cars abandoned by folks who'd decided walking might be safer. Still the snow and freezing rain fell. He lost count of the times he had to stop and clear the glass.

All this was nervewracking drive he'd had in the back of his mind the grail of hills Ackerman's Field lay within and the knowledge that if he got up them it would be on foot. He thought longingly of Mother Halfacre's vomitflecked couch, cheery waves of heat rolling off the woodstove. But when he got to the long hill on Highway 13 it had been salted and there were black strips of macadam visible through the ice like remnants of an ancient and more temperate world. He drove on and finally into the ghosttown of Ackerman's Field, the town square white with blowing snow and so utterly deserted it might have been beset with plague and abandoned.

He called from a payphone but the phone rang endlessly somewhere in a house he'd never seen and he finally gave it up. He guessed every-one of right mind was somewhere covered with blankets asleep. Only fools abroad this night and apparently only one of them.

When he could make no further headway in the frozen night he had fetched halfway to the top of a steep hill with the ice coming straight at him out of heavens so black they negated the headlights, the rear wheels spinning impotently and the car sliding sideways and backward onto the shoulder of the road. The door would not budge. Finally he turned in the seat and kicked bothfooted until it opened in a hail of flying ice and he got out cautiously, hanging onto the door, his feet skating crazily on the slick incline.

Here was a world so alien he seemed to have taken a wrong turn somewhere and wound up in an arctic wasteland, the wind howling down through the frozen trees like wind through the strings of an enormous illtuned harp, the rain coming slant and hard and freezing upon everything it touched. The earth glowed with an eerie blue phosphorescence that seemed to be flickering somewhere beneath the transparent ice and tended away into the blurred mauve trees. He'd seen childhood snows every winter of his life but nothing that had quite prepared him for this. He reconsidered the wisdom of the derelicts huddled in Itchy Mama's parlor, and he thought, a man could die out in this shit. Really die, wake up stiff as a poker in some other world. You'd have to thaw to even ease through the golden portals.

He had a thought to stay in the car but immediately abandoned it. He had to keep moving. No move is the wrong move, Warren had said that night, and Warren though drunk may have stumbled upon some philosophy that had escaped Sophocles or Plato. Life is motion, stasis is death. *Got to keep moving, got to keep moving, blues falling down like hail,* he remembered his grandfather singing in some old bottleneck blues. Another, perhaps more applicable, *I'm the man that moves with the icicles hanging on the trees.*

He hammered on the trunk with the jackhandle until he shattered the ice in the lock and finally got the key to turn, fully expecting it to break off in his fingers. His hands felt useless as blocks of wood. He'd have liked to shove them deep into the cleft between Itchy Mama's enormous breasts where she'd heated the whiskey to its body-accommodating temperature. He'd have wallowed in her arms, drunk the heat from her body like blood. Lain in her stricken grasp like a man fallen asleep in the warm embrace of a grizzly.

He found the blanket and wound it about himself as best he could and staggered off into the night toward home. With the blanket about him and cowled over his face he looked like some crazed young monk or an acolyte testing the temper of his faith against the elements.

He cut through the woods over terrain he'd known all his life but even this familiarity was perilous. The weight of ice and snow caused huge branches to split away from the trunks of trees and they fell all night with sounds like highcaliber riflefire. His feet were beyond cold, finally beyond feeling, clumsy chunks of insensate matter trudging woodenly through the snow. He fell and got up and went on. Once he sat leaned against a tree and thought he'd rest a while then go on. Somehow it seemed to be warmer here, a more temperate part of the blizzard, perhaps the eye of the storm. The room where its heart was housed. His mind seemed to be shutting down as well, coming and going, shorted voltage dancing across the circuits in flickering blue light.

Once he thought Boyd and his mother had returned in his absence. They'd built up a huge fire and the walls of the house were amber with its glow and the heat-saturated air jerked him inside like a warm embrace. Your supper's in the warming closet, his mother said. We eat while you were traipsin around in the woods like a crazyman.

When finally he fell through the door the cold and darkness rolled on him wave on wave like black water. He wanted heat worse than light and before he'd even lit the lamp he crammed the stove with paper and pine kindling and by feel found the kerosene can and threw on oil as well. He kept breaking matches or dropping them but finally he had it lighted. He could hear the heat from the kerosene roaring in the flue and he sat before the stove with his hands upraised to it like a supplicant.

THE WEATHER had been holding below a viable painting temperature so Albright had decided to do all the scraping and caulking then paint when the weather moderated. He had scraped cornice and gables and shutters and caulked everywhere cold might gain entry around the windows. Some of the windows had long needed reglazing and he was finishing that when Mrs. Woodall came out the front door.

Mr. Albright, I'd like to see you a few minutes when you get time off from your work.

Well, to tell you the truth I'm about through here. I've about got her except for paintin and it's too cold for that. It keeps tryin to sleet or snow or somethin but I didn't see any need of comin back tomorrow to glaze three or four windows, I thought I'd just knock her out tonight and go.

Well, you'd know more about that than I would. We have plenty of time. At any rate, I want to talk to you. Just come in the front door, it isn't locked. Don't bother knocking, there's no one here except me.

When he'd finished the windows he capped the can of glazing and stowed his tools in the bed of the truck and went up the flagstone walk to the front door. The door was an ornate entrance of mahogany that had been let go almost too long. But Albright had stripped and sanded the wood and the carved cherubim that mantled it and sealed everything with preservative and he was well satisfied with the way it looked.

He went into a living room with a floor of pale polished oak. Rugs thrown about here and there. Pictures on the walls. He looked about cautiously as if his mere presence might begin breaking things. The room looked cozy and comfortable and he could feel a warm rush of air blowing discreetly from somewhere.

Have a seat in that easy chair in there and warm, she called from another room. I imagine you're about chilled to the bone.

He seated himself in the chair as told. He was cold indeed and the soothing heat seemed to be soaking itself into his pores like some rich oily liquid. He leaned back and closed his eyes.

When he opened them again she was standing before him with a squat glass of icecubes in one hand and a decanter of amber fluid in the other. Are you a drinking man, Mr. Albright? she asked.

He was eyeing the decanter. I been known to, he said.

She poured two inches or so into the glass. Gene would never drink anything but this Kentucky bourbon, she said. It's supposed to be mighty smooth.

He sipped the bourbon and slowly began to be warmed within and without. He needed to be off and gone while he was still feeling good about the progress he was making in squaring himself with the widow

Woodall, but he lingered over the bourbon and she seemed ever ready to replace each sip as he removed it from the glass.

Supper will be ready in just a moment, she said. You've worked so hard around here recently I wouldn't feel right about things sending you off without feeding you.

He protested weakly about getting a sandwich at home but she would not hear of it and presently he was ushered into a dining room where on a gleaming cherry table service was laid for two and a crystal chandelier lit the room with a pale diluted light. When he was seated at the table with a knife in one hand and a fork in the other she dished up grilled steaks garnished with fried onions and mushrooms, baked potatoes dripping with butter and sprinkled with chives, a crisp garden salad.

There'll be pie later, she said, attendant at his shoulder.

Pie later, Albright thought in a bourbon-diffused wonder, slicing into his steak. It seemed to fall away in tender strips before the actual touch of the knife and at its center it was the exact shade of pink he would have chosen had he a say in the matter. He sliced off a section and chewed. He closed his eyes and for once seemed at a loss for words to express himself.

I can tell you're pleased, she said. She had seated herself at the other end of the table and spread a napkin over her lap and was forking salad onto her plate.

It's the beat of anything I ever put in my mouth, Albright said.

Gene couldn't stand the sight of me and he grew to loathe my touch, but he never had a derogatory word to say about my cooking or my money.

Albright could not come up with a fitting response to this and so kept on eating. More bourbon was served during the meal and Albright grew expansive, regaling her with his adventures in the taxi business, his brief career as a metal crimper.

When they had finished the apple pie and cheese he arose when she did and went back into the living room. Albright was making ready to go but she urged him to linger on.

I have so little company, she said. Most of the friends we had were Gene's friends and seldom come around. And of course Gene was very busy, he had his mistresses.

Albright was seated in the easy chair without quite knowing how it happened. One moment he was eyeing the door and the next he was leaned back into the soft upholstery and she was scooting a hassock in front of the chair.

Would you like to watch television?

No, he said, I've seen it before. All them gray folks bouncin around makes me nervous.

Gene bought it to watch the wrestling on, she said. I'd rather read a book, wouldn't you?

Mmmm, Albright said.

I usually have a cup of coffee or a little cognac after the evening meal, Mrs. Woodall said. Which would you prefer?

I'm not much of a coffee drinker, Albright said.

He sipped the cognac and decided he'd never had anything like it. He was already rehearsing in his mind the story he was going to tell Fleming Bloodworth about this and he was searching his mind for a way to describe the bouquet the cognac had when he lifted the glass to drink.

She refilled their glasses and seated herself across from him in a bentwood rocker. Albright was noticing that she had done something to her hair. He did not know what, but it looked somehow softer, less like a lacquered wig. Perhaps it was the cognac but she was looking considerably less froglike and more like a kind, well-educated woman.

I don't understand your obligation to Gene, she said. But these last few days I've been thinking how rare a quality honor is. You felt an obligation, financial or otherwise, and you're honoring it the only way you know how, with the sweat of your labors. Honor is a very attractive quality in a man; it distresses me to admit that Gene did not possess it. Not an iota of it, or any empty space where honor had ever been. When I met Gene I was teaching English in a college up in East Tennessee. My father was well off, a well respected man in that part of the state. Gene was hired to do some work for him. He was just an itinerant carpenter then, building decks, pouring concrete sidewalks. I fell in love with him. He seduced me and married me, which I admit required very little effort on his part, and in no time he was in the construction business.

Truth to tell he was good at it. All he needed was a start. I was that start; he betrayed me almost immediately, and he's betrayed me a thousand times over.

Through a shifting cognac haze Albright wondered where this was going. Why she was telling him. How he was supposed to respond to it. He sipped cognac and gave occasional sympathetic and encouraging nods.

It made me bitter and meanspirited, she said, refilling the brandy snifter she held. A man seduced me and used my money to change himself from a jackleg carpenter who did not even possess his own wheelbarrow into a successful businessman with a literal harem of women. Then he refused to even share my bed. What would be your opinion of a man like that?

I'd say he was a worthless, coldhearted son of a bitch.

She nodded. He was that and more, she said. I've been admiring your hair in the light. Do you mind if I touch it?

What?

I've been looking at your hair. Admiring it. It looks like spun gold. Is it all right if I touch it?

Why Lord yes, Albright said. You help yourself.

She rose and ran the fingers of her left hand through Albright's tangle of white curls. Then she just stood for a time with her palm resting on his scalp. She eased her fingers gently out of his hair and drank the remaining cognac in her glass. She crossed through a wide arched opening into the kitchen and he could hear her rinsing the glass at the sink.

When she came back into the room she paused before him. When Gene died I was his sole heir, she said. I inherited his business, all its assets, all its liabilities. I also inherited whatever outstanding obligations were owed the company, or to Gene himself. I must apologize to you, I've drunk more brandy than I'm accustomed to and it always goes to my head. I'm going to bed. You're an attractive man, Mr. Albright, in your own way, and I'd like you to stay the night, if you'd care to. My bedroom is down the hall and to the right, and I'll be in it. If you decide to stay, I'd assume you'd want to bathe. There are towels and soap in all the bathrooms, just wander around until you find one.

She was watching him with something that was almost amusement. Whatever you decide, I am hereby absolving you of all responsibility toward any debt owed Gene Woodall or Woodall Construction Company.

She turned and went. He heard a door open, a door close. Goddamn, he said. He set the glass aside and sat for a time staring at the dead television screen. What to do. Absolved of all responsibilities had an official, free-and-clear ring to it, but there seemed a question of authority here. Some things went beyond wills and heirs and lawyers.

At length he arose and went in search of a bathroom. A man who could climb a shaky forty-foot ladder ought to be able to find a bathroom, he thought, even in a house of this size.

They lay in a comfortable semidarkness. The windows were black and Albright could see snowflakes listing against them. Hear a winter wind keening beneath the cornice. Lying there beside her Albright was beset with a bleak postcoital despair. He felt that all he had accomplished had been for nothing. All the chipping, scraping, sanding had been negated and he was deeper in debt than ever. He was driving Gene Woodall's pickup and had eaten his food, drunk his special bourbon and an inordinate amount of fine cognac. Now he had lain with his wife, and there was no way he could ever pay off such an insurmountable obligation.

Finally he told her the story of the crimper. Of the legal papers, the judgment. Lastly of the fifty-dollar curse Brady Bloodworth had levied that had resulted in a plane being so destroyed you could have packed it away in a shoe box.

She lay propped on an elbow listening to all this with an attentive look on her face. When he had finished she said, And you got all that for fifty dollars? I wonder why sand is so much more expensive.

What?

Let me describe a hypothetical situation. Are you familiar with the word hypothetical?

No.

She told him. Then she said, Let's hypothesize a woman with a grievance. A bitterness. Suppose further that there is another person with a grievance, a mechanic, perhaps, who has a great deal of familiarity with airplane engines. What makes them function well, what makes them not function at all. If a sum of money changed hands, say a thousand dollars, a substance might be added to the fuel tanks. An airplane will not run on sand.

They Lord God, Albright said.

Of course this is all hypothetical, she said, laying a hand on his shoulder. I just thought it might make you feel better. Now go to sleep.

Albright lay quite still until she was asleep and then he eased out of bed. Dressed himself rapidly, found his shoes. He went down the hall and through the living room. He opened the front door and went onto the porch. A wind was whipping snow in a white dervish and the windshield and sidewindows of the pickup truck were covered with a layer of ice. The wind mourned coldly in the bare tree branches, windbrought ice sharp as mice's teeth stung his face.

When he crawled back into bed she stirred sleepily against him. Where'd you go, she asked.

Albright was settling himself into the warm covers. Just got up to make sure all the doors was locked, he said.

BELLWETHER SAT looking at his shoes. They were military low-quarters shined to a rich black gloss. Bellwether had been in the war just long enough to get shot and win a medal and then he was discharged. He was shot almost immediately, as if his assassin had been waiting on him, standing at the ready with his piece already cocked, waiting for the paperwork to be filled out. Along with the medal Bellwether had acquired a military bearing, a military neatness. If he had slogged through the entire war perhaps he would have lost this along the way but he had not. He had formed the habit of spitshining his shoes and civilian life had not broken him of this habit.

Just what kind of deal is this he's cooked up? Bloodworth asked.

Something pretty sorry, I guess, Bellwether said. It gets pretty complicated with the legalese but what it boils down to is that he's claiming you're incompetent. That you're a danger to yourself and a danger to others. He wants to put you in some kind of a home, and he's petitioning the court to be made your guardian and have a power of attorney.

The old man seemed only to hear the word home. A crazyhouse? Hellfire. He's crazier than I am.

Well, I'm not braggin right now about my own sanity. I've got no business even telling you this in the first place. Or even being out here, as a matter of fact. But I knew you when I was a boy, and you've always been square with me. I think any man deserves a warning. They were out there at the courthouse talking to some people from the state and I nosed around and found out what was going on.

I just may show some folks how much danger I can be to other people. Wait a minute. You said they. Who else is in this? Not Warren.

You ever heard of a fellow named Coble?

Well I'll be damned, he said. He grinned ruefully. The sky was black with chickens coming home to roost, he could see them settling about the trees.

And you can just forget about this business of being a danger to folks. Are we right clear on that?

The old man was silent a time, thinking all this over. How can I fix this? he finally asked.

It was cold in the trailer and Bellwether kept thinking the old man might get up and stir the fire but Bloodworth seemed not to notice so finally he rose himself and took down the poker from where it hung on a nail behind the heater. There was wood stacked along the wall and he guessed the boy had done that. Bellwether raked the coals toward the front of the heater and laid sticks of split oak atop them and closed the stove door. There was a small window above the juryrigged flue for the stovepipes and he stood for a moment looking out at the day. Small dark birds he didn't have a name for but just called snowbirds foraged the ice with an air of unfocused agitation. Beyond the treeline the sky looked the color of blued metal and as cold.

It's beginning to spit snow again, Bellwether said.

Let it come, Bloodworth said. Ass deep to a tall Indian. I'm cozy as a badger in its den. Young boys to tote wood in for me, officers of the law to load up the heatin stove.

It strikes me you're taking this a little light for a man puts as much value on his freedom as you always did.

You never did tell me how I could fix it.

I don't know that you can fix it. You need to get Warren up here on the double. Trouble is, he hasn't been around here like Brady has. Brady claims he's been watchin you. Claims you shot one of his dogs and waved a gun around threatening him. Coble told them his wellworn story about the Black Angus cows. All about the preachin and the bab-tizin. You might have thought that was funny at the time, but it's come back on you like a bad check.

A fool is just so hard to resist, Bloodworth said. How about that boy? He'll speak up for me.

The way the law looks at it he's a minor. I could speak up for you myself, but I'm not your next of kin. That's who the judge issuing pa-pers is going to be listenin to, and right now that's Brady. He's your next of kin, and you seem to have pissed him off pretty good.

Then if it's up to him I'm in a hell of a shape.

I guess you are. All I can think of to do is call Warren for you. Do you know how I'd do that?

He's got a telephone. He lives in a place called Town Creek, Alabama.

Bellwether wrote that down. He put on his hat and adjusted it. I'll let you know what I find out. Any papers'll be served through my office.

I appreciate it, Bloodworth said, Whether I acted like it or not.

Bellwether nodded. He had the door open and a foot on the top step when Bloodworth thought, Florida. Hellfire.

Hey.

Bellwether turned.

What if I had a different next of kin?

How's that again?

If you'd do me one favor I don't guess you'd balk at two.

I probably wouldn't.

I need a telegram sent to Little Rock. He had found paper and was rummaging in a drawer for a pencil. I've got me a plan to knock Brady's legal papers into a cocked hat.

What are you doing, calling up the reserves?

Two chances is twice as good as one by my arithmetic, Bloodworth said, handing Bellwether the paper. Let me give you some money to pay for this.

When Bellwether closed the door and went down the steps the day was colder yet and the yard beneath its layer of ice lay in frozen whorls. He could hear sleet in the trees again and it rattled onto the roof of the cruiser like shot and lay there without melting.

WHAT WOKE the old man was not the engine but the long drawnout sound of wheels slurring on snow and ice. When the noise stopped he came fully awake. The car had halted before the trailer but he could still hear the engine, idling now, a car door closed.

Visitin hours are about by God over, Bloodworth thought. Since the night he'd killed Brady's dog he had kept the pistol beneath his pillow instead of in the guitar case and now he slid it out. He had come to believe that before this was over he was going to have to shoot somebody. Brady, Coble, who knew. Just start with dogs and work up.

He heard footsteps on the ice and just as someone pounded on the door death came swiftly into the trailer like a physical presence. It came swiftly up the steps and turned the knob and so through the door, crossing the linoleum with a sure firm footstep toward where the old man sat on the bed with the pistol in his hand. Death's presence was overpowering in the tiny trailer, its weight on Bloodworth's chest was such that he could hardly breathe, he had to struggle against it to get his shoes on, take up a heavy wool peacoat from the night table. Long ago the old man had been helping to dig a grave in a family plot on Grinders Creek and they were inadvertently digging the woman's grave too near her husband's casket and Bloodworth's shovel had disappeared into the rotten wood and the smell that had risen out of this ancient and sacred earth had been the same odor that saturated the trailer and Bloodworth had stood with the shovelhandle in his hands breathing death in a kind of appalled outrage, thinking, so this is what it amounts to, this is what it all comes down to.

He was at the back door when the pounding came again, moving in a kind of panic, some primitive instinct for survival demanding that he be somewhere else, anywhere else but here. He slid the pistol into the peacoat pocket and put on his hat and took up the stick from where it leaned against the doorjamb. He eased the door open and went cautiously down the metal steps. He closed the door soundlessly and felt the lock click and stepped into the yard.

It was cloudy but there was a pale glow rising from the icy earth. He could feel snowflakes melting on his cheeks and hear their soft faint hush falling into the leaves. He moved as swiftly as he could while still maintaining his balance toward the arbor of vines and trees where the line of darkness lay like the border of a foreign country he could slip across and vanish into. He was listening for the back door to open and death to come down the steps after him but all he heard was the idling of the car in his mind, a long low hearse with the rear door sprung open, a faceless man in a black coat standing on the doorstep with a folded paper in his hand.

He paused only a moment to catch his breath in the clearing where the sitting room was. He could see the pale snowy outlines of the lawn chairs. He angled toward the slope of thickening woods, with only a vague idea of where he was going; he figured it was Brady at the door delivering another load of craziness and he had no need for it. It occurred to him that he might cut through the woods and come out on the road and into the field where the cedar row led to the house. If he was at the cedar row there was no way he could miss the house, even in the dark. Besides, a light would be burning, he could almost see the yellow light flaring across the smooth icy field.

Climbing the snowy slope he had a thought for the spotted horse clambering up the hay bales long ago and smiled a small sardonic smile to himself, thinking of flesh calling to flesh not across distance but across vast gulfs of time. He wondered what he would say, what he would do. He had no idea what the circumstances would call for but he had no doubt that he would be able to handle whatever was required, throw his fate on such mercy as they possessed and make amends, kill them all.

SOMETIME AFTER midnight Julia's eyelids trembled as if jerked from the turbulence of some unsettling dream. Then the lids opened, though at first there was nothing to see save darkness, and she lay trying to get a fix on where she was, on when she was.

Time seemed wormholed and faulted, honeycombed in mazes that crossed and recrossed. She knew there was someone in the room with her. A hand had lain on her forearm. Gentle but cold as ice, and a voice had said: *Julia*.

She raised on her left elbow, felt on the nightstand for her glasses. Even before she found them objects were beginning to surface from the purplegray murk the room was drowning in: a chifforobe, a cedar wardrobe, the worn dull pewter of a mirror. The objects tilted and swirled, rocked once and righted themselves.

She fumbled for the lamp, but in her haste to put an end to all this darkness her hand knocked it off the table and the glass base shattered and she struggled up, swung her feet off the side of the bed, her glasses on now and her eyes already searching the wall for the lightswitch.

There was just a ghost of light through the window, just enough to lighten the walls, to make the black rectangle of the open door even darker, to suggest an exit into who knew what, a world so unfeatured and undimensioned that it was beyond her power even to conjecture upon it. She turned toward the window: beyond it everything was pearl-white and glowing, the diametric opposite of the world of darkness the doorway had become.

When she found the lightswitch and clicked it on objects in room sprang at her with an otherworldly clarity, gaudy and vibratory and larger than themselves, but the dark monolith had become the doorway to the living room. She passed through it and went through the house turning lights on then she came back to the front door and opened it and stepped onto the porch.

For a moment the cold took her breath away, a wind with teeth sang off the eaves and rattled beads of sleet onto the floorboards then swept them away and sucked from her such meager warmth as the shift provided and mourned like something grieving in the pine branches. Across the field the snow was already sticking and blurred by white motion it shifted with the wind. In the garden dead weeds clashed softly against the barbed wire and she thought of the pale figure stooped to cross it so long ago. When the wind stilled momentarily the snow sifted down through the pine branches, falling thickly, falling faintly in its eternal almost nosound through the trees.

A rush of warmth struck her when she went back in and closed the living room door. She thumbbolted it against the cold and turning saw that the floor was smeared with blood, bright and wet against the white linoleum.

E.F. has been here, she whispered to herself.

She had no word for what she felt but she knew the world or her perception of it had altered and that it had altered forever.

When the lights finally woke Brady he rose to see why they were on and the first thing he saw was a bloody footprint on the living room floor and he rushed into the bedroom. His eyes took in the broken lamp, the floor strewn with glass, Julia standing before the mirror. Her feet were bloody and she was clutching before her a black dress, an old crepe with three-quarter sleeves, and she was studying her reflection with a look of speculation on her face, as if trying to decide did the dress fit her anymore.

THE WHITE BUICK had been parked with the left front wheel driven up onto the sidewalk, the driver's side door swung wide. Fleming stood for a moment studying the house Neal had rented in Ackerman's Field in bemused speculation, then turned and started up the cracked concrete sidewalk. Halfway to the porch he saw a dropped purse, its contents strewn on the frozen grass. He stooped and picked up a compact, a lipstick, a handful of coins. He looked for an uncertain moment as if he might take them on to the house but then he dropped them back on the earth where he'd found them and went on.

The house was a two-story clapboard with the paint peeling away in great yellow slashes. He went up the stoop and crossed the porch and hammered with a fist on the edge of the screen door. The door rattled loosely on its hinges. The front door was open behind the screen but the house seemed steeped in silence and he could make out nothing through the dirty screen wire.

Neal, he called. It was very cold and he stood hugging himself and stamping his feet to keep the blood flowing through them. He grasped the door by its handle and slapped it loosely against the frame repeatedly and when that drew no response he opened the door and went in.

He was in a hall that apparently ran the depth of the house. A door on the left hand, a door on the right, both standing ajar. Dark paneled doors razed with dull opaque varnish. There was no one in the room on the right, only stacked cartons of what looked like fruit jars and old newspapers.

In the room across the hall a naked girl lay atop the tousled covers of a bed fashioned from gleaming tubular brass. He turned away in awkward haste and made to close the door but something about the girl drew his eyes back to her. She was very still. She lay profoundly still and seemed not to feel the cold though there was no heat in the room and his breath plumed in the air like smoke.

He approached the bed. The room smelled like vomit, on some level he'd been aware of it since coming through the front door. The girl had vomited on the bed and on herself and there was vomit in her curly red hair. Her eyes were open. They were blue. A vase had been overturned on an old sewing machine cabinet set beside the bed for a night table and five roses lay on the bed and a single longstem rose lay across the rounded marble of her abdomen. Its stem was woven into the snarled red tuft of pubic hair. It was very cold in the room and nothing seemed to exist anymore save this room. He could hear himself breathing. He leaned to study the girl more closely, as if to see was she sleeping. She lay staring at the ceiling and as motionless as if she were holding her breath. Thorns on the rose stem had indented but not pierced the alabaster flesh of her stomach and when he clasped her ankle it was as cold as the curving tubes of brass.

He was going out the screen door when he heard the noise of someone retching in the back part of the house. He turned and went down the hall. At the end of it a stairway led away to another floor and to the left there was a bathroom where Neal knelt on the white tile floor. He was on his knees with his arms wrapped about the toilet as if it was something he'd arise with and carry off and his face was pillowed on the cold porcelain.

What's the matter with you?

Neal raised his head and turned. There was bloody froth at the corners of his mouth. His eyes were blurred and unfocused. Sick, he said.

What's made you sick?

Bad whiskey, Neal said. Why don't you just get the fuck wherever you were going and leave me alone.

I'll get a doctor.

Don't get a doctor, don't get any fucking body. Whoever you got would just call the law. I don't believe I need no law here this morning. What are you even doing here? What time is it?

I don't know, early, seven maybe. I came to ask if you know where the old man is. To get you to help me hunt him. He's gone out of that trailer and I've hunted the place over and I can't find him. Albright pulled the car out last night from where I had it stuck and I went to see about him but the doors were locked and I never could get him to the door. This morning I tried again and finally prized the back door open with a tire spud. He wasn't there and there wasn't any fire. We need to find him before he freezes to death.

Hell, you don't even know he's out in the cold. Besides, I ain't studying that old man. He can take care of himself, sink or swim. I'm sick as I ever been. Sicker than I ever been.

I think something's happened to him.

Something's going to happen to you if you don't get the fuck away and leave me alone.

There was a calendar on the wall that marked a date five years gone. Fleming stood staring abstractedly as its flyspecked print of September Morn.

I think that girl's dead, he said.

What?

There's a dead girl in that front room.

Oh, Jesus, no, Neal said. He tried to rise, settled back bonelessly against the toilet. Oh shit. How can this happen to me?

The boy was silent a time. I think it mainly happened to her, he said.

Well, you'll just have to help me. If I can get up. When I can get up.

Help you what? I told you there needs to be a doctor here. Somebody. Where'd you get bad whiskey?

That fucking Early. He laid for me. I slipped in there this evening, yesterday evening, and stole another jug. The son of a bitch. He poisoned one and hid it out and I got it. I'll kill him. I aim to kill him, just as soon as we hide that girl.

I'm not hiding any girl. You can forget that crazy shit.

Neal's face was very white. His cheekbones and nose looked like those of an effigy cast from wax. His eyes were glazed and his forehead slick with greasylooking perspiration.

Well, we don't have to hide her. Just take her out on a road somewhere and dump her. Just get her away from me.

He fell silent, in a deep concentration. Who all did we see last night, Neal asked himself.

I'm not hiding any girl, Fleming said again.

You worthless little shitass. Think you're better than anybody else. Think you know every Goddamn thing because you read a book one time. Here I am with my back to the wall and you fold on me. Blood's got to hang together.

What about your blood?

What?

You don't mind letting your blood slide. You turned your back on it and just walked away.

You little fucker. That's what you're pissed about. You just can't stand it because I screwed your little Raven Lee Halfacre. Well, I did, and I enjoyed every Goddamned minute of it. I never heard her complaining, either. I'm going to sit here a minute and rest and then I'm going to get up and stomp your ass. And then I'll go and screw her again, just for spite.

The boy was silent. Neal turned and spat into the stained toilet bowl. He wiped the back of his hand across his mouth. You've got to help me, he said.

I'll see you around, Neal, Fleming said. He turned and went up the hall. Neal rose and staggered across the room and fell against the doorjamb and slid down it.

Fleming went into the room where the pale dead girl was lying in state. There was a folded bedspread on a chifforobe and he shook it out and spread it over her. Then he went out of the room and out of the house.

THE TRAILER'S BACKYARD was windswept ice trackless as a wasteland but after he'd crossed its expanse snow was drifted in the woods and he found the old man's tracks. It had snowed more since he'd made them but still they were there to read, the right footprint firm and clean, the left dragging, not even clearing the surface of the snow. Pockmarks in the ice where the walking stick had gone. He went on around the slope through a childhood fairyland of ice. Each fork filled with snow, each leaf encased in ice. He moved through utter silence save the carillon tinkling of the icy leaves. Small black birds flitted about the ice with a curious decorum, their tiny bright eyes unreal as bits of obsidian from a taxidermist's hand.

He went on through the woods, and the going grew heavier. The old man seemed to have just forged a straight path into the woods, taking what came, places where the wind had driven the snow into kneedeep drifts, windfall branches he'd had to work his way across. Of course the first thing he'd noticed was that there was no return set of footprints. He knew they had to stop somewhere and he was beset with a rising dread about what he'd find when they did.

When he began to come upon dog tracks he paused and studied them with some interest. They crossed and recrossed, huge tracks like the spoor of wolves. The tracks bore left and they bore right but followed the same general course the old man was taking.

He paused to rest, breathing hard, the icy air like fire in his lungs. He couldn't fathom how the old man had done it. Here the earth sloped so steeply the old man must have dragged himself from the trunk of one poplar to the next. A hare erupted by him in an explosion of snow and when it topped the slope Fleming turning to watch its flight suddenly saw the old man's hat. It was lying on the ridge crested with an inch or so of snow on the crown and tipped slightly sidewise with the brim frozen in the ice. He clambered up the slope, falling, his feet sliding on the ice beneath the snow, rose and struggled on.

The old man's black coat was what Fleming saw first, stark against the snow. He was lying on his left side, his face in the snow, his knees drawn up toward his chest.

Fleming whirled to run. Brady, he was thinking. Brady was closest and there was a telephone. Before he had even started his descent there was a sound, a groan, then a low keening moan that went on and on without cessation or variation. He saw that Bloodworth was trying to turn himself in the snow, clawing at the ice with his right hand in an attempt to wheel himself around facing Fleming. He'd start to turn then cease with his head lolled back and Fleming saw with horror that the long black strands of his hair had been frozen into the ice.

He ran to him. He didn't know what to do. He tried freeing the old man's hair, flailing at the ice with a fist. At last he took out his pocket knife and began to saw the hair off above the ice. The old man was trying to talk. His mouth frothed with spittle. He walled a terror-stricken eye up at Fleming, a wild black eye with the yellowlooking cornea shot with clotted red. Once when he was a child Fleming had with Boyd come upon a wreck in which a trailerload of horses had been capsized. The horses were screaming in voices nigh human and one horse trapped on the bottom had rolled upon Fleming a wild outraged eye that demanded that he do something, anything, and that eye had looked like this.

Bloodworth kept trying to talk. He sounded as if he were cursing, praying, calling upon someone for something. Then help me, help me, Fleming understood. He kept trying to move around, to get up. Fleming noticed for the first time that the old man's pistol was lying in the snow. Bloodworth kept trying to pick it up and lift it toward his face but he couldn't work his fingers. They were frozen or he'd lost the use of them or both and he'd bring the arm up and the pistol would tilt away and once he managed to bring the barrel against his temple but the finger through the triggerguard lay lax and useless. Help me, he was trying to say.

Listen, the boy said, laying a hand on Bloodworth's shoulder. I'm going after help, we'll get a doctor, it'll be all right.

Bloodworth struggled to look at him. His entire face had slackened, all the muscles dead, no more animate than cold wax. With his wild eyes and lolling mouth and long hair hacked off by the pocket knife he looked like something that would come at you out of a nightmare.

No, he said quite clearly. Help me.

I can't, the boy said. Goddamn it, I can't.

Bloodworth looked away, toward the treeline. The trees were brittlelooking and cold and they looked like surreal and patternless ironwork some crazed sculptor had wrought against the heavens.

He saw that the old man was crying silently, tears welling up and coursing onto the ice. Fleming lowered his face to the rough wool of the old man's shoulder. He could not bear this. He could not bear this. Through the thick coat he could feel the old man shaking with the cold. Then he raised his face and wiped an arm across his eyes and without forethought or hesitation picked up the pistol and wrapped Bloodworth's hand around it and rested the barrel against Bloodworth's temple.

He was looking away through the trees when the explosion came and when it did a soft avalanche of snow fell like an afterthought and blackbirds scattered with wild startled cries from all the frozen trees.

IN ORDER to get the dead girl into the trunk he had to back the Buick up to the edge of the porch. The Buick came wheeling crazily across the ice, straddling the sidewalk, the spinning wheels peppering the front of the house with bits of black ice. Neal hadn't been able to lift her. He had her wrapped in the bedspread and he managed to drag it by one corner down the hall, standing on the porch then and looking up the street and down, seeing nothing but the frozen street and trees then hauling her with a thump across the threshold and onto the porch. He sat for a time resting, sick at heart, staring at the still shapeless mass beneath the blanket. Finally he rose and struggled with her, getting her head and torso into the trunk then lifting her legs in but when he tried to close the lid he was left with two bare feet resting on the edge of the trunk opening. Try as he might he could not adjust her so that the lid would latch. At last he sat with his forehead against the icy bumper trying to think what to do.

He rose and went into the house and came back out with a coathanger. He arranged the blanket over the naked feet and drew the lid as near to closed as it would come and wired it from the inside with wire from the hanger. By now he was in a state of disassociation and the threat of someone walking upon a man loading a dead girl into the trunk of a car did not even occur to him. He was so tired that he thought she was bought and paid for. His state of exhaustion seemed to justify any small wrongdoing he might be guilty of.

He was far out on the Natural Bridge road rolling toward the river when night began to fall on him. He'd thought it morning but the light was just dimming down. Then the day lightened, like the advent of a bleak and cheerless dawn. He drove on. The world darkened again, night fell so that he turned on the headlights but they weren't working and he drove along in the dark with the brake half in and half out and when day came again he was on the shoulder of the road and the trees he was driving toward looked like trees in an inksketch left in the rain. The first sideroad he came to he cut into it, bumping along over the rough earth, the world through the windshield shifting and fading as if reality itself was out of control.

He drove until the road had deteriorated so that he was driving over brush that stood headhigh in the headlights, stopped where the logroad began to incline toward a hollow. He got out and unwired the trunk. Then he slid down the quarterpanel and sat on his feet, his cheek resting against the corner of the bumper.

When the man in the green coveralls came up out of the woods Neal had managed to get out a cigarette and light it though he was not smoking it. He just sat holding it. You taken drunk a little early in the day, ain't ye buddy? the man in the green coveralls asked. When he saw the blanketcovered form his eyes went curiously blank for a moment. He did not set the deer rifle down as he'd started to but shifted it to his right hand with his thumb laid across the hammer and with his left turned back a corner of the blanket. They Lord God, he said.

E. F. BLOODWORTH LAY in state like fallen royalty, like a ruler an assassin's bullet has stricken down. The undertaker had not been able to make him any more benign or approachable than he had been able to make himself in life. He was a fierce-looking corpse to the end, doomed reprobate patriarch whose lineage had gone strange and violent, he lay sternfaced and remote, at a cold remove from his seed that had bloomed finally in poisonous and evil flowers.

Everyone seemed to be there save Fleming but if his absence was noted no one commented upon it. Bellwether came. The old men who haunted Itchy Mama's porch were well represented and they all had pronouncements to make. You won't see his like again, they said. They broke the mold when they made E.F. The old stories were told again and death made them new, gave them a validity they had not possessed before. Albright came with a woman who nobody knew and who did not introduce herself. She was a boxlike woman with bright orange hair and she stood looking down at E.F.'s scornful visage with a dry and bitter eye. Then she turned away, without looking at anyone, and Albright followed her out of the house.

The body lay in Brady's front parlor. Forbidden its thresholds in life in death he was hauled forth like an exhibition, like a trophy in an elaborate and expensive showcase. The old woman had drawn a chair near the casket and from time to time she would look at the old man's face. Brady had permitted her this. This time, Brady's face seemed to say, he's not going anywhere at all.

Warren had little to say to Brady or to anyone else. He stood looking down at the enigmatic old man but he was as inscrutable in death as he had been in life. He studied with something akin to detachment the reconstruction of the old man's temple, wondered what had been used to implement the undertaker's art. Then he turned away. He leaned and kissed his mother's cheek and went out the door into the night. He stood for a time beneath the pine tree. It was very cold and he could smell the astringent odor of the pine and it reminded him of when he had been a child. He looked up and through the pine branches the stars looked the same tonight as they always had, from then to now the cold uncaring constellations seemed to have altered not one iota. He took a halfpint bottle out of his hip pocket and unscrewed the lid and canted the bottle against the stars and drank.

In the house Brady was the consummate host, his shoulders mantled with a new and unaccustomed dignity. He spoke platitudes in a low somber voice. He saw that everyone received a cup of coffee, a slice of cake. He said, yes, it was a shame, but he was thankful that he had brought the old man back to die among his own people. Blood called to blood, Brady said. Blood would not be denied.

His face burned with the light of the redeemed. He was redeemed, but the old man was the redeemer; see him, Brady's face said, see what it has come to. He used his life as a weapon and when there was no one left to hurt he turned it on himself.

FROM THE HILLSIDE where he sat he could hear faint singing. He had his father's binoculars trained on the white double doors of the church and when they opened outward he watched the pallbearers come down the steps with the casket. Albright to the right front, his fair hair like a torch in the winter sun. Sharp on the left. Brady following behind the pallbearers, the grandmother on his arm. She was wearing a hat with a veil and the wind cartwheeled it away across the graveled parking lot and a child ran to fetch it. In the spare sun the hearse was a deep sinister mauve and it seemed to be drawing all the light into itself.

They progressed toward the dark rectangle beneath the canvas awning. He followed them with the binoculars. They assembled about the grave. A man with a Bible read words Fleming could not hear. In the stiff wind the preacher had to hold the pages flat with both hands. Fleming wondered what he read. He smiled to himself. I seen a pretty woman in a red dress, the old man had said once. And then I seen her take it off. What else is there? The awning flapped in the bitter wind. Women clutched the hems of their dresses, men their hats.

He lowered the glasses and the scene distanced itself to animate dolls at some undisclosed rites. He sat for a time in the cold, in the quiet. Trees moved above him, tossed in the wind. When he looked through the binoculars again they were filling in the grave. He rose to go. He did not want to be the last mourner to leave. He did not want to be the one to leave the old man alone on that lonesome hillside with night coming on the way it was.

He lay on the bed and he felt he might never rise from it. He lay in an enormous torpor. The world was too heavy to bear and it was settling itself onto his chest. He felt old, old. Civilizations had risen and fallen in the brief time that he had lived. He felt that when the old man's head exploded across the snow he should have turned the gun on himself.

He felt he should rise and make a pot of coffee, cook a meal, build a fire. Instead he lay without volition listening to the house whisper to itself. It whispered in the voice he had used as a child, it took on the sibilant murmur of his mother's voice, Boyd's burred monotone. Old imprecations and recriminations and placating words rose and fell and trembled in the dead air as if words once sequenced into phrases were never done with but recycled themselves in perpetuity. Ghosts went about their preordained rituals. The house was full of the dead, of the dead in life. The windows lightened, they darkened. He heard banjo music that seemed to be rising out of the earth itself like ground-fog.

Brady came. He was still wearing his dark suit, as if he were becoming a professional mourner, hiring himself out for the solemn occasions of others.

You've disgraced the family by not showin up at your own grandaddy's funeral, he said.

The boy just lay with his fingers laced behind his head and watched with cold eyes. Leave me alone, he said. Get away from me.

Why don't you have a fire in here? Brady's breath smoked in the cold air. What's the matter with you? Are you sick?

I'm sick.

What's the matter? What are you sick with?

I'm sick of you, Fleming said. I'm sick of all of you, of all your crazy bullshit. I won't put up with it anymore. I want you out of my house.

Brady seemed not perturbed by this outburst. In fact he seemed almost amused. How does it feel to be a cat's paw? he asked.

What?

How does it feel to be a tool that does my bidding, Brady said. That

I can pick up and use to do something I want done but don't want to dirty my hands with. How does that feel?

I don't know what in hell you're talking about. I doubt that you do.

That old man never killed himself. I shot him, with you for a cat's paw. Do you remember that cigarette butt I showed you that time? That Harwood thumped out?

The boy noticed for the first time that Brady was carrying a paper bag. Brady opened the bag and withdrew a book. Fleming sat up on the side of the bed. Is this yours? Brady asked. He reached Fleming the book. Thomas Wolfe, the spine read. *Of Time and the River.* The boy flipped the pages. The only word his eyes registered was October. He suddenly drew the book back and slammed it as hard as he could into Brady's face. It struck with the force of a fist. It burst Brady's nose and opened a cut at the corner of his left eye. It staggered him back against a sewing machine cabinet and he fell, hands splayed out to break his fall. Fleming was up instantly from the bed to recover the book. He threw it again. It struck Brady in the forehead, the red waves of hair springing up, his glasses spinning away and skittering across the floorboards.

Brady was trying to cover his eyes with his hands and he was working his way in an awkward backward crawl to the door. You've gone as crazy as he was, he said.

Fleming picked up the book and laid it on the cabinet. He stood breathing hard and he was dizzyheaded with the effort it took not to fall upon Brady and kick him to death with his boots. He could not rid his mind of the image of Brady somewhere watching the old man dying like an animal in the snow. If he'd not seen it in fact he'd seen it crouched behind and peering through the twisted bracken his mind was clotted with.

Brady was up and fumbling with the doorlatch. Don't think this is the end of this, he said. He raised a hand and pointed a quivering forefinger at Fleming. I've got other possessions of yours, he said. Don't think you can abuse me and talk to me like a dog and get away with it. I own the rest of your life. I'll cast spells day and night so that nothing goes right for you, the rest of what little time you've got left. I'll thin your blood till it seeps out of your pores like water. Your seed will dry up and you'll be as useless to a woman as a gelding. You'll die in one of the wars with your lungs filling up with salty water.

Fleming so wanted done with this madness that he rushed Brady and turned him and shoved him through the open door onto the porch. He slammed the door and latched it then hooked the chain that secured it and went back and sat for a time on the side of the bed. Brady did not leave immediately. Fleming sat listening for the sound of footsteps crossing the porch. They didn't come. He imagined he could hear Brady breathing through the boxed walls of the house. Time passed. When he had begun to think that Brady had covertly eased off and gone Brady suddenly shouted, Don't fall asleep in there. I'll set this mess afire and it'll fall in your face while you sleep.

He lay watching dust dance in the mooted light from the window. After a while Brady seemed to come to some decision and Fleming heard him get up and descend the steps. It seemed an interminable time before he heard a car engine crank at the bottom of the hill.

Then he rose himself and began to build a fire in the woodstove. When he had it crackling cheerily he put the coffee pot on to boil and dumped coffee into it. He took up the Wolfe book and one other and he took from beneath the bed the leather satchel containing the records the old man had given him. He unlatched the door and went out and stowed the books and records some distance from the house and then he went back in.

By then the coffee was made and he poured himself a cup and holding it in his left hand with his right stripped the covers and sheets from the bed and piled them on the floor by the heater. He threw on magazines and newspapers and dumped the picture box on for kindling, photographs drifting like dry leaves, folks frozen for an instant in some curious life that no longer bore any relevance to his own. There was a kerosene can on the porch with perhaps a quart of fuel in it and he brought it in and poured it all over this tinder. He set the can aside. He looked about once as if he'd commit this place to memory for good and all then he tilted the wood heater over into the floor. Stovepipes fell in a clatter, in a rush of soot that drifted like anthracitic snow. The kerosene caught immediately and flames leapt up and the paper on the ceiling began to curl and smolder.

He stood by the flames for a moment refilling his cup at his leisure and then he went out of the house for the last time. He recovered the books and the records and since he could already feel the heat from the dry pine he retreated some farther distance and stood drinking the coffee and just watching it burn.

He sat with the old woman on the south end of the house where the thin sunlight was. The weather had moderated somewhat and the day was cold but bright. The grandmother would not allow herself to be kept inside all the time and she seemed to have reached some point in her life where the weathers were of no moment. They sat in wickerwork chairs against the wall where the light fell and the old woman had allowed a shawl to be draped across her lap. The boy wore a heavy dark coat that hung oddly to the right side for he had recovered the old man's pistol and it was his intention if Brady said a single word to him to shoot and kill him.

His other intention had been to give her a word of farewell or at least some news of his going but this was not one of her better days. She had known him at first but when he had mentioned leaving she had confused him with E.F. and seemed determined to maintain this confusion and see it through to its end.

She studied his face in a cold appraisal, eerily like a young woman peering through the ruin time had made of her face. You're a good-looking man, she told him. But you're not the only man in the world. Far from it. You'll turn up some time from you whiskeymakin or your musicplayin and be mighty surprised.

She fell silent and watched him out of her fierce hawklike face. I'm not goin to put up with it anymore, she told him. Jails and shootin laws and bein treated like trash. If you go this time that's an end to it.

He looked away, out across the garden with its dead and windtilted weeds. Where the wraith had leaned to raise the wire and so accommodate its passage. A flock of blackbirds moved like a shapeshifter against the blue void.

This old music, she told him, it's drove you crazy. It's got inside your mind until you think that's all there is. More than me and what's worse, more than them boys. Do you think kids raise theirselves?

No, he said. No, I don't think that.

Then what are you goin to do about it?

I don't know, he said.

No. I expect you don't.

All I can do is just do the best I can, he said.

It would need to be some better than the way you've lived so far, she told him.

He rose abruptly to go. But he turned back and leaned over her where she sat and kissed the papery skin of her cheek. She looked up in mild astonishment, recognizing him, then waved him away. Get on away from here, she told him. Quit wastin your time with an old woman, go do whatever it is young men are supposed to be doing. He grinned and turned to go, resting his hand a moment in passing on her bony shoulder, still breathing the smell of her skin where he'd kissed her. There was a dry acrid smell about her, and the fugitive smell of death biding its time, and a compound of spices, cinnamon and cloves and nutmeg that made him think of Egyptian mummies in their sarcophagi, their viscera jarred and the sacred flesh preserved for eternity with exotic spices, far underground, waiting while the sands shift ceaselessly above them and the millennia roll.

She seemed somewhat surprised to see him but not displeased. I thought I was shut of you for good last time, she told him.

No, you'll probably never be shut of me, he said. I'll probably aggravate you for the rest of your life.

I suppose I could learn to live with that.

She was heavier yet through the abdomen and he thought he should inquire about her health but as this was a matter of some delicacy he did not quite know how to go about it. Finally he said, Are you uncomfortable?

She gave him a wry smile. I don't believe I'm as uncomfortable as you are.

They were sitting in the yellow Dodge outside Raven Lee's house. Fleming kept glancing to see was Mother about but she did not make an appearance.

I'm going off for a while, he said. I've got some stuff I need you to take care of for me. Funny as it might seem to you, I don't have anybody else to ask.

What is it?

A couple of books. Those records we played that time. The old man's banjo.

Oh, Jesus, Fleming. He didn't die, did he? He died.

So he told her his tale, staring out toward Clifton where not a soul seemed to be about this cold December day. He told her all of it, and when he was done with it she just sat quietly beside him for a long time. Finally she leaned her face against his shoulder and closed her eyes.

So what are you going to do now? Where are you going?

I'm going in the Navy. I'm seventeen and Warren signed for me and I'm leaving for Memphis sometime tomorrow.

God, when you make a move you really make a move. Are you sure this is what you want to do?

He thought about it a while. There were a lot of things he could have told her but they seemed somehow beyond articulation so finally he just said, I can finish school and they'll help pay college tuition. I've got to do something, no move is the wrong move, Warren always said.

It sounds like you'll be aggravating me from a considerable distance, she said.

He took six folded fifty-dollar bills and laid them beside her on the seat. You may be needing this, he said.

What's all this? She was fanning the bills out like a poker hand, studying their unusual denominations.

It's till I can send some money. You'll be needing money for doctors and all that. I guess it's just for whatever you need it for.

Lord, where'd you get it? Rob a bank? And why on earth are you giving it to me?

I borrowed it from Warren. Actually he offered it and I took him up on it. He said he'd just piss it away on loose women anyway.

Is that what you call what you're doing with it?

No. No, I don't, and I don't want to hear anymore about it.

All right.

He sat for a time in silence. It seemed to him somewhat ironic that Warren had given him money to pay for a grandchild he didn't know existed but he did not say any of this. He just sat comfortably beside her, until this sense of comfort began to bother him a little; he was aware that he experienced it only when he was with her, and it had occurred to him that it might be some time before he experienced it again.

Where's the banjo and stuff you wanted me to keep?

In the trunk. I just went and got it out of the trailer. No one else wanted it.

Life would be so much simpler if I'd met you before I started fooling around with Neal, she said. I wish this was your baby.

He was silent a time. She was still leaning against his shoulder and he was trying not to move so that she would stay there. I'll take it then, he said.

What?

I want it. It's mine. Neal doesn't want it and he doesn't want you. Anyway he got out on bond and headed out. I want you any way I can get you, and I'll treat the baby the same as if it was mine.

You are crazy.

No I'm not. I was crazy, before, but I'm not now. I'm finally not crazy anymore. Can you believe that?

I don't know what to believe.

Then he did twist around in the seat, so abruptly that she straightened and pulled heavily away from him.

Listen, he said vehemently. Somebody's going to have to say what they really mean and then do what they say they will. All this lying. All this bullshit and pretending. It's just wasting lives, wasting time, everything's just a waste.

She was looking at him curiously. That's just the way people are. The way the world is. What are you trying to do, fix the world?

I don't want to fix the world. Fuck the world. Just the little part of it that I have to live on. You and that old man. Folks starting babies and walking off like that's got nothing to do with them. People walking off while you're asleep and never coming back. Leaving a note. A God-damned note. Old people living half a mile apart and wanting to see each other and dying without doing it. Now that's crazy for you. That's what's crazy.

Hush, she said, touching his face. You hush, now.

He got out of the car into the cold air. A wind with ice at its edge was blowing off the river. He went around and unlocked the trunk. She opened the car door and called him to wait. Get back in here, she said.

He sat behind the wheel.

So are you asking me to marry you, or what? I can't quite follow all this, it's a little confusing. Is that something like what you meant?

Yes. That's exactly what I meant.

Could you maybe say it then, in actual words?

I want you to marry me.

All right, I'll marry you, see how easy that was? When?

When I get out of bootcamp. Three months. I'll get leave then and we can get married. We can get the allotment papers filled out so that you can be drawing some money. If I get stateside duty you can come wherever I am.

Wherever you are, she said. I like the sound of that, unspecific as it is. Of course you know that we could get married first.

Out of all this I've only learned one thing. If I don't go now I'll never go.

Is that so important? Just for you to go?

I've got to go.

I guess you know there's a war on.

Folks keep telling me about it.

You know, Fleming, in all our wandering around at night we never did manage to spend all of one together. We could use some of this money and rent one of those tourist cabins down by the river. What would you say to that?

You know what I'd say. But could we do that, I mean could you do that? With the baby and all?

I would say that you could, she told him.

HE HEADED OUT just at twilight, the Greyhound bus rolling toward Memphis past barren endless fields stitched together with powerlines bellying pole to pole. He watched the known world fold under purple dusk with a cold unease.

He had no faith in the permanence of any of this. What he'd seen of life had shown him that the world had little of comfort or assurance. He suspected that there were no givens, no map through the maze. Here in falling dark with the world rolling simultaneously toward him and away from him everything seemed no more than random. Life blindsides you so hard you can taste the bright copper blood in your mouth then it beguiles you with a gift of profound and appalling beauty. There were things that he had to do that he could not even begin to articulate but the hunger for the taste of her mouth was an addiction he could not be shut of. Nor did he want to be. But there seemed little chance he could have them both, no guarantee that he could get or hold onto even one.

The glass was darkening and his face was appearing over the drowning landscape like an image in a slowly developing photographic plate and he closed his eyes against it. Of all the things he'd been told of life there was little that seemed salvageable. Just do the best you can and let it roll, the old man said one time. The slap of Brady's cards on an oilcloth tabletop told of a future preordained but the boy suspected that future events swirl like smoke and are as hard to hold in your hand for every event is connected to every other event like the veins in a leaf. He could not wash blood out of snow and the undone curl on Raven Lee's forehead formed with her left eye a question that he could not decipher, let alone answer.

In the end he was left only with the fireflies he had seen that summer night in Clifton, their fragile and provisional light endlessly echoing the movement of the dark water, visionary and profoundly mysterious as a glimpse he'd been permitted into the secret clockwork of the world itself.

FOR SOME TIME now Boyd had been journeying through a land so despaired of by men that they had decimated its trees and they had labored over the earth itself as if to shape it to more manageable contours then torched their homes and fled. Taking their dead with them or pursued by them for he had passed by where the graveyard had been. It was a wonder to him. Even the dead were gone. In a world of variables and perpetually shifting horizons he'd thought death the one constant but apparently this was not so and even the most fundamental givens of existence seemed to invite skeptical reconsideration.

These days he was traveling much under the cover of darkness by inclination as well as necessity and he had been forced to leave where the fences began an automobile not registered to him but which he now numbered among his few possessions. All this land was posted keep out with strong no-nonsense warnings and threats but Boyd had so distanced himself from the ways of men and their laws and makeshift order that he regarded them as invitations with the wording slightly altered and so went on.

When he came to the foot of the hill there was no poplar where the mailbox had been nor was there a mailbox. He crossed the ditch and began the hill's ascent with his feet so ingrained by habit and by the unreckonable number of times he'd climbed it in the past that they seemed to adhere to the footpath with no help from him so that he was looking ahead into the semidarkness with something that was almost apprehension. At the point where the roof of the house should have intersected with the horizon it did not. There was a sharp intake of his breath, no more.

He kicked through the rubble where the house had been. As if he'd unearth bones, artifacts from the curious folk who'd lived here. Pieces of a puzzle that would compose themselves into a coherent whole that would explain how a world could so alter itself. For a superstitious moment it seemed to him that by turning his attention elsewhere and his back on the place of his past he'd doomed it to fade to a point that was now useless to man as a dusty stagesetting for a show that had closed long ago.

He sat for a time on a foundation stone and smoked a cigarette. He'd have liked to know the outcome of all that had transpired here but all he could find were more questions and he had enough of these already to last him a lifetime. He toed out the cigarette in the ashes and rose. This desolate moonscape of ash and charred rubble filled him with a restless unease. His life was motion now and the world was wide with horizons beyond numbering that shaped themselves against the sky in